Praise for *The Me I Used to Be*

"Jennifer Ryan takes family drama to a new level in this tangled emotional web of a novel. Secrets come to light, love is rekindled, and redemption is found—all in the glorious golden sunshine of the Napa Valley. I loved it!"

— Susan Wiggs,
New York Times bestselling author

"*The Me I Used to Be* is Jennifer Ryan at the height of her storytelling best. Page-turning, powerful, with high-stakes drama and unforgettable romance. I couldn't put it down!"

— Jill Shalvis,
New York Times bestselling author

"Gripping and emotionally compelling, *The Me I Used to Be* is a beautiful story of losing yourself, starting over against all odds, and coming out triumphant. I was hooked from page one!"

— Lori Foster,
New York Times bestselling author

"Ryan (*Dirty Little Secret*) delivers an intoxicating blend of hair-raising suspense, betrayal, and true love with this gripping contemporary set in the rich vineyards of Napa Valley. . . . Ryan's fans will devour this outstanding tale, as will the many new readers she's bound to win."

— *Publishers Weekly* (starred review)

Praise for *Sisters and Secrets*

"Jennifer Ryan's *Sisters and Secrets* should win an award for being the most unputdownable book of the whole year. The drama will keep you on the edge of your seat, and the emotional roller coaster will touch every emotion."

— Carolyn Brown,
New York Times and *USA Today* bestselling author

"Sibling rivalry comes to a head in a masterpiece of family and secrets."

— Fresh Fiction

Lost
and
Found
Family

Lost
and
Found
Family

A Novel

JENNIFER
RYAN

wm

WILLIAM MORROW
An Imprint of HarperCollinsPublishers

LOST AND FOUND FAMILY. Copyright © 2021 by Jennifer Ryan. All rights reserved. Printed in the United States of America. No part of this book may be used or reproduced in any manner whatsoever without written permission except in the case of brief quotations embodied in critical articles and reviews. For information, address HarperCollins Publishers, 195 Broadway, New York, NY 10007.

HarperCollins books may be purchased for educational, business, or sales promotional use. For information, please email the Special Markets Department at SPsales@harpercollins.com.

FIRST EDITION

Designed by Diahann Sturge

Title page and chapter opener image © Dmytro Mykhailov/Shutterstock, Inc.

Library of Congress Cataloging-in-Publication Data has been applied for.

ISBN 978-0-06-300351-4

21 22 23 24 25 LSC 10 9 8 7 6 5 4 3 2 1

*For all those hard-working women out there who
do it all the best they can for the ones they love*

Lost
and
Found
Family

W hy now?" Sarah sank deeper into her office chair, wallowing in her desire to be defiant, knowing this reckoning disguised as a visit was a long time coming.

Sarah stared at the letter Margaret's attorney, Luke Thompson, sent her two weeks ago basically telling her to either allow Margaret to see the boys voluntarily or face a court battle.

All Margaret had to do was ask.

But no. She had to be difficult and get a lawyer.

"Why can't Sean's mother come here if she wants to see the boys? She can make the drive just as well as I can. Why demand such a long visit when the kids have school and I have a business to run?"

Her best friend and assistant, Abby, kept her features and response neutral. "You haven't taken a vacation in four years."

Sarah rolled her eyes. "Spending time with Sean's mother is not a vacation. It's an endurance race through hell."

Sean's mother and sister knew nothing about the man Sean had become before his death, and treated her with open hostility, making it clear they hated her. She'd endured their disdain followed by two years of cutting silence, and now, out of the blue, Margaret had demanded to see her grandsons.

Sarah despised Sean for making her keep his deep dark secrets.

She did it to spare his family, for the sake of her children, and the company they owned and had built into a thriving enterprise.

But keeping the secrets weighed on her mind and heart.

Abby pressed her lips into a flat line. "Maybe you'll resolve the differences between you. Put the past to rest, then she won't be so unkind."

That was a tepid term for the scathing words Margaret liked to spew.

"She doesn't want to be friends, or even play nice for the boys' sake. She blames me for Sean's death and thinks I stole his company from him."

After the company's IPO and Sean's sudden death, the stocks were up and down like a roller coaster. She did what she had to do to stabilize the business and show the investors the company was still solid. "We came so close to losing everything. The boys deserved some small piece of their father to survive."

Abby folded her arms across her chest. "*You* are Spencer Software. Everything this company is only exists because of you and your genius at programming. *You've* always held the company's reins. *You* catapulted us to where we are now."

Sarah found it difficult to accept the accolades she'd worked hard to deserve but wasn't comfortable flaunting.

"Spencer Software is the best in the industry, and there are your successful side businesses as well." Abby prodded Sarah to see her life for what it really was, not how Sean's family saw it, and how she hid it. "People are banging down the door to get you to do their projects. The boys will have some legacy. Thanks to *you*. Not Sean. Stop letting him take credit for *your* work. You should have left him long before he started treating you like an employee instead of his wife and the mother of his sons."

No sense arguing. Sarah had saved the company and, most important, everyone's jobs. "You're right. So why the hell did I agree to spend *six* weeks with his mother, who hates me, and pretend that all the things I allowed her and the world to believe are really true?"

"Tell. Her. The. Truth." Abby held her hands out and let them fall. "What difference does it make now? He's gone. You shouldn't have to pay for his mistakes and misdeeds forever."

Sarah didn't see an upside to revealing Sean's true character. "He was everything to her. The perfect son, who could do no wrong. I can't take that away." She understood Margaret in a way. "As a mother, I look at my boys and want to believe they're perfect in every way. Let her have her untarnished memory of him. I wish for the boy's sake he'd been that person."

And telling Sean's mom everything opened the door to the boys remembering things better left forgotten.

Abby let it go.

Sarah glanced at her calendar and worried about all the meetings she'd have to take remotely. "Did you call Margaret and give her the details about our arrival?"

Abby rolled her eyes again. "Yes. And Margaret wanted me to tell you"—she released a frustrated huff—"and I quote, 'She could have taken five minutes between lunch with friends and spending Sean's money to call me herself.'" Abby might get a headache from all that eye rolling.

"And so it begins." Sarah waited for the tide of resentment to pass.

Abby made a disgusted face to let Sarah know what she thought about Margaret's attitude.

Abby leaned over the desk and put her hand over Sarah's. "I just wish, for once, someone gave you as much as you give to others. Only the good things you do in the name of the company are public knowledge. But that all changes at the benefit next month." Abby gave her a mischievous smile, excited Sarah would be publicly celebrated—mostly against her will.

"I just want to focus on the job I love. I get people want to celebrate a woman in my position and that I'm a role model for young girls who want to be in the tech industry. But I hate doing press."

"As co-CEO you should take credit for all you do and not let Evan hog the spotlight."

"He can have it." Sarah held the position so she had a say in how the company was run, but she left the majority of the public aspect of the CEO job to Evan, who knew how to run the company and loved being the face of Spencer Software.

She and Evan ran the company the way she'd hoped she and Sean would have done if Sean had been a different kind of man.

"Your new security program will innovate the market. And though everyone knows a woman is behind the bestselling Andy's Antics games, the press and consumers can't wait to find out that it's really you behind the obscure photo and bio on the website."

Because Andy's Antics wasn't a public company, Sarah had been able to keep her identity somewhat secret. Insiders knew, but she'd kept the narrative on the games, not who made them.

"It's about time you had your coming-out party." Abby held up her hands. "That's all I have to say. You should get credit for all you've accomplished."

"Margaret won't like it when I do. I don't even know how much Margaret knows about what I've done with Spencer Software, let alone if she even knows about Andy's Antics."

"She'll know soon enough. If you come clean to Margaret about Sean, you could get all the secrets out of the way in a matter of weeks."

"Some skeletons are better left buried. You should go home. It's late."

"How much longer will you work tonight?"

"Not long. I've got a call for the Knox Project, and then I have to pack up the laptops for the trip."

"How many are you taking?"

"Only three. I have the Knox Project to finish, the Knight's Revenge game for Tyler to test, and another data storage project for Cadence Medical." She liked to use a different computer for each project to keep everything straight and because it was easier to hand off to her team when she had the programming done and they could test it, work out the bugs, and implement it for the client.

"Assign some of the work to the programmers downstairs and take some time to yourself during this trip."

"They're as overworked as I am. Besides, look around. There are twelve laptops representing my various projects." She took on the big, complex projects that had catapulted the company's name and profits. "Be thankful I'm not taking more than the three."

"Only twelve right now." Abby opened her mouth in mock surprise.

At any given time there could be more than twenty laptops in Sarah's office. Twelve wasn't so bad. The fact that she'd only work on three projects while away meant she might get more than four hours of sleep at night. Maybe. Probably not.

Abby headed for the door. "I'm out of here. Make your call, then go home, see your kids, and get some sleep tonight because tomorrow is going to be one hell of a day."

"Thanks, Abby. Go have some fun for both of us."

She wished she could ditch work, cancel the trip, and go to Hawaii with the boys instead of Carmel.

She picked up the letter from Luke again and cursed Margaret for going to an attorney when a simple phone call would have sufficed. She did not look forward to the long car ride tomorrow, facing Sean's mom, and dredging up all those memories of him, what had happened, and a past she tried to bury but always seemed to find a way to rise to the surface.

$\mathcal{E}$xcitement warred with anxiety in Margaret's stomach. "They'll be here tomorrow. I can't wait to see my grandsons. It's been too long." She regretted that in her grief and because of her anger and resentment, she'd let so much time go by.

"I told you the letter would work." Luke stood in the kitchen, wearing a tailored suit, tie loose. Luke was a defense attorney. When she asked Luke for help with her Sarah problem, he'd convinced her to start with a letter requesting to see the boys.

She was surprised it worked.

And she had Luke to thank for it.

He and Sean had been close as brothers growing up, though they'd gone their separate ways after high school. Still, she thought of Luke as a second son.

But she'd kept the bad blood between her and Sarah private until now.

"Two years is a long time to let this go on." Luke didn't understand.

Depression had stripped her of any sense of time. One day dragged into the next. "At first, my grief was too great to see anyone. A mother shouldn't outlive her child. When Sarah took over

Sean's company, I got angry. After the funeral, she didn't grieve him, she just took everything and shut us out."

Sarah got everything Sean worked so hard to build and erased him from the boys' lives.

They probably didn't even remember him. Their own father. It made her sick.

So she put her foot down and insisted on this visit. She deserved to see her grandsons.

The company envelopes Sarah sent monthly sat piling up on the credenza behind her desk in the library. They reminded her of all Sarah had taken and Sean had lost.

She refused to open them and allow Sarah to rub it in her face.

"I bet you miss the boys. Take this time to try to mend the relationship with Sarah so it's easier for you to visit the kids." Luke's sympathetic tone didn't lessen the turmoil roiling inside her.

"She wants nothing to do with me or Bridget." Her daughter, like her, hadn't liked what Sean told them about Sarah either.

"No one really wins in court. Everyone pays a price. Remember, Sean loved her."

Margaret waved that away. "And look where that got him. Dead. She and Sean came from different worlds. It was obvious she only wanted to use Sean to elevate herself from a poor foster girl. She had no family and little education before she ended up at MIT."

"Really?" Interest lit Luke's eyes.

Margaret had a brilliant idea. "You should look into her teenage years. She got into trouble. Sean didn't know all the details. Find out what really happened. If she's got a criminal past, that will help my case."

Luke's eyes turned thoughtful. "I'll look into it, but juvenile records are sealed. And you should really try to come to an agreement you can both live with."

"I want to be prepared. Just in case."

Luke pressed his lips tight. "All right. If that's what you want, I'll see if I can find out anything."

"I want her to pay for what she's done. Short of that, I want to see my grandsons whenever I want."

Luke sighed. "Do you know anything else about her life before she met Sean?"

"No. Not really. They met at MIT. She wasn't doing well in school."

"Sean told me how hard and competitive it was there. Lots of people dropped out or couldn't cut it. Most graduates are head-hunted for top companies and the government."

"Exactly. He had a bright future ahead of him. But he fell for a pretty face, her charm, and then she rushed him into a wedding at the courthouse. Not even a proper ceremony with family and friends."

"I remember hearing about it from a mutual friend." Just out of college himself, Luke had gone to work for the family law firm, building his reputation for winning difficult cases.

"The poor girl married well and got the life she always wanted when Sean used the money he inherited from his father to start his own business. He said she constantly pushed him to make more money, so she could keep spending it. Just before he died, he told me he wanted to divorce her and take the boys. She was too busy doing God knows what to be bothered with them. But she got it all, and now she's head of the company—but I assure you someone else is doing the work for her while she continues to reap the rewards. Those boys probably never see her because she's at the spa, shopping, and lunching with friends."

"Some people care more about money than who they use and hurt." Disillusionment filled Luke's words.

Margaret smacked her hand on the table. "That's her."

Luke put his hand over hers. "It's happened to me many times. Someone finds out who I am, and how much I'm worth, and something changes. They don't see me, but what I can do for them." Luke sat back with a sigh. "Sean must have been disappointed by her and the marriage. I get why you're angry, but why do you hold her responsible for his death? She wasn't driving the car."

Margaret clenched her hand into a fist. "No. But he was working late into the night, making deals to keep her happy. He should have been home with the boys, enjoying the life he had already made for them."

"Focus on your grandkids. Enjoy your time with them. Take this opportunity to watch how she interacts with them and see how they're doing. I imagine this will be the most time you guys have spent together."

"I'm surprised she went along with the six weeks. But that will be long enough for me to really get to know the boys and them to become comfortable with me." So that if she had to take them from Sarah, they'd be happy to stay with her. "But I'm not sure I can endure *her* that long. She refused to send the boys alone, so I have no choice. You're right, though, this is the perfect opportunity to make sure those boys are being taken care of properly. She couldn't even cook when she and Sean got married. I only hope she's put aside her selfish behavior and finally put those boys first."

"Maybe it's time to sort the whole mess out. At least for the kids' sake. Without lawyers," he added, trying to get her to back down.

But she wouldn't. Not when it came to Sean's boys. "I'll spoil those boys rotten while I can, but I won't make nice with her." Margaret would make sure Sarah remembered just what she had taken from her. If those boys weren't happy and healthy, she'd follow through on her threat to take them away from their mother, no matter the cost to herself. They were all that mattered.

"I'll come by tomorrow for moral support if you'd like." Luke stopped by several times a month to check on her.

She lived alone in a secluded area. As she grew older, it seemed that over the past couple of years she went fewer places, had fewer visitors, and the house and land had fallen by the wayside because she physically and financially couldn't keep up with them. She appreciated so much that Luke kept in touch. Especially since Bridget only stopped by because she needed something, usually money or a babysitter.

Luke returning to the neighboring ranch where he'd spent summers had been a wonderful surprise and a much-needed gift in her life.

She patted his hand. "I'd love the moral support. Face it, you're curious, aren't you?"

"You like most people, so the fact that you despise her intrigues me."

"You'll see tomorrow. I'm sure she won't disappoint either of us. A leopard doesn't change its spots, even when it is camouflaged in a Chanel suit." Margaret eyed him and prodded, "You'll see when you run the full background check and dig up every speck of dirt on her."

Margaret wouldn't let Sarah get away with taking her son and her grandsons from her.

Chapter Three

Margaret believed Sarah had taken her son away. She thought Sarah was a terrible wife and mother. She thought Sarah kept Sean and the boys from her. She blamed her for Sean's death.

And because of all that, she wanted to punish Sarah for everything.

But Sarah wasn't the one to blame. She hadn't done anything wrong.

At this point, she didn't think she could convince Margaret of that no matter how hard she tried.

Back in college, Sarah believed Sean wanted to make a life with her. He loved her.

Or so he'd said.

But life doesn't always work out the way you hope.

People aren't always what they seem.

And what Sean said was not always what he did.

Her marriage to Sean turned sour long before his death, because the Sean she thought she loved was just an illusion.

He didn't want her or a family. So she'd tried to be mom and dad to the boys long before Sean's death.

She worked hard to give them everything they needed.

Thanks to her, they would never know a day of desperation for food, shelter, or love. Not the way she did growing up.

Jack leaned forward in his car seat and tapped her shoulder. "Mama, will Grandma remember us?"

"Of course. She can't wait to see you."

"Will we be able to watch TV and play in Grandma's yard? Does she have a swing? What about a slide?" Jack liked to ask a lot of questions. And apparently he already missed his things at home.

Sarah took the left onto Carmel Valley Road. Her stomach tied into a knot as they drew closer to Margaret's home and six weeks of what was sure to be torment. "I'm sure you can watch TV and play in the yard, but I don't know if there's a swing. If I remember right, Grandma's property backs up to a horse ranch, so maybe we'll see some of the horses." She thought fondly of the ranch she'd transformed after her horrible time growing up there. Her private getaway—that she never got away to because of work.

Still, it was there waiting for her when she needed it.

"I've never seen a horse." Nick frowned, despite the excitement in his eyes.

"Maybe we'll get to see lots of new things on this adventure." She hoped with all her heart this trip would be good for the boys and not bring up sad memories.

Both boys went back to watching their tablets. She used the time to settle her heart and mind. She reminded herself that no matter what had happened between her and Sean, he had given her the greatest gifts in her life. Jack and Nick were her world and her greatest accomplishments.

She followed the GPS directions. It had been a while since she'd been to her mother-in-law's home. A wedding gift from

Margaret's third husband. Custom built on six acres with a grove of trees surrounding it. Of course, husband number three hadn't lasted long and Margaret retained the house in the divorce settlement. She said he loved that house and there was no way she was going to let him have it. After all, he owed her.

For what, Sarah didn't know. It seemed he ended the marriage simply because he and Margaret didn't have enough in common to hold it together when they bickered all the time.

At least he wasn't as bad as her second husband, a workaholic who sometimes liked to drink a little too much and turned out to be a mean drunk. Sean had actually really liked him because he taught Sean a lot about business when Sean worked for him in the office during his high school summers. The guy also bribed Sean and Bridget with gifts so they'd forgive the epic shouting matches he had with Margaret.

Margaret had Sean and Bridget with her first husband, who had an affair when the kids were young and Margaret was trying to be a good wife and mother to two rambunctious little ones. Sean remembered his father fondly as the guy who showed up on weekends in expensive sports cars and lavished him with extravagant gifts and always had a beautiful woman in his life, though they never stayed long. His dad passed young, when Sean was in his first year at college. He died in a tragic boat fire while on a scuba diving trip.

Sean grew up to be a lot like how he described his dad. Then he died young, too.

Three failed marriages and two children who turned out to be self-centered had left Margaret unfulfilled and unhappy.

Sarah couldn't change the past. She couldn't bring Sean back. But she could try to make this visit as pleasant as possible for her kids' sake. So she vowed to be herself during this visit and not let Margaret get to her.

At least, she'd try.

She wound her way down several back roads and finally reached her mother-in-law's magnificent tree-lined driveway. The leaves shown in beautiful golds and reds. Fall was Sarah's favorite time of year. The white house with dark green shutters flanking large windows came into view. The huge porch wrapped around the first floor. French doors opened onto the second-story balcony, providing wonderful views and a quiet place to sit in the rocking chairs and relax.

As she drew closer, she noticed the whole place had a weathered and neglected feel. The paint was peeling, the gardens were overgrown, the lawns had gone to weed, and the drive needed to be re-graveled.

Margaret had always been particular about the appearance of her home.

Sarah almost thought she had the wrong place until she parked in the drive and noticed Margaret sitting on the porch with a visitor. The other person remained hidden in the shadows, but she couldn't help but see Margaret's frown.

She glanced in the rearview mirror. Sure enough, the boys had fallen asleep. She exited the car and waved. "Hello, Margaret."

"You're late. Where are the boys?" Margaret's sharp, clipped words grated.

Not even a hello. "Asleep in back." Sarah opened Jack's door and woke him with a gentle rub on his chest.

"Mama, are we there yet?" Jack rubbed at his eyes.

"Yes, honey. Let's go see Grandma."

Sarah turned around and Jack climbed onto her back. Sarah

went to the other passenger door, opened it, and gently woke Nick.

Nick opened his big green eyes, and as he did upon waking most days told her, "Daddy played with me while I slept."

Sarah's throat clogged, as it always did. She brushed her son's golden hair away from his brow, gave him a smile, and said, "Daddy will come back and play when you go to sleep tonight. Wanna see Grandma?"

Nick nodded.

She set Jack on the ground beside her, then hooked her hands under Nick's arms and lifted him from his seat and held him close.

Sarah walked toward Margaret with her getting-heavier-by-the-day load and Jack right beside her with his little arm wrapped around her leg. The guest stepped out of the shadows to the porch railing and leaned against the post, staring down at her. She wished he'd remained hidden. Tall, handsome, he conveyed strength and confidence in his worn boots, faded jeans, and chambray work shirt. He was made to draw a woman's eye with that gorgeous face and wide shoulders, and she found herself staring for a moment before she caught herself and realized the unfamiliar sensation running through her was attraction.

She couldn't remember the last time a man made her feel any kind of personal interest.

Sarah guessed he probably worked at the nearby horse ranch. His intense gaze studied her. Margaret had probably already given him an earful about her no-good daughter-in-law, and Sarah's initial interest quickly faded because he probably already thought she was a gold-digging bitch.

She glanced back to Margaret, noticing for the first time the sixty-four-year-old woman's small frame seemed a bit frail, her complexion pale. Her graying blond hair had been cut short into a simple, sleek style. Margaret held her hands clasped so tightly, her knuckles had turned white. They appeared swollen.

Sarah knew all too well grief and pain could wear a person down. Maybe that's what she saw in Margaret as the older woman carefully placed each foot on the treads as she made her way down the steps to them. Her gaze locked on Jack, who had Sarah's same dark hair and brown eyes. He'd grown a lot over the past two years. Margaret noted the differences with surprise in her eyes.

Sarah sympathized. Time went by way too fast and her boys were growing up and changing with every passing day.

Nick lifted his face from her neck and Margaret gasped at the sight of him. While Jack took after her, Nick looked just like Sean. Blond hair, a beautiful soft face with his father's light coloring, the same mouth, slender build, and piercing green eyes.

Margaret blinked tears away. Her stoic exterior showed a tiny crack but Margaret pulled herself together and hid her true emotions again.

It couldn't be easy for her to see how much the boys had changed over the last two years and face the reminder that life went on, even when you still grieved. And let resentments hold you back.

Jack ran the short distance to Margaret. She opened her arms to him and cuddled and kissed him on the head, then immediately produced a chocolate candy. Jack snatched it and gave her a warm, sweet smile.

Margaret cupped Jack's face in her hand. "You've grown at least six inches since I saw you last. You'll be tall, like your father."

"Mama says she's going to stop feeding me because I'm almost as big as her." Jack's serious tone made it seem like Sarah had meant it.

"Well, not to worry, Grandma will feed you bunches and you'll be an inch taller by the time you go home."

"Can I watch TV? I want to watch cartoons." Sarah's boy was obsessed with TV, which meant she had to make him earn it. At home, homework and chores came first.

"Later, Jack. Let's get settled first and spend time with Grandma." Margaret's gaze drifted to Nick, still in Sarah's arms, playing with her hair. Something he always did. She cherished every stroke he made down her hair to the middle of her back.

Sarah took the initiative and closed the distance to Margaret, so she could get a better look at him. "Honey, do you remember Grandma? Please say hello."

"Hi." Her shy guy spoke softly, then whispered in her ear.

Sarah whispered back and Nick smiled. She looked right into Margaret's eyes and told her what Nick said. "Nick would like to know if he can have a candy, too. He also wants you to know that his daddy said he misses you."

Margaret gasped. She recovered quickly, hiding the shock in her eyes. "Of course you can have a candy, Nick."

Sarah set Nick down and stretched her aching back. It often hurt because she was always carrying the boys. They wouldn't be little for long and she tried hard to enjoy these moments and not take them for granted.

Nick received his candy and smiled with a mix of happiness and wariness. Margaret looked over the boys' heads and eyed Sarah up and down, obviously finding her lacking, before she scooted the boys up the steps. "Go find the cookies on the counter in the kitchen."

Sarah didn't like the boys having so many goodies right before dinner, but she held her tongue, not wanting to start off on the wrong foot.

Once the boys cleared the front door, Margaret turned on her. "How dare you say that their father misses me! You have some nerve coming here and speaking of Sean as if he's still alive." Margaret shook with anger and grief.

She obviously didn't intend to be civil.

Sarah had vowed to remain calm no matter what. She would not argue with Margaret or engage in any kind of yelling or verbal sparring. She'd had enough with people yelling when she was growing up and didn't raise her voice unless absolutely necessary. The boys deserved to know their grandmother, and she was going to make sure they got the opportunity. "Nick asked me to tell you that."

"He needs to understand Sean isn't coming back. The doctor told you that two years ago when Nick was having nightmares," Margaret challenged.

Sarah took a slow breath to calm her rising ire. She had seen Jack and Nick through their tears and grief. She had finally gotten them to accept their father's death, though they did so in different ways.

Jack always wanted to hear stories about Sean. Every night at bedtime, Sarah told him one of her memories. He especially liked the stories that included Jack and his father together. It made Sean real to both the boys, whose memories of their dad faded a little more each day.

Nick's acceptance had taken longer. Even though he was younger and everyone thought he would forget his father, that wasn't the case. Nick began having dreams about his dad immediately after Sean's death. At first, Nick woke up scared and confused and wondered why his father wasn't home. The doctor told Sarah not to encourage him, but to coax him to accept Sean wasn't coming back. Even so young, Nick seemed to understand his father was gone, but couldn't reconcile why he saw him on their nightly adventures.

Sarah took another approach and encouraged Nick to talk about his escapades with his dad. She told him how special it was that he could see his dad in his dreams.

Nick found comfort in seeing his dad in that way. As time passed, he accepted his father could only come at night and his grief subsided.

Sarah looked at Margaret and very quietly stated, "Nick doesn't have nightmares. I encourage him to talk about Sean whenever he wants. To Nick, his daddy is alive somewhere and plays with him in his dreams. I will not allow you, or anyone else, to make him feel that it's wrong in any way. The doctor and everyone else said he would forget Sean. I don't want that, and neither should you. So, if he says that his father told him he misses you, then you can believe it. Nick believes it."

Margaret pressed a hand to her chest, the flood of emotions reflected in her eyes, making her breath unsteady. "He looks just like Sean. More now than when he was a baby. I miss Sean, too."

Sarah almost hadn't heard the last sentence. She took another slow breath. "I know you don't want me here. But I brought your grandsons to see you and spend time with you in hopes that we could put the past behind us."

Margaret's eyes narrowed. "Never. You took Sean from me, but you won't keep the boys from me anymore." Margaret dismissed her with a glare and slowly went back up the stairs. She excused herself from her guest and made her goodbyes before going inside.

Sarah didn't even rate an introduction because she wasn't important.

She would always be the one who kept Sean away, and now the boys.

She didn't do it on purpose. Life had to go on, and she had to provide a good life for her sons, which left very little time for herself.

She was beginning to see that her responsibilities were wearing her down. She could seriously use a nap and a few days alone with nothing to do.

Wishful thinking.

Sarah stared up at the house, wondering what she had gotten herself into, completely aware of Margaret's guest's penetrating gaze and the temptation building inside her to look at him and take in again the imposing but intriguing man.

Chapter Four

*L*uke took in the entire scene from the porch riveted by the contrasts. Margaret angrier than he'd ever seen her. Sarah, calm and warm with her boys, nothing like he expected. Margaret described her as cold, calculating, and selfish. None of that matched anything he saw in the tired woman's appearance, eyes, or attitude.

Exhaustion hung on her like a heavy pack weighing her down. She kept up a good front, but he noticed the dark circles under her eyes and the way she stood not quite straight, her shoulders lax.

Petite compared to him, maybe five-foot-four, with long dark hair shot through with strands of red that fired in the sunlight. It looked so soft and silky, he wanted to run his fingers through it like her son had done. Her flawless skin didn't have an ounce of makeup. Nothing needed to enhance her natural beauty, especially her red lips that even at rest held the hint of a smile.

She radiated a warmth that seemed to wrap around him.

She didn't flaunt that lithe body and soft curves with revealing clothes. She seemed perfectly comfortable and at ease in her skin.

Everything, all of her, woke up his hibernating libido. And like a hungry bear, he wanted to feast on her.

Shaken by the sudden desire, he kept his outside impassive, despite the quake erupting inside him.

He'd lost interest in women over the years. At thirty-four, he was tired of always coming close to having something real only to have the illusion evaporate before his eyes when his name and business became more appealing than him to the woman in his life. He'd had the misfortune to fall for a couple of women who seemed sincere at the start but turned out to be opportunistic, leaving him feeling used, unhappy, unsatisfied, and like he'd failed to make the relationship what he wanted.

His parents and younger brother made love, family, and happiness look so easy.

Not so much for him.

So after getting burned one too many times he kept his interactions with women superficial and short-lived. He tired of dating. He tired of life in general. Boredom had been his constant companion as of late.

Sarah intrigued him.

But if she turned out to be the woman Margaret described . . .

He wasn't so sure because he expected an overly done up woman with perfect hair and makeup in an expensive outfit and overpriced shoes, dripping diamonds, not the woman standing in the driveway wearing Levi's, a simple tee, and well-worn tennis shoes.

He walked down the stairs and found a safe topic to break the ice. "Cute boys."

Sarah startled when he spoke and her gaze landed full on him. Those brown-sugar eyes did something to his gut.

"Um, thank you. I'm Sarah. I believe my mother-in-law forgot to introduce us." Her voice was like a slow song you never wanted to end.

"I think she overlooked it." Luke couldn't get over her delicate beauty. He simply enjoyed looking at her.

He caught himself staring before she noticed.

She quirked a brow and studied him with a look, clearly meant to signal an attempt at levity. "Are you the next contestant to become husband number four?"

The unexpected laugh that absurd joke evoked caught in his throat when she smiled right at him. All that warmth and humor directed right at him. Damn. "Don't believe the rumors clogging the local grapevine." His voice sounded harsher than he intended, but he was out of practice at being lighthearted and making jokes.

Sarah gave him a mischievous look. "I think she could give you a run for your money. After all, she's had a lot of practice, having had three previous husbands who couldn't keep up with her. I'm sure she'll keep you on your toes." She winked to let him know she was truly teasing.

Luke laughed out loud. When was the last time he laughed like that? "First of all, Margaret's a great woman, but we are not an item. Second, I could be her son."

The smile vanished from Sarah's face and it looked as if a curtain had been drawn in those beautiful brown eyes.

Yeah, he needed to polish his rusty social skills.

"Excuse me, I have to check on my boys."

Sarah sidestepped to go around him, but he blocked her way. "I'm sorry. I didn't mean to upset you. I see there's bad blood between the two of you regarding Sean, but I didn't mean anything by what I said. I'm sorry."

The urge to touch her, offer some comfort to make her believe he meant it, overtook him, but he locked in his control once again. He hoped he could back up without crushing her to him. His whole body begged to pull this woman close.

Sarah's rosy lips tilted in a small smile. "I accept your apology. I'm tired and a little on edge."

He nodded, glad the tense moment had passed. "Can I help you get your luggage from the car?"

"I can manage."

"I'm sure you can, but it wouldn't be very neighborly of me not to assist."

She stretched sideways and pressed a fist to her lower back. "If you don't mind, I'd appreciate the help."

"How much does that little guy weigh?"

"I think thirty-six pounds at his last pediatric visit. Maybe a bit more. My back says more." She rolled her shoulders and grimaced.

Damn. Her tight jeans and pink top concealed the strength of her slight frame.

She opened the back of the SUV, revealing three suitcases, a backpack, and two large computer cases. "Did you enjoy the drive down?"

"Once the kids settled in and I finished a conference call, I got lost in the beautiful scenery." The big yawn punctuated how tired she looked.

"Were you up late last night because of the trip down here?"

She shrugged. "Kinda. Work last night, the kids, more work this morning. A couple fires I had to put out that couldn't wait. We got a late start on the road, but I managed."

Luke wished she'd say more about work. He really wanted to know if she actually contributed to the company or just made a good show of it while others did everything. Still, all that plus a call in the car. "You must have had one hell of a day."

"Every day is one hell of a day."

Before Luke could ask her about that exhaustion-fueled comment, the boys ran down the steps calling for her.

"Mama, can I have my tablet now?" Jack asked, his eyes pleading with her.

"I'm tired. I want cartoons." Nick yawned.

"Who are you?" This came from Jack, the more curious one.

Sarah looked up with the question in her eyes, too.

He should have properly introduced himself. His mother raised him better.

"Luke Thompson. I own the ranch behind your grandma's house." His eyes fell on her again and he said, "It's nice to meet you."

Hers narrowed with anger and suspicion, but she didn't say anything about him being the lawyer who'd contacted her about this visit because Jack jumped up and down at Luke's feet. "Grandma says you have horses, and barn cats, and fields of corn. I like to take the leaves off corn. Can we see your horses? We've never seen a horse."

Luke took the rapid-fire questions and statements in stride. "Yes, I have horses and barn cats. There is a vegetable garden that has corn growing in it. You've never seen a horse? What kind of place do you live that you've never seen a horse?"

"We live in a city and Mama won't let us have a dog." Jack and Nick looked accusingly at her.

"Outnumbered again. You can't have a dog until you can take care of it yourself. Mama is too busy to take care of any more little ones all by herself. You two are more than enough." Sarah ran a hand over each boy's head. She tickled both of them and handed Jack the backpack.

"Grab your tablets out of the back seat, then back up to the house." She waved her hands to get them moving.

Luke watched the pair do as they were told, then run up the porch steps. He thought of his own brother and how they were always together when they were young. "The boys are great."

"And yet you want to take me to court and *try* to take them from me?"

Luke regretted that she'd put two and two together and blamed him for Margaret's actions. "*I* don't want to take you to court. *I* don't think it's good for anyone involved to fight over children. Which is why I convinced Margaret to let me send the letter requesting the visit."

"Yes, it was a very nicely worded *order* to bring them here."

He tried to explain why he got involved, even though he didn't really want anything to do with this family drama. "Sean and I were childhood friends. Margaret was devastated by his death and she misses her grandkids."

Sarah held her hands out wide. "Yet she's given me the cold shoulder for the past *two* years. If she wanted to see them, all she had to do was call and ask."

"Would you have brought them to her?"

"Yes. Because I'm a reasonable person."

He actually believed her. "She doesn't think so."

"Because she doesn't know me at all."

He wondered if the things Margaret said about her were really true. "Well, she'll get to know you over the next six weeks." Despite the circumstances, and because of his overwhelming attraction to her, he'd like to, too.

"All she wants to know is anything she can use against me. That's why you're here. Right? To dig up all the dirt you can to present in court."

"I came by to lend some moral support because she's expecting you to make this . . . difficult."

"Me. She's the hostile one."

"I have to say, you showed restraint."

She mellowed. "I will make sure my boys have the best time

they can with her because they deserve to know their grand-mother. But if she thinks she can take them from me, then both of you will find you're in for the fight of your life."

Luke liked a challenge, but he didn't want to fight with her. "It's my hope, and I think Margaret's, too, that you two will work out your differences for the kids' sake."

Sarah rolled her eyes. "Yeah, she seems like she wants to work things out."

"Give her a little time."

"I think it's obvious I'll be the one doing all the giving."

Luke wondered about the pampered princess Margaret de-scribed and whether she and the woman standing before him were really one and the same.

Maybe over the last few years Sarah had changed.

Maybe she wasn't at all like Margaret described.

"Now you've seen that I've delivered them to her. I assure you I will stay out of her way and let her enjoy her time with them. If you'll excuse me, I need to get our things inside. The sun is set-ting, and I need to feed my bottomless boys."

Luke wasn't quite ready to go.

He liked a good puzzle, and Sarah was like a thousand pieces sitting on a table just waiting for him to sort out and fit together. It would nag at him until he figured out who this woman truly was. And he would find out.

Chapter Five

Sarah didn't know what to make of Luke. He didn't seem quite sure of her, and she could only blame Margaret for that.

Sean had never mentioned Luke as a childhood friend. Then again, he really only liked to talk about himself. And he'd been a live-in-the-moment kind of guy. She'd liked that about him, because she often thought about her crummy past and found herself wallowing in all the bad instead of focusing on how far she'd come and all the good in her life.

Once the boys came along, she had so much good to focus on with them.

She wanted to place some of the blame on Luke for Margaret threatening to take her to court, but he seemed sincere that he thought they could resolve their issues with this voluntary visit. Even if it had been forced.

Luke didn't take the hint to leave and pulled all three suitcases out of the back of her SUV. "I'll take these in for you. You grab the other stuff."

"You don't have to do that."

He started toward the house. "I know. Just being neighborly," he reminded her.

She wondered if there were indeed ulterior motives at play.

Fine. Let him and Margaret watch her. She expected to be scrutinized by Margaret the whole time she was here anyway. So be it. They'd see. She loved her boys. She was a good mother. No one could say any different.

She grabbed the computer bags out of the back of the car, slammed the lid, and caught up to Luke on the porch. The second they walked in the front door, Margaret called out, "Take the two bedrooms at the top of the stairs on the left."

Luke followed her up the gorgeous oak staircase.

She walked into the first bedroom on the left and found a beautiful cream-colored room with a king-size bed. A stack of sheets and blankets sat atop the bare mattress. The huge antique dresser had a beveled mirror above it. Crystal vases stood on each end of the dresser and a huge crystal chandelier hung in the center of the room. A cream-colored rug stood out against the dark wood floor. Everything had a thick layer of dust covering it. Stuffy; the air smelled stale.

Margaret had definitely *not* rolled out the welcome mat for her.

The pictures of Sean overwhelmed her with feelings of resentment and anger. Several stood grouped in old silver antique frames on each dresser and night table. They showed him as a boy up until his college graduation.

Clearly his life before she had stolen him away.

"Set the suitcases down anywhere. I'll go through the bathroom and check out the boys' room before I move their stuff in there." Dust bunnies skittered across the floor as she walked toward the Jack and Jill bathroom.

Concern filled Luke's eyes. "Maybe Margaret meant the rooms on the other side of the staircase?"

No, she didn't. "Thank you for bringing up the bags. I appreciate it, but you don't have to stick around." *And witness my embarrassment.* "I'll be just fine."

"Let's see the other room first. Margaret's arthritis has been getting worse, but I can't believe she'd allow company without getting the rooms ready."

Sarah knew better and continued on through the bathroom and found two twin beds in a forest-green room. A nightstand stood between the two beds with a crystal lamp, pictures of Sean, and the same gorgeous wood floors that were throughout the house. An antique dresser and chest of drawers lined the walls around the room and above the dresser was an oil painting of a little boy playing with a dog in a field. Jack would be happy to find the television and DVD player with the small love seat in front just waiting for him to plop down and enjoy. She could hook up one of her computers to it so they could watch Netflix on the TV screen.

Each bed had a new-looking blanket. A toy chest in the corner held several wrapped packages waiting to be opened.

Unlike her room and the bathroom, this room had been cleaned and made ready for two little boys. "It's perfect. They'll love it."

Luke hooked his thumbs in his jeans pockets. "She's certainly made sure to let you know who's welcome and who isn't. Aren't you going to say anything about your room?" Luke seemed to be waiting for her to throw a tantrum like a spoiled child who required everyone to jump at her every whim.

That wasn't her, never had been, no matter what Margaret's opinion.

Or Luke's, for that matter.

And she wouldn't give him something to use against her if Margaret pushed forward and took her to court.

Margaret must have told him a convincing tale about who she thought Sarah was. But she wasn't about to dignify Margaret's lack of hospitality with the least bit of outward frustration.

What did Sarah expect? Margaret hated her. She wasn't welcome here. Not surprising, but it still hurt.

Luke stared at her, confusion in his eyes, waiting for her to say something.

"I don't mind dusting and making the bed. I've got to get the bathroom ready for the boys' bath tonight. Thanks for your help. Please excuse me."

Luke raised one eyebrow, the earlier confusion turning to anger. "Aren't you even just a little put out that she got things ready for the boys and neglected to get the room ready for you?"

Was he baiting her? Hoping she'd lose her temper and play right into his hands? Not going to happen.

"I'm sure after marrying Sean you got used to the finer things in life."

Sarah met his incredulous gaze and held it for a good long minute. Margaret had certainly made him believe that about her.

She didn't have the energy to change his mind. She didn't really care what he thought. But maybe if she showed him who she really was, he'd somehow convince Margaret she didn't need to drag them to court for nothing.

"I'm sure she's told you I'm the wicked witch who deceived, manipulated, and took advantage of her son. She'll spend the next six weeks slighting me at every turn, just enough to get to me, but not so that the boys notice. Each time they aren't around, she'll remind me how much I stole from her.

"I didn't come from money and Sean did. So what? Do I like nice things and having someone to clean up the house? Beats shoveling manure and sleeping on the floor, that's for sure."

Luke held her gaze. "So that's how it is? You met Sean and saw an opportunity for a better life?"

"That's a little simplistic, don't you think?"

"Is that what you did? Deceived, manipulated, and took advantage to get what you wanted?" He sounded disappointed in her.

"That's exactly what Margaret would like you to believe, but that's not me. Either you believe me or you don't."

"Margaret is my friend. I don't want anyone taking advantage of her."

She held her hands out. "I brought the boys to visit their grandmother. That's all. I don't want anything from her." At the very least, she wished he'd believe that.

His lips went flat. "Every woman I ever met was after something."

"Sounds like you pick the wrong kind of women."

His hands sank deeper into his pockets. "So my family keeps telling me."

She appreciated his honesty and the reluctant admission. "We're here for six weeks. Thanks to her thoughtlessness about them having school, I'll be mom, teacher, and run my company remotely, all the while hoping she'll see taking me to court is pointless and unnecessary. Six weeks," she repeated, "then I'll take the boys home, and we'll be out of Margaret's life."

"You aren't going to let her see the boys again?"

Sarah rolled her eyes and let out a heavy sigh. "I'm not the bad guy you think I am. Margaret can see the boys whenever she wants, but that doesn't mean I'll drop everything to facilitate it the way I did for this extended stay."

Her phone rang. She dug it out of her pocket, resigned to another long night. "Excuse me, I have to take this call, and I still need to feed the boys."

"I thought you were on vacation?"

"I have a business to run." She tapped the screen to accept the call. "Hi, Abby, put me through." She left the boys' room with the phone at her ear waiting to be connected to the board meeting.

Luke followed her into the bathroom and studied her while she retrieved cleaning supplies from the linen cupboard and filled the basin with hot water all the while listening to her phone. "I could help you get things in order."

She tapped the mute button, but continued to listen as the minutes from the last meeting were read to all the members of the board. "That's very nice of you, but I'll take care of this. Really, I expected much worse."

Luke touched her arm. "It's not right."

She appreciated the sentiment. "Her son is dead. She holds me responsible. I can't change that. To her, I am the person she believes me to be. I promised the boys six weeks with their grandmother and that's what they're going to get. If she wants to see them, then I come as part of the package. Thank you for the help with the bags. I can manage from here."

She couldn't quite make out the mixed emotions in his eyes, but she appreciated the hint of sympathy.

She unmuted her call. "George, could you go over the quarterly figures with everyone. I want the latest numbers." She kept her gaze on Luke as she addressed her CFO and he recited the company's financial information.

She yawned and the sympathy in Luke's eyes turned to concern.

She muted the call again. "Please, just go. I've had a really long day and it's going to be a long night." Overwhelmed by Margaret's hostility, Luke's attention and need to know her intentions and digging into her past, along with the cleaning she had to do, feeding the boys, and running her company, she couldn't take it all at once and not feel the burdens taking more than she had to give right now.

"Margaret should have at least been hospitable and grateful you brought the boys to see her."

Yeah. It would be nice if they could be civil and Margaret hadn't left more work for her.

She gave him a weak smile, but had nothing to say before she unmuted her call and forged on with work because that took precedence to making a stranger like her. "George, those figures are off from the projections. What's the difference? And how did it affect our profits?" She listened to George's explanation and scrubbed the sink and counter, all the while watching Luke watching her in the mirror.

Held in his uncompromising stare, she felt like he was looking for something within her.

He wouldn't find the woman Margaret described to him.

The boys pounded their little feet up the stairs and appeared in the bathroom doorway next to Luke.

"Can we see your horses?" Jack asked, his eyes pleading with Luke.

Since she was distracted listening to the financials George rattled off, Luke got the jump on her. "Sure you can. In fact, your mom can bring you over to the ranch tomorrow at eleven and we'll go riding."

"Yes!" Jack smiled from ear to ear.

Nick's eyes filled with excitement, though he was too shy to say anything to Luke.

She met the challenge and amusement in Luke's eyes with her own frustration.

She muted her call again and redirected the boys so she could have another minute alone with Luke. "Go check out your room. After this call, we'll have dinner."

Jack sighed and gave her a sad frown. "I thought you were going to be on vacation."

"I'm sorry, little man. I promise I won't work the whole time." Jack might not understand what it was going to be like the next six weeks, but Sarah anticipated a lot of phone calls and late nights at the computer.

The boys ran into the other room.

She kept her voice low so they wouldn't overhear. "Why would you do that?"

"Because I want to get to know you."

"Why? So you know just how to attack and misrepresent me in court?"

"If you're not the woman Margaret described, what do you have to lose? Prove her wrong," he challenged, then turned and walked away.

Of course, she couldn't back out. The boys would throw a fit. Having grown up on a ranch, she really loved horses and would love to teach the boys to ride. And though she shouldn't care what Luke thought, she wanted to show him that she wasn't the monster Margaret probably made her out to be.

Plus, she felt oddly sorry to see Luke go and she wasn't quite sure why, except she really did want him to like her.

It shouldn't matter whether he did or not, but it upset her that maybe he'd believe Margaret without even giving her a chance.

Still, did he invite them over to find things to use against her, or because he really did want to get to know her?

Chapter Six

*L*uke found Margaret gazing out the window in the breakfast room, her eyes filled with sadness. She looked a little lost.

Her watery, grief-filled gaze turned up to him. "Nick looks just like Sean."

Luke agreed, remembering his childhood friend fondly. "All the photos in the room you gave Sarah reminded me of that, too."

"Not just his looks, he has his mannerisms, his shyness as a boy. Sean grew out of that and became a charismatic man. I'm sure Nick will, too. Just looking at him brings back all the memories." She smacked her open hand on the table. "I hate her! She took him away, and then she robbed him of his future. He'll never see those boys grown. Sooner or later, they'll forget him."

"It sounds like Sarah tries to help the boys remember him. She encourages Nick's dreams."

She rolled her eyes. "Children grow out of such things." Her lips pressed tight. "Sean was just a means to an end. She got the business and the kids. The only thing Sean got was a greedy wife and dying before his time, thanks to her."

"Isn't that a bit harsh? She brought the kids to visit just like you asked."

Margaret gave him a dirty look for siding with Sarah. "Harsh!

No. The boys told me she'll be working from here, rubbing it in my face that she owns Sean's company."

"Take that time to get to know the boys while she's out of your way," he suggested, trying to get her to focus on what was important.

Margaret's eyes went bright. "That's what I like about you, Luke. You always find the silver lining. Maybe the boys will open up about what it's really like at home and we can use that in court to make sure she lets me see them whenever I want."

"That's not what I meant." He wanted Margaret to accept her victory. The boys were here and she should focus on them, not her battle with Sarah, who seemed all too willing to put their arguments on hold. "I really don't think she wants to keep the kids from you." Sarah seemed more than reasonable.

"Just wait. In no time, you'll see what I see. Her true colors will come out. She can't hide who she really is."

He'd found that out the hard way with a few of the women he'd dated. "Regardless, I think you should give her a chance." He planned to do just that. "It's been a long time and people change." As a defense attorney, he often saw the worst people could do to each other. Surprisingly, he wanted Sarah to be more than he initially expected.

"She's self-centered and selfish." Margaret's bitterness and resentment held her hostage in her anger and grief.

"I invited her and the boys over to the ranch tomorrow to see the horses. Come with them."

She dismissed that with a frustrated frown and a telling rub of her knee. "You know I don't have the energy for walking all over that huge spread of yours. I'm sure the boys will have fun. Just make sure she doesn't burn the place down while she's there."

That spiked his interest. "Why would I have to worry about that?"

"I told you yesterday she was a troubled teen. She burned her uncle's property to the ground. Luckily, no one got hurt."

There had to be a story there.

His gut tightened at the vindictiveness of it. But his heart softened at the thought there had to be a reason, because she didn't come off as callous or cruel.

He'd met his fair share of ruthless criminals.

Tired of hearing all these terrible things about Sarah that didn't ring wholly true anymore, he tried not to put too much stock in Margaret's accusations. He may have just met Sarah, but something wasn't right. He didn't think she was a bad person. After all, the boys seemed very attached to their mom, and she to them.

"Don't let that sweet and innocent act fool you. Behind those doe eyes is a mean and hurtful person. Sean learned it too late. Don't get taken in by her, too."

He couldn't ignore Margaret's warning. "How do you know she burned her uncle's place down?"

"Sean told me. She confessed to doing it right before they got married. After the arson, she met a man who got her out of trouble and paid for her to attend college. I can just imagine what she gave that man to help her out of that kind of situation." Margaret pursed her lips and raised an eyebrow. "I'm sure you know what I mean."

His gut soured at the thought. "I get the drift."

Now she'd accused Sarah of using sex to get out of trouble.

He really didn't know what to think. "Did Sean say why she did it?"

"What possible reason could justify setting fire to someone's home?"

He didn't know, but something like that took a lot of rage. He wondered what had happened to make Sarah go to such an extreme. *If* she even did it.

He couldn't think through all the information and contradictions. "The woman you describe, and the woman I just met don't add up. I guess I'll see who she is when she comes to the ranch tomorrow."

"Not everyone is as they appear. You know that."

He'd met people who looked like they wouldn't hurt a fly but had done some heinous things. He'd met guys who were handsome enough to easily get a date, but instead of treating women with respect resorted to harassment, assault, and worse.

Nothing people did really surprised him anymore.

And because of the people he dealt with he read people well. While he had reservations about Sarah, he wondered if they were rooted in what Margaret told him and his desire to help his friend rather than in anything substantive.

His initial impression of her seemed real. She was a beautiful woman, a warm and patient mother, a reasonable person, and not one to back down when challenged, but also not someone looking for a fight.

"If anyone met you right now, they'd look at you and see a rancher. How would they know you and your family own one of the most successful and lucrative law firms in the country?"

"I see your point. I guess I'll get a better sense of her tomorrow."

"You'll see, I'm not wrong about her."

"Enjoy your evening with the boys. Have fun with them. Don't let her get to you. I'll check on you later in the week."

Luke was almost out the door when Sarah came down the stairs, cell phone to her ear as she carried on her business conversation. The boys stomped and scuffled upstairs. All he could think was that she looked lovely gliding down the stairs punctuating her conversation with one hand while holding the phone with the other. For a fleeting second he thought how nice it would be to have a home full of noise and life and a woman walking down the stairs to him.

Her eyes met his. She gave him a cautious smile and continued on into the kitchen.

He needed to get a grip. The woman was getting under his skin and she didn't even know it.

Chapter Seven

*T*he evening hadn't been as bad as she expected. Mostly because she and Margaret stayed out of each other's way. Sarah cooked dinner for everyone while finishing her conference call. She and Margaret engaged the boys during dinner but not each other. Margaret didn't even thank her for cooking and cleaning up.

The boys enjoyed playing with their new toys and Margaret. Sarah watched the boys with their grandmother and decided their happiness was worth being in the same house with her mother-in-law.

She'd discovered a few surprises last night. The pantry and refrigerator were barely stocked, the main living spaces of the house were in need of a good dusting and vacuuming, and Margaret had apparently abandoned the main suite upstairs and moved into the smaller suite off the kitchen.

She'd tried to think of a discreet way to ask Margaret about the state of the house and property, but couldn't find an opening for the conversation that wouldn't lead to Margaret taking insult or thinking Sarah looked down on her or her home.

So she thought she'd do something nice for Margaret, and keep the boys from being surrounded by all that dust, and called her housekeeper and nanny, Camille, to come in the morning and clean the house top to bottom.

Once the boys settled into bed after their bath and books, she'd stayed up until four in the morning working on the Knox Project. Not such a hardship to sit out on the balcony with her laptop. The cool night air kept her energized and you couldn't beat the view of the trees and all those stars. If she listened carefully, she could hear the horses from Luke's ranch.

She'd gotten the boys breakfast at seven, done the grocery shopping at eight, and met Camille at the door just before eleven. "You made it."

Camille hugged both boys at once. "I've missed you guys."

Jack cocked his head. "You saw us yesterday."

Camille poked Jack in the belly. "It seems like forever." She brushed her hand over Nick's head, then turned to Sarah. "The drive was beautiful." She glanced past Sarah into the house. "Everything good?"

"Sure," Sarah replied because what could she say about Margaret's expected hostile welcome?

"We're going to see the horses," Nick announced.

"I heard." Camille looked at her. "You sure that's a good idea?"

Spending the day with Margaret's attorney . . . No. Probably not a good idea. Still, she couldn't let him dare her to prove him wrong and not show up to do just that.

"We're going to have fun riding horses." Her cheerful response probably didn't fool Camille about how she really felt about facing Luke's continued scrutiny.

"Be yourself," Camille said. "He'll see you for who you really are."

"Who are you?" Margaret asked from behind Sarah.

Sarah waved Camille into the entryway. "Margaret, this is my good friend Camille. She's the boys' nanny and our housekeeper."

"What is she doing here? If you're too busy to pay attention to the children, I'm here. I'm happy to do things with them."

Sarah handed the cooler to Jack. "Take this out to the car and get in your seats. I'll be right there."

Sarah waited for the boys to do as she said, then turned to Margaret. "I'm taking the boys to Luke's. Camille is here to clean the house."

"That's not necessary," Margaret argued, but Sarah saw the embarrassment in her eyes.

"I've got a heavy workload and I promised the boys I wouldn't work all the time while we are here, so I don't have time to clean the house myself for you. It's needed and Camille will take care of it."

"I don't want a stranger in my house."

"You invited *me* here." She hoped Margaret understood that she didn't know Sarah as well as she claimed to Luke. "Camille is part of our family, so please treat her kindly and let her do her job."

Margaret silently seethed for a moment. "Fine. Of course you'd hire someone to do everything for you." With that Margaret spun on her heel and walked away.

Sarah turned to Camille. "I left the cleaning supplies in the kitchen."

Camille touched her arm. "Don't worry. I'll have the place cleaned in no time and I'll stay out of Margaret's way."

"Thank you. I know this is above and beyond."

Camille smiled. "It's no trouble. And you did pay for my upcoming vacation." Camille deserved the five-night six-day Key West vacation.

"If you want to extend your stay a couple extra days, just let me know."

"That's probably all the family time I can handle." Camille was meeting her parents and they planned to spend the week together catching up.

Sarah wished she were only here for six days instead of six weeks. "Thank you again for driving all the way out here. I'm hoping Margaret doesn't get as upset about the gardeners coming by later."

Camille looked around the yard. "It's not safe for the boys to be running around out here without cutting back the lawn and overgrown bushes."

"Let's hope she sees it that way." Sarah glanced at the boys waiting in the car. "Gotta go. I don't want to be late."

"Don't let Margaret or her lawyer get to you. You're a great mom."

"Thanks. I appreciate that." She didn't think anything would change Margaret's mind.

Sarah rushed to the car and made sure the boys were strapped in properly, then slid into the driver's seat and drove down the long drive toward Luke's place.

"I can't wait to see the horsies," Jack announced, his gaze focused on the road ahead.

"We'll be there soon." Already tired, she sucked in a deep breath, knowing even this day wasn't going to end until well into the morning hours again.

She needed to reevaluate the hours she worked, because they left no time for herself. And the constant fatigue left her feeling perpetually drained, a little bit sick, and dragging.

When she arrived at the ranch, all thoughts of sleep and long hours vanished. The gorgeous land spread out in wide pastures and tree-covered hills. Well tended, all the buildings were white, including the main house. The stable was first-class and huge. The pastures were green and vast, some outlined by white fencing and dotted with beautiful grazing horses.

Luke lived on quite a spread. The main house stood two stories tall, white with dark blue shutters, and a wraparound covered porch. The garden out front was well tended and the plants bloomed profusely in shades of pink, red, and purple. The scent of gardenias from the main house walkway floated down to the barn.

She was so taken by the ranch that she didn't register the noise coming from inside the barn until she'd gotten the boys out of the car.

"Mama, what's that noise?" Jack started backing away from the stable and the sound of the distressed animal.

"It's okay. That horse is just mad and letting everyone know it. Let's go find Luke. He's probably helping take care of the horse."

The barn was massive with at least twelve stalls on each side of the wide center aisle. At the far end of the barn outside an open stall stood a very angry stallion. What surprised Sarah was the manner in which everyone was dealing with the distraught animal. Horses were emotional creatures and needed to be handled with patience and care.

She didn't see Luke. Two men on each side of the horse held him with lead ropes, obviously trying to keep the animal under control while another man tried to get close to him without getting kicked or bit. Each time the man took a step close to the horse, he went nuts and tried to buck, pull, and otherwise get free and away from the men. Very dangerous.

The frustrated horse could injure himself and the men.

Sarah sat the boys on a bench outside an empty stall, far away from the angry beast. "Do not move."

She walked down the long aisle toward the angry horse, singing a lullaby. At first, loudly, to get the horse's attention. As she made her way toward the animal, she softened her singing and stopped five feet from him. He watched her intently. As did the surprised men. The horse's ears pricked up and listened to her clear, soothing voice. He snorted and stomped, but kept his eyes on her.

One of the men backed up and got right in Sarah's face. "What the hell are you doing? Can't you see this animal is out of control?"

Sarah continued singing and sidestepped the man, so the horse could see her.

"Step back, Doc. Let her be." Luke's smooth, low voice rumbled like whiskey and the blues rolled together. It washed over her and sent an unfamiliar warmth through her whole body.

She'd felt him come up behind her before she'd heard him. She didn't have time to think much about that because the angry horse in front of her demanded her full attention.

She continued to sing the lullaby and walked straight up to the horse's head. He stomped and shook his head up and down. Sarah reached up and brushed a hand down the horse's nose.

In her singsong voice she asked, "What's his name?"

"Ace."

"Hello, Ace," she sang, then went on with the lullaby.

Luke's anxious voice rumbled behind her again "He's the backbone of this ranch. He's a champion and worth a fortune. Nothing can happen to him."

Still singing to the horse, she turned and looked at Luke. In that moment, she could see he not only needed the horse for his breeding program, but he loved the horse. She also noticed that her boys had moved up and were crowded behind Luke's legs. They peeked at her and Ace from around him.

"What do you need done with Ace?"

Luke answered for the man, who must be the vet. "He needs some shots and one of the trainers noticed he's favoring his left back hoof."

The vet added, "He also has a cut on his hindquarter that may need stitching."

Luke restrained his fury behind his clenched jaw. "He's been cut?"

"I'm sorry, Luke. He's out of control today and he hit his rump on the gate to the stall. It was his own damn fault. That horse has no sense, and he's meaner than a rattlesnake."

Sarah continued singing and rubbed both hands up the length of Ace's nose. Once she got her arms to full length, she pulled Ace's large head down and put her nose to his. She rubbed the sides of his head and stood nose to nose with him singing the lullaby. Ace began to calm and soon he wasn't stomping, or fussing. After several choruses, she knew just when the horse had bonded with her when he nuzzled his nose against her cheek.

Still singing to Ace she stepped back, grabbed a brush from a nearby table, and began to work the brush over his gleaming coat. He stood still, but watched her carefully. She worked and worked, brushing and singing, calming him even more. Once she'd given Ace a good once-over, she turned back to Luke and found all four men silent and watching her.

It was quite a picture, turning around and seeing Luke holding the hands of both her boys. She'd never seen a prettier picture. The boys were safe in a man's hands, and the fact that the man was as strong and gorgeous as Luke didn't hurt either.

She'd provided them with everything they needed, except a good man in their life.

Tears filled her eyes and she quickly blinked them away.

Ace nibbled at her jeans pocket and bumped his big head

against her back. Luke stepped forward thinking Ace was trying to hurt her.

Sarah held up her hand to stop him. She was still singing for the horse and turned back to Ace. "It's okay. He only wants what's in my pocket." Sarah took out a roll of the cherry candies the boys loved and peeled one off for Ace. The horse took it and nuzzled her neck.

She rubbed his big head and addressed the vet. "Doc, get the shots prepared as well as the sutures for Ace's hind leg."

She met Luke's worried gaze. "Don't worry. I've got this. I grew up on a horse ranch. I'll take care of Ace. I noticed you have two horses saddled outside. I presume those are for the boys to ride. Why don't you take them out and have someone help you get them up in the saddle and riding."

"I'm not leaving you with Ace. If he gets upset again, he could really hurt you."

"You and I both know if any of you come near this horse, he'll just go off again. He needs to be tended to, and I appear to be the one he trusts at the moment. I'd really like for you to take the boys out of here while I do it." The last thing she wanted was for her boys to see her get kicked if Ace got upset when she checked that hoof and cut. She was willing to take the risk for the beautiful animal.

It didn't hurt to show Luke she wasn't afraid to get her hands dirty and do the work.

The vet planted his hands on his hips. "Good God, Luke. You can't allow this woman to tend Ace. She's not a vet. What if she hurts him?"

Sarah rubbed Ace's neck. "I know what I'm doing. Take the boys outside, and I'll be there soon."

Luke shook his head. "I'll stay. Jerry, my manager, can take the boys outside to ride."

She didn't want anyone but Luke with her boys. "Look at them. They trust you. I trust you with them. Trust me with Ace. You take care of my babies, and I'll take care of yours."

He clamped his jaw tight. "Damnit."

"Mama, Luke swore." Jack looked up at Luke with a disapproving frown.

"He's just mad. You guys go and see the horses outside. Luke will let you ride, then we'll have our picnic."

"Mama, is Ace going to hurt you?" Nick gave her those big worried eyes that made her heart melt.

"Ace was just having a tantrum." Ace decided to punctuate that statement by stomping his hooves and shaking his head up and down. "What does Mama do with boys who have tantrums?"

"You make us calm down, and if we be good, you sing," Jack said.

"If we're bad, you send us to our room for a time-out. We don't like that. I like it better when we get ice cream." Nick hid his face in Luke's leg.

She hoped Luke remembered what the boys said the next time Margaret told him a bunch more lies about her.

"Mama likes giving you ice cream better than tantrums, too. Now go have some fun."

"I think Luke needs a time-out for swearing, Mama. Are you going to send him to his room?" Jack asked.

"Only if she's coming with me," Luke said under his breath, but she caught the hushed words.

The other three men tried to suppress their laughter, but it rang out, despite their effort.

Luke held her gaze, his direct and intense, to let her know he meant those hushed words.

She could almost feel a caress heating her skin, though they stood yards apart.

He may be looking out for Margaret's interests, but he also had an eye on her. She appreciated that he saw more than faults.

But could she trust that the attraction was real and not a means for him to get close to her so he could try to find things to use against her?

Luke sighed out his reluctance and uncertainty, but finally scooped up both boys. "Don't make me regret trusting you." He carried them out of the stables.

Seeing her boys safe in his strong arms endeared Luke to her even more than how much he cared about his horse.

And she appreciated his reluctant trust.

She'd do everything possible to help Ace and do it without incident because she didn't want to disappoint Luke.

Chapter Eight

 arah went straight to work on Ace, brushing him and singing to him once again. Calm, he stood still and watched her
move around him. As she passed one of the guys, she took the
lead rope from him and nodded for him to back away, leaving only
one man holding him, giving Ace some room to breathe and the
space he needed to feel safe.

She kept singing and brushing and rubbing her hand over him.
When she finally had him completely calm, she addressed the vet
for the first time in ten minutes.

"Do you have all the shots ready?"

"Yeah, I'll just begin—"

She held her hand up to stop him. "Just stay where you are. I'll
give him the shots."

"Excuse me." His authoritative voice boomed though the massive stables. "I'm the doctor here, and I don't appreciate you usurp-
ing me, especially in front of Luke."

"Obviously this horse doesn't like you or want you near him.
Now, step back. I'll give him the shots."

"You'll do no such thing. I won't allow you to harm this horse
by improperly giving him injections."

"Step back, Doc," a man still holding a rope on Ace and supervising ordered. "Let her be. You heard Luke. He wants her to take care of Ace today." The man turned to her. "I'm Jerry."

"Sarah." She gave him a smile, appreciating him backing her up.

The doc threw his hands up in the air and let them fall. "Luke's crazy letting this woman near Ace like this."

Jerry looked him in the eye. "We're all here watching, so if something goes wrong, you can be the first to tell Luke, 'Told you so.'"

Sarah picked up all four shots and, as quickly as possible, expertly gave each one to Ace. The horse didn't even flinch, and she rewarded him with another cherry candy. He accepted it and nuzzled his nose at her neck again. She moved on and checked each of Ace's legs, stroking her hands over his strong muscles and tendons, searching for any tender spots. Nothing came of it, so she moved on to cleaning out each of his hooves, still singing Ace into a calm trance.

When she reached his back left leg Jerry spoke up. "That's the hoof we think is giving Ace trouble."

She bent to pick up the hoof. Out of the corner of her eye she saw Doc move forward to have a look himself. Before she could tell him to back off or grab hold of the horse's leg, Ace kicked out, hitting her right in the thigh, and moved his big body, blocking her from Doc's approach. Sarah went down hard, clutching her thigh, tears streaming down her face.

Jerry moved forward and Ace shifted again, just missing stepping on her as she lay on the ground holding her throbbing leg. The intense pain radiated up her hip and back and down to her foot.

All the men moved then. To save herself, Sarah called out, "Stop."

Thankfully everyone froze.

Ace stood very close, still and watchful.

Sarah took the opportunity to roll onto all fours. She pressed up to her feet. No small feat; the pain seared up and down her leg. "Doc, are you stupid or simply hard of hearing? I told you to stay back."

His eyes went wide. "You're blaming me." He pointed to his chest, not one bit sorry for what he'd caused. "You have no business being around this animal."

"You arrogant son of a bitch! Back off." Sarah wiped away the tears and slowly limped to Ace's front. He lowered his head and looked at her as if to say he was sorry for what happened. Sarah met his eyes as well and stepped close and hugged his neck, letting him know she understood he only wanted to protect her.

It took some serious strength and nerve to slowly walk to his back left leg again. Her hands shook, but she bent to pick up the hoof. Ace stood completely still and allowed Sarah her inspection. Sarah cleaned the hoof and took great pains to inspect it carefully, even though her crouched position hurt like hell. She filed down a rough spot and checked Ace's shoe to make sure it was secure and properly placed. She slowly lowered Ace's hoof and stood, taking the weight off her battered leg.

"Jerry, Ace has a small soft spot on the bottom of the hoof. Probably just a stone that had been stuck at one time but is now gone. It's really nothing."

"That's what we thought. Thanks for checking, Sarah."

"Sure, no problem. Now, let's get a good look at the cut on his hindquarter." Sarah inspected the cut and decided, while most of it was superficial and would heal by itself, there was a spot at the end that had gone deep enough to need a few stitches. She walked over to Doc's bag and took out what she needed. Without a word, she wiped all the equipment down with alcohol swabs, found the medicine she needed to numb the area, and a fresh syringe. The vet stood by glaring with his arms folded across his chest. A stout man with a wide middle, white hair, and ruddy cheeks, he reminded her of one of those garden gnomes. All he needed was a white beard, little green suit, and a pointed hat.

She sang a new song for Ace, slow and soothing, and worked on the cut, cleaning it well to help prevent infection. Then, she numbed the area and expertly closed the wound with four stitches. She swiped some salve over the gash.

Sarah picked up the brush and, still singing, worked the brush over Ace again. By the time she finished, the horse was calm and Sarah was exhausted. Her leg screamed with pain, but she still had to play with the boys and sit through their picnic.

"Okay, Ace, you're all set. Now, be a good boy and play nice with everyone. Jerry, where do you want him?"

"He's due to have some exercise outside before we put him back in his stall. He could probably use it after the morning he's had. I'll take him out to the exercise ring."

Jerry stepped forward to take the lead ropes for Ace, but Ace wasn't about to give up on having Sarah take care of him. He stomped his hooves and moved toward her.

"Okay, big guy. I get it. You're in the mood to be babied. Jerry, I'll take him for a short ride."

"Ride," he said, aghast, and shook his head. "I don't know if that's a good idea. He hasn't been ridden in a while, let alone saddled."

"Who said anything about saddling him?" Sarah took off the lead ropes, turned over an empty bucket, stood on top, grabbed Ace's mane, and hauled herself up onto his back. She gave him a soft kick and walked him out of the barn.

As soon as Ace felt the sunshine on him, he took off like a

rocket. The only thing Sarah could do was hold on. The pain in her thigh was punctuated by having to use her legs to hold on to Ace, but she hadn't felt this free in a long time. Ace was a strong horse and he was using that strength to get some energy out. With the sun and wind on both of them, Sarah simply gave in and enjoyed the ride that Ace was determined to give her.

Chapter Nine

I'm four and I know all the numbers of the alphabet." Nick said.

"It's not numbers, it's letters," Jack corrected. "He's still a baby. He gets mixed up."

Nick persisted. "I am not a baby. Mama says I'm a big boy now. I go to pre-K."

Luke had worried about leaving Sarah with Ace, but listening to the boys chatter as they made their way to the horses outside made him smile. So full of energy; it felt good to hold them in his arms with their little hands clinging to his shoulders.

Luke pretended the boys were weighing him down. "You're both big boys." He hefted them up a bit higher. "That's why you get to ride these big horses."

"I want the brown one," Nick yelled.

"They're both brown, dummy," Jack said to his brother.

"Jack, don't call Nick names. That's not nice. Now, which brown one do you want, Nick?" Luke loved how Nick concentrated with his eyes narrowed and his mouth quirked in a crooked frown.

"The one that's all brown. The other one has a white nose. I don't want that one."

"Okay, Stella is yours. Jack, you get Mandy. Both these girls are great riding horses. They're very gentle. First, we're going to

introduce ourselves to them, and then we'll go over the rules before we ride. Deal?"

In unison the boys echoed Luke, "Deal."

Luke set the boys down and walked them up to the waiting
horses and one of his ranch hands, Miguel. As if on cue, the
horses lowered their heads to the boys, ready for a pat. The boys
enthusiastically stroked the horses.

"She tickled my hand. Her nose is soft." Jack pulled his hand
back to his chest. "Nick, she tickled me."

Nick patted Stella's soft nose. "Yeah, mine tickles, too. Let's
go for a ride!"

"Okay, boys, here are the rules. You have to wear these helmets,
just in case you fall off." Luke plunked a helmet on each of their
heads. "Hold on to the reins." Luke held them up. "These straps
here. Don't pull. And no yelling at the horses. Loud noises scare
them. The last rule is that you have to do exactly what Miguel and
I tell you to do. Deal?"

"Deal."

"Deal."

"Okay. Buckle your helmets. Let's go over to the indoor training ring and Miguel and I will teach you how to ride."

Luke and Miguel settled the boys up in the saddles. Their faces
lit up with the kind of joy Luke hadn't felt in too long to remember. Nerves replaced some of that excitement when the horses
jostled them a bit while they walked down to the ring, but half an
hour later, and several rounds about the ring, the boys were back
to having a ball.

Luke nodded to Miguel and they stepped away as Jack and
Nick rode on. "You're on your own, boys."

"I'm doing it." The pride in Jack's eyes made Luke's chest tight.

"Me, too," Nick whispered, not wanting to spook his mount.

Jack laughed with excitement and Luke couldn't help but smile at the little boy. He was so cute and full of fun.

Luke remembered what it had been like as a kid getting up on a horse for the first time and trying to outride his younger brother. His father and mother taught them just as Luke had taught Jack and Nick. He remembered the pride in his father's eyes when he watched them ride.

Luke felt a pang in his heart. His brother, Jason, had found love and started a family of his own. Luke loved his niece and sometimes found himself feeling jealous of his little brother.

Yesterday, seeing the boys with their mom, he'd felt that twinge of envy again.

He'd love to see his own boys riding the horses and running around the ranch like he and his brother had done for so many years. Maybe a little girl, her long hair waving in the wind.

He really wanted a family.

Not going to happen without the right woman. And he'd tired of the dating game, because that's exactly how it felt.

Women had become a convenient date for whatever business or social obligation he had to attend and a warm body in his bed to fulfill his physical needs. Even the sex felt stale, a moment's distraction. All of it left him empty in more ways than one.

He'd let it happen.

He'd made it happen.

Which is why he'd stopped dating months ago.

He'd really wanted to try with his last girlfriend, but she lived in Silicon Valley and the drive out to the ranch in Carmel and back to Silicon Valley grew to be a chore for both of them. She found excuses to be there while he made it clear his place was at the ranch. The whole thing fizzled out. At least she hadn't stolen his credit card and racked up a huge bill like the woman he dated before her.

But the thief and the relationship-going-nowhere punctuated Luke's dating bad luck. So he focused on the ranch, giving himself time to be alone and figure out what he really wanted.

A kind, loving woman who would be a best friend and partner and a house full of happiness and sweet—and a little wild—kids.

Nick turned to him. "Are you watching?"

"I am, buddy. Great job."

Pride lit Nick's eyes and he sat up straighter.

It felt damn good to give Nick that sense of accomplishment and be a part of his life if only in a small way. Luke hoped Nick remembered today and how brave and free he felt riding.

"Sit up in the saddle, Jack. You guys are doing great. Wait until your mom sees you."

"Where is Mommy?" Nick asked.

Luke tried not to let his worry for Sarah overwhelm him. "She'll be here soon."

At that moment, Ace sprinted across the road and into the field with Sarah riding bareback low over his neck. Her hair flew out behind her like Ace's tail. Woman and horse appeared to be in flight.

His heart raced. True fear clamped his lungs tight and stopped his heart. Sarah was a little bit of a thing, and Ace was a huge stallion. If she fell, she could be seriously injured or killed at the speed Ace galloped.

Just when he was about to go after her, Jack called out to him, "Look at Mommy go. I want to ride like that."

Jack set his feet wide to kick his horse and make her take off, but Luke scolded, "Don't!" Jack slowly lowered his feet. "It's dangerous. You could get hurt. Remember the rules we talked about?"

"Yes. No going faster than a walk, or I could fall and hurt myself."

"That's right. We'll have to tell your mommy that when she gets back." Luke had a few other choice words for her about being reckless with his horse and her life.

His anger simmered, but he continued instructing the boys, watching their progress around the arena. Fifteen minutes later, Ace and Sarah returned from the field and headed for the arena entrance. She trotted in, and although Luke was steaming mad, he couldn't help but notice Sarah looked magnificent. Flushed from the ride, a huge smile graced her beautiful face for the boys. She matched Ace's pace to that of the boys and their horses.

"Hi, boys. Having fun? You look like real cowboys."

"Like Luke?" Jack asked.

"You sure do. Keep practicing, I'm going to talk to him."

He tried to keep his voice low, but he really wanted to yell. "Are you crazy? That horse could kill you, and you take off bareback on him with no regard for his safety, or yours."

"You don't have to snap at me. I'm an experienced rider, and Ace is a great horse."

"He's a very expensive horse, and I can't take the chance that he'll get hurt with you riding him like a maniac. What the hell were you thinking?"

"Listen, I took care of your horse and exercised out his frustration from the morning. I can see you're upset, but the horse is fine."

He kept his concern on the horse because thinking about her being hurt still made his anger and fear rise. "He's got a bad hoof. Did the doc take care of it?"

"The hoof is fine. Nothing but a stone. You need to fire that terrible vet. Ace doesn't trust him. I don't either, for that matter."

"Is that so?" He didn't like her telling him what to do on his ranch. But maybe she had a point. He'd been having doubts about the vet's skills and lack of enthusiasm for his job.

"He doesn't keep his tools clean, he has no patience with temperamental horses, he's arrogant, and he lacks common sense when it comes to dealing with irate horses. You should contact Dr. Fields. She works at a ranch I know about. She's great with horses and is building a reputable list of clients."

He usually didn't mind someone making suggestions, but something about her showing up and taking authority of his prized horse and sending him off to babysit rubbed him the wrong way and his mouth ran away with him. "Taking care of Ace for me is one thing, telling me who I should hire and fire is something else. *I* run this ranch, and *I* make the decisions. *You* don't get to take over just because you feel like it. Maybe that worked with Sean when you took over his life and business, but it won't work with me."

The stillness in her unsettled him.

He'd gone too far, and said things he didn't really mean.

By the look in her eyes, he'd hurt her feelings, but she quickly hid that away and blanked out everything on her face.

She swung her leg over Ace's back, slid down his side, and landed on the dirt. Her leg gave out, but she caught herself. He thought he saw a flash of pain, but she turned away before he could really tell.

He looked Ace over for any sign he'd been hurt or favored his back leg. The horse looked fine and stared adoringly at Sarah, irritating Luke even more.

She gave him that blank look again. "Thank you for teaching the boys to ride. I'm sorry I missed the lesson, but it appears they've learned a lot in a short time. I appreciate your taking the time with them. They'll never forget it." With that sincere gratitude, she turned and walked to where the two boys had halted their horses in order to watch their exchange, making him regret raising his voice and talking about Sean in front of them.

"Come down now, boys. It's time for lunch."

The boys dismounted just like he taught them, with an assist from Sarah.

Luke wanted to put a stop to this, but didn't know what to say.

She tied the horses' reins to the arena fence, grabbed both boys by the hands, and turned them to face him. "Thank Luke for the riding lesson."

"Thank you, Luke." Nick looked downright sad about cutting the day short.

"Thank you," Jack said to the ground, then turned his disappointed gaze to Sarah. "Mom, I thought we were going to see the whole ranch and have lunch with Luke."

"It's time to go. No arguments."

The disappointment on the boys' faces cut Luke deep.

Before he could say anything else, Sarah turned her back on him, and took the boys with her. He should go after her and apologize for yelling and . . . and what? Being stupid. The truth was he had no idea why he was mad, except that ever since he'd seen her yesterday, he couldn't stop analyzing his life. And he didn't like what he was thinking.

Ace fussed again, so Luke turned his back on Sarah and the boys to calm the horse. He ignored the sound of their car driving away and the loneliness that settled over him.

"Where'd they all go?" Jerry asked, coming up behind him.

"They left." Luke's tone and stance should have warned Jerry he didn't want to talk and was working on a good mad.

Jerry ignored the danger signs. "Well, I hope you thanked Sarah for what she did. She was amazing with Ace. She sings like an angel, too."

"Yeah, she does." He feared her voice would haunt him forever. "She told me I should fire the doc. Can you believe that? She's not here more than an hour and she's telling me what to do, like she runs the place."

Jerry stuffed his hands in his front pockets. "I agree with her. I don't know what the doc was thinking, but every time she told him to stay back he'd get closer to Ace, agitating him. She'd calm Ace all over again. When she gave Ace his shots, he didn't even flinch. He just moved closer to her, so that he could touch her. Besides all that, she had to clean several pieces of Doc's equipment before she used them on Ace."

"I thought Ace just got nervous around the vet because he knew there'd be a poke or pain." Luke rubbed his hand down Ace's nose. "You really stood still for her?" He spoke to the horse, but Jerry answered for him.

"Yep. He didn't even try to nip her all the while she checked every inch of him, nose to tail. Ask me, he'd have never cut himself if the doc showed any patience toward him. Doc hated that you asked Sarah to tend to Ace and did nothing but cause trouble the whole time she was working on him. Doc treated her downright rude."

"What'd she do? Bitch and moan about it the whole time."

"Nope, not a word. She kept singing to Ace, keeping him calm, and doing everything that needed to be done. She must have brushed him from head to tail four, maybe five times."

He eyed Jerry, seeing the admiration in his eyes. "So you like her?"

"What's not to like? She's beautiful, sings better than any person I've ever heard on the radio, and treated your stubborn horse like a precious baby. Why are you being so hard on her?"

Luke wanted to kick his own ass. "I don't know." Because she might have screwed over Sean.

Because she got under his skin and he wasn't sure he could trust her.

Jerry shook his head in dismay. "Ask me, you should've been a little more hospitable to your guest, especially after she worked her ass off for you."

He raised a brow at Jerry's tone. "Is that so?"

"God's truth. I never seen Doc work that hard on Ace, on any animal, or for you."

The rebuke properly cowed him. "Shit. How am I going to make it up to Sarah?"

"Seems to me a thank-you would do. I think she'd appreciate a simple kindness. She showed enough of it."

"I don't know any woman who only wants a simple thank-you."

"She's not like other women." Jerry gave him a you're-an-idiot look, hooked a lead rope on Ace, and walked him back toward the stables, calling over his shoulder, "It's not like you to run off a good-looking women. Ask me, that one was a keeper."

Was she? Margaret didn't think so. In fact, she blamed Sarah for Sean's untimely death. She painted a very disturbing picture of Sarah's past.

But was it true?

He pulled his cell from his back pocket and hit the speed dial despite the fact he didn't want to go down this road. "Dean, it's Luke. I have a job for you."

"You haven't taken a new client in a while," his top investigator said.

Yeah, he'd been focused on the ranch. He needed time away

from helping people who broke the law circumvent the system, outright get away with their crimes, or serve far less time than they deserved. He had some innocent clients, but most had earned the charges against them and paid him a ton of money to get them out of trouble.

He not only wanted to know, but needed to know which side of the legal line Sarah stood on.

"I'm helping out a friend who is having difficulty getting regular visitations with her grandchildren." True. But also not exactly a clear picture of the situation. Sarah had brought the children as requested. "Anyway, I need you to dig up everything you can on Sarah Spencer. She runs Spencer Software. I'm particularly interested in an arrest for arson when she was a teen."

"Those records are probably sealed, boss."

Luke sighed. "I know you can get them." Whatever Luke asked for, Dean produced. Dean had contacts everywhere.

"It'll cost you."

He had no doubt. "Whatever it costs. I need those records and any others you find."

"On it. Bad moms are the worst."

He felt like shit for doing this. From what he'd seen, Sarah was a good mom. She'd done nothing to warrant this kind of intrusive probe into her past.

He just couldn't live without knowing who she really was. He wasn't even sure he'd share whatever he found with Margaret.

"Just get it done discreetly and quickly."

"I'll let you know as soon as I know." Dean hung up.

Luke wondered if he'd just made a huge mistake.

He glanced around the arena. All of a sudden, the ranch felt quiet and empty.

He wanted it to feel like home, not just a place to hang and sleep. But he feared it would never really feel that way because home included the people who loved you.

And he lived alone.

Maybe he deserved it for some of the shit he'd done in his career. Like picking apart a woman's life for no good reason. He was proud of most of his cases. He'd helped a lot of people, but a few of his clients left a black mark on his heart.

He really hoped he didn't make things worse with Sarah.

He took Stella's and Mandy's reins and led them out of the training ring toward the barn to put them back in their stalls so he could check on Ace and deal with the vet. But all he really thought about was how badly he'd handled things with Sarah.

Chapter Ten

S arah heard the doorbell downstairs. Though she expected Sean's sister, Bridget, and her daughter, Sophia, to arrive sometime in the next half hour, she still had to tamp down the anticipation that it might be Luke. She hated the way they'd left things yesterday, and especially didn't like that he thought her reckless and anything like the woman Margaret made her out to be.

Since school had started a few weeks ago, the kids were working on the packets their teachers had given her before they left for the trip. She hated taking them out of school for this extended time but Margaret hadn't left her a choice.

She handed Jack his math worksheet. "Do all the problems you can on your own. I need to go see who is at the door." She checked on Nick, lying on the bed with his clipboard in front of him. "How are the b's coming?"

Nick stopped tracing the next one on the sheet and looked up at her, smiling. "I did it." He'd traced the dotted letters about twenty times now.

"Great job, buddy." She handed him a blank sheet. "Now try to write them on your own."

He took the paper and did the first one, then showed her the shaky but definitely proper lowercase b.

"Don't forget to do a line of uppercase ones, too. I'll be back soon."

Sarah rushed down the stairs just as Margaret came out of the kitchen. "I'll get the door."

"About time," Margaret snapped, like Sarah had somehow become the butler.

Sarah opened the door, disappointed to find Sean's sister, Bridget, standing on the porch and not Luke.

"About time," Bridget snapped in the same tone Margaret liked to use on her. "What took you so long?"

"I was helping the boys with their homework."

Bridget walked in, making Sarah have to stand back and out of the way before she got run over.

Sarah was getting really tired of the cold shoulder and outright attacks from Margaret. She didn't need more of them from Bridget, too.

Bridget went to Margaret and hugged her. "Hi, Mom. How are you?" She glanced back at Sarah, then focused on Margaret again. "Everything okay?"

Like Sarah would do something to harm Margaret. She rolled her eyes, not even trying to hide her irritation.

"Yes. I'm fine. Just waiting for the boys to come down so we can have some fun with Sophia."

Sarah's gaze fell on the pretty ten-year-old who walked in behind her mom. "Oh my God, Sophia, you've grown a foot since I last saw you."

Bridget pinned her with an angry stare-down. "It happened when you refused to let Sean visit his family. You could care less if the kids really get to know each other."

Bridget's hostility made Sophia uncomfortable, and the little girl took a step away from all the adults.

"Sean did whatever he wanted." A fact Margaret and Bridget never accepted. Since she couldn't make any headway with them, she focused on her niece. "How have you been, sweetheart?"

"Good, Aunt Sarah."

"How is your dad?" she asked, hoping to show Sophia that she still cared about her and her family.

"Hopefully crying over his new girlfriend dumping him if she's smart." The venom in Bridget's voice made Sophia's embarrassed and hurt gaze drop to the floor.

Sarah took a step closer to Sophia. "I was really sorry to hear about your parents' divorce. That's got to be really rough."

Sophia's head came up and she nodded.

"The boys are upstairs in their room. They can't wait to see you. I might have also left a present upstairs with them for you."

The sadness in Sophia's eyes disappeared behind her excitement.

"Go on up and get it." Sarah waited for Sophia to leave before she turned to Bridget. "What is wrong with you?"

"Me? You're the one who sent Sean over the edge and kept the boys from us all this time."

"If you wanted to see them, all you had to do was ask."

"Like you'd bring them."

"They're here," she pointed out.

Bridget pressed her lips tight. "And *you're* here." The snide tone irritated Sarah. "But we both know it's only because Mom threatened to take you to court."

"All either of you had to do was ask. We don't need a lawyer or judge. It's unnecessary and a waste of money when a civilized conversation would do."

Margaret joined in on the attack. "Sarah loves spending Sean's money. She had her housekeeper drive in to clean *my* house and called a gardening service."

"You're welcome," Sarah shot back, because Margaret should thank her for fixing up the house and yard. "The house and yard needed to be clean and safe for the boys."

Margaret's gaze dropped to the floor. Maybe she regretted jabbing at Sarah with the unwarranted accusation.

"We know you're just showing off." Bridget dared her with a look to contradict her.

Sarah really didn't want to fight.

Bridget didn't back off and spewed even more indictments. "Now you're buying off my daughter with gifts so she'll still like you." Snotty. And untrue.

"The gift is because I feel bad for feeling like I couldn't reach out to her the last two years to give her birthday and Christmas gifts because you and Margaret made it clear I wasn't welcome. I wasn't sure that if I sent her something, you'd actually give it to her."

"Of course I would." Bridget sounded sincere, but Sarah didn't quite believe her. "I'm not a monster like you."

"So talking about her dad like that is you being nice."

"Enough." Margaret turned to Bridget. "I understand you're upset that the divorce was just finalized and he's seeing someone new, but talking that way . . . It's not good for Sophia to hear things like that or see you so angry at her father."

Bridget's eyes glassed over. "The divorce was only final yesterday. But he's been seeing that bitch for weeks."

"You two have been separated for a long time," Margaret gently pointed out.

"I hoped he'd change his mind," Bridget admitted. "Instead, he just agreed to everything. The alimony. Custody arrangements.

He just wanted it done. He didn't care if Sophia and I ended up in a tiny apartment I can barely afford."

"That had to really hurt." Sarah sympathized, knowing exactly how it felt to be with someone who didn't want you anymore. She also knew what it was like to end up with nothing and have to start all over.

"Oh please." Bridget rolled her eyes. "You don't care about me and Sophia."

"I do." She hoped Bridget believed her and they could somehow get past all this hostility. But Sarah didn't hold her breath because she knew Sean had confided in his sister a lot and loved to tell Bridget things to get her sympathy and the attention he loved. "I know what it's like to have your life turned upside down by the loss of your husband and partner." Maybe their situations weren't exactly the same, but it still boiled down to being left alone and having to start over.

Bridget narrowed her gaze and shook her head. "Don't do that. Don't compare what happened between you and Sean and what happened in my marriage. You ruined him. You took everything from him. You never cared about him. You made his life a living hell. That's not the same as two people growing apart over the years."

"You only know what Sean told you. That's not the whole story."

"Like I'd believe anything you have to say about it."

Neither Bridget nor Margaret wanted to know what really happened.

Sarah's cell phone rang upstairs. "Believe whatever you want." She turned to Margaret. "I bought and set up all the ingredients in the kitchen for you to make and decorate cupcakes. I'll send the kids down and get back to work so you can enjoy your time with them."

Sarah turned for the stairs just as Sophia ran down them, her brand-new tablet in hand.

Sophia launched herself into Sarah and hugged her. "Thank you so much, Aunt Sarah. I love it. I've been wanting one forever, but Mom said it was too expensive."

Sarah held Sophia and kissed her on the head. "I'm so glad you like it. Now you can play games, read books, and use it for schoolwork." Sarah stepped back and took the tablet. She clicked on the store icon, then handed it back to Sophia and pointed out, "See here? You've got a fifty-dollar credit. Use it wisely and not all at once."

"Are you serious?" Bridget fumed. "That's too much."

Sophia turned to her mom. "I'll be responsible. I won't spend all of it at once, like she said. And there's this sci-fi book series I've been dying to read. All the kids at school have all five books and I have no idea what they're raving about. Now I can read them."

Bridget reluctantly nodded for her to go ahead and get the books. "But you can't get anything else until you read all of those first."

Sophia beamed. "Yes. Okay. Thank you." She turned to Sarah again. "Thank you, thank you, thank you."

Sarah smiled. "You're welcome. Now go make cupcakes with your grandma. I'll send the boys down."

Sarah started up the stairs when Margaret said to Bridget, "At least she spent some of Sean's money on his niece. He'd have wanted to do that for her."

However Margaret and Bridget wanted to justify the tablet for Sophia without giving Sarah credit for doing something nice, fine. Sarah didn't really care. Let them think Sean would have done it. She knew the truth. Sean hadn't bought anything for any of them in all the years they were married. She sent all the birthday and Christmas gifts. She had to remind Sean to call his mom and sister on their birthdays. And when he did, he played it up big-time that he remembered them and was so glad they liked the gift he picked out just for them. They ate it up. Sean kept his good-guy, best-brother-and-son status because of her.

They really didn't know him at all.

Not the way Sarah did.

Chapter Eleven

*L*uke's surly mood simmered for the next day and a half. He didn't know what to do with the information it took Dean only a few hours to obtain and send to Luke. Sarah's adult record was clean. No arrests. No parking or speeding tickets. She'd been an upstanding citizen as an adult.

But apparently sixteen-year-old Sarah *Anderson* had indeed burned her uncle's ranch to the ground and stood there and watched it go up in flames until the police arrived and arrested her at the scene. She didn't deny doing it. In fact, she'd confessed to the crime to the responding officer.

The only explanation in the police report for why she'd done it was because she was angry her uncle had sold their horses.

The reason on the surface didn't warrant her retaliation.

He didn't know what to make of the information.

He thought of a thousand scenarios that would set her off and make her rage at her uncle and burn the place down. None of them was as benign as the sale of some horses.

He didn't think she had a quick-trigger temper. He'd never seen her even raise her voice with the boys. Margaret hadn't mentioned any fights she knew about between Sarah and Sean. She hadn't called to tell him Sarah had done anything disturbing during her visit.

So what really happened? What provoked that kind of rage?

It ate away at him and consumed his thoughts.

Everyone knew the boss was in a bad mood and they avoided him. So it was surprising when Jerry sought him out in the barn and stood in the doorway. Luke had let several of the horses, including Ace, out into the pasture while he cleaned a few of the stalls. He'd been working out some of his frustrations since before dawn, same as he'd been working himself to death the last couple days.

"Luke, you better come out to the pasture." Jerry stood back, giving Luke space, but he had a look in his eye that worried Luke.

"What's going on? Is Ace all right?"

"He's fine. Agitated, because the men got too close to his prize."

Luke's eyebrow shot up. "What?"

"Come take a look."

Frustrated, he pushed the pitchfork handle against the stall wall. "Just tell me what's going on."

"You have to see it to believe it. None of us can get close enough, but I think Ace will let you."

"That damn horse is going to be the death of me. Can't he behave?"

They made their way out to the pasture. Luke counted three men with seven horses, Ace among them, all standing around something in the field.

"What's that on the ground inside the circle of horses, and why won't they let the men get close to it?"

"You'll see. It's the strangest thing. I couldn't get past any of them animals. They've turned into guard dogs."

Luke's worry rose the closer he got to the horses. He was finally getting a clear picture of what the horses were doing. Seven horses surrounded a body on the ground. Luke's heart pounded; he was sure the horses had trampled someone. They wouldn't allow anyone near whoever had been hurt or killed. Luke quickened his pace until he was right in front of Ace, trying to get past him. The huge animal wouldn't budge. Ace shifted and blocked Luke again, but he caught a glimpse of the woman.

Sarah.

His heart stopped. He had no idea if she was alive. The devastating thought made his heart pound so hard and fast, he couldn't catch his breath. He needed to get to her.

Since Ace wouldn't let him pass, he stopped in his tracks, thinking about the best way to get to her through the horses.

"Did anyone see her get trampled?" Luke held on to his control by a thin thread.

"I don't think she's injured," Jerry called out. "We just can't figure out what she's doing out here."

So far, she hadn't responded to any of the noise around her. Terribly pale, she didn't move, but he caught the slight rise and fall of her chest.

"I don't think she's hurt," Jerry called again.

Saying it didn't make it true.

Luke was about to lose it. He'd never lost control in any situation, but seeing Sarah lying limp on the ground nearly did him in. Sarah needed help, but if Luke didn't keep a rein on his emotions, he was going to make things worse.

Luke ran a shaking hand through his hair and kept his eyes on Sarah. He took a deep breath and approached Ace, standing a few feet in front of him with Sarah a good ten feet behind her guard horse.

He reached up and stroked Ace and gave him some soothing

words. As he stroked Ace, he moved with him closer and closer to Sarah. Although he was talking to Ace and running his hands down his long neck, he kept his gaze on her.

Her arms lay on the grass above her head and her knees were bent and laying to her left. Her long dark hair spread about her head and arms. She looked peaceful, but for the exhaustion etched on her face.

She wore a white tank top and blue plaid flannel shorts. There didn't appear to be any dirt on her clothes, or her bare legs, so he assumed she hadn't been trampled. God, he hoped she was all right.

He hadn't seen her since he'd yelled at her in the training ring, but he hadn't really stopped thinking about her either.

The closer he got the more worried he became and the knot in his stomach wouldn't let up. He couldn't remember ever being this scared, not knowing if she was okay.

What would he tell her boys?

The thought squeezed his heart.

About five feet from her now, Ace stood still right beside him, trying to keep Luke away. Luke wasn't having any of it and kept walking, using his weight and strength to finally push Ace off to the side.

Finally close enough, he fell to his knees beside her. Ace nudged at her legs with his nose and Luke swatted his big head away. With one shaking hand, he brushed a strand of hair from her cheek and said her name as a fractured, ragged whisper. He laid his palm on her forehead. So cold, goose bumps covered her arms and legs. He wanted to take her in his arms, warm her soft skin, and hold her, safe and protected.

He gently laid his palm across her abdomen and leaned down to her ear. "Sarah, wake up. Are you okay?"

She didn't stir. She simply lay there breathing evenly, but not moving. He didn't realize that he gently stroked her hair and held his palm over her heart, feeling its steady beat.

"Sarah, come on, wake up. You're scaring the hell out of me. Open your eyes."

Sarah came awake with a start, her eyes wide open, surprise and uncertainty filling the depths. "Are you okay, Luke?"

"Am *I* okay? No, I'm not okay!" In the blink of an eye, fear, relief, and finally anger settled in his mind. "What the hell are you doing here?"

"Am I sleeping on your kitchen table?" With her lying below him, his face inches from hers, she couldn't see the sky behind him.

"My kitchen table would be an improvement. You're sleeping in the middle of my pasture with several horses ready to trample you! How the hell did you get here?" He didn't mean to yell, but she'd put him through a hell of a lot the last two days. Including a few erotic dreams that kept him up at night and left him aching with a need he couldn't slake.

Her cold hand settled on his wrist. He'd laid his hand on her stomach earlier to feel her heartbeat and the soft, shallow rise and fall of her ribs.

Her cheeks pinked and her eyes turned shy. "Help me up?"

He took her hands in his and hauled her up, but kept her at arm's length, resisting the urge to crush her to him and give in to his relief that she was okay.

She slowly surveyed her surroundings and did something he didn't expect at all. She laughed.

"What the hell is so funny?"

"Well, I was just thinking this isn't a bad way to wake up. I'm surrounded by horses and men. Two of my favorite things." She gave him a brilliant smile, obviously trying to alleviate the tension in the air.

He ran a hand through his hair in frustration, while the guys around him let out a crack of laughter. Unable to reconcile his emotions, he wanted to shake her for scaring him. He also wanted to pull her into his arms and hold her and hope that some of the brightness of her smile warmed up all the cold, dark places inside him.

Instead, stupid reigned and he snapped at her for making him crazy. "Start talking."

Her chin tilted up, all beauty and defiance in a tiny, taut package. "Sometimes when I'm under a great deal of stress, and I haven't gotten enough sleep, I sleepwalk."

He didn't expect her to say that either. "That's how you got here?"

"Yep." She looked him right in the eye, daring him to . . . He didn't know what.

"That must be . . . scary."

"I've woken up in some odd places," she admitted. "And yes, sometimes it's scary. At home, I take precautions so I don't leave the house or hurt myself."

Luke's eyes swept from her head down to the gruesome bruise on her leg. She'd been lying on her left side, so he hadn't seen the bruises that covered almost her entire thigh and disappeared under her shorts.

"What the hell happened to your leg?"

He knelt, grabbed her knee, and gently ran his fingertips over the dark bruises, studying them and the all too familiar pattern they made. A horseshoe.

"Your vet spooked Ace."

Damn. He had no idea and wanted to kick the doc's ass. "Why didn't you tell me you were hurt?"

"You were too busy snapping at me for being reckless with your prize horse and telling you how to run your ranch. Remember?"

He stared up at her, hoping she saw the remorse he couldn't hide and the apology lodged in his throat because words didn't seem enough.

Her eyes softened. "It hurts like hell, but I'm fine."

"I really don't know what to say."

Jerry stepped forward. The other guys had already abandoned the pasture to get back to work. "Why'd you ask Luke if you were sleeping on his kitchen table?"

Sarah relaxed her stance and turned her attention to Jerry. "On one of my sleepwalking . . . adventures, I woke up to my neighbor cooking breakfast for her family. I had fallen asleep on their dining room table. The funny part is, it was their daughter's seventh birthday. I had taken her beautiful birthday cake out of the fridge and used it as a pillow."

Jerry busted up laughing.

Luke felt sorry for the little girl.

"What did your neighbors say when they found you?"

"Good morning."

Anything could have happened to her. Where were the boys? Home alone?

Jerry went along with the amusement of it all. "Just, 'good morning'?"

"It was the third time they'd found me on their property. Of course, this was the first time I'd picked the lock on their door and ended up on the dining room table with cake in my hair." She waved that all aside. "They took it all in stride. I had a beautiful cake delivered that afternoon for the party. Pink roses and blue and lavender butterflies, just like their daughter wanted. Later, I also had a crystal-covered cake dish made for them with a Sleeping Beauty handle on top that looked like she was sleeping on top of the cake. They got a huge kick out of it."

Jerry smiled, obviously a little in love with Sarah. Which irritated Luke to no end. "That's a great story. The cake thing was clever and thoughtful."

Luke thought so, too, but he wanted to know about something else she'd said. "How'd you know how to pick the lock?"

"Contrary to what most people think, you can do just about anything when you're sleepwalking. I've even heard of people driving. Picking the lock was a snap. I acquired a great many unseemly talents as a teenager." She eyed him. "I'm sure Margaret gave you all kinds of juicy tidbits about my sordid teenage years."

And he'd learned a lot from her sealed juvenile records. They painted a dark picture. But her record after living with her uncle remained spotless. Because she got what she wanted from Sean? Did financial security change her? Maybe it was having the boys.

Whatever it was, it didn't change the facts.

"I'll add criminal to the list of things she called you, including arsonist, master manipulator, and gold digger."

She fell back a step, then caught herself. "Do you believe all that?"

He shrugged, and said, "Jury's still out," without thinking.

Sadness filled her eyes.

Why the hell did he say that?

To protect himself from being disappointed by yet another woman? By her?

He owed her yet another apology, but before he could find the words, Ace stuck his head between them, demanding her attention. He'd waited for her to wake up and had kept her safe and now he wanted his reward.

"Jerry, how about a leg up."

Jerry cupped his hands and Sarah stepped into them with her bare foot and he lifted her to Ace's back.

She grabbed Ace's mane and before Luke protested, she gave Ace a kick in the sides, and they took off across the field.

"She sleepwalks into my field, scares us half to death thinking she's been trampled to death, and now she steals my horse." He threw his hands up and let them fall and slap his thighs. He took a step toward Jerry. "And why the hell didn't you tell me about Ace kicking her! Did you see her leg?" A punch of regret replaced his waning fear.

Jerry gave him an incredulous look. "What the hell is the matter with you? Couldn't you see she was embarrassed? She couldn't help what happened this morning any more than you can help being a stubborn ass. I didn't tell you about her getting kicked because I thought she was okay. The kick looked bad, but she got right up." He shrugged and admiration shown in his eyes. "That girl's tough."

"Yeah, she is." He felt terrible that his horse hurt her. "Can you believe she broke into her neighbor's house?"

"You know just as well as I do that people who sleepwalk have no control over what they do. Sounds to me like she more than made up for it. She gave the little girl a decorated cake and the mother a fancy cake dish to make things right."

"That doesn't excuse that she broke the law."

Jerry's hands went up and dropped. "You're impossible. Stop looking at her like she's every other woman you have coming and going in your life. What did you see when you found her?"

The wash of fear came back again. "I thought she was dead."

"Yeah, she was pale as a ghost, has dark circles under her eyes, and probably hasn't slept more than a few hours a night for weeks. She's exhausted. That is why she sleepwalks."

"You think I didn't notice all of that. She brought several computers with her and plans to work while she's here. Hell, she hadn't even been at Margaret's more than fifteen minutes when she took a business call."

"Really? So, she brought her kids to see a woman who hates her, by your account, continues to keep up with her work, comes over here and tends to your prize stallion, has been doing God knows what for the last couple days, *except* sleeping, and all you can think to do is insult her and yell at her because she didn't tell you your horse kicked her while she was doing *you* a favor. I know you're better than this. But so far, you've been ungrateful and insulting to the lady and all she's done is take care of your horse and sleep in your pasture. Seems to me, in addition to the thank-you you already owe her, now you owe her an apology, too."

"I wonder what a thank-you and an 'I'm sorry' is going to cost me."

"If you're smart, it'll only cost you a little of your pride. Take a good look at that girl. She's not what you think she is, and she certainly isn't anything like any of those other women you've kept company with. She's special. If you can't see that, you're more stubborn than I ever thought. If I was ten years younger, I'd snatch her up if she'd have me."

The spurt of jealousy came out of nowhere. "Don't even think about it, old man."

"Is that so?" Jerry turned and walked back to the stables and left Luke to ponder what he'd unwittingly admitted out loud.

He wanted Sarah.

Chapter Twelve

*L*uke found Sarah in the barn ten minutes later, singing and brushing down Ace. He stuck to the shadows, watching and listening to her beautiful voice. He didn't need Jerry to tell him she was special. He saw it and wanted to know more about her.

She probably wouldn't believe that since he'd been fighting himself and the pull drawing him to her. He couldn't keep denying his attraction, or that acting on it meant opening himself up like he hadn't done in a long time.

After she and the boys left the ranch the other day, he'd let anger, instead of his true feelings, reign because all the life they breathed into this place that day left with them, leaving him lonely once again.

Walking into an empty house each night and rising in his lonely bed every morning had been wearing on him longer than he cared to admit.

On the ranch, in his law practice, it was easy for him to see the fruits of his labor, yet he couldn't seem to find that kind of success and satisfaction in his personal life.

Perhaps the beauty standing before him could change that.

Sarah stretched her back and favored her hurt leg. Carrying

those boys around was taking a toll on her. She needed to take better care of herself before she made herself ill.

What kept her up at night?

He couldn't help but wish it were him.

He was tired of fighting it.

And Sarah deserved better from him than the unwarranted antagonism he'd given her. So he relaxed and went with a little levity, hoping to show her he wasn't rude by nature, but a good guy. Someone she could open up to and confide in, because he really wanted to know everything about her.

"You plan on standing around my barn in your underwear all day?" The amusement in his voice got him a hint of a smile from her.

She gave him barely a glance before turning back to Ace. "Now, Luke, we both know I'm not wearing underwear."

Fire flashed through his system. Sultry, erotic images filled his mind. His hands itched to reach out and touch her. He could practically see her dusky nipples through the skin-tight tank. Although the flannel boxers weren't exactly lingerie, they drove him crazy. Her long slender legs could stop traffic. And the fact that her toenails were grape-juice purple made him smile. Her tousled hair framed cheeks flushed from her early morning ride, and the muscles in her arms went taut as she worked the brush over Ace.

He saw the strength, not only in her body, but in her.

"You have an amazing voice."

"Thanks."

He wanted to keep her talking and erase what he thought he knew about her with something real. "Did you sing at school or church when you were a kid?"

"No."

He waited, hoping she'd go on.

She met his steady gaze, made some silent decision, and went back to brushing Ace. Finally she confided, "When I was young, I lived on my uncle's ranch. Not a ranch as nice as yours, but a run-down place. The barn was falling apart, the house and outbuildings were all dilapidated, but the horses were well tended. My uncle raised them and sold them to keep the ranch, but he never seemed to profit. He spent his life trying to hold on."

He couldn't believe she'd open up about the one thing he really wanted to know about without him prompting her.

She sighed. "It made him mean, that constant battle to keep the bank from taking everything." She kissed Ace on the nose and stared into his eyes. "Anyway, one of the ranch hands had a radio he brought to work each day. I'd listen to the songs and sing along. It was the only form of entertainment I had. I loved music." Wistfulness filled her voice. She went quiet for a moment. "When he got fired, I missed the music, but I had a knack for remembering the songs, so I would sing while I worked. It gave me comfort. The horses never seemed to mind if I got a lyric wrong or couldn't hit a note." She gave Luke a half smile over her shoulder.

"Why'd the guy get fired?"

"For bringing the radio and making me happy." The matter-of-fact way she said it didn't hide the anger and resentment and remorse. "Like I said, my uncle was a mean man."

Luke wanted to ask how mean. He wanted to know if he'd hurt Sarah.

The answer was clear in the way she spoke.

"When he found out the guy liked my singing and I liked the music, he got rid of both. He said I was distracting his men. I needed to concentrate on my job, and not some fanciful pastime. Since I'd cost him a worker, too, I had to do my job and his."

"How old were you?"

Her hand stopped brushing Ace and her eyes stared back into the past. "Thirteen. There was never any more music on the ranch. I only sang when I was alone at night in the barn with the horses."

"Why were you in the barn at night?" He hazarded a guess, but he wanted to hear her say it.

"I slept in a small room on the floor in the back of the barn." Not in the warm house, in her own room, in a soft bed.

His throat went tight with sadness. "Did you go to school?"

"Why do you care?"

Because it kills me to think of you living in a crap barn, cold and lonely with no music. Those words wouldn't come out of his mouth. "Because I want to know who you really are."

Why did you burn the place down?

She stared at him. "I'm not who Margaret described to you."

"It appears you're not."

She pressed her lips together, then answered. "My first three foster families sent me to school, but when I was eight, my uncle showed up and took me to the ranch. He needed me to take care of the horses. I didn't go back to a real school again until I was eighteen. Senior year at MIT, I met Sean."

"Where were your parents?"

"My mother drank herself to death when I was four. My father didn't know I existed until I was sixteen."

Wow! "That must have been really hard."

She nodded. "It was." The way she said it meant he hadn't even scratched the surface of how she felt about her tragic childhood.

"Did you like living on the ranch?"

"I liked the horses. They were all I had growing up." Sadness filled those words. Not anger or rage.

It didn't add up to her setting fire to the ranch.

She set the brush on the nearby workbench. "I've got to get

back before the kids wake up. Sorry I caused you so much trouble this morning."

He stepped in front of her before she retreated. "Why did you burn the ranch to the ground?" He had to ask. She'd had a rotten childhood, but that didn't justify what she did.

She slowly looked up and right into his eyes. "Didn't Margaret tell you *why* I did it? Of course, I never even told Sean why, so I can only imagine the explanation she gave you, besides her general opinion of me, which is that I'm evil and therefore I do evil things. Right? I burned down the ranch. I killed her son. I took his business. I keep her grandchildren from her. Everything I do is just for spite and my own selfishness."

So, she'd never told Sean why she'd done it. It surprised him, and made him want to get the answer all the more.

"It wasn't some whim. You had a reason. And don't tell me it was because your uncle sold the horses like the police report says. That's bullshit."

Her head tilted and her eyes filled with anger. "You got my sealed records?"

Shit. "Yes." What else could he say?

"Let me guess, so you can use it against me in court to take my kids from me. You want to make my whole life about something I did when I was just a hopeless kid."

No, he didn't. He wanted to know the truth. "Why did you do it? What would make you do something so drastic?" He demanded the answer with the same urgency of his questions.

"Because I was in a rage!" Her whole body vibrated with anger and resentment that he'd insist on an answer and that he'd violated her privacy based on an unsubstantiated claim from Margaret. "I couldn't take one more thing being snatched away from me."

"What did your uncle take from you?"

"The only good thing I had left."

"The horses," he guessed, sadness tightening his gut and clenching his heart, because if that's all she'd had in her life without school, friends, or a family who loved her, then yes, she'd been hopeless.

The pain in her eyes ran deep. "He stood in front of the barn talking to a wealthy rancher about selling the last of the horses. My uncle had either drunk or gambled away the last of the money. He needed the quick cash the ten horses provided. They didn't know I was listening from inside one of the stalls, but I heard everything they said." She fought back tears. "I couldn't lose them." She sucked in a breath to wash away the desperation he saw in her eyes and heard in her voice. The anger came raging back. "Turns out the guy wanted to buy more than the horses, and my uncle was only too happy to take the extra five hundred to get rid of the smart-ass mouth he couldn't afford to feed. Not that he did a good job of that to begin with."

Aghast and overwhelmingly furious, he blurted out, "Your uncle tried to sell you for five hundred dollars?" Luke seethed. Everything inside him screamed to protect her. From what? It was done, and he was left helpless. Not a good feeling. He ran both hands through his hair and let them drop to his sides, balled into tight fists.

Sarah let out a half-hearted laugh. "No, Luke. Not *tried*. He did sell me." She shrugged, but it didn't erase any of the turmoil in her eyes. "The guy loaded up the horses he got on the cheap and the girl he couldn't wait to get home into the trailer. Locked me in so I couldn't run."

"What happened?" He didn't really want to know.

"I picked the lock on the room the guy put me in at his place and hitchhiked back to the ranch. And for that final act of cruelty my uncle inflicted on me, I burned his ranch to the ground. I stood in the middle of the front yard and watched the barn and the house go up in flames.

"My uncle was, of course, down at the bar. But when he got home, he had exactly what I had. Nothing."

She sucked in a breath; the retelling had taken a toll on her emotionally, and he hated seeing the pain written all over her face. "I got to see his face before the police hauled me away. That was the most satisfying moment of my life. Three years later when he died of a heart attack, I was the only living relative, so the land came to me. He actually had a life insurance policy and I was able to use the money I received to pay off the debt. I still own it," she said, matter-of-fact. "It's actually not far from here."

She shrugged again and her eyes narrowed. "So now you know. I'm a spiteful bitch. I take everything the men in my life have. I took my uncle's ranch and I took Sean's company. Feel better having all those stories about me confirmed?"

He didn't believe that one damn bit.

And something else disturbed him even more. "How long were you with the man who bought you?" Just saying those unbelievable words filled him with fury.

"A couple of days."

Days! The thoughts that ran through his head made him sick. "Did he hurt you?"

The far-off look that came over her told him yes—deeply.

"He didn't rape me. But there are lots of ways to hurt someone. Don't ask, because I'm not going there with you."

He didn't really want to know. He wished he could erase it from her mind, heart, and life.

His heart ached and his fury flared. He wanted to find the guy and beat him half to death just so he'd know how it felt to be in that much pain.

Just like the pain vibrating around her, consuming the joy he'd seen in her.

"There's nothing about any of that in the police report."

She gave him a very insincere smile. "You can't be that naive. The cops had their *criminal* in custody." She used that word to remind him he'd called her that not even a half hour ago. "My uncle denied it ever happened, the guy who bought the horses denied it happened, and I was the one who burned down the ranch. I didn't have any proof. My word against theirs, and I was just a dumb kid. If you were a cop, who would you believe?"

Her. Because she didn't seem to have a problem admitting what she'd done. "So what happened? Did you go to juvenile detention? Jail?"

"I spent several days behind bars while I waited for the system to do its thing without any concern for me. Then someone unexpected showed up. He saved me from the fate I deserved."

Luke represented people who deserved what they got, but Sarah wasn't anything like them. Yes, she'd done something wrong, but the system had failed her for so long she didn't believe anyone would ever help her. Even the cops didn't believe her story. They only cared that they'd gotten her for the arson. "Who saved you? Your father?"

"I've answered your questions. You either believe what my uncle did, or you don't. No one else did, so I don't expect any better from you."

He wished she did, because he didn't want her to see him as another person against her. "I do believe you."

"I don't care."

"Yes, you do, or you wouldn't have told me something you never even told your husband." That had to mean something.

It meant something to him.

She gave nothing away. "You and Sean used to be friends, so I guess that's why you felt you needed to dig up those records."

"I knew Sean from grade school to high school. After that, life had us going our separate ways. College and the family business for me. Sean went to college, met and married you, and started a family and his own business."

"And you think he did that on his own?"

"You tell me."

She sighed. "That's just another long story."

He'd let it go for now. "Do you miss him?" He really wanted to know if she still loved Sean.

"I wish the boys had the father they deserve." She dropped that loaded statement and left it hanging. "If you'll excuse me, I need to make breakfast for my boys and I have a full schedule today." She started backing away. "Thanks for letting me ride Ace."

"I didn't. You took him. Again."

That got him a reluctant smile.

"You have some really nice horses, but . . . Why haven't you found a mare that compares to Ace?"

"I tried to, but the owner refused to sell to me because I didn't meet their experience requirements."

"You should contact Blaze Ranch. It's not far from here, and they have outstanding horses."

"That's who I tried to buy from. How do you know about Blaze Ranch?"

"I know the owner. She just wants to make sure the horses go to a good home where they'll be treated well. If she doesn't know the ranch, she doesn't sell."

"I can't fault her for being careful about her horses. There are some pretty disreputable places, and people aren't always nice to their animals."

"We agree on that." She took another couple steps away, though he felt like he'd gained some ground in getting her to open up and like him after his bad behavior.

"You can stop digging in my past. There's nothing else to find. But I suppose you wouldn't take my word for it."

He already knew there was nothing else to find. His investigator would have uncovered it. "I'd rather just spend more time with you and get to know you better the normal way." He wanted her to open up to him.

"You should have just talked to me instead of investigating me."

He knew that, but because Margaret had asked him, he'd decided to help a friend instead of going with his gut and believing that if he asked Sarah she'd give him a straight answer.

And while she wasn't hiding anything else in her past, he wondered about her cryptic statements about Sean.

"Goodbye, sweet boy." She wasn't talking to him and gave Ace a pat goodbye. She walked down the aisle toward the barn doors. Barefoot, wearing her pajamas, and limping. He shook his head at her boldness, and in this case, overconfidence.

"How do you plan to get back to Margaret's?"

"Same way I got here. Walk," she said over her shoulder.

He shook his head again and pulled his keys from his pocket. "Get in the truck, Sarah."

"I don't want to put you out," she called back to him.

"Get in the damn truck." Amusement mixed with his exasperation made her stop and turn back.

She huffed out her own frustration, but with a hint of her elusive smile tugging at her lips. "Fine."

They climbed into the front seat. He was wholly aware of how small the space felt and how close she was to him. He drove her back to Margaret's in silence, trying to reconcile her past, her marriage to Sean, with the woman she was today. Sarah had certainly gotten herself far away from growing up a poor foster child. She really did rise from poverty and abuse to become an MIT graduate and a business owner.

Not to mention the mother of two great boys. Ah, those boys. He'd had such a great time teaching them to ride. So full of life, they brought back so many memories of him and his brother and summers on the ranch.

"Bring the boys back to the ranch. I'd love to hang out and take them riding again."

She eyed him uncertainly, and he didn't blame her after the way he'd acted.

"I'd like to prove to you that I'm not the ass I've acted like since we met."

"Are you sure you can manage that?" she teased.

"Yes. And I promised the boys I'd show them around the ranch. I hate breaking a promise."

That seemed to soften her a bit.

He tried to tempt her more. "Jack wants to pick corn out of the garden. You could bring them by this afternoon."

She gave him one of those crooked smiles he was getting used to seeing hesitantly tilt her tempting lips. "You make me laugh, Luke. Some woman must have really done a number on you. You don't even realize that you just invited my boys over and as an afterthought remembered I come with them." She held up her hand to stop him from saying anything. "I'll bring the boys, because they spent all day yesterday begging me to go back and see the horses. I'll even try to stay out of your way while you play with them. I have several meetings scheduled this morning, but once I'm done, I'll bring them over."

She reached for the door handle to exit the truck, but he touched her shoulder to stop her. She turned back, he leaned in, and he found himself inches from her beautiful face.

He didn't mean to kiss her. Need overtook reason and the pull between them drew them together until his mouth landed on her warm lips. The intimacy of the simple kiss stunned him.

All but one thought escaped his mind. *Hold on*.

He hooked his arm around her middle and pulled her into his chest. She felt so good pressed up against him. Her hands slipped up around his neck and she buried them in his hair. When she opened her mouth to him, he took her into the fire.

Pressed against him, her soft breasts rubbed against his chest each time he moved and he slanted his mouth over hers to take the kiss deeper. She tasted sweeter than he imagined, her skin warmer and softer than in his dreams.

She gave everything over to the kiss. When his tongue smoothed over hers again and again, she grabbed fistfuls of his hair to hold him to her and her tongue met his with equal strokes.

Raw need and the rightness of her in his arms made him want to hold on to this moment, her, forever. A low growl escaped from deep in his throat.

She jolted and planted both hands on his chest and pushed back. "I thought you hated me." The dazed look in her eyes satisfied him.

"Not even a little bit." In fact, she might be everything he'd been missing in his life. And that realization hit him square in the chest and he stared into her eyes, wonder running through him as he traced his fingertips along the side of her beautiful face.

She touched her fingers to her kiss-swollen lips. "Don't do that again."

He wanted to do it, and a hell of a lot more, a million more times.

She tried to get out of the truck, but he touched her shoulder to get her to turn back again.

"Why not? You liked it. You kissed me back."

"I don't get involved with anyone. It's not fair to the boys to have someone else come into their lives only to leave again."

That surprised him. "Are you saying you haven't been with a man since Sean died?"

"You're the first man to kiss me in almost five years." With that bombshell sitting between them she scooted out of the truck and casually walked up the porch steps.

Just as she closed the front door behind her, it hit him what she had just confessed.

Sean died two years ago. Nick was four. Which meant she hadn't been intimate with her own husband since before she gave birth to Nick.

She'd admitted that something had been seriously wrong between Sean and her long before his sudden death. That realization came with a great many questions.

The one he wished he knew the answer to the most . . . Did Sarah simply use Sean to elevate her life from poor foster kid to rich wife?

He didn't want to believe it, which made him wonder what really happened between her and Sean.

Chapter Thirteen

*S*arah parked in front of Luke's house and wondered what she was doing.

He worked for Margaret. Not in a continuing way, but he had sent her the letter demanding their visit. He not only did some kind of background check on her but somehow got his hands on her sealed juvenile records. His actions made her angry, but in a way she was also relieved. In the back of her mind, she'd always known the bigger her public image at Spencer Software and Andy's Antics, the more people would want to know about her. It was only a matter of time before someone found those records.

She'd just thought it would be some tech genius who hacked the system to get them.

Not the lawyer for the woman who hated her most.

But despite all that, Luke didn't seem to be trying too hard to prove Margaret's case—that she had married Sean only for his money. He seemed genuinely interested in getting to know her for real, not just to pick out all her faults.

He actually believed her side of what happened with her uncle.

She thought she didn't care, but she did.

And while she appreciated his change of heart, and the way he listened to her story without the judgment he'd shown her earlier, she really didn't know if there was anything but attraction pulling them together.

Most relationships started that way, but Luke seemed averse to relationships that came with commitment, judging by the way he wanted to push her away, even as he reluctantly pulled her closer.

It confused her.

She really didn't know if he actually liked her.

He shouldn't have kissed her.

She never should have kissed him back.

But the temptation had been too great to ignore. And it had been a long time since she felt that kind of desire.

And she'd never been kissed like that. It overtook her. It settled her and shook her up all at once.

Luke, and his many facets, intrigued her. At first, the only thing pulling her to him was the physical attraction. But now, she found common ground with him. He loved the horses as much as she loved them. He worked hard. He was a lawyer and a rancher. She liked running Spencer Software and the work she did there, but she found satisfaction in her gaming projects that she did for fun because they fulfilled another part of her.

Maybe he'd had an attitude with her in the beginning, but she didn't hold it against him. She often held back because she didn't trust others, so that he did the same was something she understood.

Luke had accepted Margaret's opinion of Sarah because he'd known Margaret for most of his life. He didn't think she'd lie. And Margaret didn't. She believed what she thought of Sarah. Luke at least took the time to dig deeper and get to know her better to form his own opinion.

She appreciated that.

Nick pulled her out of her head. "Mama, I want to see the barn cats."

She set aside her reservations about seeing Luke again and slipped out of the car and unbuckled Nick from his booster seat. "Let's see if Luke is ready for us." She turned, let Nick jump onto her back, and closed the car door. On her way to the porch, she changed direction and followed the thwacking sound coming from the side of the house.

She rounded the corner and found Luke standing tall, his arms over his head, hands gripped around the ax he brought down, splitting a log in two. The pieces fell off the stump.

Nick wriggled on her back. "Awesome!"

Luke spotted them and pulled the earbuds from his ears. "You made it." The bright, open smile made her stomach flutter. But the rest of him held her attention. Suddenly, she felt too warm in her tank top, jeans, and hiking boots.

Bare-chested, he smelled like freshly chopped wood, and his hair was tousled from running his hands through it, like he'd done in frustration a number of times when with her. Usually, because he was angry with her. His snug jeans rode low on his hips. Who could miss his chiseled six-pack? Not an ounce of fat on him. With each movement he made she watched the play of muscles as they rippled under his bronzed skin. Ranch work did a body good.

She hadn't been this close to a half-naked man in a long time. For some reason, she found herself drawn to Luke and the strength he radiated despite their tumultuous start.

And she thought again about that kiss he'd laid on her.

His gaze dropped to her lips, then met her eyes again. His filled with desire, stark and urgent. "It's good to see you." His warm words felt welcoming and settled the butterflies in her belly. "Where's Jack?"

"He woke up this morning with a cold. I gave him some medicine after lunch, and he fell asleep. Margaret said she'd bring him if he woke up and we weren't back yet."

"I killed him." Nick bounced with excitement on her back.

Sarah smiled and explained. "Video games. Nick is an excellent driver and killed it at the stock car race."

Luke grinned. "Oh yeah. I've got a whole mess of video games. Maybe we'll go head-to-head sometime, little man."

"Do you mean it?" Nick didn't usually take to strangers, but he liked Luke. "You'll play with me? Mama plays, but she wins cuz she makes games."

Sarah didn't want Luke asking about her business, so she quickly changed the subject. "Nick can't wait to see the barn cats."

Luke pulled the ax up again and thwacked it into the log, making it stick. "Let's head down to the barn."

He picked up the red flannel and pulled it on, then started buttoning it. Sexy as hell half naked, he even looked good putting his clothes back on.

She caught herself staring and turned toward the barn.

"Five years is a long time," Luke said from behind her.

She glanced over her shoulder, caught his knowing look and the sheer male pride that he knew she liked what she saw in him.

Who wouldn't? The man was pure cowboy perfection.

But he also had a sharp lawyer's mind, she reminded herself, and so far he'd only confused her about his motives. Was he spending time with her for professional or personal reasons? Was this all about Margaret's threat to go to court, or was he really interested in her?

Either way, he made her nervous and unsure and she didn't like it, so she held strong to the inner strength and confidence she used in business.

She reminded him why they were here. "You promised Nick barn cats and vegetable picking."

"I can multitask. Because I'm all about spending time with you."

To distract him, she handed him the box she'd brought with her. "These are for you. Apology brownies. Sorry for sleeping in your field."

"You didn't have to do that." He raked his fingers through his hair and gave her an apologetic frown. "I overreacted. It's just that seeing you out there with all those horses . . ."

"I know." She didn't want to think about what could have happened.

Luke handed a brownie to Nick, then took a big bite of another. "Where did you get these? They're outstanding."

"I made them."

Nick swallowed the last of his square. "Mama makes the best brownies and cookies. I like chocolate chip best."

Luke stopped just inside the barn and cocked his head. "I thought you couldn't cook."

She stood beside him and raised a brow. "Why would you think that?"

Luke shrugged. "Margaret."

"I should have known." She rolled her eyes. "Are you going to make me explain some lie Margaret told you every time you see me?"

"It's called a conversation." He smirked. "I'm interested."

She shook her head, but gave in and told him the truth. "You know my mom died when I was very young. The foster families I stayed with only ever gave me the bare essentials. My uncle over-cooked or charred everything he ever made, which is why we ate a lot of pizza and fried chicken out of a bucket. I imagined real families had moms who cooked healthy meals and baked cookies for after-school snacks."

"I doubt they all do, but mine did." Luke gave her a glimpse into his very different childhood.

"There's a restaurant close to our office. I love eating there. So much so, they know me now. So when I found out I was pregnant with Jack, I asked the chef if he'd teach me how to cook and bake. We struck a deal and he taught me."

Luke looked intrigued. "What deal?"

"I revamped his restaurant inventory and ordering systems. I set up a database for his customers' orders and billing information. Now, he can see who his most loyal clientele are and what they like to order. When they make a reservation, he can have special menus ready for them."

Luke tilted his head. "I frequent several restaurants in San Francisco and Silicon Valley, but there's this one place where the chef caters to his exclusive clientele."

"Gerard's," she answered for him, loving that he knew the place.

"You learned to cook from a Michelin star chef." He sounded impressed.

"Yep. He was really appreciative of the work I did. He always keeps a table for me. I still eat there several times a week and every once in a while he lets me back into the kitchen to help him cook."

Luke cocked his head. "Isn't there like a four-month waiting list for a reservation?"

Sarah shrugged one shoulder. "Not for me."

Luke swallowed another big bite of brownie, set the box on a table, held his hands out to Nick, who immediately went to him. "Sounds like he got quite a deal for the work you did for him." Luke settled Nick on his hip.

"I don't have a single memory of anyone ever making me cookies. So if you ask me, I got the better end of the bargain. You can't put a price on the memories the kids and I make when we get in the kitchen, make a huge mess, and cook something yummy."

His eyes filled with admiration.

Good. She'd blown apart another of his misconceptions about her. "You know, you'd figure me out a lot faster if you'd forget everything you *think* you know about me."

"I want to know everything." He held her gaze, completely sincere.

Sarah wanted to believe that, despite the fact he'd once believed she'd used Sean to rise out of her dire circumstances, only to take his money and company in some selfish power grab to steal all his wealth.

She took this as a sign he trusted her in some small way.

She hadn't lied when she said she'd sworn off men, but looking at how sweet Nick looked in his arms, and remembering how good Luke looked without a shirt, maybe what she really meant was she was only interested in getting involved with the right man.

But was that Luke?

Maybe. He was certainly the only man in years who'd grabbed her attention.

"Kitties, Mama." Nick looked from her to Luke.

Luke headed over to one of the cupboards outside the horse stalls and pulled out a can of cat food and two small paper plates. He set Nick on the ground, put the two plates out, then popped the top on the cat food can.

The sound brought meows from two different directions and Nick smiled. "They heard it."

Luke pointed at the top of one stall where an orange tabby

walked along the wood then jumped down and came running to the plate. "Say hello to Tiger." Luke rubbed his big hand over the tabby's back and received several head-bumps. "He's a real sweet boy."

All of a sudden, a gray cat with a black-dots-and-lines pattern ran and leapt onto Luke's shoulder, rubbing his head against Luke's head.

"Hello, Monster."

"Monster," Nick repeated, laughing. "That's not his name."

Luke smiled at Nick and gave Monster a pet. "It sure is. He gets into everything and loves to shred the toilet paper roll in the bathroom. But he's a great mouser."

Monster jumped off Luke and chowed down on his food.

Nick petted the cats while they ate.

Luke ruffled Nick's hair, then stood next to her. "I'm glad you brought him over. Sorry Jack missed out. But you can bring them back anytime you want. Though I hope you'll keep it to Thursday through Sunday."

"Why?"

"Because I drive into the office Monday to Wednesday and I'd hate to miss spending time with you. And the boys," he added.

"Tell me about your lawyer work?"

"You don't want to hear about that."

"It's called a conversation," she mimicked him.

He chuckled under his breath. "I work with my family. Grandpa started the business. He practiced criminal law and built quite a reputation. Dad and I followed in his footsteps. Jason, my brother, practices corporate law. We have a few other junior lawyers working in-house who handle things like tax law and intellectual property."

"I imagine they work closely with Jason."

"That's right. He loves the business. So does Dad, though he's cut back a lot the last couple years. Recently, he's hardly been practicing at all, so his retiring isn't a surprise to his clients."

"And you?"

"I used to love it. Still do sometimes, but I wanted something more. I wanted this to balance the demands of the job. Here, no one's life is hanging in the balance. If I get something wrong, no one gets hurt. I didn't put a dangerous or hurtful person back out on the streets."

"If you're not happy as a defense attorney, why not change your specialty?"

"I like defending people in court. I've just stopped taking high-profile, complex cases. Though lucrative, they suck up a lot of time and take a toll on my life."

"All work and no play," she guessed, finding common ground with Luke.

"If I wasn't in the office or court, I was barely getting any sleep at home before I went back to the office. When I made time for personal relationships . . . they fizzled out or ended badly because of my overscheduled life. I burned out at work and in life. My parents owned this place before I took it over. When I was young, we spent summers here, riding horses, camping, fishing, and hiking. Then the place mostly sat empty for years. I took it over and turned it into a working ranch. I loved this place. Still do. I've lived here the past three years."

"It suits you." She'd seen it in the way he loved his horses like they were his children.

A horse nickered and kicked at a stall gate.

"That's Ace," Luke said. "He must want to see you, too."

She bent and rubbed Nick's back as he giggled at Tiger, who had flopped down between his legs on his back and held Nick's hand to his belly while Nick petted him. "I'll be right down there." She pointed to the last stall.

Nick nodded. "I like him."

She kissed Nick's head. "He likes you, too." She stood and met Luke's steady gaze. "Watch Nick. I'll go say hello to Ace."

"Just don't steal him again," Luke teased.

She headed down the aisle and called out, "No promises."

Luke mock-groaned behind her. Soon she heard his low voice as he played with Nick and the cats.

She reached Ace's gate just as he kicked it again. "Hey now. That's enough of that, big guy."

Ace turned and put his head over the gate. She gave his neck a long stroke. "There, now. That's a nice boy." She wished she could take him out for a ride, but settled for babying him with lots of pats.

A phone rang in the distance.

"Hey Sarah," Luke called.

She turned and found him standing next to Nick holding up his cell. "Sorry. It's work. I need to take this."

She nodded, gave Ace another rub down his long nose, then kissed his face. "Be good. I'll see you later."

She headed back down the aisle as Luke walked away from her and Nick. She met her son in the middle and picked him up. "Did you have fun with the kitties?"

"I love them." He tucked his hands between her and his legs. "I have to go."

"Okay."

Luke stood at the end of the barn, his back to her. She rushed toward him, knowing Nick probably couldn't wait long to go to the bathroom.

"What did you find out about the car accident?" Luke's question stopped her in her tracks. "I want to know everything about it and the woman in the car with him."

"Mama. I have to pee."

Luke spun around, his eyes filled with guilt. He pointed to a closed door next to an office.

She took Nick, opened the door, set him down, and made sure the light was on before he closed the door and did his business.

"I need to call you back," Luke said, then turned to her. He opened his mouth to say something, but immediately closed it.

"Nothing to say? Let me. I thought after our talk you dropped this, but you're still digging into my past. It doesn't matter what I say or do, you're going to continue to believe everything Margaret says about me for a friend you didn't even keep in contact with past high school. You're more loyal to a woman obviously bent on revenge even though I've done nothing to warrant it and a dead man you don't even know anymore. Do you really believe I'm such a terrible person and mother?"

"Mama." Nick stood in the open bathroom door, his gaze bouncing between her and Luke.

She held her hand out to him. "Time to go home."

"But we didn't pick vegetables," Nick whined. "Jack isn't even here yet."

Sarah picked up Nick and walked toward the barn doors. "We're going back to Grandma's."

"Sarah, wait. Let me explain."

She turned but didn't meet his eyes.

"After our talk about . . . " Luke glanced at Nick, then said, ". . . your uncle, I completely forgot I asked my guy to look into Sean, too."

She appreciated that he didn't say anything in front of Nick about what she'd done as a teen, but it didn't excuse that he was still digging into things that had nothing to do with whether or not she was a good mother to her boys.

So she had the final word. "What happened when I was a kid, what happened with Sean, they made me want to be the best mom I can be. That's all you need to know. My marriage is none of your business. He's gone. I've moved on. So should you."

With that she turned and left, a knot in her gut that if he kept digging he might expose what she'd spent the last two years keeping secret.

Chapter Fourteen

*S*arah pulled the large tote bag up to her shoulder and took both boys' hands in the parking lot just off the Carmel public beach. Margaret carried the chairs and Bridget pulled the rolling cooler.

Margaret and Bridget went ahead. The boys moved slowly over the sand, but they made it to the spot Bridget chose just as she spread out a blanket.

Sarah pulled out the bucket and tools she'd brought and handed them to Jack. "Pick a spot close by to make sand castles."

Jack and Nick moved a few feet away, plopped down in the wet sand, and started playing.

"There's Sophia," Bridget announced. "Why is he walking her all the way here?" She wasn't enthusiastic about seeing her ex.

While Bridget came to the house to drive with her and Margaret, Sophia had spent the night at her dad's place because it was his weekend to have her. Rob agreed to drop her back with Bridget to spend a few hours with all of them today.

Sophia ran over, dropped her towel on the blanket, and said, "Hi, Grandma. Hi, Aunt Sarah," then ran to play with the boys.

Sarah turned and watched Bridget with Rob.

"You're late." Bridget held her hand out for Sophia's bag.

Rob handed it over, checked his watch, then stuffed his hands in his shorts pockets. "By three minutes. Parking on a Saturday at the beach . . . not easy. And this is supposed to be my day."

"I'm sure Little Miss Tight-ass-no-brains will keep you company."

"And I'll enjoy every minute of it because she won't be spewing this kind of BS at me." Rob walked away from Bridget toward Sarah. "Sophia told me you were here." Rob wrapped her in a quick hug. "It's so good to see you."

Finally, someone was happy to see her. She and Rob had always gotten along. "It's good to see you, too. Thanks for bringing Sophia. The boys loved playing with her when she visited their grandma."

Rob smiled and nodded at Margaret. "Good to see you."

Margaret nodded her hello, but didn't say anything because Bridget seethed beside her with her arms crossed over her chest.

Rob lowered his voice. "Looks like Bridget forgot to bring a chair for you." Rob shook his head. "If it helps, I get even worse treatment."

"I'm fine on the blanket," she whispered back.

"It's a slice here and there and before you know it, you're bleeding to death. And she wonders why our marriage fell apart."

"I heard you're seeing someone new."

"It's nice to be with someone who sees me." Rob's gaze got lost out at sea.

Sarah understood all too well. In the end, Sean only looked at her as a means to an end. Not a real person. Not someone he used to love. If he even ever did.

"How's the construction business?" she asked so Bridget could hear and stop staring daggers at them for whispering together.

"Great. I just got a huge contract to take over the new Oak Park custom home development."

Bridget sat forward in her chair. "You said you didn't get the project." She got a suspicious look in her eyes. "Or maybe you just held off taking it until the divorce was final because you didn't want that kind of big payday included in our settlement."

Rob rolled his eyes. "Another construction company got the contract when I initially bid on it, but they had some issues come up and lost the deal, so the developer recently gave it to me. But please, make this into something it isn't. I've missed that so much." Sarcasm dripped from his lips.

Bridget fell back in her seat. "I haven't missed the way you lie so easily."

Rob shook his head and stared up at the sky.

Sarah didn't want to take a side, so she just went with being nice. "Congratulations on the contract."

"Thanks."

Jack ran up to them. "Can we go horseback riding at Luke's when we get home? Sophia wants to come."

Sarah sighed. "Honey, I told you Luke has to invite us. We can't just show up at his place. And Sophia's daddy is picking her up in a couple hours to take her home with him." Not that she wanted to play another round of contradiction, with Luke being nice only so he could compare what he saw right in front of him with whatever he dug up next. "Can you say hi to Uncle Rob, please?"

"Hi Uncle Rob."

Rob smiled. "Hey buddy. I heard you've been hanging out with Luke." He turned his gaze on her. "Lucky guy."

She blushed, despite the fact she and Luke weren't a thing. Though for a moment she'd thought . . . But it wasn't. She hadn't seen or heard from him after the scene in the stables.

Like all her other interactions with him, he left her wondering where she stood. He didn't hide his attraction to her. He'd kissed her. But then he questioned things that had nothing to do with who she was now. Did he really want to use her past against her? Or did he see that what happened to her as a child and her marriage to Sean made her who she was today?

And what did his investigator tell him about Sean's accident?

Did he know the truth?

If he did, he hadn't shared it with Margaret.

Which made her wonder if he'd dropped the whole thing or if he was just biding his time to use it against her if she refused to let Margaret see the kids in the future.

She hated not knowing what he really wanted from her.

Bridget called out, "She hasn't been back to Luke's place and he hasn't been to Mom's in days."

Margaret must be keeping Bridget up to date on everything Sarah related. *Great.*

Bridget sneered. "He saw her for exactly who she is. Too bad Sean didn't sooner or he'd still be alive."

Jack stared at his aunt, dead quiet and still.

Sarah wondered if Bridget was right.

Rob stepped in front of Jack and stared down Bridget. "You never know when to keep quiet. Not in front of Sophia or Sean's sons. You used to be nice. Now you don't seem to care about anything or anyone's feelings."

Bridget looked angry and remorseful all at once.

Sarah touched Jack's back. "Go play with Sophia and your brother."

Jack ran back to them.

Rob turned to her. "I'm sorry her anger with me has spilled over onto you."

"She doesn't like me either."

"It's no excuse to say something like that in front of Jack. Or at all," he called over his shoulder, knowing Bridget hung on their every word. Rob lowered his voice. "If it wouldn't cause another fight, and Sophia wasn't so excited about spending a couple hours at the beach with the boys, I'd just take her back with me."

"I'll keep an eye on her."

Rob nodded. "Thanks. Ask me, Luke's a fool. I never believed even half of what Sean told Bridget."

She touched his arm. "Thanks."

"Isn't your girlfriend waiting for you?" Bridget called out.

Sarah removed her hand, angry that she couldn't even get away with a simple gesture of gratitude without Bridget thinking it meant more.

Rob turned and called back, "I'll be back at three to pick her up." He turned and started backing up from Sarah. "You agreed to six weeks of this." He shook his head, gave her a "you're crazy" look, then turned and walked off.

Sarah sighed. Then she pulled her shirt over her head, grabbed the sunscreen she'd sprayed all over the boys before they left the house, and applied a generous amount on her arms, chest, belly, legs, and her back the best she could.

"You're so pale, you're going to fry out here." Margaret awkwardly scooted out of her low chair and stood.

Bridget brooded and didn't even attempt to help her struggling mother up.

Sarah would have tried, but Margaret usually snapped at her for trying to help.

Margaret held her hand out for the can of sunscreen.

Sarah gave it to her.

Margaret surprised her by moving around her, pulling her

ponytail off her back, and spraying her down thoroughly. She handed the can back.

"Thank you."

Margaret acknowledged that with a tilt of her head, then struggled to sit in her chair again, mostly falling into it.

"Are you okay?"

"I'm old." Margaret tried and failed to hide a wince of pain and went back to watching the kids.

Sarah sat on the edge of the blanket, kicked off her flip-flops, and sank her toes in the sand. She pulled her phone out of her cut-off jeans shorts back pocket and tapped the screen, sighing when she saw 123 new emails from yesterday to today.

"More work?" Margaret asked, an edge to her voice.

"Just a few emails," she said, hoping to not have another argument about how she didn't pay enough attention to the boys.

"Mom! Can we go in the water?" Jack called, all three kids standing and waiting to splash in the waves.

Sarah stuffed her phone in her tote bag and got up. "Wait for me." Before she joined the boys, she turned to Bridget. "Do you mind if Sophia goes in the water?"

"I mind that she'll be staring at you in that skimpy bikini top."

Jealous much?

Sarah's suit wasn't any more revealing than those of any of the other women sunbathing on the beach.

Bridget wore a simple one-piece tank-style suit. She looked cute in it, but obviously didn't feel that way and kept a sarong tied around her hips and covering her thighs to her knees.

"But she can swim, right?"

Bridget waved her away. "Yes. Go strut your stuff."

Sarah rolled her eyes. She didn't strut anywhere. But she did join the kids down the beach where the waves crested on the sand.

She took Nick's hand and walked with him farther into the surf. He was too little to keep his balance in the rolling waves. Jack did better, but Sophia had to help him every once in a while. But the kids had a blast and Sarah found herself laughing and kicking and playing in the sand and surf with the kids and really enjoying herself like she hadn't done in a long time.

She needed more of this.

She definitely needed more sleep.

But instead of doing that the last few days, she found herself leaving her laptop in the boys' room with the camera on so she could keep an eye on them on her phone while they slept, and she snuck out of the house in the dead of night. She didn't think Margaret would hear them from downstairs if they awoke for some reason. She walked in the fresh air and under the stars so she could wind down and finally sleep after work. Inevitably, she found her way to Luke's place and the horses that drew her there as much as thinking about him did.

She didn't know what it was about him that had her turning over their every interaction to figure out what she'd said or done to make him react the way he did around her. Or what she should have said or done to make him like her.

She thought they'd gotten to a better place, but then he'd received that call and she got scared that he'd dig up things better left buried.

"Watch out," Sophia called, racing with Jack toward her as a big wave followed them in.

She picked up Nick just in time to save him from toppling over and spun him around as the water rose up to her thighs.

Jack and Sophia made it up the beach and out of the worst of it.

Sophia ran back to her as the water receded. "Nice save."

"Thanks." She smiled and laughed with Nick as he splashed her legs.

"You're really pretty," Sophia blurted out.

"Thank you, sweetheart. So are you."

"I hate this suit." The princess on the front was a bit juvenile for a ten-year-old. "Mom won't let me get a two-piece. Not even one of the tank ones."

"Yours seems to be getting tight on you. Next time your mom takes you shopping for one, if you can't get what you want, look for a one-piece that is a solid color or a pattern. It will make you look your age. More sophisticated," she added, earning a huge smile from Sophia.

"Thanks. Good to know."

She was happy to help, but no way was she going to tell Bridget how to parent her child. Or suggest an appropriate two-piece wasn't the end of the world to make Sophia feel like the young lady she was blossoming into.

"You're way cooler than my mom."

"Only because she's your mom. Mom's aren't cool to their kids."

"I think you're cool," Nick said, holding on to her leg as another wave washed in.

"Thank you, buddy."

He smiled real big and hugged her close. "I'm glad you came and played instead of working."

She bent and kissed him on the head. "Me, too, bud."

"How come your dad didn't stay?" Jack asked Sophia.

"My mom wouldn't let him," she said plainly. She looked up at Sarah. "They hate each other now."

"I hope not." She meant it. "They're both hurt. I hope they find their way back to being friends."

Sophia kicked at the wave that rolled in. "I don't think that's possible."

Sarah hugged Sophia to her side. "Anything is possible if you try. Always remember that, sweetheart."

"Will you try to get Luke to ask us to come over again?" Jack's mind got stuck on one thing sometimes.

"*If* I talk to Luke again, yes, I'll ask if you guys can go over and ride the horses. But I don't know if I'll see him again." She hoped she would, but she couldn't promise her boys anything because Luke's silence and absence spoke volumes.

"Let's have lunch," Margaret called out to them.

The kids ran to get something to eat. Sarah took a minute and turned to the ocean. She let the breeze blow over her and took in the beautiful view, but all she saw in her mind's eye was a gorgeous man who was always pulling her close and pushing her away at the same time and she got nowhere with him.

She didn't expect to ever hear from him again.

He obviously wasn't missing her the way she missed him when she allowed herself to think about him.

So she did what she'd been doing for days, wiped that image of him out of her head, and went back to her boys and the 120-plus emails waiting for her. Because he wasn't.

Chapter Fifteen

*L*uke spent every waking moment of the last week and a half since he'd seen Sarah sweating out his frustration about the state of his life and analyzing every interaction he'd had with her.

He'd spent a good portion of every day since he met her wanting her and not knowing how to go about getting her. New for him. While he hadn't laid on the charm—at all—he knew that would only work to a point.

Sarah wanted real, because she was herself around everyone. She didn't put on a show or pretend to be anything other than herself.

Refreshing and sexy as hell in his book.

She certainly didn't put up with his BS.

And he liked that she called him out on it instead of just going along to keep him happy.

He'd just scratched the surface with her and he wanted to get to know her better, because the more he learned, the farther away she got from being the woman Margaret described and became more of the woman he wanted but didn't think existed for him.

Everything in him said she was the one he wanted.

The kiss they shared started a fire in him.

Every interaction they shared held the promise of something

great building between them, but then he'd ask about her past, Sean, and ruin it.

It wasn't just that he'd been investigating her. The two times she and the kids came to the ranch, he hadn't done what he promised and showed them around or picked vegetables in the garden. Simple things.

He'd blown it with Sarah and the boys.

And that's why Sarah didn't date. Because she didn't want some guy making promises to her kids and not keeping them. She didn't want to let the boys get close to someone, only to have them disappointed when that person left because they weren't committed.

He cussed himself out for disappointing the boys and called himself ten kinds of stupid for giving Sarah a reason to believe he wasn't the honest, reliable guy she and the boys deserved.

As he had that epiphany, Jerry found him in the stables and saw everything written all over his face. Luke could still hear the laughter in his voice from this morning.

"So, you finally figured it out. You let her get away. She didn't go far. She's here singing to Ace every morning at the crack of dawn. She thinks she's alone most of the time. I stay out of her way and let her enjoy the horses. She looks terrible. Can't be getting more than two, three hours sleep a night. Makes a person wonder what's so important that she has to stay up all night to get it done." After that disturbing news, he added something Luke desperately hoped was true: "Maybe she's missing you as much as you're missing her."

Hope that he could make things right and spend more time with her sent him after her because he was getting nowhere staying away from her.

He stood in Margaret's backyard with a present in his hands, looking up at the second-story veranda and Sarah working on her computer. Classic rock rang out from her phone. Led Zeppelin. Nice.

Lost in total concentration staring at the computer screen and typing a mile a minute, she didn't notice him. He couldn't help staring at her beautiful face.

He wasn't used to missing anyone. He always went after what he wanted. But he'd stalled out with Sarah because he'd never had to work this hard to get a woman's attention. But he thought Sarah was special and he wanted her and he meant to show her how much.

Completely engrossed in what she was doing, he didn't think she noticed him walking up the back steps and standing a few feet behind her, watching her work. In addition to the laptop on the table in front of her, two more sat at her bare feet on the floor. Just inside the French doors, he spotted one on the bed and two on the dresser. All the computers looked like they were running something. He had no idea what, but they were all busy flashing this and that on the screens. Files and papers sat neatly organized on the table. She glanced at some of the papers as she typed.

Sarah wasn't typing a letter or proposal of any kind, but some kind of strange code language. Most of the words were recognizable, but there were other abbreviations and symbols that didn't make any sense. She typed so fast, he couldn't believe she actually knew what all the strange characters, words, and symbols meant. Amazing.

And he wanted to know more. About her job. About her.

He wanted more of the truth to erase who he'd been told she was, because he really liked the glimpses she gave him of the woman who intrigued him like no one had in a long time.

* * *

"Are you just going to stand there all day staring at me, or are you going to say hello?"

After their last encounter and the days that had passed, it surprised her he'd come at all.

Stupidly, she'd spent the last week missing him.

That was the plain truth.

She thought about their kiss and couldn't help but want to feel his arms around her again.

But here she sat, typing on her computer, trying not to let him see just how much his mere presence affected her.

"Hello." His deep voice held a trace of uncertainty about his welcome. "Are you really busy?"

She hit Save on the computer and turned to face him with a raised eyebrow before she surveyed the six laptops surrounding her. All different projects she'd been working on for months. She'd only brought three with her, but some problems had come up and Abby had sent her another computer by overnight delivery almost every other day for the past week.

Was she busy? Always. But she tried to cut the tension and teased, "No, not really."

God, he looked great. Black boots, snug worn jeans, a black T-shirt stretched across his broad chest, the sleeves straining over the muscles in his arms, and today he wore a black cowboy hat. He looked dangerous, despite his open and warm expression, though some concern shown in his eyes as he watched her.

"Are you headed to a birthday party or something?" She pointed to the present Luke held, wondering why he hadn't left it in his truck.

"This is for you." He held the package out to her, but she hesitated to take it. He tilted his head and studied her. "You look like no one's ever given you a gift."

Gifts had been few and far between in her life as an unwanted child. "I . . . um . . . Why did you get me a present?"

"I owe you two thank-you's and three 'I'm sorry's.'" His earnest eyes turned stormy with uncertainty, because she still didn't take the present.

He set the gift in her lap and dropped his hat on the table.

She pressed her hands on top of the box, thrilled by the kind gesture, but she didn't want him to think he owed her anything. Or that she expected him to buy her things.

"Why don't you just say 'thank you' and 'I'm sorry'? You didn't have to buy me anything."

"I wanted to." He hooked his thumbs in his front pockets and shifted from one foot to the other, then let out a big sigh, sat beside her at the table, and leaned in close, setting off a swarm of butterflies in her belly. "Thank you for taking care of Ace. I'm sorry I yelled at you when you took off on him the first day. I'm sorry I was angry and called you a criminal when I found you sleeping in my field. I completely overreacted, but you scared me half to death." A flash of that fear crossed his eyes even now. "I think you took ten years off my life when I saw you lying in that circle of horses." He took a breath. "Thank you for trusting me enough to tell me the truth about what happened with your uncle. I want you to know it meant a lot to me that you'd tell me something you haven't shared with anyone else.

"Finally, I am so sorry that I ever agreed to investigate your past for Margaret or had any part in threatening to take the boys from you and forcing a visitation." The sincerity in the apology touched her.

"Also, you should know, I know about Sean and the accident, everything, and I understand now why you want to put the past behind you and move on." He held her gaze.

She guessed at what he'd found out about the car accident, but wondered if he really knew "everything" that came after it.

"And will you share the information you uncovered with Margaret?"

He didn't answer that, but asked, "Did you come here to also try to mend the relationship so the boys can spend more time with family?"

Luke understood her better than she'd thought.

"Yes."

"Then I think she should hear about the Sean you were married to from you." Meaning Luke didn't recognize the man Sean had turned into either.

"Margaret isn't ready to listen to anything I have to say about Sean."

"When she is, I know you'll deliver the news gently because you're not out to hurt her."

"I never was."

"I know. Time's a bitch. It allowed her anger to build into a wall between you, you to move on, and me to use work and the ranch to get stuck trying to figure out a way to fix things between us when all I really needed to do was get over the fear that you'd refuse to see me and hear me out and come and talk to you. Because deep down, I knew you'd give me a chance, because that's who you are."

"I let work get in the way of things I should be doing sometimes, too." She had to apologize to her boys a lot lately for working too much and not spending time with them.

"Don't let me off the hook so easily. I stuck my nose in your business when I should have just spoken to you."

"I'm sure you don't take your client's word for everything." She understood he needed an unbiased and straightforward accounting of what happened. Still, she didn't have to like why he'd done it.

He'd only done it because he believed what Margaret told him. Now he knew the truth and she hoped this was the end of it.

"I also made you and the boys a promise and I didn't keep it. It won't happen again."

She believed he really meant it. "You've thanked me and apologized." She pushed the present in front of him. "You don't owe me anything else."

He pushed it back. "Open it, Sarah. I want you to have it." He put his hand over hers on the package. "Please. I picked it especially for you."

She took the present into her lap and unwrapped the pretty, delicate paper. White roses over a golden background with a gold ribbon tied around to match. She carefully folded the pretty paper and placed it on the table. She lifted the box cover, pushed the tissue aside, and revealed the gorgeous carved wooden box.

Tears filled her eyes.

She pulled the gift out and admired the details. Roses, lots and lots of carved roses. A silver plaque engraved with her name in a very feminine script adorned the lid. With trembling fingers, she lifted the lid and found the inside lined with deep red velvet, and the lullaby she had sung to Ace on the first day she'd gone to the ranch played in soft tinkling notes.

Tears trailed down her cheeks. No one had ever given her something so lovely and personal. Ever.

Luke took her hand and kissed her palm.

"Don't cry, Sarah. It was meant to make you happy. I know you like music and this song especially. You sang it so beautifully to Ace. I thought you'd like it."

She squeezed his hand. "I love it. It's the nicest, most thoughtful gift I've ever received. Thank you."

"You're welcome. I'm sure Sean bought you some really nice

things, but this reminded me of you. Sometimes when I go to sleep at night I think I hear you singing. Your voice haunts my dreams."

"You probably do hear me. I've been sneaking into your stables at night. Well, the early morning."

"Jerry told me. Why don't you ever sleep? You look completely exhausted. I'm worried about you." Concern and caring filled his eyes and voice.

She hadn't been taking very good care of herself. She'd gotten buried in work and often forgot to eat.

The Knox Project was coming down to the wire, and now that Abby had sent her three more problems to fix that stumped her team of programmers, she just couldn't find the time to do everything that needed to be done. Losing ground on all fronts, her anxiety jacked up high, she couldn't sleep.

The boys were begging for more attention, Margaret's hostility grew the more she worked, and she spent hours on the phone attending meetings as one of the faces of the company.

She had a lot of people depending on her, and sometimes it all became too much.

Luke looked like he'd had a rough couple of weeks, too. Maybe they both needed some quiet time.

Before she gave Luke an answer, her cell phone rang. She sighed deeply when she glanced at the caller ID. "It's my office. I've been waiting for this call. Only take a minute, and then we'll talk."

"Okay, but I want an answer. I'm about ready to slip a sleeping pill into your iced tea."

She appreciated the sentiment but rolled her eyes and answered the phone.

"Hi, Marcel, did you get it?" She picked up one of the laptops at her feet and began typing to bring up the files she had just sent to the office.

Luke kept watching her.

Marcel jumped right in. "I got it. This is the best encryption code I've ever seen."

"If it works, it will be the most secure system ever created. Now, use your considerable talents to try to break my encryption and find the back door. If you find it, I'll give you a twenty-five-thousand-dollar bonus. If you break the encryption, you can have my job."

"I don't want your job. I have a life."

"I have a life." She scoffed. "It's not a very fun one," she admitted, earning an affirmative nod from Luke. "Get to work. We only have a couple weeks left to finish this. Oh, I'm sending back two of the laptops tomorrow. I fixed the problems with the Petticoat Project and updated the North Pole Project. Contact the customers and let them know they'll be there in a couple of days, then contact David and tell him once he gets the laptops to go to the customer sites for the install. He can take as many people as he thinks is necessary to complete the jobs. Let's see, did I miss anything?"

"How's the new game coming?" Marcel's excitement revealed his anticipation. "Will it be finished for the holiday release?"

"You aren't going to believe it. I came up with another scene and added it last night. I sent it to the team to test. Find out if they like it. I'd like an unbiased opinion. I'm going to give it to Tyler at the benefit at the end of the month."

"Sounds good." Marcel hesitated, then added, "We can't wait for you to get back. The phones are ringing off the hook with customers requesting bids."

"Soon. How many of the calls are worthy of a proposal from us?"

"You'll have to ask Abby. I'll get started on the Knox Project and call you when I'm done."

"Sounds good. Remember, find the back door and win the prize." She couldn't help the smile he couldn't see, but she hoped he heard it in her voice.

"For that kind of money, I'll find it." Marcel's cocky tone only made her smile more. "Once I do, I'll document everything."

She hung up and fully focused on Luke's warm hand still holding hers. It felt good, right, so she linked her fingers with his. "Sorry. Working long-distance has been . . . trying. My staff gets antsy when they can't actually see me coding. They constantly wonder how much progress I've made. There's always a deadline looming."

"I had no idea you're so involved in doing the actual work. I assumed you just oversaw management—but you're hands-on in a way most CEOs are not. You work your ass off for your staff and clients."

She didn't know what to say. It was all true. So she simply shrugged it off.

One side of Luke's mouth drew back in a half frown. "Can he break your encryption?"

"No," she said emphatically, then backed off even if she did believe it. "At least, he better not. He's the best hacker there is. I hired him after the FBI arrested him for hacking into a very secure bank, emptying out several accounts, and returning the money to the many seniors an unscrupulous crook swindled out of their life savings, including his grandparents."

"A modern-day Robin Hood."

"Yeah, well, it was still a crime and the FBI gave him an ultimatum to either go to jail or work for them. He does the work they want, but prefers working for me."

"So, I guess you don't have to worry about paying him the twenty-five grand."

"Oh no. He'll find the back door. I made sure of that."

Luke cocked his head. "I don't get it. Why do you want him to find it?"

"I'll see just how well my program works. If he finds the back door really fast, then I need to make some adjustments. If he's got to work for it, then I've done my job."

"How long will it take him to find it?"

"Probably two days if he really attacks the problem. Once he finds it, I'll put in the remaining safeguards to block it. It's just a test to see how secure the program is. In this case, the program has to be better than anything out there." She rolled her shoulders, easing the tension in them and her neck. "The Knox Project has been kicking my ass, but I've finally made some headway. I should finish it on time and under budget."

He stroked a hand down the side of her face. "No wonder you look so tired."

She raised a brow. "You suck at sweet-talking women."

That sexy grin came out again. "I'll work on it. But right now I'm worried about you." His thumb brushed her cheek and she couldn't help leaning into his touch. "I didn't expect you to be so thoughtful and caring after talking to Margaret."

"Hearsay, Counselor. Inadmissible for good reason. It's unreliable at best. Lies at worst."

"Point taken. So tell me more. The company must be doing well if you can hand out twenty-five-thousand-dollar bonuses."

She eyed him. "I'm surprised you haven't dug up all those details."

"I planned to," he readily admitted. "And it's not hard to discover the financials on a publicly held company. But like you, I got busy with lawyer work and ranch stuff and driving myself crazy trying to come up with a way to apologize to you."

She ran her hand over the beautiful gift. "You did very well."

"I'm just glad you haven't kicked me out."

"I understand work taking over your life. It's why my companies are doing exceptionally well. The Spencer Software stock has been up every quarter and profits have increased considerably. My success with Spencer Software has allowed me to start another business. It's extremely successful, too, which is why I work all the time."

"Why do you do it? You could have sold the company or had someone else run it when Sean died. Instead, you kept it going and started another company."

She shrugged. "I couldn't let it go. At the time the company was in the midst of going public. Sean's death worried the investors, but there were other problems I had to fix, or the company would have imploded. And I made a promise to Margaret."

"What promise?"

"That no matter what, I'd keep the company going, so that when the boys grew up they'd have something of their father."

"What if the boys grow up and don't want any part of the business?"

"That's fine with me. They can do whatever makes them happy. The money from the business will give them the opportunity to spread their wings and find that thing they love to do."

"Yeah, but it won't be a piece of Sean. It's all you. *You* run the company, and *you* do the work that keeps it alive."

"Try telling Margaret that. She's so focused on Sean's death and being angry with me, she hasn't taken the time to even ask about the company. I suppose she doesn't really care about the details. I love what I do, but sometimes the amount of hours I work feels like the punishment Margaret wants to inflict on me." The loneliness of it overwhelmed her sometimes.

Luke brushed his thumb over the back of her hand. "Then take a break and spend the evening with me. Let me make everything up to you and show you that I really am a good guy. We'll drive into town, I'll take you to a great restaurant, and we'll get to know each other even better." Luke glanced into her room. "I hope Margaret can watch the boys. Otherwise, we'll take them with us."

She appreciated that he was so willing to include them. "Actually, Margaret took them over to Bridget's place for dinner and a movie." Sarah hadn't been invited, which suited her. "They won't be back for a while. You just missed them." She yawned. "I'm not really up to going out tonight."

Luke's face fell in disappointment.

She just wanted to be alone with him. "I have another half hour of work to get done and sent back to my office. Let me do that and I'll meet you at the ranch. You have a really nice firepit by the garden. Get a fire ready, and I'll bring dinner. We'll have a cookout and watch the sun go down."

His eyes lit up with excitement and anticipation. "Sounds good to me."

He stood, and since their hands were still linked, he brought her up with him. "I've missed you so damn much." He pulled her hand up over his shoulder and leaned down to kiss her. Soft, warm, his mouth touched hers and she was lost in him. Completely intoxicated, she dove in for more, sweeping her tongue along his, tasting him, taking him in.

He held her so close and she felt so safe in his arms. Time, work, all the pressures in her life disappeared and for the first time in a long while she felt like only a woman, wanted and needed by a man who made her feel those things and so much more.

His lips left her mouth and he kissed his way around her face. One on her jaw, he moved up to her temple, kissed her on the forehead, and gave her one last kiss on the lips before he pulled away. Dazed, he held her by her shoulders while she regained her head.

"I'll see you in about an hour or so. You sure you don't want me to cook, or take you out?"

"Huh? What?"

"Dinner," he reminded her, his grin even more vibrant—and smug.

She didn't mind. He'd earned it. "Wow, you have to stop kissing me like that. I completely lose all coherent thought."

A laugh rumbled out of him. "Good to know."

She smacked his shoulder. "I'll bring everything."

"Hurry up. If I only get a couple hours, I want every minute of it." He gave her a light kiss, then cupped her cheek and held her gaze. "I really am worried about you."

"I'll be okay. Dinner will reenergize me. You'll see." She squeezed his impressive biceps. "Thank you for my gift. I'll keep all my treasures in it."

"I'm glad you like it. I'll see you in a little while. Don't keep me waiting."

"I won't." She watched him leave down the back steps, excited for their date and the possibility of something more, even if she hadn't dated anyone in forever.

She sat at the table to finish her work, but the music box held her attention and she ran her hands lovingly over the wood.

Luke had been wrong. Sean had never given her anything as nice as the music box. In the beginning, she thought he just didn't want to spend what little money they hadn't sunk into the business on extravagances she didn't need. Later, when they had more money, all the gifts had been work related. He'd get her a new cell phone or some new upgraded laptop. All the gifts were so she could work more efficiently, or do her job better, but she'd wanted something just for her, as a woman, as his wife.

The only piece of jewelry he'd ever bought her was her gold wedding band. She'd never had a diamond ring.

Birthdays and anniversaries they spent out to dinner at a fancy restaurant, which was nice but impersonal. It wasn't the same as a gift chosen with love especially for her.

It hurt.

And Sean had done it to get back at her. Because although he'd had the idea for the business and loved wining and dining potential customers, she got the credit and praise for the programs. Clients started asking for her. And Sean didn't like not being the center of attention or getting the praise he so loved.

Sean knew she wanted a family. He was only too happy to give her what she wanted so she'd be happy—and work more. He expected her to produce at the same level as before she had the boys. He managed everything during her eight weeks' maternity leave with Jack, but the same burnout he'd had in school came back when he had to take over her projects during that time. He preferred being the salesman. The second she was back to work, he piled it on, despite her objections and pleas that he hire someone to help with the load. But they were barely getting by, with small margins on projects to build a name for the company and keep the investors happy.

When Nick came along, Sean gave her barely two weeks before he was pushing her to complete one very important project after the next. It seemed everything was dire. The work needed to be done better and faster than the competition could do it.

That's when he stopped pretending her cared about her at all.

He stopped treating her like a wife and treated her like an employee. He wouldn't give an inch on her schedule and expected her to meet every deadline. When she didn't, or took time with the kids, he'd yell at her, give her the cold shoulder, and argue with her, amping the enormous amount of stress and pressure on her.

He'd given her the family she wanted, hoping it would be enough to keep her happy and working. But Sean barely spent any time with the boys. They hardly ever did anything together.

And the dream of having the family she never had as a child evaporated and she knew her boys would never have that either with Sean.

She knew she needed to get out, but sometimes that's easier said than done when there are little hearts involved, there's no money, other people are depending on you for their job and income, and investors want to see a return on their investment.

To make matters worse, Sean didn't hide why he stopped being nice to her. She'd known almost to the minute the affair started. It wasn't hard. The woman worked in their office. They didn't hide it, but flaunted it in front of her. Sean left the office early with her, took her out to dinner and to exotic places for long weekends. She'd seen the bank and credit card statements documenting their affair. And all the extravagant gifts he bought her.

The expensive jewelry hurt her the most.

Trivial, yes. But it broke her heart to realize she'd been used to build the business he'd wanted but couldn't pull off because he didn't have the stamina to do the actual work.

It took her far longer than it should have to realize he'd never loved her. He'd simply needed her drive and talent to succeed.

Sean got caught up in his own ego and thinking the company would be the next big Silicon Valley success. But without her, it would have all come crashing down around him. His mistake was in thinking the woman who only wanted to be loved would do anything to get it from him.

She had more pride and self-worth than that, even if Sean had stomped all over them.

She'd worked hard to earn her degree and change her life.

She'd never settle for anything less than real ever again. She wouldn't settle for a man who wanted everything from her and gave nothing in return.

Sarah ran her hands over the music box, pulled it to her chest, and thought of Luke, a man who said "thank you" and "I'm sorry" with his heart.

Chapter Sixteen

*T*ime was passing too quickly on Sarah's visit, and though there were still four weeks to go, Luke had no idea what he was going to do when she left. The ranch was his dream and he was finally living it. He didn't know what he'd do if they couldn't work out some way to see each other. Hell, he didn't even know if she wanted to be with him. But the long drive back and forth from Carmel to Silicon Valley wouldn't be easy for the long haul. He'd tried that in the past and failed. Plus, with the hours she worked and needing to be home with her kids, he feared they'd become some weekend thing.

And for the first time, he wanted more.

Maybe he could convince her to stay at the ranch and work from there. With technology today, she could probably do her work from anywhere. Despite what she said about needing to be at the office, if she'd just admit it, she didn't have any real trouble working from Margaret's.

But he was getting ahead of himself. First, he needed to convince her that they should be together. If she walked away before he had a chance to show her how much he wanted her to stay . . . It'd be like tearing himself in two. Part of him would go with her. And he'd be left wondering what might have been forever.

A soft knock sounded behind him. He turned and found Sarah standing at the back door, smiling at him through the window. He'd left a note on the front door for her to come around so that he didn't miss her while he set up the backyard for their dinner.

He opened the door and smiled back at her. "I'm so glad you came." He took the cooler from her hand. "Hungry?"

"Starving."

So was he. For her.

"Let's head on back to the firepit."

He followed her down the porch steps and around the path to the back garden. She wore faded jeans, a lightweight baby-blue sweater, and short brown boots. Her hair was up in a ponytail. No makeup again. She looked tired but at the same time fresh and natural. He loved that Sarah didn't hide behind all that stuff. She was perfectly comfortable in her own skin. And he found that exceedingly sexy.

Family and friends thought he didn't want to commit to anyone. Not true. He just wanted to find the right woman.

And he was pretty damn sure she was standing in front of him.

Making a commitment to Sarah didn't scare him half as much as losing her did. That's why he'd struggled with how to apologize and show her that he really did want to be with her for the right reasons.

* * *

Sarah's shoulders slumped the second her phone rang. She wanted one work-free evening and time to explore this thing happening between her and Luke.

She turned to him. "I'm so sorry. I have to take this."

"No problem."

She appreciated that he meant that, but still wished she didn't have to interrupt their date. "Hi, Abby." She sighed, not hiding her disappointment about the interruption.

"Are you okay?"

She hated making Abby concerned. "Sorry. Yeah, I'm fine. What's up?"

"You tell me what's up." Abby knew her too well. Last they left things on their call before Sarah headed to Luke's, Sarah had expressed how happy she was about making up with Luke.

"I'm trying to have a date with Luke, but *someone* interrupted us."

"Oh crap. Sorry. And yay! He's the first man you've been interested in since Sean. This is so great."

Sarah chuckled under her breath. "I love the enthusiasm, but if I don't actually get back to the date it will end without it starting."

"Okay. Sorry. I wish I could get this done some other way, but . . ."

"Abby, what is it?"

She sat in the Adirondack chair by the firepit. Luke hadn't lit the logs yet, but he'd taken the time to bring the two chairs down from the porch. He'd even cut some flowers from the fading garden and placed them in a vase on a low table set for two with stoneware plates, silverware, and red linen napkins. Very simple and pretty. It had been a long time since she'd shared dinner with a man when she wasn't conducting a business meeting.

She felt his strong presence behind her. Just like earlier in the day, she could feel him staring at her while she talked to Abby.

"Evan is meeting with clients, so I need your help. Accounting just notified me that Mr. Larson hasn't paid his final installment. David's team completed the installation two days ago and we should have received the money that day via wire transfer. Accounting checked with our bank; they don't have anything pending."

"Remind me how much the final payment is."

"You're not going to like this."

"How much?"

"A million two."

"Great. What's the contract say about penalties?"

"Stan, in legal, said if they don't pay today, there's a five percent penalty."

"Five percent on the final payment or the total?

"The total. Stan let George know what was going on, but Larson wouldn't take his call. You'd think George, as CFO, could handle this problem, but he can't get Larson on the line. Larson will only talk to you."

"Has legal released the licensing agreement?"

"No. They said they never release them until the final payment is verified, same as all the other contracts."

"I just wanted to make sure they hadn't already sent it. Okay, tell Stan and George I'll deal with this. Put me through to Mr. Larson's office."

Abby connected the call through to Larson Marketing. Sarah listened to it ringing, glanced at Luke waiting patiently, and mouthed, "I'm sorry."

He shook his head, set the cooler down by the firepit, and took the seat beside her, relaxed and unbothered by the delay.

Larson's assistant finally picked up. "Larson Marketing."

"Connie, this is Sarah Anderson."

"Hello, Sarah. I'm afraid Mr. Larson is in a meeting right now."

"Get him on the line. Now. He's given my staff and our CFO

the runaround for two days. Tell him time's up, or I shut him down."

"Just a minute, please." Sarah was sure she heard understanding in Connie's voice.

Sarah only had to wait a few seconds before Tom Larson decided that his meeting wasn't as important as talking to her.

"Sarah, it's so nice to hear from you. I thought you were going to be here to do the final installation. You know how I've been looking forward to meeting you."

"Tom, you knew very well I had no intention of being there."

"Why are you hiding from everyone? I just want to meet you in person. You always send someone else."

"Because I'm busy working on the next project. Now, you owe me one point two million dollars and you have," she looked at her cell phone to check the time, "fifty-four minutes to make the transfer. If you don't, you owe me another three hundred thousand and I won't release the licensing agreement until I get paid."

"Sarah, come on. The installation was just completed. Please be reasonable. At least give me thirty days, like any other accounts payable item."

"I am not any accounts payable item. You knew that when you signed the contract. I'm the one who revamped your entire computer system, which I'm sure is working beautifully."

"Yes. It's even better than my staff or I expected. Everyone has been so pleased the last few days and the installation and transfer of the old system's information took no time at all."

"I'm so happy you're pleased. Now, let me remind you of a few things. You are in violation of our signed contract. Final payment was due two days ago when we completed the installation and as I told you, I expect it in less than an hour. The five percent penalty fee goes into effect tomorrow. You've been running my software on your system for two days without a license to do so. Now, you have less than fifty minutes to make your payment, or I pull the software. If there wasn't a lawyer sitting right next to me, I might threaten to hack into your system and drop a really nasty virus that will shut your entire system down in a matter of minutes. But there is a lawyer beside me, so I'll only say that I expect to hear from my accounting department in an hour that payment has been received or my lawyers will start breathing down your neck. Do I make myself clear?"

"I'll send it," he quickly assured her. "Still, it's too bad we can't get together. Everything I've heard about you intrigues me. I've tried to get an invitation to the benefit at the end of the month, so I can meet you. Your voice alone is enough to keep me up at night," he admitted, and she cringed. "Apparently, it's impossible. You should be pleased that you've created quite a stir. Your business is about to explode."

"Remember that when the software I completed for you needs to be upgraded in another year. Six million will look like a bargain when you find out what I'm going to charge you for the upgrade. You should have negotiated that into the original contract, and you shouldn't have tried to cheat me on the final payment. Give me your word that the money will be sent today and I may overlook your adolescent behavior."

"It is on its way as we speak."

"Very good. Thank you, Tom." She hung up and dialed Abby back.

"Abby, Mr. Larson will make the transfer. Tell legal to verify with accounting the payment is received, then have the licensing agreement sent over. Let me know if there are any more problems with Mr. Larson. I might have to unleash Fido on him if he doesn't make the payment."

"Well, now I hope he doesn't make the payment."

"You're really twisted, Abby. I'll talk to you later."

"Enjoy your date with Luke!"

Sarah hung up and smiled at the man smiling back at her.

Chapter Seventeen

S arah stared at Luke and just took him in. God, he was so handsome. He wore the same jeans and black T-shirt from earlier, but he'd put on one of his favorite flannels. Faded from washing, it looked really warm and comfortable. Exhausted after another long day, she wanted to rest her head on his chest and wrap her arms around his strong back and hold on to him. She wanted to borrow some of his strength and feel his warmth wrapped around her.

"Will you light the fire?" She stood as he did. "I'll get the food out of the cooler."

Before she moved, he wrapped her in a hug and pressed a soft kiss on her hair. "I'm so glad you came tonight." She let go of all the tension in her neck and shoulders, burrowed into him, and held on tight. She closed her eyes and sighed.

He rubbed his hands up and down her back. "Are you finally starting to relax?"

"If I relax any more, I'll be asleep." Snuggled up against him seemed like a great place to rest and recharge.

"I'd say I'll take you inside and put you to bed, but if I get you anywhere near a bed you won't be sleeping."

She leaned back and stared up at him, amusement at his bluntness making her smile. "Is that right?"

He traced a finger along the side of her face. "You've been haunting my dreams. I know I've been really stupid, demanding explanations for things I never bothered to simply ask you about. I broke my promise to your boys. I'm sorry. I'm going to fix that. I really love having all of you here. I want you to spend more time here, so I can show the boys the ranch and you and I can be together."

She pushed away, but her hands held his waist and his remained on her shoulders. "I'd like that."

"From the moment I met you, and despite my completely wrong impression of you, I saw and felt something growing between us. I can't deny the strong, deep feelings I have for you. Missing you these last many days has shown me that not having you here made me miserable. Ask anyone in my office or down at the stables, I've been impossible to be around." The honest admissions touched her and showed her that he really meant everything he'd said.

Every time she'd tried to concentrate on work the past week and a half, she'd only get distracted and think of him. The boys had begged her to take them back to the ranch so they could hang out with Luke. They liked him. But she held back, not wanting to throw herself and the boys at Luke if he didn't want to see them.

But he did. And that was the best news she'd received in a long time.

"I've missed you, too," she admitted. "I have strong feelings for you, Luke, but I also have two boys to think about, and so do you. It's not just me you're asking to come into your life. They come with me. I told you before, I don't get involved with men. So if you're in, I need to know it's not some casual thing, because with you, I want more. And if you're in, I'll expect it." It wasn't easy to put herself out there like this, but she wanted to start over with Luke, so they had a real shot at what she hoped they both wanted.

"I'm in. All the way. I've got four weeks to convince you. And I will."

"Then let's start with dinner and conversation and see where we go from there."

Luke relaxed and he brushed his fingers through the side of her hair. "I'm relieved to hear you say that. I was afraid I'd lose you before I ever had you."

"I'm too tired for you to have me now. Ha. Ha."

"I bet I could change your mind." He kissed her again, blanking out her thoughts and making her press into his strong, tempting body. He ended the kiss and pressed his forehead to hers. "But I don't want to skip ahead and rush things. I want to know you, Sarah. What you want. What you need. What makes you happy. Everything."

Her stomach rumbled. She'd gotten lost in work and missed lunch. Again.

Luke leaned back and smiled. "Sounds like you need dinner."

"Start the fire. The boys will be home soon, and I need to be there to put them to bed."

Luke released her and kneeled by the firepit. "What'd you bring for dinner? I'm curious to see what a five-star chef taught you to make for a cookout."

"It's a surprise. The table and flowers are lovely. You didn't have to do all of this for me. Paper plates would have been fine."

"You know what I like about you? You just chewed out a guy for not paying you a million two and you're okay eating off paper plates."

"I grew up alone with nothing, Luke. Fine china and fancy

restaurants are nice, but dinner by a fire with someone I care about is better. At least, I think so."

Luke sat back on his heels. "I just want to spend time with you. Dinner is a bonus."

She appreciated the sweet sentiment and the honesty behind it so much. "Then let's spend time together."

Chapter Eighteen

Luke lit the fire and peeked under the cooler lid Sarah opened and saw a couple bottles of his favorite beer and several foil packets of food.

"So, what did you make? All I see is foil, salsa, and tortillas. Tacos?"

"Just wait. Put the foil packets on the grill grate. Everything is cooked. It only needs to heat."

She reached in and pulled out a beer for each of them. She cracked one open and handed it to him and did the same with another for herself. She clinked her bottle neck to his and took a long swallow of the cold beer and let out a satisfied sigh. "God, that's good. Do you know how long it's been since I had a beer in the great outdoors?"

"Too long to remember how good it is." He took a sip of his beer and sat in the chair beside hers. "So, this is what you like to do when you have free time?"

"What? Oh no. Well, yes. But this is all for you. Here's what I do when I have free time."

She grabbed her purse and took out a bottle of bloodred nail polish. She kicked off her shoes, pulled off her sock, and put her foot up on the end of the chair and painted her toenails. "This is the best invention ever. Nail polish that dries in less than two minutes." She wiggled her toes to help them dry.

"Are you telling me that the only thing you do for yourself when you have free time is paint your toes? And the most amount of time you actually take for yourself is, what, two, maybe three minutes?"

She swiped her pinkie toe, then closed up the nail polish bottle. "Welcome to my world."

He turned his head toward her. "Tell me about your world. What's a typical day like for you?"

"Let's see. I get up at seven with the boys. Camille, our nanny and housekeeper, who is amazing and the boys love her, arrives at the same time. She makes the kids breakfast and gets them ready for school while I shower and get ready for work. I usually take at least one call during this time depending on the clients I'm dealing with and what time zone they're in. I drive the boys to school at eight and head into my office. I take care of whatever meetings I have for the day—board meetings, client meetings, conference calls, etcetera. At noon I pick up Nick from preschool and take him home to Camille, who's already made our lunch. Nick and I eat together. It's our one-on-one time. Then I go back to work. My office can have more than twenty laptops going, representing each of the projects I'm solely responsible for. At three I pick up Jack and take him home. We do homework for half an hour and I go back to work again. I work on projects and deal with whatever calls or meetings come up. At six I pack up however many laptops I'll need for the night. Camille cooks dinner most nights. Sometimes I pick something up or we order pizza. The kids and I eat together. Camille goes home. The boys and I spend time playing, then I give them their baths, and put them to bed by eight. Then

I work until three, maybe four in the morning, sleep, and do it all again the next day at seven."

"You put in a twenty-hour day, five days a week. Are you crazy? No wonder you look like you're exhausted all the time."

"Since I've been here, I haven't gone to bed before five. I've been sneaking into your stables at night. Remember? That's why I'm so tired."

He gave her a disapproving scowl and used tongs to take the food off the grill. She wrapped the tortillas in foil and tossed them on the grill to warm. "I suppose you catch up on sleep on the weekend."

"I wish. Sometimes, if I'm really lucky, the boys sleep in until seven-thirty. I spend the day with the boys. But once they go down at eight, I'm back to work until the early morning again."

"Now I want to take you to bed for a whole other reason. I just want to watch you sleep for a full eight hours."

She laughed. "I haven't slept eight hours straight in, I don't know, ten years."

"You kept these kinds of hours even when Sean was alive and running the company?"

"Yes and no. Yes, I kept these hours, but instead of taking several hours a day to play with the kids, I worked all those hours. In the beginning, we were trying to get the company going, and then we took the company public, in addition to the fact that I gave birth to two boys. Then, Sean was gone and there was only me to make sure the company stayed open. I had stockholders and employees to consider." She shrugged one shoulder like it was nothing. "I just do it. Over the past two years, I've grown the business considerably and expanded into other areas. We used to handle small jobs, but now I take on projects worth millions, as you heard on the last call I took. The Knox Project that I'm doing now is worth over twenty million."

He was impressed. "What's the Knox Project? Are you working for Fort Knox?"

She gave him a crooked smile while she took the tortillas from the grill. She opened all the foil packages and made him a burrito of chorizo and eggs, cheese, and salsa. She gave him a big scoop of fried potatoes and onions and handed him his plate.

"Hey, this is my favorite breakfast when I go camping. How did you know?"

"Jerry. He knows all kinds of wonderful things about you. I love breakfast for dinner, so I threw this together. Not exactly five-star-chef, but really good all the same."

Luke's grin made her stomach tingle. "So you asked about me, did you?"

She smiled and his eyes warmed as they watched her. Instead of answering that loaded question, she steered the conversation to an easier topic, her work.

"Every project I take on I give a name. It gets tedious referring to the projects by the company they belong to, or the person who hired us to do the job. I try to pick a name that's both fun and describes the project. Most recently, I had the Petticoat Project. That one was for a lingerie chain. The Knox Project is for a financial and investment firm. It's the largest and most demanding project I've ever taken. The company hired me to secure their systems. I've worked on several smaller companies' security programs, but this is like securing Fort Knox. Hence the name. Once the installation goes through and the company goes live with my product, it will be the newest and most secure security program available. The encryption and safeguards can't be matched."

"I had no idea you were such an expert. The way Margaret

spoke, she made it seem like Sean had tutored you through school, and you were just going along for the ride with the company. That isn't true, is it."

More lies Sean told. "I graduated MIT with honors. On my own. Growing up the way I did, I learned an important lesson. You can't depend on anyone else to do things for you." It made her angry to think anyone would think of her as some helpless female. She worked hard to get through the challenging school, where so many failed or burned out.

"Instead of going with one of the many lucrative job offers we received at graduation, Sean wanted to build our own company. Sean had big dreams. He sold me on the idea and the life we'd have together once the company hit big. At first, we shared the workload. But about a year into it, Sean burned out on the time-consuming and technical coding and shifted his focus from the projects to bringing in clients."

"Sounds like a good balance. But let me guess, it wasn't for you."

"Don't get me wrong, convincing people to take a chance on a brand-new startup took time and effort. Sean excelled at wining and dining potential clients. And we started winning a lot of bids."

"But doing the actual work was a lot more time-consuming and demanding than what he did."

"Eight-to-ten-hour days turned into fourteen-to-eighteen-hour days. While Sean was schmoozing people, taking meetings, and attending conferences, I delivered the product and slowly became more and less important to Sean."

Luke held her gaze. "Work became more important than your personal relationship."

"When I voiced my concerns, tried to pull back on work so we'd have more time together, he was all about the company. I became just an employee."

"I'm sorry, Sarah. That had to hurt."

"I got lost in Sean's dream. I tried so hard to make him happy."

Luke put his hand on her knee. "But you weren't happy."

"I wanted a home and family. But having the boys didn't give me the home I wanted for us. And then Sean was gone and everything fell to me."

"And you're still doing the bulk of the projects," he pointed out.

"Not exactly. We have nearly two hundred people at the company. Most of the programmers handle the meat and potatoes. Web design, data processing programs, system security, networking, that kind of thing. We're a comprehensive software company."

"So if that's the basis of the business, what's your focus?"

"I work on the big-ticket, complex projects that take a high-level, expert programmer. It's kind of my thing."

"How did you even get into programming?"

"When I went to live with my dad, he hired a full-time tutor because I was so far behind in school. He got me a laptop to do my schoolwork. I'd never used a computer. So I started asking questions about how it worked. I got basic answers from him, a bit more from my tutor, but I wanted more, so the tutor found me a couple online computer classes to do on my own."

"And you were hooked."

"It just made sense to me. Since I spent so much time alone as a kid, spending hours on a computer seemed like a great job to me. Getting the computer to do what I wanted it to do . . . I loved it."

"But you can't keep up this kind of pace. Believe me, I know. It's why I backed off from my law practice. Don't you want more balance in your life?"

"With the business growing so rapidly, I simply haven't had time to hire programmers who are at my level. I've hired some key staff under me to take care of implementation and testing once the software's written, but I haven't had the time to interview or search for the talent that I need to do the projects like I do. I have a few software developers who take on pieces of the coding, but it's just the basic stuff.

"The Knox Project is completely new territory. Once it goes live, my company is never going to be the same, and my life will change, drastically. As it is, the press is hounding Abby and the rest of the board of directors trying to get to me."

"Don't you do interviews?"

She shook her head. "Not my thing. I like my privacy. Whenever there's a press conference or some kind of public engagement that requires someone from the company to speak, I send Evan. He's co-CEO and loves the limelight and being the face of the company. But it's the same thing that happened with Sean. People aren't satisfied with talking to a figurehead. They want to talk to the person generating the success.

"Plus, my time is valuable. I hardly attend customer meetings, unless it's absolutely necessary. I do most of the meetings via conference call or email. Whenever it's necessary to go to a company site to look over a system, I usually sneak in unannounced, get what I need, and leave before upper management has a chance to find out I'm in the building. People love to talk and hold meetings that go on and on and cover the same ground. I learned early on an email that takes me five minutes to write usually takes care of something much better than an hour-long meeting."

"I can relate. When I meet with clients, they want to go over things again and again. I mean, they're paying for my time, so I'm happy to talk until they feel secure that I'm doing everything I can on their case. But when I've said the same thing five times, I'm ready for them to get out of my office and let me do my job."

"Exactly. It doesn't help that I started a side business, which took off immediately, and that just added to the speculation because no one knew where the work was coming from. I hide behind the company name. More recently, the foundation I started after Sean died has gotten a lot of press for our charitable work."

"And Margaret knows nothing about any of this." Luke sounded surprised, but he shouldn't be.

"She doesn't want to know anything about me."

"The boys must be extremely impressed."

"Not really. I'm just Mom. They have no idea of the success I've had. I don't want them seeing their mother's face plastered all over the Internet and in business magazines. Unfortunately, I've made it impossible to maintain that much longer. I'm attending a charity benefit at the end of the month and the press is expecting me. Abby calls it my coming-out party. I think it's ridiculous, but it's good publicity."

Luke swallowed a bite of burrito and wiped his mouth on a napkin. "Do you need a date for this charity benefit? Or do you already have one?" Those words must have left a bad taste in his mouth if the sour expression on his face was any indication.

"I'd love you to come with me, but I'm afraid I might bore you to death. In addition to the benefit that evening, Abby has several meetings set up before the dinner. I'm doing double duty that night. I'll be the attendee and the CEO extraordinaire. Still want to go?"

"Absolutely." His eager response made her smile and set the butterflies in her belly to fluttering wildly. "What day is it?"

"The twenty-seventh."

Luke perked up. "The Rockford Benefit?"

"Yes."

"My family goes every year. We buy our own table." Which meant Luke believed in giving back just as much as she did.

"Then we'll be there together." She took a huge bite of her burrito and savored the yummy taste. "So you'll be taking off your cowboy hat and putting on your lawyer one?"

"Something like that." He'd demolished his first burrito and made another. "You might be the only person who sees me as two different people."

"I know you fit here. I'd love a glimpse of you all suited up as a lawyer."

"I prefer jeans, but I'd put a suit on for you any day of the week." The warmth in his voice shot right through her.

"I can't wait to see it." She wanted to know so much more about him. "So tell me about your childhood."

"Well, it was always me and Jason together growing up. Just like Jack and Nick. We were best friends as well as brothers. Like you, Dad ran a successful business and had the money for us to live in the biggest house imaginable, but they wanted us to grow up having had a normal life. Education was the highest priority and we went to great schools, but we were raised in an upscale but not outrageous house in the Bay Area. We spent summers here. Mom, especially, loved the ranch. She likes open spaces. They travel a lot now, and Dad only goes into the office a couple days a week. I work three twelve-hour days during the week in the office and a couple of hours each night the other days here. I sometimes have to go into court the other days."

"It must be nice to have so many people to count on."

"We're a close family. Always have been. Do you see your dad a lot?"

"Once in a while. We keep in touch over the phone, but our relationship is . . . complicated."

"How's that? He's your dad. Were you angry that he didn't find you sooner?"

"Actually, no. My mother never told him about me. As I understand it, they met and had a very brief affair. It didn't even last a month. She went back to her tumultuous family. I never met my grandparents, but it's obvious they weren't nice people. My mother turned out to be a wild child, drinking, getting into trouble, ending up pregnant young and not even telling the guy. My uncle was as neglectful as my mother and a mean drunk. It's no wonder the relationship between my mom and dad didn't work out. He came from a stable family and had plans for his life that didn't include the perpetual party my mom enjoyed and used to cover up her misery."

Luke shook his head. "That sucks."

"Yeah. Anyway, my dad went on to a very successful career in finance, got married, and had a family. I have a half-brother, he's seventeen and completely in love with what I do. He's extremely talented with a computer. I hope he'll finish college and come to work for me. I give him some of my products to test."

"I feel like you're leaving something out. Do you spend holidays with them? Does your dad's wife accept you? Are you part of the family now?"

"Again, it's complicated. He didn't even know I existed until I was arrested and my uncle contacted him, hoping he could make right what I'd done with a big fat check. I didn't even know my uncle knew who my father was, but the moment my dad saw me, he knew I was his, and he accepted me. He believed me when I told him what happened and told my uncle to suck it. My dad and his wife took me into their home, but it was awkward and difficult at first. He wanted to make up for sixteen years by being a parent to me, but I'd lived a lot of life in my sixteen years and had pretty much taken care of myself for most of it. I didn't need someone to micromanage my life. I needed someone to help me move on.

Once he figured that out, he let me lead and we became close friends. That was enough for me.

"He hired a top attorney to get me out of the trouble with my uncle's ranch. Two years' probation and community service. I was grateful. It still bothers him he didn't know about me, and that I grew up the way I did. He has regrets. I have regrets. Our relationship isn't like most fathers' and daughters' but it means the world to me to know that he's on my side. He could have walked away from the whole thing when my uncle called him and kept his family in the dark that he had an illegitimate daughter, but he didn't. He chose me and the harder path over taking the easy way out."

"Do you and the boys spend time with him and his family?"

"Not as much as we'd like. Everyone's so busy. But I really love it when we're all together."

"If you stopped working so much, you'd have more time to spend with them." He said it with a teasing tone, but she heard the gentle reminder to take better care of herself and stop working like a maniac.

"I'll take that under advisement, Counselor." She smirked at him. "Tell me about growing up here with your brother. It must have been heaven."

She leaned back in her chair and looked at the beautiful landscape. The ranch was really lovely. The old oak trees stood tall and green. She could imagine being a kid on the ranch and running around the pastures, climbing the trees, and just being young. She felt she'd never been a child. Not since her mother died and she'd been shipped from one horrible foster home to the next until she ended up working her childhood away on her uncle's ranch.

"I imagine my childhood was the exact opposite of yours. My brother and I ran wild on this land. My father spent a lot of time

with us. We'd go camping in the woods and fishing at the creek.
My mother was always home, waiting for her men to return, with
a hot meal prepared and a smile for all of us. Where Dad was fun,
she was strict and kept us all in line, but in a good way. She still
tells us all what to do. We always do what she says. We spend the
holidays together no matter what else is going on in our lives. We
try to get together for dinner at least once a month. I see my father
and brother at the office the days I go in, and sometimes when she
knows we're all there together she'll come down and force us to
eat a healthy lunch."

"Definitely the complete opposite of my upbringing. It was
hard when I first had Jack. I had no idea how to take care of a
baby. I read all kinds of books, but they don't really tell you how
to be a good parent. I didn't have anyone to ask how I was doing.
I questioned everything I did. I drove myself insane thinking I
was going to mess up and do something that would damage him
for life. After a while, I finally took some advice from my father
and started paying more attention to the cues Jack gave me and
relaxed."

"Sean must have been a big help. He'd grown up with his mom
and sister. Surely he was able to lend a hand."

"Sure."

Not exactly convincing.

Luke already doubted everything he'd learned about Sarah
from Margaret. What his investigator had discovered about Sean
spoke of a shitty husband. Apparently he'd been a crap father, too.

Sarah never quite lied about him, but it was evident she never
told the whole truth either.

As a lawyer, Luke was very familiar with the tactic. He'd let it
go for now. She'd learn to trust him, and he'd find out just how
big of a bastard Sean had been to her. Because everything he'd

learned in his investigation showed Sean had checked out of the marriage early on, and that sucked for Sarah, who deserved a hell of a lot better. But what Sarah also deserved was a fuller life. She could let go, but she was afraid to. Her reasons for not hiring top-notch staff who would be able to take some of the work off her shoulders sounded like excuses. He needed to discover why she had such a hard time letting go.

"Tell me something you like."

She eyed him. "What do you mean? Like chocolate?"

He smiled. "Every sane person likes chocolate. What else?"

"Ice cream, rainy days, but only when I get to be inside by a roaring fire reading a book. Horses, but you knew that. I like your garden. It's very peaceful, and although it's faded now, I bet it looks spectacular in the spring. I don't know what else. Most of my time is spent working, instead of enjoying life. I like being a mom. I feel that's when I'm at my best, when it's just me and the boys and we're laughing and playing."

"What kind of ice cream?"

"Rocky Road. Coffee. Vanilla with fudge. One of these days I'm going to take an entire day off. It will be raining, I'll have my raging fire, and I'll sleep for at least twelve hours, then I'll read a sexy romance novel and eat a gallon of ice cream. Now, that would be a great day. It'll never happen, but it would be a great day."

"Where are the boys on this great day?"

"With Camille, the nanny. Every mom deserves a day to herself once in a while."

"Well, how about on this great day of yours, you share it with me and we sit on a soft blanket by that raging fire after you've had at least twelve hours of sleep. We'll eat ice cream, then I'll make love to you until you're completely satisfied and devoid of energy. I'll kiss every inch of you and run my hands over your soft skin.

I'll finally get your hair out of that ponytail you like so much and spread it across the blanket and run my fingers through it, while I completely ravage your mouth with mine. I'll bury my hands in all that hair when I fill you. I'll be so deep inside you that you'll think we couldn't possibly be any closer. Then, I'll take you on the ride of your life where we'll both end up tangled in that blanket and hotter for each other than any fire could ever burn. Your sexy romance novel will blush at the things I'll do to you."

She blushed from the tips of her newly painted toes to the top of her head. No one had ever looked lovelier or smiled bigger.

"Your dream day is far better than mine."

"I'll make it your favorite dream day."

"You're going to have to work up to that rainy day with me. It won't be tonight."

"I knew you were going to say that." Still, the disappointment hit him hard.

She pointed to the sunset sky. "No rain," she teased. "But perhaps the cookies in the cooler will appease you for now. Will you get them out?"

He grabbed the plastic container and opened it. He glanced up at her and smiled. "Just how much did Jerry tell you?"

"Enough. I hope you like them."

Peanut butter cookies loaded with peanuts, just the way he liked them. He felt spoiled for the first time in a long time. She'd made him one of his favorite meals and baked his favorite cookies in between everything else she had to do. "You've got more than a full plate, yet you took the time to do all of this for me. Why?"

She met his gaze. "Because I wanted to do something nice for you. That's all." She shrugged, then stared into the fire.

She was so simple in the nicest ways. He couldn't remember a time when a woman had done something for him just because she wanted to be nice. Ulterior motives usually came with anything good someone did for him. Sarah's sincerity touched him deeply. "Tell me what you don't like."

She pinched her lips, then looked at him. "I don't like people who hurt others for sport."

Like Sean?

"I hate the smell of jasmine perfume."

Because Sean came home smelling like it?

"I don't like being stuck in traffic. I don't like people who harm animals, or children. You could probably guess that one. I don't like peas, cooked carrots, or tomatoes."

"You don't like tomatoes? Not even in spaghetti sauce?"

"Spaghetti sauce is fine, but I don't like fresh tomatoes. They squish and squirt in your mouth. It's gross." She made a sour face and stuck out her tongue like children do when they don't like something.

Luke laughed, loving her smile, and the way she made him relax and enjoy the moment.

They sat in the garden eating cookies, talking, and laughing together for the better part of two hours. They talked about everyday things and stories from their childhoods. They both avoided talking any more about work because they wanted to concentrate on getting to know each other aside from what they did for a living.

Sean didn't come up again. He'd caused enough trouble between them, so Luke steered clear.

The sun set and the light faded. He helped Sarah pack up the leftover food and put the cooler back in her car. And when it was time for her to go, like always, he didn't want her to leave.

She stood outside the driver's side door. "I had a really good time." She pressed her lips together and took a steadying breath. "There's something I want to say."

She stared at his chest for the longest time.

"You can say anything to me," he coaxed.

She finally met his gaze again. "I have a complicated life. I know we've just begun to get to know each other, but . . . I've never felt this way about anyone. I hope we do this again."

"I don't just want to do this again, I want you to stay, even if we don't know what that looks like right now. But I have four weeks to convince you."

He closed the distance between them, pressed her up against the SUV, and kissed her until her hands wound around his neck, and she pulled him in tighter. They lost themselves in the kiss and each other. He savored the feel of her body pressed against his and completely lost his mind to her and the heady scent of her citrusy sweet perfume.

He broke the searing kiss, pressed one to her cheek, then whispered in her ear, "Stay with me."

Her hands slid down his neck and shoulders and landed on his chest. "The boys will be home soon," she reminded him.

Disappointed but understanding completely, he pressed his forehead to hers and stared into her gorgeous eyes. At least she knew he wanted her. "Promise me you'll get some rest."

"Are you trying to take care of me?"

"I'd like to, if you'd let me." He brushed his hand down her arm and took her hand. "You haven't given me your promise to rest."

"I don't make promises I can't keep." She squeezed his hand to halt his protest. "I'll *try* to get more rest. I've been giving a lot of thought to cutting back on my schedule and hiring some new people. It's going to take time, but I know I need to do it. For myself, and for the boys. Okay?"

"For now."

She ran her hand down the side of his face and leaned up and gave him a soft, lingering kiss goodbye. He wanted to wrap her in his arms and hold on to her. Instead, he reluctantly released her and waved goodbye as she drove away, realizing this was the first time he'd ever regretted ending a date.

He already missed her and couldn't wait to see her again.

Chapter Nineteen

Two weeks later . . .

S arah dragged her butt into the kitchen. She'd been up all night finishing the Knox Project. She brushed her mussed hair from her face and found her thermal mug in the dish rack where she'd left it last night after doing the dinner dishes.

Margaret walked into the kitchen.

Sarah pressed the back of her hand to her mouth to cover a huge yawn. "Can I get you a cup of coffee?"

"Can you manage? You look like you're about to keel over." The harsh words felt like a slap after all she'd done to keep Margaret's home clean and give her the time she wanted with the boys.

Sarah turned and leaned back against the counter, blocking the coffeepot. "Do you have to do that every time we speak to each other, even when it's about something as simple as me offering you a cup of coffee?"

"You're in a mood," Margaret shot back.

"I'm tired of you swatting at me all the time."

"Poor Sarah. You don't like it, you can leave."

"I'd be happy to pack up the boys and go right now."

"You can go. The boys stay. Or I will take you to court and use everything I've learned about you to ensure I get to see those boys whenever I want. Maybe they'd be better off here anyway. Look at you. You're barely keeping it together."

"Yeah. Thanks to you."

Margaret eyed her. "What do I have to do with you not sleeping? It's your own damn guilt that keeps you up at night."

"You would think that because you don't want to face reality. So let me impart some on you right now. What do you think the boys will think of their grandmother dragging their mother into court for visitation when I went out of my way to bring them here for weeks? What will a judge think of me changing my schedule, working remotely, being mom and teacher to the boys, all so you could have your visit? Do you think those things make me look bad? Or is the truth that I want the boys to spend time with you, therefore I made it happen at your request."

Margaret stared at her. No response.

"I feel guilty that the boys didn't have the father they deserved. I feel guilty that in keeping a promise to you it takes time away from them. I don't feel guilty about Sean's death. It was his own damn fault. And you'd know that if you actually wanted to know what happened and who Sean really was."

"He was a good man," Margaret shouted.

The doorbell rang.

Sarah turned, poured her coffee, and faced Margaret again. "I wish he were the man you think he was."

Margaret gaped at her.

"I'll get the door."

* * *

Luke smiled when Sarah opened the door, but it vanished the second he saw the anger in her eyes and the dark circles beneath them. He didn't like how pale she looked. "Hey. Are you okay?"

"Not really. I'm sorry. I know we're taking the kids riding, but they're not up yet and I'm running a little behind."

"You look like you're running on empty."

She held up her mug. "That's what this is for." She gripped his hand and tugged to get him to come in. "Come upstairs. I need to get dressed and wake the boys."

Luke followed her. "Did you sleep at all?"

"Not really." She took another big gulp of her coffee.

Luke stepped into her room behind her and found three laptops open and running on the bed. Another lay running on the nightstand. Files and papers littered the bed.

His heart tripped when he spotted the open music box, filled with pictures from the boys and a piece of the wrapping paper and ribbon the box had been wrapped in, among all the work stuff. One of the pictures showed a huge heart that said "I love you." His heart melted as he remembered that she'd said she'd put her treasures inside. Sarah hadn't filled the box with jewels. She'd filled it with what was most important to her.

Dressed in blue flannel boxer shorts and a cranberry-colored lace-trimmed camisole, she surveyed the bed with a wistful look.

"Sarah, honey, I'll take the boys riding and you can stay here and get some sleep."

"No. I promised them."

"You need to rest."

"I will. After our ride. The boys have been looking forward to it. And so have I."

"Okay," he reluctantly agreed. "But I'm worried about you." He'd keep a close eye on her.

She wrapped her arms around his neck and pressed her body to his, her breasts against his chest. He knew exactly how they felt in his hands, thanks to the many make-out sessions they'd secretly shared during their stolen moments over the last two weeks.

What he wouldn't give to get her naked and in a bed under him, all that soft skin pressed to him.

He shook off thoughts of deep kisses, soft caresses, and the building desire that needed to be slaked soon.

Luke kissed her softly and held her close because it seemed like she needed some affection and his warmth. "You okay?"

"Perfect. I'm exactly where I want to be."

"Mama," Jack called from the other room.

Sarah sighed. "They're up."

Luke leaned back. "I'll get them ready while you get dressed."

She gave him a soft kiss. "Thank you." She went to the dresser, opened drawers, pulling out clothes before she closed them again. A lace bra, purple T-shirt, and a pair of jeans dangled from her hands. She dumped them on top of the dresser.

He studied her, trying to read her mood and just how fatigued she was, despite her trying to hide it.

To his utter surprise, she stripped off her camisole with her back to him, but his eyes locked onto her reflection in the mirror. The site of her full breasts made his mouth water. Her dark hair spilled down her back. The thought of moving in behind her and cupping her breasts and feeling their weight in his hands drove him mad. She slipped her arms through the lacy bra straps and connected them at her back. She pulled her hair free and her breasts pressed against the lace. She pulled the T-shirt over her head. He didn't think he could take much more without touching her. Then she took off her shorts and revealed the lace panties hidden beneath, hugging her slightly rounded rump and slim hips.

She slid her legs into the jeans and pulled them up with a wiggle of her bottom.

Disappointment lanced through him to see her creamy skin covered.

"Is this some kind of payback?" he joked.

A sexy grin tilted her tempting lips. "Well, I need to get dressed so we can head to the ranch. For our ride," she teased back.

He'd like to take her on an entirely different kind of ride. "You're killing me." Need, sharp and heady, settled in and made his dick hard and achingly uncomfortable behind his fly.

She laughed and sat on the bed to pull on her socks and boots. "You act as though you've never seen a woman put her clothes on."

"After two weeks of you and the boys coming out to the ranch to ride and hang out, I'm dying because all I want to do is take your clothes off and get my hands on you. God, you're stunning."

Her gaze locked with his. Surprise and absolute appreciation shone in hers. "Thank you. That's probably the nicest thing anyone's ever said to me."

He couldn't blow that off as something most women would say to be humble because everything in the way she looked at him and said it told him she really meant it.

Her cheeks pinked and she dropped her gaze, grabbed her hair at the nape of her neck, and pulled it through a ponytail holder a couple times. Once done, she walked to him, wrapped her arms around his neck, and pulled him down for a kiss. Before he could take her under and they got lost in the moment, she broke the kiss. "Let's get the boys."

"Yeah. Sorry. I, uh, couldn't take my eyes off you."

She smiled again. "You're sweet."

Luke opened the bathroom door and found both boys dressed

and brushing their teeth at the sink. "You guys look like you're almost ready to go."

"We finally get to ride on the trail." Jack's excitement showed in his wide, toothy, toothpaste-drooling grin.

"Rinse and spit, buddy."

Nick finished first and gave Sarah a big hug around her legs. "Hi, Mama."

"Hey, baby. Ready to go have fun with Luke?"

"I dreamed we rode right up to the moon last night."

Luke knew Nick usually dreamed about his dad. It touched him deeply to know he'd had a fun dream about him. It showed Luke just how much Nick liked being with him.

Sarah's gaze met his and she gave him a soft smile that told him she got it, too, and it made her happy.

Luke was becoming important not just to Sarah but to the boys, too. He didn't take that lightly.

"Well, Nick, I don't know if we'll make it to the moon this morning, but I bet you'll like the ride."

"Let's go," Jack ordered, his enthusiasm taking him out of the room on the run for the stairs.

Sarah grabbed her coffee and cell phone and followed him and Nick out of her room.

Margaret stood at the bottom of the stairs with Jack.

Luke didn't miss the glare she sent Sarah when her cell phone rang and Sarah answered, "Hey, Abby, hold on a sec."

Luke hoped she didn't have to stay behind and finish some work. To help make sure that didn't happen, he put his hand to her back and steered her toward the front door.

"I'll bring them back after our ride and breakfast," he told Margaret, not caring one bit about her disapproving look.

"Are you already in the office?" Sarah asked Abby as she climbed into Luke's truck and he took his seat. The boys sat between them, using one buckle for safety though they were only going from Margaret's driveway down his long one. "Why do you want me to put you on speaker? Luke doesn't want to hear about my work."

Luke raised a brow, wondering why Abby needed him. "What does she want me to hear?" He drove the truck toward the ranch.

"I don't know. She's lost her mind." Sarah put the call on speaker and draped her arm across the seat and her boys, and placed her hand on his shoulder.

All squished together in his truck, it felt so right to think they were really becoming a family. "Okay, Abby, spill it. What's going on?"

"Marcel got your email way too early this morning, but he was expecting it and couldn't wait to open it. He called the team in and they compiled the program and ran it with the test data. Sarah, it works! It really works!"

A roar of cheers went up in the background from Sarah's employees.

"The whole team tried to break your code. They can't. You've done it!"

Luke slowed the truck and stared across at Sarah. She stared straight out the window, a huge smile on her face. The pride in her eyes intensified as the cheers washed over her and filled the truck cab. After all the hard work she'd put in, she deserved to take in this moment.

Sarah grinned, let out an excited giggle, then filled him in on what had been happening. "Marcel found the back door, but he couldn't crack the encryption. I spent the last couple of weeks verifying all the security levels. All we had to do was run it with the test data from the company." She paused, that giddy smile on her face growing bigger. "It works."

"You did it," he repeated Abby's exuberant words.

Another cheer went up from her employees.

She picked up her cell from her lap and addressed her staff. "I didn't do this alone. You guys are the best, and we did this together as a team. I know you guys are excited about what this means for the company, but remember we still have a lot of work to do."

"'Team,' my ass, Sarah. This was all you. We just sat back and watched in wonder. We've got to celebrate when you get back."

"We will. And thank you, Marcel, but you guys did help. I'll throw a big party for everyone at Gerard's when I get home."

Everyone cheered again.

She smiled and shook her head. "I was going to call later and set up the testing and implementation teams, but since you're all there, I'd like Marcel to head the test team and David to head the implementation team." A round of congratulations and well wishes went out to Marcel and David. "Right now, I want you all to head over to Joe's Café and have breakfast on me. I'll talk to you soon."

"I'll call you in a few hours," Abby shouted over everyone else. "We'll coordinate the next steps."

"Sounds good."

"Luke," Abby called to him. "You have no idea who the woman with you is. She's just done the extraordinary. Her name and face are going to be everywhere. Newspapers, magazines, every tech website on the planet. She'll be on every TV news program. Sarah, you won't be able to hide behind Evan anymore."

They arrived at the ranch and Luke cut the truck engine, then stared over at her. She didn't seek the limelight, but she was about to be in it. He couldn't be happier or prouder, but he wondered if this would somehow take her away from him.

Sarah shook her head at the phone. "Really, Abby. Get a grip. Luke doesn't care whether the press or industry goes nuts over my program."

"He should know what you've accomplished. Eight months of you going without sleep and working every possible moment. You've achieved something very few can accomplish on their own and in such a short time. You've made history."

"Thank you for being my cheerleader. Now, I've got to go see about a horse. Call me later."

Before Abby started up again, she hung up.

Luke made no move to get out of the truck.

"What? I thought you'd be happy I finished the Knox Project."

"Good job, Mommy," Nick said, snuggling into her side.

"Thank you, buddy."

"I'm really happy for you." Luke meant it. "So the whole thing is complete." Maybe now she could take some time to herself.

"Well, except for final delivery to the client. Now I'll have more time to spend with the boys. And you. I have a couple other projects to finish, but the Knox Project was taking up the majority of my time," she rambled, not taking credit or basking in the win.

Her first thought was spending more time with her kids and him.

He loved that most.

He tried to wrap his brain around this amazing woman. "Your staff is completely dedicated to you. They look up to you. You've just accomplished something amazing that will put your company on the map and you say it's nothing. I'm completely impressed, and so proud of you. You're . . . phenomenal."

Stunned, she went completely still.

"Come on. Let's ride."

Sarah got out on her side while Luke lifted both boys down on his.

"Ace, stop!" Jerry called out.

Sarah ran toward the barn doors just as Ace came to a halt in front of her.

He reared up on his hind legs, kicking his front hooves and chopping at the air.

Magnificent.

His display of strength and anger was awesome.

And scared the crap out of Luke.

Ace came back to all fours and shook his head up and down and snorted his frustration just a couple feet from Sarah.

"What do you think you're doing?" she snapped at the huge beast. "You know what you need? A girlfriend. Come here and say hello."

Ace moved forward into Sarah's arms, putting his massive head over her shoulder. She wrapped her arms around his neck and stroked his coat. Ace shivered and relax.

Jerry came to an abrupt halt at the stable doors. "Luke, I'm sorry. He saw Sarah and ran for her."

Luke's jackhammering heart finally slowed. "It's okay. I think he's in love with her."

"He ain't the only one." Jerry made that comment to Luke in a low voice as they watched Sarah soothe Ace.

"I'm falling pretty damn hard and fast for her. I don't know what to do about it," Luke confessed.

"Tell her."

"Just tell her?" He wasn't so sure about that. "It's only been a few weeks. I need more time to show her how I feel, so she'll believe what I want us to have together."

"She always looks happy when she's here. The boys love being around the horses and running through the fields."

"This place isn't the same when they aren't here. I've grown so attached to them." So much so that even in this short time he couldn't imagine life here without them anymore.

Chapter Twenty

*L*uke left Ace out in the pasture after Sarah spoiled him with a brush-down and an apple. Then he took Sarah and the boys riding. Jack and Nick had become very proficient, even if Stella and Mandy were more likely than not to follow Luke's horse and pace. Sarah brought up the rear of their little line of horses. While the boys chatted with each other and about anything and everything around them, Sarah remained relatively quiet.

He wondered if her mind was on work, but he hoped she was simply enjoying the early morning ride across the dewy fields.

"I'm hungry," Nick announced for the tenth time.

"We're almost there. Just up and over this small hill."

"Will you make pancakes?" Jack asked.

"That's the plan."

They rode into the yard outside the stables. He dismounted and went to Jack to help him down. Sarah plucked Nick off his horse.

He caught her slightly swaying before she caught herself. "Hey, sweetheart, are you okay?"

She gave him a weak smile. "Head rush."

"Why don't you head up to the house? I'll put the horses away."

Sarah shook her head. "Really. I'm good."

He wondered how often she said that to herself and others when it wasn't really true.

"Come on, boys, take the reins and lead your horses to their stalls."

He walked his horse and Sarah's in, then called out to two of the hands cleaning stalls. "Take these horses to their stalls. Brush them down and make sure they've got feed and water." They hadn't gone on a long or strenuous ride, so the horses would be fine in their stalls until they were let out into the pasture later.

Nick and Jack ran back to him and Sarah.

"Can we go up to the house and get something to drink?"

Luke held his hand out toward the stable doors. "Go on up. There's some juice boxes in the fridge. Your mom and I will be there in a few minutes." He waited for the boys to take off for the house.

Once they were out of sight, he turned to Sarah, cupped her face, and leaned down and kissed her softly. "You need to go to bed."

"Is that an invitation? Because . . ." She pulled her buzzing phone out of her pocket. "I've got fifty-seven new emails. And as patient as you've been doing the whole dating thing and taking time to get to know me . . ." Exhaustion hung on her; she was too tired to even smile at him.

"Sweetheart, I'm serious." He brushed the wisps of hair that had escaped her ponytail away from her face.

"I like it when you do that."

"Touching you is my favorite thing to do."

A soft smile tilted her lips, but her cheeks remained pale. "That. But also when you call me nice things. No one has ever called me 'sweetheart' or 'honey.' You do it a lot and I like it."

"Didn't Sean have a sweet name for you?"

She stared at him, taking a moment to consider whether or not to confide in him. "Sean was only sweet when he wanted something, which means he was sweet all the time. I found out too late that the charm was insincere and manipulative. After a while, I didn't respond to it because it turned my stomach, so he just demanded."

If Sean were here, he'd deck him for treating Sarah so callously. "I'm sorry he treated you that way and disappointed you. But I'm not him."

"I know you mean what you say and how you say it. I know you care about me."

Hearing the way she said those words, that she meant them, relieved him. "I care more than you know." He wanted her to see that and believe it. "I can't promise that I won't disappoint you. I'm sure I will at some point. But I can promise that I won't deceive you because I want something from you. And all I want is you and a life with you. It's that simple."

Tears and weariness filled her eyes and she began to pace back and forth in front of him. "I've been thinking a lot about what to do about you."

"Keep me," he suggested.

She hesitated for a split second, then smiled softly. "I have a lot going on right now."

"I know. I'm trying to be patient. Which isn't easy for a man like me, because I'm used to getting everything I want. But you're worth the wait, sweetheart. And the torture." Because he wanted her in his bed, too, desperately.

She sighed and paced away and then back to him again. "I'm trying to work out how to schedule everything I need to do, and how I can be with you here at the same time. I just don't know how it's possible. I've finished programming the Knox Project but

I still have to travel all over the world to finish the installation."
She stopped midstep and pressed the back of her hand to her forehead. She dropped her hand and stared at him. "I have a dozen
other projects, a company to run, people who depend on me, and
I'm in love with you." She paced again and threw her hands up
and let them fall. "I don't know what to do about that either. I
have to take the boys home soon and they're going to miss you
terribly. I don't know if I can take missing you. I have a charity
benefit to go to and I don't even have a dress." She rolled her eyes
and kept going. "The press will be there, wanting me to answer a
multitude of questions about my businesses and how I did it all."
Her hands flew up and fell down once more, slapping her thighs.
"Quite frankly, I don't want to tell them anything."

"Sarah, stop." Worry quickly overshadowed the soaring elation
he felt when she said she loved him. Everything about her was in
action. Her body, mind, emotions. Seeing her spin out and spill
her thoughts and worries in a tumble of words concerned him.
This wasn't her.

She spun to face him and wobbled but caught herself. "Luke."

"Sarah?"

Her eyes narrowed in concentration that seemed to be difficult for her to hold. Then her eyes rolled back and she mumbled,
"Catch me."

With the words barely out of her mouth, her knees buckled. He
lurched forward, fell to his knees, and caught her before her head
hit the cement floor. He hugged her to his chest and held her on
his lap and called out, "Jerry!"

He came running from the office. "What happened?"

"She collapsed." He ran a shaking hand over her face and hair.

"I'm not surprised. That girl needs a vacation from this vacation. Should we call an ambulance?"

"I don't think so. The exhaustion finally caught up to her. I'll take her up to the house and put her to bed."

"The crew and I have things covered."

"Thanks. Today I need to take care of her and the boys."

"No problem."

Luke stood with Sarah in his arms and stared down at her pale but beautiful face. "She said she's in love with me."

"That's great. Now you two can really be together."

"I wish it was that simple. She was ranting about work and having to leave and not knowing how to schedule everything and still be here with me. I don't even know if she realizes she told me she loves me."

"At least you know she does." Jerry congratulated him with a tap on the shoulder. "Now you can tell her you love her and the two of you can figure out the rest as you go."

Easier said than done, but he wanted a life with Sarah more than he'd ever wanted anything.

Chapter Twenty-One

*L*uke took Sarah up to the house and straight to his room. He laid her on his bed and stared down at her, so tired that she didn't even stir. All he wanted to do was make her feel better. So he gently took her shoes and socks off, slipped off her jeans, unhooked the bra at her back and pulled the straps down each of her arms, and tugged it out of her shirt like he'd seen other women do themselves. He tucked her under the covers and stared down at her, his heart aching for her.

What would have happened if she'd been somewhere else when she collapsed? What if she'd been alone with the boys and they didn't know what to do for her?

Those thoughts and a thousand others disturbed him.

"Luke?" Jack stood in the bedroom doorway, Nick right behind him. "Is Mama okay?"

Luke didn't want to worry the boys. He was glad he got Sarah settled before they saw her.

He went to Jack and Nick and kneeled in front of them. "She worked a lot last night. The ride made her tired, so she went to sleep. Let's go have breakfast."

He took their hands and led the boys down to the kitchen, leaving Sarah sleeping soundly in his bed.

"So, pancakes?"

Jack looked at Nick. Nick stared back at Jack. Some silent communication going on.

"So . . ." Jack said, eyeing him. "Can we have the chocolate cereal in the cupboard?"

Luke hid a smile and held back the laugh bubbling up his gut. The boys had snooped in the cupboards while he'd been carrying in their mom.

Before he said yes, Nick confessed, "Mama doesn't let us eat that."

Luke leaned down and gave in to the boys because he didn't think Sarah would mind a treat for them under the circumstances. "I won't tell her you ate it if you don't."

The boys gave him huge toothy grins.

He'd confess to Sarah later and let her know it was his idea. It was his favorite cereal.

Okay, sometimes he ate like a kid.

"Take a seat at the bar. I'll get the bowls."

Luke set a bowl in front of each of them, poured the cereal and milk, handed both boys a spoon, and they all dug in. While he fed the boys, his mind was on the woman upstairs in his bed. Sarah deserved a nice long nap.

"Will Mama be up soon?" Jack asked. "Cuz we don't have to do school today. We could just play."

Luke hid his smirk. "We could, but then you'd have double the work to do tomorrow and you wouldn't get to play as much. So maybe we'll go to your grandma's and make sure you get today's work done so you can play today and tomorrow."

Jack scrunched up one side of his face. "If we have to."

Nick tipped up his bowl and drank all the chocolate milk. "Done." He let out a big burp.

Jack laughed.

Luke couldn't help but join in. He'd had his fair share of burping contests with his brother, Jason, over the years. Being with the boys always took him back to those happy times and made him want them to be his family.

"Let's head over to your grandma's now." He took all the bowls to the sink. He heard a phone ringing upstairs. "Hey, give me two minutes to grab your mom's phone. I don't want it to wake her."

Luke left the boys in the kitchen and ran up the stairs just as the phone stopped ringing. He found it in Sarah's jeans pocket and stuffed it in his own. He stared down at her sleeping soundly, her breath slow and even, the dark circles under her eyes still very prominent. But damn, she looked good in his bed.

He kissed her forehead then headed back downstairs. The boys were sitting on the leather sofa staring up at the wood beams on the tall ceiling.

"Let's go, boys."

They bounced off the couch and ran for the front door and his truck. He wished he had that much energy.

Jack managed to open the door and climb in. Nick needed a boost.

Sarah's phone rang again as he settled behind the wheel. He started the truck, checked the caller ID, accepted the call, then turned the truck toward Margaret's.

"Hey, Abby, this is Luke. Sarah's asleep right now."

"It's nice to meet you, Luke. Can you wake her? I've got a few items that can't wait."

"They'll have to, because she literally collapsed from exhaustion and I'm not waking her for at least eight hours."

"Luke, seriously, we've got a lot going on right now."

"I get that. But there can't be anything that can't wait a day. If there is, I'm sure someone else, or you, can handle it."

"But Sarah—"

"Deserves a few hours of uninterrupted sleep after working her butt off for months," he interrupted. "You're the gatekeeper at work. I'm doing it today because she needs someone to take care of her physical and mental health." He wanted to make that his job permanently.

"No one knows better than me that she needs to get some rest—"

"Then let her." He pulled into Margaret's driveway. "Listen, I've got the boys and we're at their grandmother's. I'm sure she'll be up soon," he said to reassure Abby and the boys, but he was still concerned about Sarah.

"You're right. Okay. But tell her to call me as soon as she wakes up."

"Will do." He'd probably wait until Sarah ate a decent meal, then tell her.

He said goodbye to Abby and helped the boys out of the truck. They beat him to the door. He knocked and waited.

He wondered if Margaret had gone out, but then a couple minutes later she finally answered. "Luke. Boys." Margaret's eyes narrowed. "Where's Sarah?"

Luke didn't think Margaret would take this well.

Jack beat him to the punch. "Mama's sleeping at Luke's."

Margaret raised a brow and gave him a disapproving look. "Really?"

"Yes." He touched the boys' backs. "Go upstairs and get your homework out."

Jack and Nick took off.

Margaret stared at him, waiting for an explanation she probably wouldn't receive well.

"Sarah is exhausted. She collapsed at the ranch. I'm going to let her sleep as long as she wants, because she definitely needs it."

"Do you see? She doesn't take care of herself. Anything could have happened if she was out with the boys."

"But she wasn't. She was with me. And I don't think she would have gone out in her condition if she hadn't promised the boys and knew that I was right there to watch over them." He didn't give Margaret time to harp on it and got to his point. "The boys just had breakfast. They need to do their homework."

Margaret glanced at the stairs. "I suppose they could bring it down and I can help them."

"Okay. I expect Sarah to sleep most of the day."

"What?"

"I'm pretty sure she was up all night finishing her project." Even if she woke up before dinner, she could use a little time doing nothing.

Margaret looked confused and irritated at the same time. "We'll be fine."

"Great. Then I guess I'll see you later when I bring Sarah back." He wanted to check on Sarah as soon as he returned to the ranch.

Margaret frowned. "I hoped you'd come to your senses by now."

He held her sharp gaze. "I hope you don't come to regret treating her the way you have and not getting to know who she really is. Because the more I learn about her and her life with Sean, it's clear, you don't know either one of them."

"What is that supposed to mean?"

"That Sean didn't tell you the truth about her, their marriage, or their life together."

"Of course she made Sean out to be the bad guy and blamed him for everything. You can't believe her. You knew him." Her gaze pleaded with him to side with her.

He couldn't. Not when he knew and loved Sarah the way he did. "I thought I knew Sean. But we were teenagers the last time I saw him. Even then, he always took the easy way and used others to get what he wanted. He did it with a smile and charm, but that didn't mean he didn't leave several disgruntled people in his wake."

Sarah was one of them and clearly deserved her ire, because Sean had been a son of a bitch to her.

"Back then, I liked hanging out with Sean. He was fun. The life of the party. But he could be jealous and competitive and push others out of his way to get what he wanted."

"Being competitive got him to MIT. It's how he created such a successful business." She defended Sean, but he saw the uncertainty in her eyes.

"Yeah, well, he used Sarah. He hurt her just to get what he wanted."

"He ended up dead because of her."

"Do you actually know what happened?" He had the facts from the accident, but he'd planned to ask Sarah about the details when the time was right, because she'd taught him not everything you thought you knew was the truth.

"I know he died unhappy." Pain etched lines in Margaret's forehead and filled her eyes.

It had to be hard to know your child died before they reached their full potential and found their happiness.

But Sean had made his choices, and most of them hurt Sarah, Jack, Nick, and others. Margaret included.

Poor Sarah. She'd been dealing with a lot of unwarranted hostility.

Margaret was beyond listening to anything that didn't fit into her perception of who she thought Sarah was and Luke refused to waste time trying to convince her Sarah was nothing like Margaret thought. He needed to get back to Sarah and make sure she was all right.

"Call me if you need help with the boys." He turned and walked down the porch steps.

"She'll ruin you," Margaret called after him.

He turned and faced her. "Be careful you don't ruin your chance to keep the boys in your life." He may have known Margaret longer, but he was on Sarah's side and she didn't deserve to be subjected to this kind of hostility and hate when she'd done nothing wrong.

Chapter Twenty-Two

S arah opened her eyes and found Luke staring at her. She was surprised to see him, and disoriented, but his warm smile and the feel of his hand brushing over her hair grounded her and made her heart trip.

"Good morning, darlin'."

She loved the sound of his deep voice and the warmth in his words. "Hi. Am I sleeping on your kitchen table?"

The charming grin made her belly flutter. "Yes, you are."

"Great." Embarrassment warmed her cheeks. "How long have I been here?"

Luke leaned in. "That's a complex question. You've been asleep for nearly a whole day. You got out of bed about an hour ago and sleepwalked down here to the kitchen. But if you want the bigger question answered, according to Jack, you're really old, thirty-two. So that's how long you've been here."

"Are you laughing at me?"

"A little bit. You sure are pretty when you're rested and lying on my table."

Not inclined to move from her spot in front of him—and Luke looked content to have her there, offered up like Thanksgiving dinner—she rolled to her side and laid her head on her arm to look at him. Luke sat back and she drank in the sight of his sexy bare chest, beard-scruffy jaw, and tousled golden hair.

"Is Margaret really mad?"

"She's definitely riled. Since you didn't wake up by dinner, she called and asked if I'd take the boys because she was afraid to put them to bed upstairs. If they woke up in the night, she wouldn't be able to hear them. And I think getting up those stairs is simply too difficult for her with her arthritis. I think she was afraid she might fall."

"I've noticed she never goes upstairs. I'm glad she called you. Are the boys okay? They must be worried."

"They're asleep upstairs. They worried about you for about five minutes."

She raised a brow.

"They got a good look at you sleeping while the doctor checked you out."

She pressed her hand to her head. "I vaguely remember someone poking at me."

"You did not want to wake up. The doctor gave you a once-over, including a vitamin shot, and said to go ahead and let you sleep. It was the best medicine."

"You didn't need to call a doctor to come out here."

"You collapsed and then you wouldn't wake up," he snapped, letting his deep concern show. "Sorry."

Her heart ached. She hated that she'd scared him. "You were really worried."

"More than I can say." He raked his fingers through his tousled hair. "Once the boys knew you were okay, we played ball, video games, and roasted hot dogs over the firepit. Once they were sufficiently dirty and tired, I gave them a bath in the big tub, full of bubbles, read them a couple stories, and put them to bed." Luke grinned. "We had a great time. I love those boys."

"You do?" She believed him. She just didn't expect him to express it so easily.

"What's not to love? Their mother has done a great job raising them. They kicked my ass at some of the video games. They know a bunch of secret codes to make themselves invincible. I couldn't get them to reveal the codes. Anyway, we have a lot to talk about. Are you fully awake now?"

"Yes, why?"

"Because I want to tell you that you scared the hell out of me!" His voice started out soft, but by the time he got to the end of the sentence the anger spilled out with his words. "When I think of what could have happened if you weren't here with me . . ."

Sarah raised up and faced him, leaning on one arm. "Luke, I'm sorry I frightened you. Don't you think it scares the hell out of me to wake up on your kitchen table not knowing how long I've been asleep, or what might have happened to my boys? They're everything to me. Don't you think I'm sitting here thanking God that you were here to take care of us? Don't you think I have a thousand different scenarios going through my mind about what might have happened to them if I'd hurt them, or myself? This is killing me and I'm so sorry that you've had to put your life on hold to take care of us."

Her words set off a deep frown on Luke's handsome face. "I love having you and the boys here. I've told you several times now that I don't want you to go. Apparently, that hasn't sunk in yet. So, let me say it again. I want you and those boys here with me. I want *you* to be with me."

"I want that, too."

"Then help me make it happen. Work *reasonable* hours. I know it's a long commute from here to Silicon Valley, but I could set up an office for you here. We'll figure something out, depending on what you need. And Abby has called way too much. I finally had to threaten to sue her for harassment if she didn't stop calling every half hour to see if you were awake. She's really great. She cares a lot about you. Anyway, I took care of what I could. She'll call later today to update you on what's happening."

"What do you mean *you* took care of what you could?"

"Apparently Evan leaked to the press that you've finished the Knox Project and it far exceeds expectations. They want to set up a bunch of interviews immediately. I told her not to schedule anything, that you didn't want to do the interviews anyway, and the press would see you at the benefit. As far as the dress you need, I asked Abby to get you something. She'll send it tomorrow."

"Oh God. You have no idea what you've done."

"You said you didn't want to do the interviews. Putting them off a week won't matter, will it?"

She waved that away. "No, not that. Thank you for putting that off. It's the dress. You have no idea what Abby will pick. She's wanted to make me over forever. I have no idea what she'll send. She thinks I dress too conservative."

"Well, if you don't like it, you'll have time to get something else."

Luke settled back in his seat, an empty coffee cup and plate between them.

"I guess I should get the boys back to Margaret's, so you can have your house back and get to work."

"Sarah, it's about three in the morning. The boys are sleeping."

She looked around the kitchen and at the dark windows. "Is it that early? Why are you having breakfast now? Are you going somewhere?"

"No, sweetheart. I'm up because you got out of bed and sleep-walked down here to make me breakfast."

"What?" She'd done some bizarre things while sleepwalking.

"When you got out of bed, I followed you down here to be sure you didn't go outside. You pushed me into this chair and proceeded to make breakfast. I thought you were hungry after sleeping so long, but you put the plate in front of me, folded your arms, and waited for me to dig in. Once I did, you got up on the table and went back to sleep. Breakfast was great, by the way. I love French toast and eggs."

She couldn't believe he'd been so thoughtful. "I can't believe I slept so long."

"My opinion: since you finished the Knox Project, your subconscious knew it was a good time to take a break." Luke stood and stared down at her. "So let's go back to bed." He scooped her up into his arms and headed out of the kitchen to the stairs without giving her an opportunity to protest or think.

Luke took the stairs like her added weight didn't faze him and stopped outside his bedroom door. He set her down, sighed with a wistful look at the bed, and took her hand and led her down the hall to one of the spare rooms. Luke pushed the door open, revealing the boys sound asleep together in the queen-size bed. Luke had brought the boys' night-light from Margaret's house, their toys littered the floor, and their clothes were stacked neatly on the dresser, their tiny shoes on the hardwood. He'd thought of everything.

She gave each of her sons a kiss on the head before she and Luke left the room.

Luke took her hand again and led her to his room.

She stopped and tugged on his hand. "Luke, I can't sleep with you. What would the boys think?"

"Jack told me I needed to stay with you, that you needed lots of hugs."

"Really?" Her heart melted that her little boy wanted Luke to take care of her. "They must be wondering what's going on."

"I promised them I would keep you safe. Jack said he liked sleeping with Nick, and that you always sleep alone, even his dad didn't sleep with you. Odd that a wife doesn't sleep with her husband. Then I remembered something you told me. You said I was the first man you'd kissed in five years. Nick is only four so that put Jack's comment about his dad not sleeping with you in perspective. So, I'm going to ask you something. Did Sean love you? Because it's obvious he wasn't *in* love with you."

Sarah sighed and raked her fingers through her already sleep-tousled hair. "Why would he love me? No one else ever did." She stepped away and wrapped her arms around her middle; then, knowing he was looking for more answers, she gave him the unvarnished truth. "I mistook his needing me for love. But it wasn't. And Sean stopped pretending it was more than just business. It was always, 'You have to get these projects done, so we get paid. Here're another five projects, hurry up or our employees won't get paid.' He got what he wanted, and I got a piece of what I wanted."

Luke's gaze narrowed. "So he got the business and you got . . . what? You grew up poor, but money doesn't seem to be your motivator."

"I grew up alone," she corrected him.

Luke's eyes went bright with understanding. "You wanted a family."

"I had the boys, but we were never a family. Sean was all consumed with the company and money. He was never part of the family life I created at home with the boys. He was too busy out having a good time. Sure, he'd drum up business. He liked to schmooze the clients. But there was also a lot of travel to exotic places. He liked to live the life of a wealthy mogul."

"But the boys have dozens of wonderful memories about their father."

"Jack was about four and Nick wasn't even two when Sean died. How much do you think they really remember? I didn't want them to remember that Sean was never there, or that when he was, he couldn't be bothered with them. That's no way for a son to remember his father, so I took what little time Sean did spend with them and made it seem like that was how he was all the time."

"You lied." He seemed surprised and upset by it.

"Yes. No child should ever feel like they aren't wanted." She'd felt that way all too often. Even now, she had to remind herself that she had a good life, the boys, and that was enough. "I didn't want the boys to grow up remembering Sean couldn't even take the time to hug them."

Luke brushed his fingertips down the side of her face and placed his hand on her shoulder. "That's not right. They deserve better. And so do you, sweetheart."

"I've had to fight and work for everything in my life. I want the boys to have everything I never had."

"They have you to love them the way you were never loved. They feel that. They know it. They're happy." His hand swept up the side of her neck and his thumb brushed along her jaw. "All I want to do is make you happy."

She leaned into his touch. "You do."

"Why did you stay with him so long?"

"I'd planned to leave, but certain circumstances warranted my caution in just walking out."

"What circumstances?"

"The boys, for one. I needed to have the means to support them when I left. I'd started doing some side work. Something fun and creative. I loved it and wanted to change my focus. When it sold big, I knew I could make a decent living. Sean found out what I was up to and threatened to use the boys to get me to continue to work for him."

Luke frowned. "He tried to blackmail you with a custody fight?"

"Without me, the company would have folded before it went public."

Luke held her gaze. "It must have been really frustrating, disappointing, and heartbreaking to be used like that. And then he threatened you on top of it."

"Sean didn't care how he got what he wanted or how I felt about it. In the end, there was no love, if there ever was any, or kindness left between us. I was just a means to an end. The boys just pawns in his games."

"Life hasn't been kind to you."

"But you are. The gift you gave me . . . It's the nicest thing anyone's ever done for me."

Luke cupped her face. "You gave me something I never thought I'd have and believe it was real."

She tilted her head and stared up at him. "What?"

"You might not remember, but you told me you love me."

A wave of understanding overlapped her initial shock. She couldn't believe she'd blurted out such a thing. And the reality of how much she loved him hit her right in the heart.

She and Luke may have lived very different lives, but they wanted the same things. Love and family.

He kissed her softly, then ended the sweet, tempting kiss too soon and pressed his forehead to hers. "Say it again. Please." All his need filled that plea and she couldn't deny him something he'd always wanted and seemed happy to finally have.

"It's true." Her heart simply couldn't deny it, even if at one time she'd thought herself in love with another. But that had been nothing but lies and manipulations. In the end, she realized that she'd never loved Sean, because she never knew who he really was until it was too late. She loved the dream of them. Reality shattered that.

But Luke was real. What she felt for him made that dream come to life in her mind in a new and real way that gave her hope, because Luke wouldn't promise something he didn't mean.

So she looked him in the eye, took a chance, and laid her heart on the line. "I love you."

His eyes went bright with a joy that lit up her heart.

"Good, because I'm so *in love* with you." The words held an honesty only Luke could make her believe.

A huge grin spread across his face. "You know, sleeping next to you and not being able to touch you has driven me past the point of my endurance."

Yet he didn't make a move.

The building anticipation made her desperate to touch him. "I wish I remembered sleeping next to you." She wanted to feel his big body pressed to hers.

His fingers slipped to the back of her neck and he pulled her a little closer so their breaths mingled and she saw all the desire blazing in his eyes. "Is that all you wish we'd done?" One finger swept up her neck, sending a shiver down her spine.

"That would have been really nice. But I want—"

His lips swept over hers in a barely there kiss that left her burning. "What do you want?" The husky whispered words turned up the heat.

"You."

He pulled her in as she went up on tiptoe to meet him in the middle. His mouth captured hers just as her breasts pressed against his hard chest and her arms went around his neck. The second he touched her, all her attention focused on how wonderful he felt against her. She loved the feel and texture of his mouth as his tongue slid along hers. He tasted like coffee, maple syrup, and temptation all mixed together, while the scent of him, some kind of tangy soap that hinted toward lime, filled her nose.

He hit all her senses, leaving her enveloped in everything Luke.

His hands roamed down her back, over her hips, and cupped her backside, pulling her closer and molding her to his hands. Her belly pressed against his hard erection and she moved against him, smiling against his lips when he moaned with pure pleasure. She'd never felt more powerful or sexy in her life than she did in his arms.

He picked her up and laid her down in the middle of the already rumpled bed and leaned over her. "Say it again."

She ran her hands up his wide bare chest and felt his heart pounding against her palm. She looked him in the eye and gave him what he wanted. "I love you." She could live on his joyous grin.

"I'm going to show you how much I love you." The searing kiss sealed that promise. Luke's big hand sliding between her breasts and down her stomach made her anticipate every sensual moment to come.

He kissed the line of her jaw and down her neck. She turned her head to give him better access and slid her hands along his broad shoulders and back, up his neck until her fingers slid through his soft golden hair.

One of his work-roughened hands swept up her thigh, over her hip, up her belly, to her breast, and cupped it in his warm palm. She moaned and arched against his hand, giving him all the freedom he wanted to explore her body. He pulled the shirt over her head and kissed the top of her breast and around to the soft underside. She begged for more with soft whimpers and moans. His tongue circled her hard nipple a second before he took it into his mouth and sucked, sending a warm shiver through her body and straight to her already wet core.

She raked her nails up his back. He growled something low in his throat and gave her other breast equal attention. That wonderfully deft and warm hand ran down her ribs and spread across her stomach, then roamed lower. Her damp panties were no barrier to his questing hand. He slid them down her legs and tossed them away. His fingertips skimmed up her long legs, tracing her sensitive skin. Up, up, until he found her wet center and she moaned with relief as he swept his fingers along her folds. She moved against his hand. He smoothed two fingers over her slick opening and drove them in deep, filling her and sending another wave of pleasure through her body.

It had been so long since she'd felt this good, since a man held her close and made her body come alive.

She sighed and tilted her hips to meet the thrust of his fingers.

"I love it that you show me how much you like that." His words rumbled at her ear a second before he licked the lobe, then planted an open-mouthed kiss on her neck.

"More." She rocked her hips into his plundering fingers.

The pad of his thumb rubbed softly over the sweet spot that made her body tighten and pleasure soar. She hit the crest and flew over it, calling his name. Lost in the pleasure of it all, she dug her nails into his shoulders. She buried her face in his neck and rode out the aftershocks, feeling connected to him in a whole new way.

Swept up in the moment and sheer desire, she pushed his shoulders, sending him to his back beside her, and covered him with her body. His hands ran from her backside to her shoulders and down again. She kissed him deeply and moved down to his throat and his bare chest. Her hands moved over the hard muscles of his biceps and up to his shoulders. Her mouth roamed down his chest to his hard stomach. She grabbed the waistband of his pajama bottoms, sat up, and pulled them out of her way. His erection stood proud, and although she hadn't been with a man in a very long time, she ached to have him inside her.

His hands clamped onto her hips. "Sarah."

She leaned down and kissed him. Desperate for him, she sank down on his hard cock and filled herself with him and every bit of pleasure he'd promised.

Circling her hips and making him moan this time, she rose and fell on his hard shaft and he thrust to meet her again and again.

Luke hooked his arm around her hips, rolled them over, and settled his big body between her thighs. Still joined, he thrust deep and stared into her eyes as his hard length pumped in and out of her tightening core.

She pulled her knees back, taking him in deeper and loving the moan that slipped through his soft lips and the heavy-lidded stare he gave her.

"You drive me crazy."

She rocked her hips against his and smiled up at him. "I know."

He dove in for another searing kiss. She wrapped her legs around his waist and held him close. The tempo changed with a surge of need. She gripped his shoulders and held him to her as he thrust hard and fast. Her back arched and her heavy breasts pressed against his chest. She rocketed over the edge and his body shuddered with his powerful release.

With Luke collapsed on top of her, his warm body pressed to hers, she found a kind of peace she'd never felt in her life.

She felt safe and wanted and necessary.

Luke pressed his face into her neck and kissed her softly, then pressed up on his hands and stared down at her. "God, you're beautiful."

She reached up and cupped his face in her hands. "And you're gorgeous."

He gave her another soft kiss, then settled on his back beside her, drawing her close to his side. She cuddled into his chest and rested her head under his chin, her hand over his heart.

Luke kissed the top of her head. "I'll never break a promise to you, Sarah, because I don't want to ever lose you or this."

She didn't put a lot of stock in other people's promises. They broke them all the time.

But she believed Luke.

And that scared her because he could really break her heart. But it also gave her hope for a future unlike anything she'd ever really given herself the freedom to imagine was possible.

Chapter Twenty-Three

S arah stood at the top of the stairs, staring down at Luke, Jack, and Nick. Luke pretended to struggle to get free as Jack and Nick tugged on his hands, trying to pull him two ways at once and getting nowhere. Luke suddenly pulled both boys to his sides, hooked his arms around their middles, picked them up, and tossed them over the back of the couch. The boys screamed, bounced on the cushions, and laughed uncontrollably. Jack popped up just as Luke turned his back but didn't move away, giving the boys time to come after him again. Jack grabbed him by the shoulder, Nick took his other arm, and together they pulled Luke backward. In reality, he sat on the back of the sofa and fell onto the cushions, groaning for dramatic effect, then sucking in a breath when both boys landed on his belly and chest. He wrapped his arms around them and tickled them unmercifully as his long legs dangled over the back of the leather sofa.

Sarah's heart melted at the sight of her boys roughhousing with Luke and the sheer delight in Luke's eyes as he played with them. It really was true. Men remain little boys on the inside.

She walked down the stairs and stood just between Luke's dangling feet and stared over the back of the couch at all three boys. "What's going on down here?"

All of them stopped and stared at her. Caught.

Jack and Nick looked unsure and ready for her to scold them.

Luke got a mischievous look in his eyes. "I think your mom missed at least a dozen kisses yesterday while she slept." He untangled his arms from the boys, reared up, took her under the arms, and dragged her over the couch and on top of him. He planted half a dozen kisses all over her face. The boys dove in and kissed her on the head.

She laughed so hard, it drove them to kiss her even more. They smothered her in love that ended with all of them hugging her close, Jack and Nick at her sides and draped over her back. Luke holding her close against his chest, her knees and feet still hanging off the sofa.

"Good morning, sweetheart." Luke smiled up at her.

"Yes, it is." She smiled at each of the boys. "Are you guys having fun?"

"Luke is the best!" Jack proclaimed.

"He's silly," Nick added.

She brushed her fingers over the side of Luke's face. "You're both. And crazy, you know that?"

"Definitely crazy about you." He brushed his nose against hers, then turned to the boys. "Go get your mom's surprise set up."

The boys scrambled over the couch again and ran for the kitchen.

Luke held her close, his head not even on the sofa, and kissed her good morning like he'd kissed her more than a dozen times last night. Her body heated with the memories of making love with him. "How do you feel?"

"Good. Rested."

"I hope so after all the hours you slept." Luke shifted, trying to hold his head up and take her weight on top of him.

She rolled over onto her back, much like him, pulled her legs down and around, and sat up on the sofa.

Luke made the same awkward move. "That used to be easier when I was younger."

She laughed. "You guys were having a good time."

"I know they need discipline, too. It's just . . . They're a lot of fun."

"They've never had anyone but me to play with, and I'm not that great at the wrestling and roughhousing. And there's something about boys. They just love to be tough."

"So we can impress girls." Luke's grin made her belly flutter.

"Mission accomplished. If we were alone, I'd show my appreciation for the way you look playing with my boys. The sheer joy in you and them." She surveyed him up and down. "All those muscles rippling when you pick them up and toss them."

"Oh yeah." Luke leaned in, bracing his hands on both sides of her as she fell back onto the sofa arm. He stared down at her. "When I saw you coming down the stairs from our room and I thought about how this could be every morning, how you could be here, in our bed, every night . . ." He kissed her again, this time letting loose all the passion he'd restrained when he and the boys attacked her with kisses.

His forehead touched hers and he looked deep into her eyes and said, "I love you."

Her heart felt so full she thought it might burst with joy, hearing those words from him. Tears filled her eyes.

He sat up and pulled her up with him. "Hey, what's with the tears? Talk to me."

"I'm happy."

Relief lit his eyes. "That's good."

"I haven't been this happy, well, ever. Except when the kids were born, of course. I just don't want this moment to ever end. I don't want the rest of the world to intrude on you and me right here, right now, just like this."

Sarah thought about what he'd said about them being together all the time. She imagined waking up every day to his gray eyes, filled with so much warmth and love for her that she ached with the need to hold him to her and never let him go.

"No one can take our happiness."

She wished that were true, but everyone who'd ever come into her life that mattered took what little happiness she'd been able to make for herself.

With Luke, she felt the potential to finally have it all. Love. A real family. A father the boys deserved. A man she could count on.

If only she could make it all happen.

"My time here is coming to an end soon. The kids love it here, but they also miss home, having their things around them, and their friends."

Instead of telling her he wanted her to stay again, Luke surprised her and asked, "What's your place like?"

"We live in a big house in a gated community, so they know we're better off than most. I wanted them to have room to play and be outside where it was safe. We live on a third-acre with a pool and a play yard. They have a tree house with a slide. It's really cool. We have a huge lawn for them to run and play ball. Everything little boys need to use their imaginations and spread their wings. I never had anything like that growing up, so I spoiled them with it. And they have half a dozen friends in the neighborhood, who come over all the time."

"You worked hard to give them a good life. You always put

them first, despite the long hours and sacrifices you make for them. I can see why you'd want to spoil them."

"I want Jack and Nick to have the best in life, but that doesn't mean they get everything they set their eyes on. I want them to appreciate real things. Family. True friends. Honesty. Trust. Love."

"All the things Sean never gave or taught them." Luke brushed his fingers through her hair. "You're a good mom. You're conscious about the decisions you make. You always try to do right by them. That's admirable."

"I just want them to know they're loved. Buying them the latest and greatest toy or game won't show them how much I love them. But playing tag in the backyard . . . I hope they'll remember that for a lifetime."

Luke took her hand. "Do you want to have more children?"

"I'd love to have a couple more."

His eyes went wide. "Really? A couple?"

"I love being a mom. Based on how much you love playing with the boys, I'm guessing you'd like to have your own children."

"I would."

"Our enthusiasm for each other last night overrode good sense. We got carried away. You may get your wish." She waited for hesitation or anger. She even braced herself for an accusation that she'd done it on purpose to trap him. But he appeared absolutely pleased by the idea, judging by the smile and thoughtful look in his eyes.

"I've never been in love like this before, where nothing matters more than being with you. I'm usually so careful. I always use protection, but last night, and this morning, I just got lost in you and how you make me feel and I wanted to experience every bit of it."

"I feel the same way."

"But?"

"I'm afraid we're moving too fast without taking the time to plan for our future."

"That you believe we have one is enough. I want you to trust that I'm here for you and the boys, and making us a family is what I really want."

"My life is so . . . busy. And overwhelming sometimes. I know you love me. I know I love you. I just need some time to figure out how to be everything to everybody and not let anyone down."

Luke hooked his hand at the back of her neck and looked her in the eye. "You already are everything to me and the boys. We'll work the rest out together. I know it's not fair, but I love this ranch. My place is here. It's what I've always wanted. Please consider moving in here with me. If you're concerned about the boys, we can put in a pool, build a tree house, whatever they want. There's a great private school not far from here. We could have it all."

She leaned in and kissed him for his enthusiasm and absolute belief they could be together and build a life after knowing each other for literally weeks. Her wild heart wanted to leap. But the woman who'd been lied to and cheated on and the mom inside of her needed to be cautious. She kissed him again because he made her believe in him and the possibility of them. "I love your crazy, let's-just-do-this attitude."

"I know what I want, Sarah. It's you and the boys and whatever life gives us in the future. I want it right now. But I know it'll take time to put our two lives together."

She breathed a small sigh of relief.

"We have all the time in the world," he assured her. "But you should know something."

"What?"

"I'm used to getting what I want, and now that I've found what I never thought I'd have with anyone, I'm not very patient when it comes to having you, with me, all the time. And I'm a lawyer, so whatever argument you have for stalling or dragging this out won't work. I'll give you every reason to say yes and do what we both know you want to do."

She chuckled. "You think you know me so well."

"I'm working on it. In fact, stay here with me. We'll plan the next steps together and I'll help you with the logistics."

"As much as I'd love that, I can't. I promised Margaret six weeks with the boys and I want her to have them. It wouldn't be right to cut her time short. I hope you understand. I gave my word."

"I get it, but I don't have to like it." He pulled her close and kissed her with the same passion that had swept them away last night. But this time, he cut it short and left her wishing they were still in bed. "Are you thinking about last night?" The need in his eyes said he definitely remembered every detail of their night together.

"Yes."

"Good. Because when you move in, we'll have that for the rest of our lives. Until then, sweetheart, make yourself at home. Come and go anytime you want while you're visiting Margaret. And know I'll be here waiting for you."

She pressed her hand to his face and took in the honesty of his words and in his eyes. "I'll make it happen. Because it's what I want. For me. For the boys. For us and the future you promised."

Luke smiled. "Should I call the pool company?"

She laughed. "Why don't you start by designing a tree house with the boys?"

He beamed. "I will."

She loved that his plans included the kids. Not only that, but he knew the best way to get her here faster was to make this place theirs. After what they shared last night, the love he'd shown her, it already felt like home.

Because Luke was here.

Chapter Twenty-Four

S arah and Luke walked into the kitchen holding hands.

Jack noticed immediately. He stared for a moment, eyes filled with questions and concern, until he looked up at Luke's smiling face and all the worry went out of him and he moved on. "We made you breakfast, Mama."

She smiled at the bowl of berries, glass of orange juice, and the plate of pancakes. "You did this for me?"

Jack nodded, pride in his eyes. "Luke said you need to eat a good breakfast."

"I poured the juice without spilling," Nick announced, his sweet smile making her grin back.

"You did a fantastic job."

Luke touched her back to get her to sit at the counter. "I fed the boys earlier." He took the pancakes and popped them in the microwave to heat.

"You did all this while I was in the shower?"

"The boys helped." Luke gave her a sheepish look. "I wanted to do something nice for you."

"Thank you." It touched her deeply, and she hoped Luke saw that she really meant the gratitude and appreciation.

"Taking care of you is my pleasure." The purr in his voice made her think of how he'd taken care of her last night.

Luke set the warmed pancakes in front of her along with a tub of butter and a bottle of syrup.

"I could get used to this."

"Stay. I'll make it worth your while." Luke's sexy grin promised heaven.

"What are you talking about?" Jack asked, his gaze bouncing from her to Luke and back.

Luke took the lead. "I like having all of you here."

"We have fun," Nick added.

Jack studied Luke. "Can we play baseball again tonight with all the guys?"

Luke filled her in. "I put together a game with the ranch hands before dinner last night."

Of course he did.

"Luke taught me how to throw a wicked fastball," Jack announced, pride lighting up his whole face.

"Let's go riding again." Nick bounced in the seat next to her.

She swallowed the bite of fluffy pancakes. As much as she'd like to stay . . . "We have to go back to Grandma's." Margaret probably couldn't wait to tell her off and chide her for exhausting herself and putting the boys at risk. Like she didn't already feel bad enough about what happened. "She's probably waiting for us right now."

She hated putting that disappointed expression on Luke's rugged face. The boys' faces matched his. But she couldn't go against her promise to Margaret. "We'll come back and see Luke every day before we go home. I promise."

Luke leaned on his forearms on the counter in front of the

boys. "Your mom and I . . . We really like each other. In fact, I love her. And I want us to be a family."

Jack sat back. "What does that mean?"

"Well, your mom and I have a lot to talk about and work out, but eventually, someday soon, I hope that you will all live here with me. How would you guys feel about that?"

Jack linked his fingers together in his lap and nervously kicked his feet back and forth. "Do you mean all the time?"

"That's right."

"What about our house?" Jack looked to her to answer that.

"The house is still ours, sweetheart. We aren't moving immediately. Like Luke said, someday soon." She turned her gaze to Luke. "There's still so much you don't know . . . things I need to tell you. About Sean. My life. The company."

"We will talk about all of it," Luke assured her before turning back to the boys. "Your mom and I just want to know if you guys would like living here with me."

"Yeah, I guess that would be okay." Jack shrugged.

"I guess so." Nick responded with more enthusiasm.

Sarah assumed Nick's enthusiasm was partly because of Luke, and partly because of the horses and kitties in the barn. Jack's approval seemed more hesitant. She'd talk to them more about the future she wanted with Luke and all of them being a family and what that would look like.

She stood, kissed both boys on the head, put her dish and silverware in the dishwasher, while the boys plied Luke with a dozen questions about making the rooms upstairs theirs. She found their constant chatter endearing, especially since it showed how much the boys loved Luke's attention.

Sarah had finally gotten a good look at the house. The great room was her favorite. The white walls with the wood floor and ceiling with the chunky beams made the room so cozy and inviting.

"Luke, I really love the house. This kitchen is amazing." She loved the big dark gray island with the white quartz countertops. The farmhouse sink was charming and went with the white Craftsman-style cabinets.

"I had the place redecorated several months ago. I'm glad you like it. I hope you'll be comfortable here, but if there's something you don't like, we can change it. Anything you want, I'll make it happen."

She smiled at him, her heart expanding with an abundance of love. "It's perfect." They'd be really happy here.

"I hope my family thinks so, too. They're coming for dinner Sunday night for our monthly get-together. I want you and the boys to join us." Luke wrapped his arms around her waist and held her close. "Please say you'll come. I want you to meet them. I want everyone to see us together and how happy we are."

How could she resist him? "Okay, we'll come to dinner. Are you cooking?"

"No. I have a personal chef who does everything."

"Oh really?" Sarah eyed him.

He smirked. "I totally get why you have Camille. And I'm with you. When you work hard, you deserve to splurge once in a while. And this way, all we have to do is show up and eat."

A truck and trailer arrived outside and distracted her. "Today is Friday."

"Yeah."

"You have a delivery." She smiled up at him.

Luke gazed out the window. "I didn't order or buy anything."

"It's a gift." She helped the boys down from their stools. "Come, boys. You can watch cartoons while I show Luke another part of who I am." The boys gave her a strange look, but she had Luke's full attention.

* * *

Luke left Sarah to settle the boys in front of the TV and reached the truck in the driveway just after two men got out. One was in his fifties, gray hair, a good strong build, and about six feet tall. The other was in his twenties with dark blond hair to his shoulders and a strong lean build of about six-foot-two. Given the similarity of their looks, Luke guessed they were father and son. Two horses nickered at him from inside the trailer. He approached the men and caught sight of the sign on the truck door. Flames rose behind the black words "Blaze Ranch." The same ranch he'd tried to buy horses from a while back.

"Can I help you guys?"

The older man eyed him. "Are you the owner? Luke?"

"That's me. What can I do for you?"

"We're here to deliver the horses."

"That can't be right. I called about buying some horses a long time ago, but the owner wouldn't sell."

"I guess she changed her mind."

Luke didn't know what to make of this. The older man looked like he was sincere about delivering the horses. "But I didn't buy any horses."

"You'll have to talk to her about it."

"Well, where is she? How do I get in touch with her?"

The man waved his hand out. "She's right behind you."

Luke turned and found Sarah standing there, smiling.

She ran past him and launched herself into the older man's arms. "I am so happy to see you."

"Me too, squirt. We brought your ladies. How are you? It's been a while."

"I'm fine. How are my girls?"

"Right as rain, squirt."

The second the older man released her, Sarah hugged the younger one. A shot of jealousy ran through Luke unlike anything he'd ever felt.

The young guy picked her up, leaving her feet dangling at his shins. "Hey, how you doin'?"

"Just fine." She leaned back. "Did you finish school yet?"

"Almost. One semester left." He let her down. Luke felt the surge of jealousy rise.

Back on her feet, Sarah tapped her fist into the young guy's gut. "Behave." She turned to Luke. "This is Tim and Randy Reed. They run Blaze Ranch, and they are here to deliver your new mares."

Luke raised a brow. "I need the extended version of that explanation."

She sighed. "I feel like I'm always explaining myself to you. I told you I managed to hold on to my uncle's ranch. I expanded it while I was in college by doing some website design work." She held her hand out to the sign on the truck door. "Blaze Ranch. Get it?"

Understanding dawned in his eyes. "Because you burned it down."

"Just a little joke on myself. Tim is the ranch hand who used to bring the radio to the stables. He was always kind to me, so when I needed someone to help me get the ranch up and running, I hired him. His son Randy works for me when he isn't attending school, along with several other people."

"You should come more often," Tim chided.

"If I had time . . ."

"You need to make the time," Tim coaxed.

Sarah rolled her eyes.

Luke wondered about the ranch. "Did Sean know about it?"

"He knew I had the land when we were in college. I told him I wanted to build something out of it and he dismissed the idea." She shrugged. "I should have taken that as a warning of what was to come." She scrunched her mouth into a derisive frown. "I don't like being ignored or told what to do, so I built the ranch on my own. If something happened, like my marriage to Sean falling apart, I knew I had a place that was all mine."

"So when you divorced him you weren't going to tell him about the ranch?"

"Well, Counselor, I owned it before the marriage, so it wasn't part of the community property."

Luke wasn't thinking like a lawyer but like a man who'd been used for what he had for too long. "I'm sorry. You're right."

"She's always right," Tim said. "You should get used to that now."

Luke chuckled under his breath. "It's starting to sink in."

Sarah turned shy. "I'm sorry I wouldn't sell you one of my babies when you called about them. I want to make sure my horses go to good homes."

"Are you telling me I spoke to you before?"

"Yes. Though I don't remember."

"If you'd only sold me a horse, we would have met a long time ago."

"It's strange how things work out. It's like no matter what, we were meant to meet."

They shared a long look that said so much, because it really felt like the second she stepped into his life, everything felt different and headed in the right direction.

Sarah's smile brightened. "Want to meet Ace's new girlfriends?"

He got caught up in her enthusiasm. "I can't wait."

They walked to the back of the trailer where Tim and Randy had backed out the horses. Luke stopped, stunned when he saw them. Magnificent. Ace was a gorgeous brown quarter horse stallion, but the ones Sarah had sent him were amazing. One sorrel, the other brown. Sarah walked up to each of the horses and gave them a good rub down their noses and the sides of their faces.

"Tim, the ladies look wonderful. How'd they do on the ride over?"

"Just fine. We have a couple new foals. I emailed you photos."

Sarah turned to him. "Meet my princesses. The brown is Jasmine and this is Gweneviere."

"Sarah, the horses . . . they're outstanding. But you can't be serious about giving them to me." He knew they were worth a fortune. And no one had ever given him anything like this. The foals these horses produced would be the best on his ranch—any ranch in the state, for that matter.

Sarah's eyes turned defensive. "I'm not giving them to you."

Luke narrowed his eyes. He should have known better. "How much do I owe you? I'll pay you whatever you're asking."

"Really. Whatever I'm asking?" She raised a brow. "I suppose I have the perfect excuse to steal you blind on these horses."

"How much?" Luke wasn't buying her ruse to gouge him. He knew she'd be fair. He could all but see the twinkle in her eyes.

"Kiss me, big guy."

He didn't have to be asked twice and planted a kiss on her that said how much he appreciated her and this gesture that would ensure his ranch thrived.

To his dismay, she pulled away far too soon and looked him right in the eye. "These horses are a gift for Ace. Although you have some really nice mares, you don't have any that compare to my princesses."

He cupped her beautiful face. "There is nothing that compares to you." He kissed her, loving her for her generosity and kind heart. She loved her horses, that was clear, but she'd given them to him, knowing he'd take care of them. He'd love them the way she did.

She trusted him with the horses, her kids, and her heart.

All he wanted to do was make her happy.

He feared ever disappointing her or losing her.

There was no one like Sarah.

His life was better with her in it.

Now all he had to do was make it permanent.

Chapter Twenty-Five

S arah had loved making Luke outrageously happy this morning. The love and appreciation she'd seen in his eyes when she gave him the horses stuck in her mind and heart. She wanted to make him feel and look at her that way every day.

But how was she really going to make that happen? It seemed so easy to talk about and wish for it, but the reality for Sarah was a lot harder.

She needed time to think, plan, and figure out a way to run her businesses in Silicon Valley *and* be with Luke in Carmel. She also wanted to make sure the boys were really okay with her relationship with Luke and the possibility they would move to the ranch permanently.

While Luke made it clear he wanted them to be a family, he'd never mentioned marriage.

Did she want to get married again?

Yes. Being Luke's wife, having a real partnership and love, would make her really happy.

Luke talked about more children and a life together like he could already see it all.

She'd always wanted a big family. The need grew out of her loneliness as a child. She'd wished she'd had a sibling. Someone to share everything with. Someone who understood her like no other.

She loved her father, but their relationship was more a friendship since he'd found her when she was nearly an adult in age, though she'd had a lot of heartache and had to grow up faster than most kids. Abby was more like a sister than just her assistant. And Tim was like an uncle, Randy a cousin. Her team at Spencer Software felt like a family.

But she wanted more with Luke. She wanted that deep connection and a lifetime of memories from a bond that would never break.

Still, she'd been disappointed before, and allowing herself to believe in Luke's vision for them was hard to do without doubts creeping in.

Luke drove them down the drive to Margaret's house. The boys sat between them, buckled together on the bench seat, wishing they could stay at Luke's instead, to go riding and play and hang out with the man they'd become close to, too.

They stopped outside Margaret's home. A sense of déjà vu came over Sarah when she spotted Margaret sitting on the porch, waiting like a sentry for the enemy to arrive, and spoiling for a fight, just like the first day she'd arrived.

Luke reached across the boys and laid his hand on her shoulder. "You didn't do anything wrong."

Tell her that. She didn't say anything because of the boys.

She slipped out of the truck and held the door for the boys to climb down. "I want you two to go upstairs and put away your things. You can watch TV for an hour, then we'll do homework and have lunch."

"Okay," Jack said, heading toward the house, Nick right behind him.

"Hold it," she called to them. "Thank Luke for taking care of you while Mommy rested."

They ran back and threw their arms around Luke's legs. "Thank you," they said in unison.

Sarah's heart melted.

Luke put a hand on both boys' heads and gave their hair a ruffle. "You're welcome." He released the boys and hooked his arm around her shoulders just as Bridget pulled into the driveway.

The boys raced up the porch steps, said hello to their grandmother, and went in ahead of everyone.

Luke greeted Bridget as she met them on the walkway up to the porch. "Hey, Bridge. Sophia at school?"

"Yep." Bridget eyed Sarah. "You look fine to me. Kudos on the dramatic performance to get attention. You got Luke to swoop in and play your white knight."

Luke looked at Bridget like he was seeing her for the first time. "What the hell, Bridget."

She rolled her eyes. "Why does sex make men stupid?"

Luke gave her an incredulous look. "What is the matter with you?"

Sarah knew. Bridget's divorce and her ex-husband's new girlfriend had turned Bridget bitter and resentful of couples. But it didn't make it easier to take her snide comments and rudeness.

Luke didn't appear happy about being called stupid.

Bridget walked past them and up the steps to greet her mom.

Sarah and Luke followed, only to have Margaret greet them with her own brand of snark. "Nice of you to bring my grandsons back where they belong."

Sarah didn't want to fight. "Don't start, Margaret. It was one night."

"Oh, it's more than that. It's your campaign to reel Luke in and ruin him."

Luke took a step closer to Margaret. "So you both take me for a fool?"

Margaret gave him a sad, condescending frown. "I love you like a son. I don't want her to hurt you, too. I thought you'd see through her lies and manipulations, but apparently even you have fallen for her . . . charms."

"She's never lied to me. She hasn't manipulated me. I simply took the time to get to know her. You should do the same, instead of believing what Sean told you and what you've assumed."

Margaret waved that off. "My son died unhappy. Because of her insatiable need for money, he was working late again, and he was probably so tired he didn't see the accident coming."

"That is not what happened." Sarah shook her head and sighed. "You really have no idea who Sean turned out to be."

"How would I? You kept him away from us. You couldn't be bothered to visit. You didn't want to bring the boys, it was too much trouble to travel even a couple hours with them."

"Not true."

Bridget waved that off. "Of course you'd blame Sean. He's not here to defend himself."

Sarah had enough. "Apparently I'm not allowed to defend myself either." She glanced up at Luke. "I'll see you later. I've got work to do."

Margaret stepped in front of her, blocking her from entering the house. "The lawn could use a mowing again. Perhaps you could at least take care of that today."

She'd had Camille clean the house and had the gardeners come when she and the boys arrived. Since then, she'd kept up with the maintenance, but she'd be damned if she took orders from Margaret. "Why don't you permanently hire a gardener to take care of the yard? Lord knows, you need one for this big property. You could use a housekeeper, too." Sarah really couldn't keep doing everything, or she'd end up passed out from exhaustion again. "Perhaps Bridget could do the work, since she doesn't have a job right now. I'm sure she'd like to earn a little extra money instead of you just bailing her out all the time."

Bridget glared at her.

Margaret sucked in a surprised gasp that Sarah had actually fought back for once. "Thanks to Sean, you have the means to have people wait on you and take care of you. You've even got Luke going out of his way to please you. Some of us have to take care of ourselves. And it's not easy when you're alone. I can't afford this house, let alone hire someone to help with the yard and housekeeping. And as my condition worsens, the medical bills pile up." Worry and resentment filled Margaret's eyes.

Bridget touched her mom's arm. "Why didn't you say anything?" At least she had some compassion for the one person who took care of her, even at Margaret's detriment.

Margaret gave a one-shoulder shrug, unable to say anything about what so obviously devastated her. "It's gone. Sean needed money to start the business. I've helped Bridget here and there. *I* take care of my family."

"So do I," Sarah shot back.

"Right. You took everything of Sean's, bought a big, new house, put the boys in private school, and probably spend all your money on fancy clothes and cars. Just look at that brand-new SUV."

Sarah had replaced her older model six months ago and given Camille her old one because she needed something more reliable than her rattle-trap sedan. But Margaret didn't know that. She didn't know a lot of things, and that was Sarah's fault, because she'd kept her mouth shut about Sean, his death, and how he lived.

"I work hard to provide for my children. I try to give them

everything I never had growing up. I've even made sure that you were taken care of because you're Jack and Nick's grandmother, but you don't appreciate anything I do for you. And I'm tired of it and you constantly blaming me for everything."

"What have you done for me? Cleaned the house and yard. You want a thank-you? Fine. Thank you."

"I did it for the boys and because despite your objections, I could see you needed the help. Bridget is so angry and lost in her own pain, she can't see your failing health, let alone the state of your home."

Margaret put her hand to her chest. "You haven't said anything."

"Because you don't care to hear anything I have to say. But you are going to listen to me now, because this"—she pointed from herself to Margaret and back—"can't go on. Not if you want to be a real part of the kids' lives."

"I do. I want them to know me. And Sean. I don't want them to forget him."

"Then you are going to have to meet me halfway and stop ignoring me and everything I do for you. I don't deserve it, and you'd know that if you stopped being so stubborn."

"I know no such thing. Sean would have taken care of me. He would have made sure to keep in touch. He'd have sent pictures of the boys. He wouldn't have just left me here all alone." Margaret's grief came out in full force, her eyes filling with unshed tears.

"You could have all of that, if you'd only open your mail."

"What?" Confusion clouded Margaret's eyes.

Of course Sarah had to clean this up, too.

She threw up her hands and paced a few steps back and forth. She glanced at Luke and then to Margaret and Bridget. She had to set things straight, but the thought of having to explain herself, yet again, made her so angry she wanted to punch something. "Come with me. I'll show you how I take care of family. There's something you need to see in the library."

She didn't wait for them to reply. She walked in the front door and headed straight for the library Margaret clearly never used, except to hide away the things she couldn't face.

The basket full of large envelopes all with the Spenser Software return address and logo sat on the credenza behind the desk. Sarah had discovered them the first week she'd arrived at Margaret's when she'd vacuumed the downstairs rooms. It infuriated her to discover that not a single envelope, except the first she'd sent, had been opened.

She slammed the basket down on the desk as Luke, Margaret, and Bridget entered the room. "Shut the door. I don't want the boys to hear this."

She waited while Luke shut the door and Margaret and Bridget moved into the room and faced her across the desk. Margaret eased herself into the chair; her slight frame had gone thin and frail the last two years. Her own damn fault. She just didn't know it. Because Sarah had provided.

She'd taken the high road and done the right thing despite how hard Margaret made it to remain kind and not angry all the time.

Bridget stood with her arms folded, ready to do battle over her brother, even if he didn't deserve it.

Sarah shouldn't have let this go on for so long. She had her own excuses and reasons why she put Sean's family on the back burner. He'd left her enough to clean up and take care of. She could only do so much.

More excuses and reasons that didn't matter to Margaret, who suffered because of her own stubbornness and Sarah's.

"You love Sean. You remember him a certain way."

Margaret cautiously nodded, while Bridget glared at her sister-in-law.

"I have tried to allow you to keep your memories of Sean just as you remember him. Most of it is real. But what he told you about college, our marriage, the company . . . It's all half-truths and lies. You're so angry with me about what he told you, and I've allowed you to believe, because I didn't want you to think less of Sean. Having two sons, I can see why you'd want to believe that Sean was a wonderful person without any flaws. But we all have flaws."

"Some of us more than others," Bridget shot back.

Margaret gave her one of those harsh looks she liked to level on Sarah, but it quickly faded and her gaze turned thoughtful. "He was wonderful until you came along and ruined everything. He had such a bright future ahead of him. The business was everything to him. He told me how you made him work so hard that he was never home. You were never happy because he couldn't make money as fast as you wanted. He told me how you spent everything he made. You were so busy out having a good time that you couldn't be bothered with the boys. He said you never let him come to see me, and kept the children away from us here. And I've seen you while you've been here. You're constantly on the phone or computer, probably online shopping and chatting with your friends." She said all the words, but the heat and certainty behind them waned as doubt crept in.

Luke didn't react to anything Margaret said, surprising Sarah. He gave her a nod to prod her on.

"Yes, you've seen me on the phone and the computer. I'm working. Always working. Because I'm not just the name behind Spencer Software, *I* run Spencer Software. I always have. Sean had a dream but didn't want to put in the hours and hard work it takes to build a company. So he used me to do it and took all the credit.

Without my hard work and technical know-how there wouldn't be a Spencer Software. "

She pinned Margaret in her gaze. "Everything you said about me wanting more money, always going out and having a good time, spending money we didn't have, all of it applies to Sean. Not me."

Margaret sucked in a breath in shock, but Sarah continued. She was going to make Margaret understand if it was the last thing she ever did. "Sean wouldn't have gotten through his last year of college if it hadn't been for me. He'd burned out and turned to drinking to cope, which made it even harder for him to get through his classes. He wanted to leave and start the company without finishing his degree. *I* convinced him he'd be better off with the degree in hand, that it would open doors. *I* got him through his last year of school. If you'll remember graduation, you'll recall I graduated summa cum laude, while Sean didn't even graduate with honors."

Margaret's eyes turned thoughtful. Sarah assumed she was thinking back to graduation, and hopefully, to what her son was like when he attended college.

"He was quite the charmer back then. I never realized he was using me until it was too late and everything was a complete mess. He knew I had talent and he used my abilities and me because he saw an easy mark. A young woman alone and lonely; pay her attention, she'll eat it up and try to please to get more." It embarrassed her to remember how she'd been back then.

"Sarah." Just her name on Luke's lips conveyed all his sympathy and understanding.

She wasn't that girl anymore. She stood up for herself now. "Yes, we started the company together, but early on, Sean just couldn't keep up. He found it a lot easier, and much more fun, to be the salesperson and drum up business. I'm not saying that isn't worth anything, but without all the work I did to back it up there would be no company today. And when that work made clients come to us and Sean didn't have to sell so hard to keep the orders coming in, well, he liked to travel and have the time of his life. At first, he made it seem like the trips were for business, and then he just simply took off whenever he wanted. He was spending money like it would never run out, and I was trying to keep the company afloat." She looked at Margaret with regret. "If you sent Sean money, I can tell you, it didn't go into the business. He probably spent it on a trip, or . . . something else."

Bridget had a question in her eyes that she didn't voice, and then her gaze reflected whatever revelation came to her mind. Still, she said nothing.

Sarah wondered if Bridget had always known more about the real Sean than she let on.

She didn't think Bridget would share, so she went on enlightening them to the realities of Sean's life. "We'd been approached by venture capitalists to take the company public. We were in the process of doing just that when I got pregnant with Nick. I didn't feel well during the pregnancy, so I frequently worked from home. The perfect setup. I could stay home with Jack and work while I was pregnant. It left a disconnect sometimes between me and what was happening in the office. Sean would bring the contracts home and I would do the work. What I didn't know was for every five or six programs I was completing, Sean was taking credit for four of them, so the venture capitalists would continue to have confidence in his ability to run the company and continue to give the company money. We needed the investors' money so we could get to the initial public offering of the stock. Sean felt once the stock went public the company would explode like all the other tech companies, and he'd be wealthy beyond belief."

Margaret nodded. "That would have happened if he hadn't died."

"No, it wouldn't have. When Sean died I sent you a check for what was left of his share of the business and our personal assets." She opened the one envelope that Margaret had opened and pulled out the letter she had sent and the check.

"I remember that check. It's for less than four hundred dollars. It was an insult that measly check was all that was left of Sean's inheritance and the company." Her anger built again. "It was you. Ever since he met you nothing was ever the same with him."

Sarah rolled her eyes. "That's for sure. I unwittingly allowed him to use me, so that he could live the life of a wealthy businessman, even if he had to steal it. And then he left me with a huge mess to clean up."

"What do you mean, steal it?" Margaret didn't understand the obvious.

"Luke, you're a lawyer. Spell it out for her, because if I say the words, she won't believe it."

Luke sighed, hung his head for a second, then raised it, and looked Sarah in the eye. "Are you trying to tell us that Sean was embezzling money from the company?"

"Exactly."

Luke swore. Margaret gasped. Bridget's eyes went wide.

"When he died there was barely enough money left to make payroll. I had to sell everything we owned to pay off debts he racked up. I sold the house, the six luxury cars Sean had bought, several expensive watches. You name it, and Sean had bought it. I sold it all and still there wasn't anything left. Then I had to go to the board of directors and investors and prove to them that the work Sean had claimed was his was actually mine. I had to convince them *I* could run the company and get them their money back."

"Why didn't you let it go?" Margaret asked, still not getting it.

Sarah frowned and tried to hold back the anger bubbling up in her gut, threatening to spew venomous words out of her mouth. "Let it go? I had over a hundred and twenty employees who depended on their jobs and the money from the company going public. I had a board of directors to answer to and the investors threatening legal action. I couldn't let all those people lose their money because of what Sean had done. I could have ended up in jail and the boys would have lost their father and me for a time.

"I'm not blameless in all this. I simply didn't care what Sean was doing anymore. I had turned my back on him and was trying to start a new company, so I could leave him."

Margaret gasped.

Bridget avoided eye contact with any of them, making Sarah think that Sean had told her something about Sarah divorcing him. Or a version of it that made Sean look like the wronged party.

Margaret shook her head. "I really didn't know how bad things were. Sean said he was unhappy in the marriage. But I never thought—"

"Yeah. You blamed me. And with all that going on, *you* demanded I keep the company for the boys. You made me promise. I didn't want you to know what Sean had become. I couldn't let anyone find out *all* he had done or everything would have fallen apart."

"If I'd known . . . I just wanted something of Sean's to survive."

"It did. The children are his legacy. As for the company, well, Luke pointed out what I'm always reluctant to admit. The company was never Sean's. It was always mine. I did the work. I made it a success."

She opened the envelope on top of the stack and pulled out the contents.

"I kept my promise to you. The company is thriving. Since you didn't cash the original check, I invested it in the company. When I was finally able to offer retirement accounts to the employees, I asked the investment specialist to diversify the money I had originally invested for you. This check represents your investment in Spencer Software and other investments I was advised to make. As for not keeping in touch with you, well, if you had opened this mail, you would know the answer to that. You were simply too angry to see the truth, and too stubborn to give me a chance."

Margaret touched her fingertips to her temple. "I . . . I don't know what to say."

Sarah wasn't done. "You blamed me for Sean's death. You were right."

Margaret's head snapped up. "What?"

Luke leaned forward. "Sarah, that's not true. Don't take that on when Sean is the one to blame."

"Maybe," she acknowledged, because Sean had turned his back on her, their boys, and his own conscience. "But I'm the one who, with the help of the chief of police, who was a personal friend of mine, covered up what really happened the night Sean died."

Bridget gnawed on her thumbnail, looking uncomfortable.

"Why would you cover up what happened?" The lawyer in Luke came out.

"I couldn't allow the press or public to find out the truth. The stock would plummet, everyone would lose their jobs and livelihoods, the boys would find out the ugly truth about Sean . . . I just couldn't let them find out . . ." She took a deep breath and finally said the truth out loud. "On the night Sean died he was racing home to confront me. Since he was never home, I left him a message that I was filing for divorce and taking the boys. Without me, there wouldn't be a company, and he'd go to jail for stealing the money. He was drunk when he crossed the center divider and hit an oncoming car. I settled with the accident victims out of court and paid for their silence." She looked at Luke. "The report you read said Sean lost control of the car on the rain-slicked road. That was only half true."

Luke's mouth drew into a tight line, but he gave her a nod to acknowledge he understood why she'd had to do it.

Margaret stared at her, wide-eyed and in shock.

Bridget bit her thumb too hard and winced.

Sarah wondered if they'd accept the truth, or hide behind denial and keep treating her like the enemy.

Luke already knew most of what she'd said, and a few other things he'd eluded to discovering during his investigation into Sean. She held those back from Margaret. Some things that would only disillusion Margaret more about the son she thought good and honorable.

Margaret needed to know, but—

A knock sounded a second before the library door opened and Jack peeked in. "Uh, Mom, Nick spilled the juice all over the kitchen counter and floor."

"Na-uh. Jack did it," Nick called out.

"Perfect. Another mess to clean up." Maybe she'd confessed enough for one day anyway. "I'm coming." She dropped the check and contents of the envelope on the desk and headed for the door.

She took Jack's hand and stepped out of the room, closing the door on any further questions and leaving a lot still unsaid.

Chapter Twenty-Six

Margaret stared at the papers spread before her and thought of all Sarah had revealed. Denial came first. "She's lying. This can't be true. Sean . . . He wasn't like what she said." Margaret tried to put it all together and understand what happened.

"People change. And sometimes they don't always show us who they really are. But Sarah . . . She's open and honest." Luke's admiration rang loud and clear in his words.

"It's just so unbelievable."

"Is it? Do you think Sean would tell you any of the things Sarah revealed?"

No. Sean never admitted wrongdoing, even when caught. She'd had to scold and punish him for lying often when he was young.

Luke drew her from the past back to the present she didn't want to face. "If Sean was the one doing all the work, how did she keep the company running and profitable after his death?"

"I . . . I don't know. I just assumed she hired people to do it. I'm trying to make sense of it." She wanted to believe her mischievous son had grown up into a good man, despite the lack of decent male role models in his life. She'd picked poorly when it came to the men in her life. And she feared Sean had learned the wrong lessons, and Bridget had learned to walk away when things got tough.

Margaret stood from her chair. It took a little extra effort these days, but she managed. She made her way around to the other side of the desk and sorted through the papers. A handwritten letter from Sarah, financial statements marked with the Spencer Software logo, and a bank statement that stunned her. She slowly sank into the chair behind her. "This can't be. She couldn't have turned three hundred and something dollars into this. It's not possible."

"How much is in the account?" Bridget asked, coming around the desk to look for herself.

Margaret had never told her about the envelopes. She held up the statement. "One million six hundred forty-two thousand eight hundred seventy-two dollars and fifty-seven cents." Margaret put her hand to her open mouth, disbelieving what she saw and admitted out loud, "I had no idea. For two years she's been sending me these envelopes, and I never opened them. I was too angry. I thought she just wanted to shove it in my face that the company was thriving while Sean missed it all. I never dreamed she sent me money."

"Just you?" Bridget asked.

Luke moved closer. "Seriously? You think you deserve a piece of what she built? It goes to her character and how much heart she has that she did anything for Margaret."

Bridget wound up, but Margaret cut her off before she spoke. "He's right. Sean left her with two little boys and not much else. She didn't have to protect his name and do this for me." Margaret thought about it and understood what Sarah intended. "She knows I'm always here to support you, Bridget. I'm sure she meant for me to help you with this money, just like I've done in the past."

Bridget picked up the statement and stared at it. "This changes everything. I could stay home with Sophia. We could move into a nicer place. She can go to college."

Margaret pressed her lips tight, not liking that Bridget wanted to do what Sean had done, live off the money Sarah made and not work for what she wanted. "Don't get ahead of yourself, dear. I've given you all I have up to now and I need to dig myself out of the hole I've put myself in."

"Yes, but . . ." Bridget pointed to the statement. "This is a lot of money."

"It is. And it's thanks to Sarah that our financial future is sound. So long as I spend wisely."

Luke jumped in. "In other words, Bridget, that money isn't your ticket to easy street and living off your mom the way Sean lived off Sarah's hard work."

"No one asked you," Bridget snapped.

"He's right," Margaret interjected, grateful Luke said exactly what she wanted to say. "I'll help, but I won't enable you to stop taking care of yourself and your responsibilities."

Bridget silently fumed.

Luke changed the subject. "Do you mind if I look at some of this?"

"Go ahead." She pushed the documents toward him. "Maybe you can tell me what these statements mean."

Margaret opened some of the other envelopes and sorted through their contents. Each one contained essentially the same items: the financial statements for both the company and her personal account that Sarah had set up, pictures of the boys and their artwork, and a letter from Sarah.

Tears gathered in her eyes and regret and self-loathing filled her gut as she read the lovely accounts of the boys' lives. "She talks about the boys' first day of school, fun things they like to do, and their accomplishments." She held the letters up. "It's like watching the boys grow up through Sarah's eyes and words."

Margaret felt terrible for ignoring all of this. Especially when Sarah had signed every letter the same, "Best wishes, Sarah." She didn't hold a grudge. She'd tried to build a bridge and Margaret had dynamited every attempt by ignoring Sarah and piling on the scorn.

None of the letters contained any hostility or said anything about what Sarah had gone through to get the company back on solid ground, or how hard she'd worked to make it a success.

Shame washed over Margaret.

Sarah had done everything to make sure Margaret knew about the boys and their lives. Margaret had been too stubborn to even open the envelopes.

She'd missed out on so much.

And it was all her fault.

Luke gave a half smile and held up the papers. "She's done an amazing job with this company. These statements show that when Sean died the company was out of money and headed toward crippling debt. After just six months, the company made a small profit. Quite an accomplishment based on what Sarah had to overcome. After the first year, she made a generous profit. She even gave out bonuses to the employees. Though she could have, and deserved it, she didn't take one. The second year she more than doubled the profits and the projections for this year are four, almost five times as much. She's projected to make almost two hundred and thirty-five million. That's the *profit*, Margaret. All of that is after she pays her staff and overhead."

Margaret couldn't think of a single thing to say.

Luke leaned in. "Did you know she does the major projects that have catapulted the company to success? She puts in a sixteen-to-twenty-hour day. While she has Camille to help with the house, cooking, and the kids, she takes the boys to school and picks them up herself. She goes back and forth between work and home with the boys at least four times a day and works well into the night and early morning. I listened in on a call between Sarah, her assistant Abby, and her team. They all adore her. And I've learned a lot more about Sarah these past weeks."

"Like what?" Bridget asked for the both of them.

"The company's main revenue comes from the lower-level programmers who do website design, database programming, and system security, but Sarah is a world-class programmer. She does the major projects that make them big bucks. She has as many as fifteen to twenty projects going at all times. She keeps to herself and rarely meets with clients directly because she doesn't have the time. She handles most of the business meetings by phone or has someone from her team attend in her place. The press is constantly trying to interview her because she has one of the hottest companies in Silicon Valley. They expect it to grow as fast, or faster, than many of the Internet companies. She refuses all requests for interviews and sends the co-CEO Evan to do public relations and press conferences. She doesn't date. Ever. She works seven days a week more often than not. She only takes one week of vacation and goes camping with the boys. For that one week, she turns off her cell phone, doesn't answer email, and spends the entire seven days with the boys.

"Did you know she also owns a ranch not far from here? She has the best stock of quarter horses in the state. I know because I tried to buy some from her a while back, but she wouldn't sell to me. She only sells to people she knows run a good ranch. She didn't know my ranch, or me, so she wouldn't sell and put her animals in possible jeopardy. She has integrity. She's not out to make a quick buck. She's mentioned that she has another business. I don't know what it is, but if it's as profitable as the other two she runs, I'd imagine she could quit it all tomorrow and never need money for the rest of her life, or those boys' lives."

Luke went on, "She's brilliant, you know. She just finished a huge project for the company. The biggest one she's ever accomplished. She did the majority of the work on her own. Her staff cheered her over the phone when they found out she'd accomplished something no one else has done. She thanked them for their hard work and told them it had been a team effort. They balked at the notion that they had done anything. They gave her full credit and still she made them feel as if she couldn't have done it without them. In my book, that alone says a lot about her character. You've completely misjudged her, and I've been guilty of the same thing."

Luke placed his hands on his hips. "She works harder than anyone I know and loves her kids bigger and better than a lot of parents I've seen. Sean didn't appreciate her. He didn't love her the way she deserves to be loved. I won't make the same mistake. I'm always holding back and pushing women away. All I want to do now is hold on to her."

Margaret had never heard Luke speak so passionately about anything or anyone. "She does all that and still agreed to take the time to come here. No wonder she collapsed the other day." Margaret felt terrible for the way she'd treated Sarah. She never gave Sarah a chance. She'd added on to Sarah's load by leaving it to her to clean her room upstairs, cook most nights, and make the yard safe for the boys to play.

"I've watched her working," she continued. "She's so intent and focused when she's at the computer. She sometimes has two or three going at the same time. She moves back and forth between them. It's funny, though. I always thought she didn't pay enough attention to the boys, but whenever they interrupt her, she stops whatever she's doing and gives them her full attention. She'll stop everything to get them a glass of water or play a game. And then, when she can, she goes back to doing her work with the same focus and intensity she had before. I didn't want to admit it to her, but I thought she was doing a good job with the boys. I don't know what she does on those computers, but I guess she really is good at her job."

She should have set aside her anger and talked to Sarah. At the very least, her grandsons deserved better than for her to just drop out of their lives. But she'd grieved deep and hard for Sean. Her only son. She'd had such high hopes for him, and it killed her to see his life cut short when he'd been on the precipice of achieving so much.

Or so she had thought.

She leaned on her elbows on the desk and held the sides of her face in her hands and stared at Luke. "I don't know what to do about all this. I've been awful to her. Cruel, even, blaming her for everything when Sean treated her terribly." She picked up several papers. "Did you see these letters and pictures? She wrote and told me about the boys every month. I didn't cash the check and she took a little bit of money and turned it into a fortune. She didn't have to do all of that. I certainly didn't deserve it after the way I treated her."

Luke gave Margaret's hand a soft squeeze. "I can't believe someone like her exists. I'm in love with her. I'm going to marry her."

Margaret gasped. She had no idea they'd grown so close in such a short time.

"You can't be serious?" Bridget's whole body went rigid. "She gets the company, all the money, and marries a rich guy?"

"You're looking a little green with envy, dear." Margaret gave

Bridget a look Bridget knew all too well. Margaret spent a lot of Bridget's youth reminding her that life wasn't a competition.

She focused on Luke. "I'm sorry I didn't see her the way you do. I guess congratulations are in order. And I really do wish you both all the happiness in the world."

Luke smiled. "She doesn't know I want to marry her yet. I've asked her to stay here with me. We haven't worked everything out, but I hope we will before it's time for her to head home."

"Nothing would make me happier than to have the boys nearby. I really want a chance to make things right. But how am I going to do that?"

"Tell her you're sorry. Tell her your feelings have changed. She'll appreciate your making the effort. Thank her for everything she's done. I've discovered that she appreciates the simple, heart-felt things the most. I'm trying to do the same because of her."

"I'll talk to her. Maybe I can do something nice, like watch the boys so you two can go on a proper date."

Luke's eyes brightened with excitement. He really had it bad. "I'd appreciate it. I'm sure she will, too."

"So she gets everything she wants," Bridget said, still smarting from not receiving her own fat check.

"Maybe if you worked as hard as she does, you'd have every-thing you want," Margaret suggested.

Bridget threw up her hands and let them fall. "Seriously, now you're comparing *me* to *her*. I'm out of here."

"Why did you stop by?" Margaret hadn't been expecting her.

"To talk to my mom about my sucky life, but you've made it perfectly clear you have no sympathy for my situation and I'll never live up to the amazing Sarah, who is so smart and kind and generous. Never mind what Sean thought about how she treated him." Bridget stormed out.

Margaret took a second to absorb her comments. "She still misses Sean. And her divorce was just finalized. She's in a bad place."

"And looking for an easy way out. I get it, but none of that excuses her for thinking Sarah owes her something or that she can take what Sarah gave you as a gift. She can't blame Sarah for everything and hold Sean harmless."

"I think, like me, she needs time to process all this." Margaret planted her hands on the desk and pushed herself up. "Let's go find Sarah, so I can start making things right." They headed to the door.

Luke let her walk out ahead of him.

They didn't find Sarah or the boys in the main part of the house. Luke glanced out the front door window. "Her car is gone."

"She just left." Margaret worried she wouldn't come back.

"I'll head back to the ranch. Maybe she needed a break and the boys needed to get some energy out so she took them for a ride." Luke headed down the steps and pulled something off his truck window, held it up, then read it out loud.

"Luke,

Took the boys grocery shopping. Invite Margaret to join us for Sunday dinner at your place. See you soon.

> *Love, Sarah"*

A half smile split Luke's face. "I invited her to meet my family."

"Don't you think you're moving a little fast?" Despite everything she'd just learned about Sarah and what happened with Sean and the company, she still wanted to look out for Luke.

"I know what I want, and it's her. Come to dinner. Watch her with me and my family. You'll see what I see."

Margaret hesitated because she wasn't sure Sarah really wanted her there or if she'd invited her just to be polite. "I don't want to intrude."

"You're not. My parents would love to see you again."

"You're this sure about her?"

"Yes." Luke sounded too sure for her to doubt him. "Please, Margaret. Join us. See what I see, so you and Sarah can truly move on and be there for the boys together."

"I'd love to."

"Great. I'm headed home to check on the horses."

"Thank you, Luke. I feel like without you, I'd have never known the truth. Sarah and I would have gone on as we always have, enduring each other. I wouldn't know about the money either. I was about to lose this house, and that would have just killed me. I love this place."

And because of Sarah, someone she'd blamed for everything and treated terribly, she got to keep her home. She had financial security, the boys were back in her life, and given time, she had someone she could count on to be there for her if she needed them.

But there was a lot of healing left to do.

"It'll be nice for all of us to be living close together someday soon." Luke waved his goodbye, climbed into his truck, and drove off with a quick honk.

Margaret's head spun with all the new information and the possibility that Luke and Sarah would live next door if everything worked out with them.

She needed time to come to terms with Sean's other life. Because it wasn't the one she thought he'd been living. She needed to reconcile what she'd believed of Sarah and the reality that all this time she'd been reaching out and helping.

Margaret wanted to believe it was to make up for the things

Sarah had done to Sean, but if that were true, she'd have stopped long ago when her attempts were ignored and outright dismissed. Yet Sarah had persisted with her notes.

Sarah hadn't turned her back on Margaret the way she'd done to Sarah. She'd stepped up to be the family Margaret didn't deserve and Sean didn't know how to be, because she hadn't taught him well.

Maybe she hadn't been the best mother. But she'd taught Sean better than stealing and using people to get what you want.

Sarah hadn't told her everything. She'd talked about what happened with the business and how Sean's accident—not so much an accident if he was driving drunk—affected the business.

She hadn't spoken about how his drinking impacted their marriage, or how his traveling strained things. She hinted about Sean being absent a lot. But had Sarah pushed Sean away? Why didn't he want to be home with his wife and children? What really went wrong in the marriage? Margaret knew all too well how easy it was for one to collapse.

Chapter Twenty-Seven

S arah walked into the kitchen loaded down with groceries. The boys headed upstairs, grumpy they didn't get to go back to Luke's this afternoon because she had to work.

Margaret walked into the kitchen, her face drawn in worry lines. "You're back."

Sarah tucked the vegetables and meat into the refrigerator. "I picked up some of that vanilla bean ice cream you like." As peace offerings went, ice cream was a good one in her mind.

"Thank you."

Sarah turned to face Margaret, surprised by the lack of hostility and taken aback by the gratitude. "You're welcome. You should sit down. Rest."

Margaret's whole body slumped with fatigue. "I admit, my arthritis and our earlier . . . reckoning kind of took everything out of me."

"I hoped to find an easier way for us to . . . leave the past behind."

"I'm still trying to not feel the way I've felt about you and reconcile who I thought Sean was with the man you describe."

"Take your time. I know it was a lot to take in. I'm sure you'll have questions. In the meantime, know that I'm not here for any other reason than to build a relationship between you and the boys."

"I appreciate that. And I should have told you how happy it made me that you brought them."

"I've loved watching them with you, and you with them."

"I spend a lot of time with Sophia. I feel like I really know her. Now, I feel as if I know the boys, too."

"That's all I want for them and you. And to show my goodwill, I took care of a couple of things for you. On the way to the store, I called the gardening service I used when I arrived. They'll be by tomorrow to do the yard, then routine cleaning once a week. I also found a reputable housekeeping service. They'll be here every other Wednesday."

"Why? After the way I've treated you, why are you helping me?"

"Because you didn't know. Because you loved Sean and grieved him the way I couldn't but a mother should."

Sarah sighed with that difficult admission, letting her battered heart settle after letting go of that hard truth. "Because now that you know, I hope we can be the family Jack and Nick deserve." Holding on to the secrets had become a burden. Without them hanging over her head, she felt lighter. Her heart didn't feel so heavy.

Except she hadn't told Margaret everything. "There's still more to tell about Sean."

Margaret held Sarah's forearm. "I think I've heard all I can take for one day." Margaret squeezed her arm, released her, and took a seat at the breakfast table. "It's hard to hear that my son turned into my ex-husband. And I became the dreadful mother-in-law, blaming you for all of Sean's unhappiness. I know better than anyone it takes two people to hold a marriage together. One can't do it alone. And only hearing one side of the story means you don't know the whole truth."

"He's your son. You took his side. I don't blame you for that."

"You should. I deserve it." Margaret held Sarah's gaze. "I wish you'd said something sooner."

In her grief, Margaret hadn't been ready to hear it.

And Sarah had been so engrossed in the boys' grief, the trouble with the company, and her own anger and resentment, she wouldn't have been able to be kind in the way she told Margaret.

Not that today went great, but time and distance had at least allowed Margaret to hear what she had to say. "Sean made sure you didn't know what was really going on. Away from here, and you, he didn't care what anyone thought about his actions. He flaunted his bad behavior. Truthfully, I just wanted out before the boys really started to understand what was happening."

"And you made sure they only saw the good in him."

"I didn't want to break their hearts, and then Sean died, and I just figured they didn't need to know everything."

"And that's also why you didn't say anything to me."

Sarah appreciated that Margaret understood. "Why shatter your image of him? I really had no idea he'd been telling you and Bridget a completely different story than the one we lived until it was too late. I hoped, over time—"

"I'd come to my senses and move forward for the boys' sake."

"I understood your grief. I knew most of your anger came from the fact that Sean died so young and would miss so much of the boys' lives and you wanted to blame someone for that."

"I wanted there to be a good reason for what happened. But the truth is, his death was senseless and preventable. He shouldn't have gotten behind the wheel in his condition." Margaret's eyes narrowed. "What really upset him that night? The divorce? Not being with his children all the time? Or you leaving the company?"

"I think you know the answer to that." Sarah didn't want to say it out loud.

"Did he ever love you and the boys?" A spark of hope lit Margaret's eyes.

Sarah obliterated it with another jagged piece of the puzzle. "Sean found someone else to love."

Margaret stared out the window for a long moment. A single tear rolled down her pale cheek. "I see."

"Sean did some terrible things, but he wasn't all bad." While Sarah still had a lot of unresolved anger, even if she had done her best to move on, she defended Sean for his mother's sake. As unfair as her mother-in-law had been, she knew it was a lot for the older woman to take in.

"Thank you for saying that, but I see now that I didn't really know him. I guess that happens when your children grow up and have lives of their own. I wish we'd been closer." Margaret's head tilted. "Then again, if I'd known what he was doing, we'd have probably been at odds when he died because I wouldn't have kept my opinion to myself about his behavior."

"I know it's difficult right now, but I hope you'll find a way to hold on to the good memories and not let what you know now overshadow them."

"Have you been able to do that?"

"Depends on the day," Sarah admitted.

"That's about as much truth as I can take right now." Margaret pushed up from her seat with a wince.

"Margaret, now that you know about the money, call your doctor. Get checked out and make your health a priority. If you're going to have lots more visits with the boys, you'll need your stamina." Sarah smiled, hoping it eased Margaret's heart and mind to know that she would make an effort to bring the boys more often.

"I'll go call right now. Then I think I'll take a little time to sort out my thoughts and feelings and . . ." Margaret stared out the window again. "I don't know what to do with all this."

"Try to work on letting it go," Sarah suggested. "Don't pour your energy into something that can't be changed. Focus on your relationship with the boys. They're the best part of Sean. They're here. They need you."

"I imagine they helped you get through everything after Sean passed."

"They are the most important thing in my life."

"And what about Luke? He said he asked you to move in with him."

"That's a bit complicated." But Sarah's heart leaped at the thought of being with Luke all the time. They just needed to figure out the logistics because she and the boys loved the home they'd made. It was close to her work. And while she could work remotely sometimes, she was still needed in the office.

They'd have to figure out a compromise between here and there.

"Maybe it's time to make your life less complicated and enjoy the happiness you've found with him." A lopsided frown tilted Margaret's lips. "You probably don't want advice from me, but I wish I'd appreciated more the good things the men in my life brought me than always focusing on inconsequential things I used to drive a wedge between us. I know you've put everything into the business, but don't let work keep you from having what you really want. What really matters."

Sarah felt that way when she and Sean were together. He wanted her to work harder. She wanted to be a mother and make a happy family with him. Yes, she got a great deal of satisfaction from her job, but she found deeper meaning in being a mom. It filled that hole in her, her childhood had left after everyone related to her either abandoned, betrayed, or died on her.

Margaret pressed her lips tight. "If Luke makes you happy, then I'm happy for both of you. For what it's worth."

Sarah wanted to say it didn't matter. But it touched her that after all the anger and resentment Margaret heaped on her, she now wished her well.

"Thank you, Margaret." She hesitated, then spoke her fear. "I hope Luke's family feels the same."

Margaret's gaze fell to the floor, then met hers again. "They're going to love you because they'll see what I denied all this time. You're strong and resilient, a good mother, kind, caring, and thoughtful. And when you love, you make the time to show that to the people in your life." Margaret surprised her with a hug. "Thank you for taking care of me. I appreciate it more than I can say."

Sarah gently squeezed Margaret. "I only did what I thought was right."

Margaret stepped back and grinned. "Even if you didn't think I deserved it."

Sarah tilted her head. "Well, you didn't. But I hoped, someday, we'd end up here."

"For the boys," Margaret added. "I'm sorry it took me so long to do right by them. And you."

"You needed to grieve."

"And I'll be doing it again now that I know about Sean. It's hard to let go of the life I thought he was living and the one I wanted for him."

Sarah understood that all too well, because while she'd been upset that her children lost their father, she'd grieved harder for the loss of the dream life she thought she'd have with Sean and their boys than she had for the man himself.

"Go. Rest. There's plenty of time before dinner."

"And let me guess, you have some work to do." This time there was no reproach in Margaret's words, just understanding that Sarah had responsibilities.

"Yes."

Margaret nodded in acknowledgment and headed out of the kitchen for her room.

Sarah put away the last of the groceries, checked on the boys, and settled in front of her laptops to get some work done.

It took her a few minutes to settle in. She worried about what Bridget would have to say and feel about the brother she also didn't see for who he really was and adored just as much as Margaret had.

Disillusioning them made her heart ache.

She blamed Sean for yet another thing he left for her to clean up.

Her phone dinged with a text. She sighed and picked it up, bracing for yet another request for her to do something.

LUKE: Miss you. Wish you were here.

LUKE: Do you want double chocolate cake or cheesecake for dessert at Sunday dinner?

SARAH: Miss you too and both! Duh! ☺

LUKE: All I want is you.

SARAH: Sweet!!! ♥

And just like that, her whole mood changed and her heart filled with love and anticipation. She couldn't wait to see Luke. And meeting his family seemed like a small thing if it meant she and Luke took another step toward her dream of a future she'd thought would never look like what she wanted but now felt very close to coming true.

Chapter Twenty-Eight

S arah watched from the back patio as the boys batted the shut- tlecock back and forth over the net of the new badminton set she set up after lunch. She'd put out a few snacks and a pitcher of lemonade. Her stomach tied itself in a knot as she waited for Bridget and Sophia to arrive.

Sarah remembered the looks of anger and disappointment in Bridget's eyes yesterday when Sarah had told the truth about Sean.

And, yet, for some reason she couldn't stop thinking that Bridget knew far more than Margaret ever did about Sean's real life. If that were the case, why did she stay silent all these years as well?

Margaret was still processing her grief, but they'd had a good talk yesterday. They were moving toward putting the past behind them. Sarah wanted to try to do the same with Bridget.

"Hi, Aunt Sarah." Sophia rushed down the back steps to the patio.

Bridget followed, looking anything but ready to put the past to rest, judging by her narrowed gaze and the firm line of her lips.

"Hi. Do you want a snack?"

"I'm okay." Sophia watched Jack launch the shuttlecock into a bush. "I'll help him get that out."

"There's a spare racket in the box next to the net."

Sophia ran to help Jack retrieve the shuttlecock.

Sarah stared up at Bridget from her seat. "We need to talk."

Bridget gripped the back of the chair she stood behind. "I don't really have anything to say to you."

"Are you sure? Because the expressions on your face yesterday said a lot."

Bridget pulled out the chair and poured a glass of lemonade. Her hands trembled, giving away how unsettled this visit made her. "I was stunned to find out all those things about Sean and that you'd made all that money for Mom." But not for her.

Sarah heard that last part loud and clear, even if Bridget was too chicken to say it. She thought she deserved a piece of the money Sarah had made. Bridget had received an inheritance from her father just like Sean. Bridget and her husband had bought a house and started the construction business. Then they'd had some lean years when the economy tanked and no one was building new construction. The money had run out, which must have put a terrible strain on their marriage.

Sarah could relate.

"I did that for her because she lost her son."

"You know, I lost my brother. As for Mom, you wanted to buy your way out of your guilt for what you'd done."

"What did I do?" She really wanted to know what Bridget thought happened.

"He gave you everything you wanted and still it wasn't enough."

"What did he *give* me that I wanted other than the boys?"

Bridget didn't look so sure of herself anymore. "The company."

"Sean wanted to start that. We both had a dozen very lucrative offers from the government and private sector after college. We would have made a ton more money than we did those early years when we started the business. I would have worked less and been happy to have a normal work and home life."

Bridget tried again. "Sean wanted to build something."

"He wanted to be rich. There's a difference. Building something takes a lot of hard work. Granted, in the beginning, he tried, but he much preferred going out with clients and being the big shot."

"That's because he wanted to get away from you."

"You seem to think I was some shrew to him. Is that really the kind of person you think I am? You saw us together more than Margaret did when we first got married. Did it seem like I was nagging him, or pushing him, or . . . I don't know, just being a bitch?"

Bridget pressed her lips tight. "No," she reluctantly admitted. "I used to think you tried too hard for his attention and took too much from him."

Sarah couldn't believe she'd say that after all the hostility. "I wanted to make him happy. I wanted to keep the peace. I wanted us to be partners and connect like we did when we first met and got married. He swept me off my feet. I wanted to know where that Sean had gone. So yeah, after a while, I stopped taking it. I stopped pretending that he didn't really mean the awful things he said to me or the way he at other times ignored me. I thought things would get better. But they didn't. It got worse."

Bridget stared off into the distance. "You snipe at each other because of frustrations and resentments. You think, He knows I don't really mean it. I don't think he really means it. But it adds up and builds until you look at him and he looks at you and you've turned into someone you don't want to be and neither of you knows how to fix it."

Sarah reached across the table and put her hand over Bridget's, feeling all the wild emotions she saw in Bridget's eyes. Anger. Regret. Guilt. Confusion. "And it all falls apart."

Bridget nodded, slipped her hand free, and crossed her arms over her chest. "At first, I believed all the things Sean said about you. I hated you for treating him so badly and making him unhappy. The more I sympathized, the more he poured it on, until . . ."

"You couldn't believe I was actually that awful?"

"You were always so kind and even-tempered. You were always nice to me. You always seemed interested in our life. I remember the way you were with Sophia. You lit up around her. You talked to her like she was a mini-adult and played with her like you relished the opportunity to be a child, too."

"I never really had a childhood."

"I know. So I wondered why you'd sabotage your relationship with Sean when it always seemed like you wanted to please him. It didn't make sense. I thought maybe you'd found someone else and Sean was too prideful to admit it. But then he'd talk about the things he was doing, trips he'd taken. He'd slip and say *we* did this or that."

"And you knew I wasn't the other half of that 'we.'"

"I didn't want to believe it. I never thought he was that guy. And you were pregnant with Jack . . ."

Sarah sat up. "Wait. What?"

Bridget's eyes went wide. "You didn't know."

Sarah knew about Trish from their office. She didn't know about anyone before Trish and at this point she didn't want to know any details. Her chest went tight. A new wave of anger and hurt washed through her. "I guess I only knew about one of his affairs."

Bridget sighed. "I'm so sorry."

"Do you know how many?" In a way, Sarah didn't want to know, but it was better to learn it all now and move on.

"When I asked, he brushed off those 'we's.' He'd say he meant a colleague who attended a meeting with him. A client he took out to impress. But I knew he was lying even as I tried to convince myself he'd never do that." Bridget twisted her lips into a frustrated frown. "I don't know exactly how many. I know it went on both times you were pregnant. And while it's completely unfair of me, I blamed you, thinking that you used your pregnancy to distance yourself physically from him during that time. I know some women don't like sex when they're pregnant. Some men aren't into it either. It's your choice. But Sean told me he resented the months you were pregnant because you two didn't . . . And he felt abandoned."

Sarah fumed. "Well, didn't he play that up for sympathy with you? Not that it's any of your business, but I never denied Sean during that time with Jack. Leading up to getting pregnant with Nick, we barely touched each other, except when we were yet again trying to put the marriage back together. Which usually meant he needed me to complete some huge project to bring in a big payday. Once I was pregnant, Sean stopped pretending to try to hold the marriage together at all and I knew he'd moved on."

"I knew it was the end for me and Rob when I started noticing the way his eyes wandered to other women when we were out. He didn't see me as the woman he wanted anymore and it seemed no matter how hard we tried to get back to that place where we loved and wanted each other, we just couldn't get there. So before one of those lingering looks turned into something more, I asked *him* for the divorce. I couldn't stand to think he'd betray me like that and just thinking that maybe he would tore me to shreds. I can't imagine how you felt knowing Sean was with someone else."

"It killed everything between us. I was crushed and devastated even though I saw it coming. I grieved for what I thought we had and what I wished we could have been. I was angry and hurt, but that was nothing compared to the fury and anguish I felt when he started seeing someone from the office openly."

Bridget sat quietly for a moment, then whispered, "Trish."

"Yes," Sarah confirmed. "I take it Sean didn't hide her from you either."

"I only speculated about the others even if the evidence was pretty clear. But with Trish . . . Sean talked about how you'd pushed him into her arms. How you were happy to be rid of him but refused to give him a divorce without a huge payout."

"There was nothing left to take at that point."

Bridget nodded. "I know that now." She stared out at the kids for a long moment, and without looking at Sarah asked, "Do you know what happened to her after the accident?"

Sarah held her breath. "What do you mean?"

Bridget finally looked at her. "I know she was in the car."

"And still you blamed me for Sean's death when you knew he had a mistress and had practically left us?"

"He knew how to shift the blame. I'm ashamed to say, I fell for most of it."

"And you never said anything to your mom about what you knew about Sean?"

"I didn't think she'd want to know that her son turned out to be a serial cheater." Bridget pressed her lips tight again. "And I blamed you. If he wasn't happy at home, that was your fault." She held up her hand. "I know. Blame the wife when the husband is the one doing the cheating . . . Not fair. I get it. But he was my brother."

Sarah sucked in a breath and tried to contain her anger.

Bridget drew back one side of her mouth. "I have a lot of pent-up anger—about Sean, Rob, that my life sucks. I took it mostly out on you because . . ." She threw up her hands and let them fall. "It was easier to be mad at you when it came to Sean." Bridget eyed her. "And maybe I was a little jealous when you showed up in a new SUV, looking like that . . ." Bridget waved her hand back and forth over the table at her. "Do you have to be so pretty? And nice? And not a bitch? I'm pretty sure Sophia is hoping you'll adopt her. Seriously, she never shuts up about you."

Bridget didn't relax as she continued. She grew tenser and leaned forward. "Anyway . . . what do you know about the baby?"

Sarah's heart stopped. "What baby?"

Bridget tilted her head. "Come on. You know. You have to know."

Sarah found it hard to breathe. "I don't know." But now she did.

"Trish's baby," Luke said, walking up beside them.

Bridget's gaze fell.

Sarah turned to Luke. "You knew about this and you didn't say anything?"

Luke held up both hands. "I thought you knew. When you found out I investigated Sean—"

"You *what*?" Bridget glared at Luke.

"Your mother asked me to investigate Sarah. To get a better understanding, I also looked into Sean's life." Luke turned his focus to Sarah. "When we talked about it, I told you I knew about him. You assumed I meant the car accident and the affair with Trish."

"And others, according to Bridget," she added.

"Bastard," Luke spat out. "No, I hadn't discovered those. But I assumed that because you knew about the affair with Trish, you also knew about the baby. Today, when you said you paid off the accident victims after Sean's crash, I assumed you paid off Trish not only to keep her quiet about the affair, but also to compensate her for the baby she was carrying but Sean wasn't here to support."

Sarah didn't know what to say or how to feel about any of this. "You and I need to work on our communication."

Luke looked contrite. "I'm sorry. I wanted to leave Sean in the past and focus on *our* future. I didn't want to dredge all this up with you because I thought you didn't want to be reminded about Sean's betrayal and the child that came from it."

Sarah sighed out her frustration and tried to think. "That child is my sons' sibling."

"Their sister," Bridget supplied. "Jamie. And I didn't know for sure she belonged to Sean." She turned to Luke. "Are you sure she's his?"

Luke tucked his hands in his pockets. "When my investigator told me about her, I had him pull the birth certificate. Sean is listed as the father. I suppose she could have lied about that, but given her behavior—not asking for anything more—that wouldn't make sense. It just doesn't seem like she's after money."

"Why didn't she ever come to me and tell me?" Sarah didn't understand why Trish would hide it.

"I wouldn't want to face my lover's wife and tell her that I had her dead husband's child." *Okay, so Bridget had a point.*

Sarah needed to get her brain wrapped around this. If Sarah didn't know about the baby, and Luke only found out through an investigation . . . She held Bridget's gaze. "How did you know about the baby?"

"After the accident, I wondered about Trish. She loved Sean. I thought that maybe I'd reach out to her. I kinda . . . you might say . . . I stalked her on Facebook." Bridget glanced away, then back at Sarah. "She should really keep her stuff private instead of public. Someone in the tech industry should know that."

"Everyone should know that by now," Sarah shot back.

Bridget frowned. "She posted pictures of a baby shower, and soon after, pictures of Jamie. She's beautiful. Looks like Sean. And Nick," she added. "I thought I was sure about Jamie being Sean's, but then Trish got engaged and posted pics of the guy, the ring, and the proposal. I couldn't ignore Jamie's resemblance to Sean, but I didn't want to be wrong, so I watched the Facebook account but never reached out to her."

"That's your niece." Sarah thought of something else. "Does Margaret know?"

Bridget shook her head. "Since I didn't know for sure, I didn't say anything and risk being wrong. It would devastate her to think Sean left behind another grandchild, only to find out Jamie wasn't his."

Sarah guessed another reason. "You didn't want her to find out that maybe I had a reason to be angry with him."

Bridget sat back. "I said I was sorry."

Luke took the seat beside Sarah and took her hand. "Sean is the one who should be sorry."

Sarah's heart felt heavy again. She didn't know what to do with this information now that she had it. She stared at the boys playing so happily with their cousin, laughing and running around and just having fun. Without their sister.

"Damnit."

Luke squeezed her hand, somehow understanding her reluctant decision. "I'll make the call as a lawyer for the family. I can let Trish know that you and Bridget have both discovered that Jamie is Sean's daughter and that you're interested in . . ." Luke waited for her to fill in the blank.

It took her a minute to define what she wanted, because having any kind of relationship with Sean's mistress never crossed her mind. "We are interested in developing a relationship between Jamie and her brothers, as well as visitation with Sean's family."

Luke squeezed her hand again. "Very well put." He touched her chin to get her to look at him. "And very big of you, Sarah. I know this can't be easy. I wish I'd been more specific—"

She shook her head. "For all of Sean's secrets that I kept, I always knew there were more that I didn't know."

"I'm sure you didn't want to know this," Bridget said.

"No. But now that I do, and if Trish agrees, I think it's best if the children know they're siblings. How I'm going to explain that to the boys . . . I don't know. But I will."

Luke brushed his hand down her hair. "I'll call her and see if she's willing to talk about letting the kids see each other."

"Maybe we could start with a playdate where she drops Jamie off and picks her up."

Bridget eyed her. "Do you really think she's going to be comfortable just leaving her kid with you?"

"Do you think she wants to spend time with me and give me the opportunity to tell her what I really think of her?" Sarah would probably hold it together and swallow all the vile things she'd like to spew at Trish, for the kids' sakes, but it would be tempting to lash out.

But lashing out would make it difficult if not impossible for Jack and Nick to get to know Jamie.

If Sarah could visit the woman who hated her most in the world for six weeks and make it work, she could do a couple of hours on a playdate with her husband's mistress.

She'd make sure to have a bottle of wine chilled for after the boys went to bed and she drank her feelings. Maybe a visit with Trish would require brownies, too.

Luke kissed the back of her hand and stood to make the call.

Sarah thought better of it. "You should send an email." She sighed, not liking what she was going to say. "If it were me, I'd rather get an email so I could take some time to think about it and process. She'll probably panic at first that we know about Jamie and think that we're going to gang up on her, or something." She hated that she was probably right and going out of her way to make this a little easier on Trish.

Luke kissed her and stared deep into her eyes. "You always find a new way to amaze me."

She scrunched her mouth into an angry pout, even if her mad was fading. "I'm still peeved about this misunderstanding."

"Are you really mad at me, or Sean for making you have to bring the boys and Jamie together?"

She gave him a mock disgruntled frown that only made Luke grin. "Why do you have to be so smart?"

"You love that about me."

She loved everything about him. She playfully shoved his shoulder. "Just do your lawyer thing without being so smug."

He smiled, and she couldn't help but smile back.

Bridget stared from her to Luke and back. "You two are really great together."

Luke stopped tapping at his phone and looked up at Bridget. "Are you two good now?"

Bridget eyed her. "I hope so."

"We are," Sarah confirmed.

If Bridget could admit that she'd been wrong and believed some of Sean's lies, Sarah could forgive.

Luke stepped away to compose the email on his phone.

"I hope things will be different for all of us now." Sarah glanced back at the boys, knowing that if Trish agreed to bring Jamie and the boys together, everything would be different again.

She'd hoped to never see or hear about Trish. She didn't know if she was ready to bring Trish back into her life and what that would look like now.

Maybe Trish would refuse to speak to her about Jamie.

Maybe she'd agree to some kind of a relationship.

No matter what, the boys had family out there and she wouldn't deny them the chance to know Jamie, whether it was in person or by some other means.

Maybe she'd have to start stalking Trish's Facebook page herself to make it happen.

Luke took his seat again. "I sent it and included your cell number. Now we wait."

Chapter Twenty-Nine

*L*uke had asked his parents and brother to arrive early, so he could tell them about Sarah and the boys. They were settled in the living room watching his niece, Emma, play.

Luke handed his mom a glass of wine—the others already had a drink—and he took a seat facing all of them.

His mom studied him for a moment. "Spill it, Luke. What's wrong?"

"Missing the office?" his dad asked. "Because we're happy to have you back full-time."

Jason shook his head. "Speak for yourself." Of course he was teasing. They'd always worked well together.

"It's not about work. And nothing's wrong," Luke assured his mom. "It's just . . . I found her."

"Who?" his dad asked.

His mom leaned forward. "Do you mean . . ."

The smile came so easily when he thought about Sarah. "Her name is Sarah. She's got two amazing sons."

"Wait a second." Jason leaned forward as well. "Are you saying you're actually serious about someone?"

Michelle, Jason's wife, planted her elbow on her knee and her chin in her hand and smiled. "Oh, I hope so. It's been so long since someone held on to Luke for more than a minute."

"Hey!" Luke said, knowing full well Michelle spoke the truth. He turned to his mom, knowing she'd understand. "I'm in love with her. She doesn't know it yet, but I'm going to marry her."

Shocked silence filled the room.

Emma broke the silence by bashing a plastic purple hippo on the coffee table over and over again. Luke wondered if she'd be disappointed when she found out there were no purple hippos in the world.

"You're serious?" Jason asked.

"Yes."

His father looked surprised. "How long have you known her?"

"Five weeks." It seemed like a lot longer.

His mom continued to study him, so he told her the truth he still couldn't wrap his brain around. "I saw her, and I wanted her, and somehow, despite my brash questions and annoying her because I thought she was something she could never be, she fell for me."

His mother gave him a knowing grin, and he went on, "She's amazingly smart and kind and devastatingly beautiful and honest and . . . incredible."

His mom put her hand on his knee. "She makes you happy."

"In a way I've never felt. When she and the boys are here, it's like . . . everything is perfect. The way I dreamed it could be. And every dream I ever had for my life and this place includes her. Them," he clarified.

"Tell us everything," his dad coaxed.

His family sat focused on him, open to everything he told them about how he and Sarah had met, Jack and Nick, her work and the company she ran, everything he could think of about her.

Jason sat back, eyeing Luke. "I have to say, I've never seen you this excited about a woman. You look happy and content for the first time in a long time. I can't wait to meet the woman who finally tamed you. Will she be here soon?"

"Any minute."

His mom took a sip of her wine, then looked at Luke over her glass. "I'm not surprised you're so eager to move things along. Jason and Michelle fell head over heels right out of college."

"He marched me down the aisle six months after I met him." Michelle leaned over and kissed Jason, so much love in her eyes.

Sarah looked at Luke like that. He hoped she saw it in him when he looked at her.

"Love at first sight seems to run in the Thompson family. Your grandfather met and married your grandmother in a matter of five months. Dad and I met and married in eight months. When a Thompson man falls in love, it's quick and deep. And it lasts," his mom added, looking at his dad.

Luke had seen the love between them all these years and didn't want to settle for less. That's why he'd waited for Sarah to come into his life. "It just hit me and all I wanted to do was convince her to stay."

"Stay?" His dad raised a brow.

"She's brought the boys to visit Margaret for six weeks. That time is almost up and then she's got to go back to Silicon Valley and run her company. But I'm hoping we can find a way to blend our lives that works for both of us. She's a programmer so some of her work can be done remotely, which I hope she'll do so she doesn't have to commute into work every day. I want her to find a balance that works for her. Right now, she's inundated with work and puts in sixteen to twenty hours a day, every day. But she's promised to cut back and work more reasonable hours once she hires more help."

"Wow," Michelle said. "How does she do it with two kids?"

"I have no idea. The last time I saw her working, she had six computers going, a dozen files, and several cell phones handy. When she was here resting, her cell phone rang practically every two minutes. All I wanted to do was tell everyone to leave her alone and wrap her in my arms and let her have the peace and quiet she needed."

"You really do love her, don't you, son?"

"Yes, Mom. She's it for me. I can't imagine living the rest of my life without her and the boys. They're so great. They remind me so much of Jason and me when we were young."

"Who's not young, old man?" Jason scowled. "I'm still young."

"You won't think that when you meet these boys. Nick, the four-year-old, he kicks my ass on the video games. Wait until he challenges you to play the race car game. He's good."

"That's my best game. No way I let a four-year-old beat me."

"Nick will. Jack is a strategist. He loves Knight's Revenge. Sarah taught him some tricks to the game and he's really good."

"Sarah plays video games with them?" Jason looked surprised.

Nothing about her surprised Luke anymore. "She does everything with them. She taught them how to play baseball. I'm telling you, she's mom and dad to those boys. She even taught them how to spit."

"Seriously?" Jason smirked. "I think I love her."

Jason gave him a wink, but Michelle took exception to his teasing. "Don't even think about it, buster." Michelle gave her husband's hair a tug while she watched her daughter practice walking. "Is she another blond bombshell like all the others?"

Luke hadn't really thought about himself having a type. But he supposed he did before Sarah. "She's almost the opposite. She doesn't need to make herself up to impress someone. She's got a natural beauty and an inner beauty that you just can't help but see. She's a lot shorter than me and has dark, long hair. Her eyes are the color of brown sugar and she sings like an angel."

"Good Lord, he's in love." Jason rolled his eyes, but the smile said he was happy for Luke. "And she knows next to nothing about us and the family business? Aren't you concerned about her finding out and . . . things changing?"

It had happened several times in the past. "Very diplomatic, Jas. But I don't need to worry about it. She's wealthy and could care less about whether I had just this ranch or a multimillion-dollar business."

Luke's mom and dad exchanged a look he couldn't really read, but he got they didn't want him to be disappointed again by a woman who wanted something other than just him. They wanted him to be happy. He was. They'd see it as soon as Sarah arrived.

He checked his watch, wondering what was taking her so long, and knowing she probably got caught on a call or was corralling the boys.

"Jason, you'd be impressed with her business sense. I saw the financial statements for her company. She runs a tight ship. She's increased her profits exponentially over the last two years and went from being in debt to generating hundreds of millions in profits."

Jason whistled, impressed.

The knock on the door stopped all further conversation. Every eye in the room turned toward the door.

Chapter Thirty

S arah stood on Luke's porch, her stomach tied in knots. Would his family like her? Had he told them about her? Did they know she had two children? Would it matter to them?

Given that Margaret was a longtime family friend of Luke's parents, Sarah wondered if they would have the same preconceived ideas about her that Luke did when he met her, because of Margaret's anger toward her.

She really didn't want to spend the whole night convincing them she wasn't the money-grubbing monster Margaret had made her out to be.

Mustering her courage, she knocked on the door, setting off a new wave of uncertainty and a billion butterflies in her stomach.

"Do I look pretty?" She didn't normally ask such things, but she wanted to make a good impression.

The black slacks and cream-colored cashmere short-sleeved sweater were comfortable and classic. Luke always saw her with her hair tied back in a ponytail. Tonight she'd secured the sides at the back of her head with a gold clip and let the rest spill down her back in long waves. Her black strappy heels would probably bring her up to Luke's nose if she was lucky. Careful with her makeup, she went with a natural look for her eyes, with subtle brown shadow and liner. The black mascara brought out her long lashes and made her light brown eyes stand out. She painted her lips a subtle wine color.

She hoped Luke appreciated the way she looked tonight and didn't think she was trying too hard. Up until now, he'd only seen her in jeans, tank tops, and T-shirts. She wanted him to see there was more to her than what he'd seen so far.

"You pretty, Mama," Nick assured her with a soft, sweet smile before he buried his face in her neck again.

Sarah looked down at Jack, standing with his back straight as a soldier beside her, holding the flowers she'd brought for Luke's mother. He gave her a reassuring smile and nod.

Footsteps drew closer to the door. She took a deep breath and waited, hoping they liked her.

Luke opened the door wide and stepped to the side, revealing his parents.

"You must be Sarah," Luke's mother said with a soft smile. "We've heard a lot about you and your sons. Come in. Come in." She waved them forward. "That little guy must be heavy."

"He's shy. You must be Luke's parents. I'm sorry, he never told me your names."

Luke's father took his wife's hand. "I'm James, and this is Lila."

Sarah shook hands as best she could holding Nick. She smiled, her anxiety easing at the warm welcome.

Luke took after his father in looks, but instead of blond hair, James had light brown hair that had turned gray at his temples. As tall as Luke, he had the same lean build. His white dress shirt was unbuttoned at the collar and his gray slacks were elegant but casual. He had a charming face with crow's-feet at his eyes and laugh lines by his mouth. Sarah imagined he laughed often and enjoyed life.

She especially liked the way he looked at his wife and had his arm around her waist. They looked comfortable with each other, like they shared something most would envy.

Sarah wanted that with Luke.

Where James radiated a quiet dignity, his wife glowed with beauty. A few inches shorter than her husband she had lovely blue eyes that softened when she gazed upon the boys. Her face was oval with beautiful, flawless skin. Her deep brown hair softly curled to just below her chin. Her peach silk blouse made her skin glow.

Sarah was pleased to see she had dressed appropriately because Lila had on a pair of black slacks almost identical to her own.

"These are my sons, Jack and Nick. Nick is the shy one." She kissed him on the head.

"Are you Luke's mommy?" Jack asked, taking a step closer to Lila.

"Yes, I am. It's nice to meet you, Jack."

"My mommy bought these flowers for you." Jack handed over the flowers and dashed into Luke's arms.

Luke scooped him up and held him close. "Hi, big guy. What took you so long to get here?"

"Mommy was busy on the email." Jack let out a long-suffering sigh.

Sarah's face heated with embarrassment. "I'm so sorry."

"Don't worry about it, sweetheart. I'm just glad you're here."

Lila touched her arm. "Thank you for the flowers. They're just lovely. They remind me of the roses I had in my wedding bouquet."

"You're welcome. I thought you might like them because of the rooms you decorated upstairs. They're romantic and lovely. You put a lot of heart in them. The way Luke talks about you and this house . . . He loves you very much. You left a lot of love here to keep him company."

Luke's mother did something Sarah never saw coming. She handed the flowers to her husband and then hugged Sarah. She put both arms around her and Nick and held her so tight she thought she might shatter from the love she felt coming from this woman she'd only just met. She couldn't remember her own mother, or anyone, ever holding her so closely, or with such reverence.

Tears clogged her throat and threatened to spill from her eyes, the display of emotion embarrassing her even more.

Lila stepped back, but held Sarah by the shoulders. "Luke didn't do you justice when he said you were incredible. That was the nicest thing anyone has ever said to me."

"I like her, Mommy. She hugs like you." Nick had finally pulled his face out of Sarah's neck.

"I like her, too." That earned her another warm smile from Lila. Sarah swallowed back the unexpected emotions and looked down at Nick. "Do you want to go down yet?"

"No." He buried his face in her neck again.

Sarah smiled at everyone and moved away from the door, so Luke's father could close it. Luke moved toward her carrying Jack. He leaned down and kissed her and held it for a few seconds. The soft kiss held a lot of promises.

Luke cocked his head toward the living room. "Come meet my brother and his wife." He leaned down and kissed Nick on the head. "Hi, buddy."

Nick looked up, grabbed Luke's shirt, and pulled him down for a kiss on the cheek. He turned back and buried his face again. Nick's show of affection completely surprised Sarah. It proved how much he had become attached to Luke.

Luke's gaze met hers and they shared a moment of connection

that said clearly how much Luke appreciated Nick's love and how much he wanted to hold on to her and this.

So did she.

And the boys obviously wanted Luke to be their dad.

Luke introduced her to the rest of his family. "This is Jason, Michelle, and Emma. Guys, this is Sarah and her boys, Jack and Nick."

"It's nice to meet you." Michelle gave her a warm smile. "Luke tells me you're an extraordinary businesswoman. He says you put my husband's work hours to shame. I don't know how you do it with two boys. I have only one daughter and still haven't managed to get back to work. I miss the challenge," she added.

"I haven't figured out how to make the day longer," Sarah confessed. "I split up my workday between them and my office. I work from home a lot. It's good to be the boss. No one can fire you for going to the school play or a Little League game in the middle of the afternoon."

Michelle acknowledged that with a nod.

Sarah tried to coax Nick out of his shyness. "Hey bud, want to give Emma her present?"

Nick looked up and handed the little girl in Michelle's arms a bag.

"Thank you, Nick." Michelle held the present in front of her little girl. "Emma, you got a present. Want to open it?" Emma stuck her little hand into the bag and pulled out the gift.

Emma showed it to her mom.

Michelle made big eyes at it for Emma's benefit, then asked Sarah, "What's this?"

"It's one of my projects. An electronic children's book with four stories. Push the button and the story will begin. You can switch it to game mode and the different-shaped buttons will rotate through saying the name of the shapes and the colors, and then it will play a song."

Luke's eyes went wide. "Sarah, you did that?"

"I came up with the idea when Jack was a baby. I finished it a few months ago and a toy manufacturer is putting it out at Christmas if I can get all the marketing material ready. This is one of four prototypes I had made. I wrote the stories and it's my voice on the recording. I hope Emma likes it."

Nick pointed to Jason and whispered into her ear, "Is he going to leave her alone, too?"

Sarah hugged him tight and looked him in his sad eyes. "Jason is big and strong like Luke. Nothing is going to happen to him. Okay?"

Luke cocked a brow. "What's this about?"

She kept her voice low so Emma wouldn't overhear her talk about her dad, even though she was preoccupied playing with her new toy on the couch with her mom.

"He wanted to know if Jason is going to die and leave Emma without a father, too." She gave Jason a half smile. "I'm sorry. He has a hard time seeing other kids with their dads." She rubbed her hand up and down Nick's back. "Not all dads go away," she assured him.

Luke put his hand on his father's shoulder. "Hey Nick, this is my dad. He's been with me and Jason our whole lives. Just like Jason will always be with Emma. And I want to be with you. Okay?"

Nick smiled at Luke. "Okay."

Luke's dad poked Nick in the belly. "I hear you're really good at the race car game. I'm not as good as Luke and Jason, but how about a game?" James's obvious love for the kids showed in his warm smile, and Nick responded: "I can totally kick your butt." Nick jumped down from his mother's arms and raced for Luke's office with Jack on his heels and James following in the rear.

Jason spun around. "I want in on this." And off he went to catch up with the boys and his dad.

Sarah shook her head. "I guess I don't need to worry about the kids for a while."

Lila tugged on Sarah's arm. "Come into the kitchen. We'll get you a glass of wine and get to know each other better." Lila went ahead.

Luke stepped in front of her before she could follow. He leaned down and kissed her softly. "I'm so glad you came tonight." He cupped her face. "I love you."

"I love you, too."

Luke kissed her right there with his sister-in-law watching with a smile and Sarah felt like she belonged because it seemed everyone was happy for her and Luke.

They'd welcomed her, Jack, and Nick and made them feel like part of the family because she and the boys were connected to Luke.

"What is it, sweetheart?"

"I really like your family."

"They like you, too." Luke kissed her again. "But not as much as I like you." Then he kissed her with all the heat and desire that usually sizzled between them.

"Luke!" his mother called. "Bring her here before you set the house on fire, dear."

Luke smiled down at her, rolled his eyes, took her hand, and led her into the kitchen, where his mother handed her a glass of wine, and clinked her glass to Sarah's. "Thank you for ending his bachelor streak."

And just like that, all the reservations Sarah didn't think she harbored about whether Luke was really serious about moving their relationship along so quickly evaporated.

Chapter Thirty-One

Sarah sipped her wine. Somehow they'd ended up staying in the kitchen, sitting at the island counter, watching the chef Luke hired cook. The young guy didn't seem to mind the company. He even threw together a cheese, cracker, and fruit plate for them to snack on before dinner. Sitting in the kitchen with Lila and Luke seemed cozy and such a family thing.

She'd never had family dinners growing up, but she'd imagined it was something like this. That's why she always made time to have dinner with the boys.

Lila stacked a slice of sharp cheddar atop a cracker. "Luke, the house looks great. I love all the changes you've made. I know things were in need of an update, but what you've chosen to do has kept the feel of the house and yet made it more modern and you."

"I'm really happy with the renovation."

Sarah loved the white Shaker cabinets, black hardware, and big, bold island he'd done in a dark gray that offset the gorgeous white countertops and played off the black chandelier over the breakfast nook. The wood barstools gave the room warmth along with the hardwood floors that ran through the house.

"My favorite is the great room," Lila said with a bright smile. "The wood and beams on the ceiling are so warm against the white walls that set off the paintings of Greece."

Luke nodded. "Raising the ceiling and adding the wood and beams made the room. The blue wall in the dining room plays off the ocean color in the paintings. The place finally feels like me. And with Sarah and the boys here, it feels like home."

Sarah caught her breath, completely caught off guard that he'd so openly reveal that to his mom. Her heart swelled with love for him. "Luke . . ."

He brushed his fingers down the side of her face and held her gaze. "I mean it."

She put her hand over his heart and leaned into him, too caught up in her emotions to find the words to tell him what that meant to her.

Lila sighed next to them. "You two seem really great together."

Luke brushed his hand over Sarah's hair and smiled. "I thought Margaret was coming with you?"

"She'll be here soon. When her doctor's office couldn't see her for three weeks, I called the local hospital and set up a video chat with their top specialist. He's the best, according to the hospital administrator, but he's also a shark when it comes to negotiating a little something extra to get him to see her immediately."

"You bribed him?" Shock filled Luke's voice and eyes.

"Can I have the rancher back, please? The lawyer in you is so uptight."

Luke gave her a mock dirty look. "Was it necessary to bribe the guy?"

"Yes. Margaret is in pain. She put this off too long. I wanted her seen immediately, so I made it happen."

"Of course you did, sweetheart. I'm pretty sure there's nothing you can't do." Luke studied her. "I guess you and Margaret are on good terms now."

"We spoke some more and I came to realize that what Margaret really wants is someone to take care of her. She lost her husband and son, Bridget is lost in anger and grief over her divorce, and Margaret feels abandoned, I think."

"You'd know something about that," Luke said, understanding her so well.

"So I took care of a few things. The doctor's visit. A housecleaning service and gardener. The house and property will be put back to rights, and she'll be a little pampered and, well, happy. Emotionally, she took a big hit. It will take her some time to reconcile the Sean she loved so deeply with the man she'd hoped he'd be. Margaret, Bridget, and I, we've turned a corner, but there's still a lot of healing left to do for all of us."

She shrugged and took a sip of the cold wine, loving the sweet taste of the Moscato Lila chose.

Luke and Lila remained completely silent, staring at her.

When Sarah noticed, Lila took the lead. "You did all of that just to pamper her and make her happy?"

"It was just a few phone calls."

Lila squeezed her hand. "It's so much more than that."

She caught Luke's steady gaze and found the love and admiration he always showed her shining brighter than ever.

Lila sipped her wine, then added, "You're a good daughter, Sarah. Margaret is lucky to have you."

Sarah managed a half smile, feeling a pinch of pain for the family she never had growing up.

"Mom, Sarah's mom died when she was very young and her father didn't know about her until she was grown. She grew up in foster care and with an abusive uncle."

Lila set her glass down. "Oh dear, I'm sorry. I didn't know. I only meant that what you did was sweet and kind."

"It's okay. Few people were nice to me as a child. Now that I'm grown, I know the importance of giving people kindness. Look at Luke. When I first met him, he was grumpy and disillusioned with his life. You seem much happier now."

Luke laughed. "I am, thanks to you."

"Grumpy. That's how you describe him?" Jason laughed under his breath, walking into the kitchen.

Luke sneered at his brother. "I'm sitting right here, you know."

"Yes, honey. We see you." Sarah leaned in and gave him a mischievous grin that he kissed right off her lips.

Margaret walked into the kitchen. "Sorry I'm late, everyone. I'm sure Sarah made my excuses."

"Margaret. Nice to see you," Luke called out over the counter.

Lila stood and embraced Margaret. "It's been a long time."

"Too long," Margaret agreed. "And look." She waved her hand toward Sarah and Luke. "My daughter-in-law and your Luke."

"They're perfect together," Lila said.

"They are," Margaret easily agreed, taking Sarah aback.

Jason took Margaret's coat. "Wine, water, soda, something stronger?" He held up his glass of whiskey.

"Wine, thank you." Before Jason made off with her coat, Margaret pulled a phone out of the pocket. "Sarah, you left this on the table and the thing hasn't stopped going off. I thought maybe you'd forgotten it."

"I did. Thank you for bringing it." The phone rang as if on cue. Lila and Margaret started talking about the house renovations Luke had done a few months earlier. Luke and Jason moved to the table to discuss some business thing Jason wanted Luke's opinion on.

Jack walked in, drawing Sarah's attention before she answered the call.

"Mommy, I want to talk to Aunt Abby. Can I answer it?"

"Sure, honey. Make sure to say hello first." She handed the phone over without looking at the caller ID. No matter how desperate Abby was to get in touch with her, she'd always make time for Jack, who answered with a cheerful "Hello."

Jack's eyes filled with trepidation. "You're not Aunt Abby?"

Luke beat her to asking Jack, "Who is it?"

Jack pulled the phone away from his ear and handed it to Sarah like he couldn't get rid of it fast enough. "It's the lady Daddy kissed the way you kiss Luke. The one who made you cry." Jack ran across the room and threw himself into Luke's outstretched arms.

Luke scooped up Jack, set him on his lap, and held him close to his chest.

Margaret and Lila stared at Sarah.

She could feel Jason's intense gaze all the way across the room.

Though the hired chef kept his back to them, stirring his pots and tending the food, she felt his attention, too.

Shit.

She'd been expecting the call, despite wondering if Trish would ignore Luke's request, but didn't expect it to come so soon.

Sarah met Luke's steady gaze. "I've got this." His encouraging nod helped ease her mind, even if her heart jackhammered in her chest and her anxiety hit an all-time high.

All she could think about was how this woman had inserted herself into her life and marriage, how she changed everything, because of her own selfish needs and wants.

Sarah walked out the back door without looking back, because she didn't want the past to taint what was so alive and wonderful in that house: Love. Family. Joy.

Everything she'd ever wanted.

Chapter Thirty-Two

Luke felt everyone's gaze, but he kept his focus on Jack. "You remember the lady on the phone?"

"Daddy used to bring me to see her."

Luke didn't think his opinion of Sean could sink any lower, but yep, it did. "Did he do that a lot?"

"No. Just sometimes because he knew I didn't like to go." Jack sighed, then looked up at Luke. "I heard Daddy fighting with Mommy. He said he was going to take us away, that we would live with the lady like he did. He said if she wanted to see us again, she wouldn't quit and keep working. Mommy cried."

"What did your mom say to your dad about that?"

"She told him he couldn't have us. He got really mad and yelled at her more."

"Then what happened?" Luke didn't really want to know, but needed to hear it all the same so he could understand Jack and Sarah even better.

"He left. Mommy wouldn't let him take us. She said if he did, she'd destroy all the computer stuff." Jack traced the grain in the wood table. "He was always at Trish's house. Mommy said Daddy didn't like her anymore and he was happier with the other lady. She said it was okay because she wanted Daddy to be happy. I guess he did like Trish because he bought her a bunch of sparkly diamonds." Jack looked up at him, anger flashing in his eyes. "He said we were going shopping, but he didn't buy me anything. He only bought the lady stuff. He took me to her house to give it to her. She was real happy, but she didn't want me there, only Daddy. I wanted to go home to Mommy. If you take me shopping, will you buy me something?"

"Sure, buddy. Did your Mom find out about the diamonds?"

"I told her. She was really sad. She doesn't have any. Daddy gave her something for her computer. I don't think she liked it. It wasn't even a fun game or anything." Jack scrunched his mouth. "You know what?"

"What, Jack?"

"I don't think Daddy was very nice to her."

"I don't think so either." Margaret came to stand next to Jack and brushed her hand over his head. "I'm very sorry your dad treated your mom that way. It wasn't right. But you know what?"

"What?"

"Your mom deserves to be happy, too."

"Luke makes her smile all the time."

Luke hugged Jack close. "And I'll never be mean to her," he promised.

Margaret held her hand out to Jack. "Let's go find your brother."

Luke met Margaret's concerned gaze. "He's in the library with my dad playing video games."

Margaret took Jack's hand. "Jack will show me the way. Why don't you check on Sarah? She probably needs you right now."

Luke gave Jack a hug and a kiss on the top of his head and sent him with his grandma. He sat at the table with his brother until Margaret and the boy left the room.

His mother stood, came closer, crossed her arms across her

chest, and dropped her voice. "Who takes their child to buy jewelry for their mistress? Who does that? I like Margaret, but her son . . . What kind of man does that?"

"He turned into an even bigger asshole than I imagined. Sarah confessed to Margaret the other day that Sean had been having an affair and embezzling money from the company. That's probably why he threatened her. In addition to the theft, he'd been passing off her work as his own." Luke fisted his hands. "If Sean wasn't already dead, I'd kill him for treating her the way he did."

Luke worried about how much pain Sarah had locked inside herself. He understood now why she was so cautious and how hard it must have been for her to trust him.

Jason tapped the table to get his attention. "I wonder how much more Jack remembers."

Luke wished Jack only remembered the good things Sarah told him. No kid, especially one so young, should think about how his father hurt his mother and made her cry. "He's a smart kid. He was about four when Sean died. I think the affair had been going on for a while."

"My God." His mother's distress was nothing compared to how he felt. "That poor girl has been through so much in her life. Go find her. She could use someone on her side for once."

No doubt. And Luke wanted to be there for Sarah, to see her through whatever happened next. He knew contacting Trish would open a Pandora's box of past hurts, but hoped Sarah was ready for it when she'd decided to try to bring the kids together.

It was one thing to know Sean cheated and had a child with another woman, but it was another to hear Jack talk about the reality of what that had been like in the moment for them.

Margaret still looked emotionally drained and utterly disappointed and disillusioned by the revelations she'd learned about Sean. He wondered how she'd take finding out about Jamie.

They'd all agreed to hold off telling her until Trish made contact—if she ever did—and agreed to meet with them.

After all Sean had put Sarah through, maybe this was too much to ask of her. She seemed to have gotten past Sean's deceit and the hurt he'd caused, but this visit with Margaret and finding out about Jamie had to have opened old wounds.

All Luke wanted to do was make everything all right for Sarah. He wanted to give her everything she'd never had with anyone else. What *he'd* never had with anyone else.

They had a connection that included a genuine affection and love he'd always wanted and never had with a woman. Just thinking about her made him smile. When she was away from him, he couldn't wait to see her again.

And when she was unhappy, all he wanted to do was lighten her heart and put the smile right back on her beautiful face.

He wanted to give her everything, but all she wanted was him. And if she gave him a chance, he'd be the best husband and father to her kids she could ever want, because she deserved it.

Chapter Thirty-Three

*S*arah walked out the back door simultaneously heartbroken because her son was crying and happy because she'd seen how Luke took care of him. Held him. Loved him.

She loved him right back for that and so much more.

With a heavy heart and a lot of reminders that this was for the boys, she greeted the woman she'd hated for years. "Hello, Trish."

"Hi, Sarah. It's been a long time." The tentative words held a lot of trepidation. "I was surprised to hear from you. Well . . . your lawyer."

"I can't believe you didn't say anything about being pregnant after the accident."

Trish paused, then sighed. "The accident woke me up in a lot of ways. I realized I'd been doing a lot of things that I made excuses for because I wanted them. I didn't think about how my actions affected other people."

"Like me."

"Yes. I told myself we loved each other so it was okay. I told myself he loved me, not you, so it was okay. I told myself that as long as we were together, everything would work out. That you'd be happy to move on because you wanted out of the marriage as much as Sean. I told myself a lot of things to justify my behavior. I just never looked at things from your perspective."

"You didn't think about me and the boys at all," Sarah accused.

"No. I didn't. Because then I'd have to think about how wrong it was to be with Sean even when he made me feel so good. Any doubts I had, he erased them with promises and romantic gestures. He showered me with the kind of love I'd never felt." Trish paused. "But there was always something there, lurking in the background, that I couldn't quite dismiss."

"Me."

"Yes. But it was more the attachment he had to you. He needed you. He refused to let you go, even while telling me how much he loved me." Trish sucked in a ragged breath. "I'm sorry. I know you don't want to hear that."

Sarah had heard Sean's pretty words of love and devotion and found them meaningless. She didn't hold much stock in him having deep emotions for Trish either, but didn't say anything about it. "Sean made it clear he wanted you, not me."

"And yet he wanted to fight the divorce. After months of assuring me he'd leave you to be with me, that we'd make a life together, he wouldn't do the one thing I'd begged him to do." Sadness filled her voice.

Sarah found that she did have some sympathy for the other woman, though it was more for her gullibility and believing in a man who'd cheat on his wife.

"Sean needed me to save the company. That's all." It hadn't been because he'd loved her or wanted to salvage their marriage. She was a means to an end.

"Even the pregnancy didn't persuade him." The admission held a lot of sadness.

Sarah wondered if Trish got pregnant on purpose to force Sean's hand, but didn't ask. Instead, she gave Trish another dose of reality. "He barely spent time with his sons because he spent all his free time with you."

"I know. And I'm sorry. They must miss him terribly."

"They miss the idea of him. Because let's face it, Sean didn't care about them. He only cared about himself."

Trish sighed again. "I know that now. I realized it in the moments before the crash. After, when he was gone, I tried to understand why I grieved but also felt . . . relieved."

Shocked by the admission, Sarah took it in and thought it through. "You realized you weren't the most important thing in Sean's life. Neither was your child. You played out what life with Sean would really look like. Him fighting to keep me at the company by using the boys as leverage. Him making promises to you again and again and again and hardly ever keeping them. Him appeasing you all the time just so you'd do what he wanted."

"Him ignoring our child the way he did his sons," Trish added.

The line went quiet as they both remembered Sean for who he was and their lost hope that he'd ever be the man they'd wanted him to be for them.

Sarah hated that they had that in common. It made it hard to hate Trish when they'd both fallen into the same trap with the same man.

"He was so angry that night in the car, ranting that you'd demanded the divorce and how he wouldn't give it to you without a fight. I didn't know about the trouble with the company. Well, some of it, yes, but not that he'd taken money from it and could end up in jail. He let that slip that night. When I told him he could turn things around without you, that we could live a good life together, he turned on me. He said I didn't know what I was talking about, that you were the only one who could save him, and all I was good for was a fuck." Trish's words held the strain of threatening tears. "I know he was upset, drunk, not thinking clearly, but those words cut deep, and I realized that he'd been using me as a fun distraction and that he really didn't have any deep feelings for me."

"I don't think Sean really knew how to love." Why Sarah offered the reason for Sean's bad behavior, she didn't know. Consoling Sean's mistress had never crossed her mind, but in the moment, it seemed Trish needed it, and Sarah commiserated with the woman for finding out too late she'd put her hopes and dreams in the hands of a man who was too selfish to fulfill them.

Trish sighed again. "He loved himself. He wanted to save himself."

"Yes, he did. But then he died in the accident and I had to save everyone from him."

"I didn't tell you about the baby because I just wanted to do the right thing and stay out of your life. I felt guilty for taking the payment you offered even as I thought I deserved it because Sean turned out to be such a shit."

"Agreed." If they were going to be in each other's lives to facilitate a relationship between the kids, then they needed to find common ground. Agreeing that Sean was an asshole seemed like a good place to start.

"For a long time, I let my guilt about the accident rule my life."

Sarah wondered about that. "Why did you feel guilty about the accident?" Aside from the fact she let her drunk boyfriend behind the wheel.

"We were arguing. I distracted him. The more I pleaded with him to leave you for me, the more furious he got. And yes, I know, I should have never let him drive that night. Truthfully,

I'd only seen him down one scotch. I didn't know he must have had several others before we left to confront you."

Sean's blood alcohol test came back showing he'd been well over the legal limit.

"He'd have gotten in that car no matter how hard you tried to persuade him otherwise."

"He was on a mission that night," Trish agreed. "And I didn't help things. I could have lost my child." The last was said on an anguished whisper.

"But you didn't. And still you didn't tell me the boys had a sister."

"I didn't think you'd care. I didn't want to intrude in your life again. I watched you rebuild Spencer Software. You didn't just move on, you thrived. It took me longer to put the past behind me."

"I imagine being pregnant with Sean's baby was a daily reminder of what you'd done and what you'd lost."

"Yes. But then I had Jamie and a new world of possibilities opened up for me. I met someone new. Someone kind, who fell in love with both of us. A man I could really see being a good husband and father. And he is."

"I heard you're engaged."

"Yes. And he wants to adopt Jamie. We'll be a family."

Because Sarah had found Luke, she understood all too well how Trish felt. "I hope you two have a wonderful life together."

"I know we will." Another tense pause ticked away the seconds. "About Jamie and the boys . . . I think it would be nice for Jamie to get to know her brothers. I'm just not sure how we'll do this after what I did to you."

Sarah sucked it up for the boys, but also because she didn't want to hold on to this resentment and anger anymore. "I don't know that we'll ever be best friends or anything . . ."

"I wouldn't expect that from you."

"But I think we can agree to leave the past in the past and be nice to each other because in a weird way, we're family." She didn't know any other way to put it. Except that sometimes you had to move on simply because what tied you together was far stronger than the bad things you could let tear you apart.

"Oh wow. Um, that's more than I deserve or expected."

"It's what Jamie, Jack, and Nick deserve. Family is important. Their connection to each other matters. I hope they will come together, be sister and brothers, and have a bond that lasts them through their lives. That they will always be able to count on each other."

"I want that for them, too. I'll do whatever it takes to help facilitate that for Jamie and the boys without making it too difficult on you."

"I appreciate that. I'll need to have a talk with the boys and let them know they have a sister. Jack remembers a lot more than I thought."

"I wondered if he'd remember me."

"Apparently he does." For better or worse, that would help him understand how Jamie was his sister. "I don't know how you feel about this, but I'd like it if for the initial visit you let me introduce Jamie to them alone. You can wait outside if you want, but I'd just really like to meet Jamie, and be present with her, without you and the past staring me in the face."

"I think I understand. You don't want to put your feelings for me on her."

"I guess. Something like that. Yes."

"Okay. I can do that, but I hope, eventually, we can all spend time together."

"Yes. Definitely." She didn't expect Trish to just drop her child and go every time. They would have to find a way to have a cordial relationship.

If she and Margaret could do it, why not her and Trish?

Sometimes, being a mom meant doing things for your kids you'd normally never do but you did them because they needed you to be a better person than even you thought you could be.

Chapter Thirty-Four

S arah said goodbye to Trish with a promise that she'd be in touch soon to set up an introduction and playdate for the kids when she returned to her home in Silicon Valley. She couldn't believe this had become her life. Cleaning up Sean's messes, reconciling with his family, now inviting his mistress to her home.

Add in work and she had way too much on her plate. All of it took an emotional toll.

She wanted to keep on hating Trish, but it was hard to hold on to anger for a woman who had made the same mistake she had by falling for Sean.

Yes, she still blamed Trish for going into the affair knowing Sean was married, but Sean was the one who'd made Sarah and Trish promises and didn't keep them. In order to reconcile Trish's role in the affair with finding a way to have a relationship with her, Sarah had to find the strength to forgive Trish, or at least set aside what she did so they could be what their kids needed them to be: a good person. A role model for finding solutions to tough problems.

But sometimes it sucked to have to be the bigger person and do the right thing.

Sometimes, she just wanted to be mad.

She picked up a rock and threw it as hard as she could. She bent to pick up another when Luke's boots crunched on the gravel behind her.

"You've got a good arm, sweetheart. I see why the boys are such good ballplayers. I definitely want you on my team next time we play." He was giving her a minute to collect herself.

The tension drained away and she found a smile for the lovely image his words evoked and the feelings running through her that he'd always pick her to be by his side.

She turned to him and sighed, so happy to see his handsome face and the patience in his eyes. "I did the right thing."

"I knew you would."

Yeah, well, it sucked to swallow her feelings. "Is Jack okay?"

"Yes. Just a little upset that the lady who made his mom cry called. I made sure he was distracted kicking my dad's ass at video games and happy again before I came out to see you."

"Okay. Good." When Luke didn't say anything else, she stared at him. "No twenty questions?"

Luke held her gaze. "You can say anything to me. I promise you, Sarah, you can lean on me and count on me for love and support whenever you need it. You don't have to put on a front when you're hurting and angry and feel like you have to do all the hard stuff while others hurt you. Talking to your husband's mistress, opening your life to her and Jamie, that can't be easy."

"It's not. I feel like I can't escape him."

"It certainly feels like he's been here the last few weeks. But you've also put him behind you in business, with Margaret and Bridget, and now Trish. You rose above all the turmoil he brought into your life. And I know it sucked that you had to fix it all, but you did it. And while you'll have to introduce Jack and Nick to their sister, I'll be there to help you and them through that. I'm here for you right now. I'll always be here with you, Sarah."

She ran to him and threw herself into his arms. "I'm so lucky to have you." She pressed her cheek to his chest and held on tighter.

Luke held her close, offering every bit of comfort she needed. "You've done a really good job keeping it all together and not giving in to what has to be a huge urge to lash out at everyone because of what Sean did. You'd be well within your rights to rage, but you've found a way to rise above it for your boys. That's what makes you so amazing."

"I don't feel amazing. That wasn't easy."

"You make handling the hard stuff look easy. But tell me. Are you okay? How did it go?"

"It went better than I thought, and I hate her a little less."

"Well, that's something."

"She really loved him. I understand her having those feelings and wanting the life Sean promised her. I suspect Trish got pregnant hoping Sean would finally leave me for her and their child." She shrugged one shoulder, not exactly sad for Trish, but understanding her desire to get Sean's full attention. Early on, Sarah had tried, but when it became clear the only thing he appreciated about her was her work output, she gave up on their relationship and focused on the boys. "Trish miscalculated. Sean had no interest in the boys. I doubt that would have changed with Jamie, but who knows."

"But he didn't want to leave you because he needed you. Sean led her on. He didn't want the divorce. He needed you to keep working, so he could keep taking the money. And as his wife, you couldn't testify against him if he got caught."

"Now you're thinking like Sean. Manipulations. Lies. Anything to get what he wanted."

"He threatened to take the boys away from you to force you to keep working for him."

"Jack told you that," she guessed, and Luke confirmed it with a nod. "He remembers a lot more than I thought he did." Her heart ached for her sweet boy. "Sean had nothing but empty threats. He didn't really want the kids. They took away from his traveling and partying. As for Trish, she wanted our divorce and fought hard for it right up until the seconds before the crash."

"They were arguing in the car?"

"Yes. She feels guilty for distracting him. He was drunk and in a rage. The roads were slick from the rain we'd had earlier in the evening. It was dark, the lights from oncoming traffic may have distorted visibility. Was it one thing? Two? All of it? None of it? Who knows? Sean died."

Sarah pressed her hand to her forehead, then dropped it. "Trish confessed that during the argument in the car right before the accident, Sean said some terrible things, including that he needed me more than a good fuck." Sarah sighed. "I'm paraphrasing, but you can see why Trish took the money I offered her and disappeared to grieve and reconcile having Sean's baby with knowing she wasn't the priority she deserved to be with Sean."

"You know a lot about how that feels." Luke sympathized.

She put her hand on his chest. "I also know what it feels like to really be loved."

Luke stared into her eyes and cupped her face. "You are everything I ever wanted. I hope you never doubt that."

"How could I? You show me how much you love me every time we're together."

He kissed her softly. "How did you two leave things?"

"She's willing to bring Jamie to meet the boys. I asked her if we could do the first one without her being there, so I could focus on the kids, not her."

"Did she agree?"

"Yes. But she hopes we'll all be able to hang out and everything will be fine. I told her we would." She met his gaze. "Because we're sort of family."

Luke's eyes went wide. "Sarah, that's really, really generous of you."

"All I ever wanted was a family. I can't deny my boys their sister. And if that sister comes with the woman I really wanted to hate forever but can't seem to manage to do that with time and perspective, then . . . Yeah. That's how it's going to be. It won't be easy, but just like I know Margaret, Bridget, and I will find a new normal, Trish and I will establish a relationship that works for us and the kids."

Luke shook his head, his eyes filled with admiration. "You amaze me. I know this is a heavy burden. And I want to be the one who shares the load with you, because you're the one I want to do the same for me. And I know you will because you love me." He brushed his fingers through her hair. "And though I haven't asked you to marry me yet, it's coming. I want you to be surprised and make it special for both of us because it's the one and only time I plan on doing it."

"We can take our time," she assured him, because she knew no matter what they'd always be together.

"But there is still one thing I'd like you to do for me."

She'd do anything for him. "What?"

"I meant it when I said I want to have a baby of our own. Whether it's one or five more, I'll leave up to you." His grin said he was teasing about five, but she understood his deep desire for a child of his own.

More than anything she loved being a mother. And it seemed Luke couldn't wait to be a dad. "Baby number three, definitely."

He gave her one of his amazing smiles. "So if I'm in, and you're in, I don't see why we have to wait to make it happen."

She couldn't come up with a single reason. "I've got nothing, Counselor."

He smiled. "Then say yes."

She didn't hesitate, not when she wanted him and a life together more than anything. "Yes."

He slipped his hand under her hair at the back of her neck and drew her in for a kiss that sealed their pledge to each other and quickly set off the passion that always burned hot between them. In his arms, she let go of all her worries, the frustration Trish evoked, the uncertainty of what came next, and fell into the promise of a life filled with love and happiness with a man she believed in and trusted, who made her feel safe and special.

Locked in the kiss and in Luke's arms, where she always wanted to be, she didn't hear someone walk up on them.

"Dinner's ready. If you two plan on hiding out here the rest of the night, I'm eating Luke's dessert." The amusement in Jason's voice broke the sultry spell around them.

Luke gave Sarah one last lingering kiss, raised his head an inch away from her, and growled, "Go away, Jason. We need another minute."

"I hope for Sarah's sake you can do better than that, bro." The door closed on Jason's chuckle before Luke could respond to the taunt.

Luke rolled his eyes, but a grin tugged at his lips.

She smiled up at him. "I like your brother."

"He's an ass sometimes. And has terrible timing." Luke rubbed his hands up her sides and back down to her hips. "Margaret is going to ask why Trish called."

She and Bridget had agreed not to tell Margaret about Jamie until one of them spoke to Trish and found out if she would agree to a meeting.

"I think we're on good enough terms now that I can tell her and she'll listen and understand."

"I hope so. She's had a lot thrown at her, too."

"At least this time I have good news. Well . . . I hope she sees it that way."

"Another grandchild, another piece of Sean. I think she'll be happy once she has a chance to process it."

So much had changed for all of them over the last several weeks. They'd been through a lot of tension and turmoil. But in the end, she'd found joy with Luke and seeing him with her sons. It was time to leave all the bad in the past and start looking toward a brighter future.

Chapter Thirty-Five

S arah stood next to Luke in the dining room feeling exposed and anxious with everyone staring at them.

Margaret looked at her with concern and remorse. "Is everything okay?" Things had really changed between them if Margaret was concerned about her.

She remembered how overwhelmed Margaret had been when they spoke before and wasn't sure now was the time to reveal another of Sean's secrets.

Luke squeezed her hand to give her courage and remind her he was there, supporting her.

She left Luke's side to walk around the table, place a hand on Margaret's shoulder, and tell her the truth about her son. "That was Trish. She and Sean were together for a long time." She glanced at Jack, who knew far more than he should, then focused on Margaret again. "She was in the car accident with Sean. To keep her quiet about their relationship so that investors and the board of directors didn't lose confidence in me, I paid her to keep quiet and she went away."

Margaret's eyes went wide, then narrowed with suspicion. "And let me guess, she wants more."

"No."

"Then what?" Margaret persisted.

"Yesterday when Bridget came to the house so the kids could play and she and I could talk about everything, she revealed that she knew a lot about what Sean had been doing. Not everything, but she knew about his affairs."

Margaret pressed her lips tight. "I see."

"She also knew something I didn't know, but that Luke had also discovered during his investigation into Sean."

Margaret stared across the table at Luke. "And you didn't tell me."

"Truthfully, I didn't know what to do with the information. I thought Sarah knew about it and wanted me to just let it be."

Margaret sighed. "I don't understand what we're talking about."

Sarah glanced at the two boys, then leaned down and whispered into Margaret's ear. "Sean had a daughter with Trish."

Margaret gasped and pressed her hand to her chest. Her eyes glassed over and she looked up at Sarah. "Are you sure?"

"Yes." She glanced at the boys again. They watched her intently, wondering what she'd told Margaret. Luke's family tried to appear uninterested, but she had all of their attention. "Now is not the time to discuss the details, but Trish has agreed to a visit."

"Why didn't she come to me?"

"I'm not sure, but I think in the end she was ashamed of what she'd done."

"And what about—"

Sarah squeezed her shoulder to cut her off. "I'm asking you to give me a little time to reveal this to *others* in my own way."

Margaret caught her meaning and nodded. "Yes. Of course. You're right."

Jack's curiosity got the better of him and he asked, "What are you talking about?"

Luke put his hand on Jack's shoulder. "Your mom found out something about your dad and she will talk to you about it later."

Jack seemed appeased by that, and Luke's tone that the discussion would have to wait.

Margaret glanced up at her. "Is that all you know?"

"Yes. Trish and I agreed to talk again soon about setting up a visit at my home."

"Okay. Well, I guess I need to have a talk with Bridget about keeping secrets. I can't believe she didn't say anything to me."

"She wasn't sure," Sarah defended. "Now we are and can move forward."

Margaret took her hand. "I can't imagine how difficult this must be for you."

"I'm determined to do the right thing. Family is important." That's as close as she'd come to revealing the truth without the chance to talk to the boys about their sister. "It's time to move on from the past and actually *be* a family." Sarah squeezed Margaret's shoulder, gave her a smile, then took her seat next to Luke.

Jack and Nick had finished eating.

Lila rubbed her hand over Sarah's back. "You've had a lot to deal with since your husband passed."

Sarah handed the salad bowl to Luke and turned to Lila. "All I ever wanted was a family. I thought I found that with Sean, but his focus was too often on Spencer Software rather than on us."

Jason choked on a sip of wine and held up a hand. "Hold it. I can't believe I didn't put it together earlier. The Spencer in Spencer Software was *Sean* Spencer. So that makes you Sarah Anderson."

Luke jumped in. "She's Sarah Spencer."

"Actually, I use Anderson. I never took Sean's last name."

Luke's eyes went wide. "You didn't? Why?"

"Anderson is the only link I have to my mother. She never gave me my father's last name, which is why I didn't know who he was until my uncle contacted him after the . . . incident."

"You really are her." Jason sat back in his chair and stared at her. Sarah eyed him. "How do you know me?"

"I drew up the contract for you to revamp Griffin Worldwide Financial's security systems. I represent them." Jason smiled, then looked at Luke. "You're dating the most-sought-after systems security programmer in all of Silicon Valley. And those video games you love, the one's from Andy's Antics," Jason added. "She's the sole owner and head software developer for that company, too."

Luke's eyes went wide. "Seriously? No wonder Jack and Nick kick a—my butt at those."

She appreciated Luke filtering his comment in front of the boys. "I kind of thought it was funny that the only fantasy games you have are mine."

"Because they're the best." Luke's praise sent another warm wave of love through her. "I can't believe you didn't say anything."

"She doesn't like the spotlight," Jason interjected.

"My work speaks for itself."

"Yes, it does." Jason saluted her with his glass.

Luke reached over and squeezed her hand. "But you can't keep working day and night the way you do."

Lila leaned in to Sarah's side. "Luke's worried about you."

Sarah glanced over and saw it plain in his eyes.

"When the men in this family love, they love deep." Lila's words hit her heart hard.

She brushed her hand up Luke's forearm, leaned in, and looked him right in the eye. "I swear, now that the Knox Project is nearly done, I will take better care of myself."

"And?" He held her gaze.

"I'll let *you* take care of me."

Luke closed the distance between them, his face inches from hers. "That's all I want to do." He sealed that promise with a soft, tame kiss because of their audience, but when he pulled back, she imagined the heat he'd unleash on her later. And she couldn't wait.

Luke's dad, James, studied her for a moment. "It's impressive what you've built in such a short time. And with two energetic boys. I don't know how you do it all."

"She doesn't sleep, that's how," Luke said irritably.

Sarah squeezed Luke's arm to let him know she got the message. "It's not easy. But I love being a mom and my work. I just need to find a better balance, because no, you can't have it all. At least, not all at once."

Michelle set her fork on her empty plate. "I wish I could find a work-at-home job. I quit to be home with Emma, but I sometimes wish I had a project or two to break up the monotony of being a stay-at-home mom and use my creativity and have a sense of accomplishment."

Sarah understood Michelle's dilemma. "I'm sure a lot of moms feel that way. What do you do?"

"I was in marketing. I did a lot of brochures, corporate documents, and product packaging design work. I can do the work at home, but finding a company that will allow you to is beyond impossible. I don't want to start my own business. That would be way too much. I like being a mom to Emma too much to take that kind of time away from her."

"I know what you mean. What's your background?"

"I graduated from UC Berkeley and then went to work for a large marketing firm in San Jose for about six years. I miss the process of putting a project together."

"Did you work on a team, or were you responsible for the project from start to finish?"

"I started out as support on projects, but by the time I left, I had my own clients and projects, and I led the team through the process."

Sarah could use someone like Michelle. And working with her meant that if things with Luke became permanent, she'd be working with family. The idea of it appealed more than Michelle's impressive credentials. "I outsource most of my marketing work for Andy's Antics and the children's toys. I have three major products coming out in the next few months. Two in particular need to have the package design and copy written for the product. I'll also need sales materials written, social media posts, and some kind of product overview. I'm fine with you emailing me your ideas and documentation. We can talk on the phone to discuss concept. I have a lot of work, so you'll be as busy as you want to be. If it's too much, just say so, and I'll outsource whatever you can't handle. You decide how many projects you want to take on. I'm flexible. If you want the job, it's yours. Name your hourly salary, or I can pay you per project."

Michelle stared at her for a moment, the silence stretching before she found her voice again. "You can't be serious. You haven't even seen any of my work."

"If I don't like something, I'll let you know. We'll work together to fix it. I can give you some of the documentation and products that I've done in the past for you to use as a brand reference, but I'd love a fresh perspective and new ideas. I'm a hands-on boss, as most of what you'll be working on is my work. I need someone to take some of the burden off of me. Luke seems to think I work too much."

"You do."

Jason sighed. "Great, now my wife is going to be too busy for me," he lamented, though the smile said he didn't really mind.

"Never," Michelle assured him. "But I . . . I just can't pass this up."

"And you shouldn't," Jason assured her. "I want you to do whatever makes you happy."

Sarah wished Sean had been more open and supportive when it came to her working and being a mom. He'd demanded she focus on one over the other instead of letting her find a balance that made her happy, fueling her resentment toward him.

"Take some time to think about it if you'd like. We can talk more about the details and your salary later."

Jason put his hand over Michelle's on the table, but addressed Sarah. "Are you sure about this? You don't have to do this just because she's Luke's sister-in-law."

"I'm not." She made sure to look Michelle in the eye so she understood Sarah meant it. "I think stay-at-home moms get a bad rap. Most companies don't believe they can contribute unless they spend eight hours a day in the office. Have you ever been to a dinner party and a woman says she's a stay-at-home mom to a group of working men and women? Immediately, most of the people ignore her, or begin talking about inconsequential matters, because they automatically assume the woman can't hold a conversation about business matters or anything of importance."

"That's happened to me at several functions Jason and I have attended over the past year. And that's with people who know I worked before having Emma. They assume I gave birth and lost fifty IQ points at the same time."

"Exactly. It's an ignorant attitude." She focused on Jason and reassured him her offer was genuine. "Michelle has a skill I need. Just because she wants to work from home doesn't diminish her capacity to do the job. Her past experience will be an asset to my projects. She's already established that she's good at negotiating.

She's made it clear she won't take on more than she can handle, because she doesn't want to take away from being the kind of mother she wants to be. She's probably a better candidate because having a child requires a great deal of patience, multitasking, and prioritizing. If I don't stop soon, I'll convince you that she's completely overqualified. Then, she'll up the salary amount she was going to ask me for by at least several thousand a year."

Michelle laughed. "I swear I'll be reasonable."

"Don't be. Ask Luke, nothing makes me happier than paying people for doing a good job."

"She does. She paid one of her employees a huge bonus just so he could buy a house for his new wife. She set up a project for him to earn the bonus knowing he'd be able to complete it. It benefited her also, but she did it to help her employee."

"That's generous. Do you do this with all your employees?" Jason's voice held some skepticism about her business sense.

"No. This particular employee has been working for me for a few years and he consistently goes above and beyond. It was his turn to be rewarded for his hard work. It was also a way to ensure he stays at my company. I don't want anyone recruiting him away from me."

Jason helped Emma with her sippy cup. "You're going to be traveling all over the world soon to do the install for Griffin Worldwide Financial. What about the kids? Who watches them while you're away?"

"I have a terrific nanny. I've made it a rule for myself to never be gone more than three nights in a row, even if that means I have to fly home from France and then back to England the next day."

"You're kidding, dear." Lila looked shocked. "Why don't you take the boys with you?"

"I try to make their lives as normal as possible. I didn't go to school all the time as a child. It's important they have a routine and stability. When they're a little older, I'll show them the world. Right now, I want them focused on school."

"Why didn't you go to school as a child? Were you sick?" Lila's eyes held a mother's concern and Sarah appreciated the heartfelt sentiment.

"When I was in foster care, I attended kindergarten to third grade. But when my uncle took me, he needed me to work on his horse ranch. I was sixteen when I escaped him." She'd survived him and his treacherous betrayal. "My father came into my life and he hired a tutor, who I worked with for almost two years to catch up. I worked very hard to get my high school diploma. Then, with a little help from him getting in, I went to MIT, where I graduated top of my class."

Margaret spoke for the first time since she'd learned about having another grandchild. "You've had a difficult and extraordinary life."

"The people I thought would love and take care of me either failed me or used me, or couldn't be what I needed them to be."

Luke's hand settled over hers on the table again. "Not anymore, sweetheart."

Lila's words came back to her. *When the men in this family love, they love deeply.*

She saw it in the way James looked at Lila, Jason supported Michelle, and Luke opened his heart to her.

Here she sat with her sons, the man she loved, surrounded by Luke's family and Margaret, a woman she never thought would ever accept her, but now did, and she felt for the first time like she was part of the family. Loved. Cared about. Important.

She met Luke's steady gaze.

Needed in the right way.

Chapter Thirty-Six

*L*uke stood by the sink, looking out the window at the garden beyond. *God. Sarah.* She wasn't like any woman he'd ever known. It barely registered with her that he was heir to the Thompson legal firm and what that meant. Other women he knew would calculate his net worth and have high expectations for what they wanted from him. Many of them seemed to quickly forget that he needed something from them, too.

A real partner. Family. Love and respect.

Sarah never asked him for anything. She found time for him, and time was something very precious in her life. And the time they spent together meant something to her because she used it to get to know him, to connect with him, and make really great memories.

Like dinner with his family tonight.

And because she thought about what he needed to be happy and build his dream, she'd had delivered two gorgeous mares for his breeding program. Under normal circumstances, he would have paid a fortune for them, but she'd just gifted them to him.

Between what she made at Spencer Software and the bestselling games she produced under Andy's Antics, she had the money to do and buy anything she wanted.

She didn't need his financial support.

Which meant she was with him because *he* mattered to her.

It had been a long time since he allowed himself to believe that. But for the first time, he knew it to be completely true. No financial strings attached.

And that meant their relationship was built on a solid foundation of respect and other intangible and infinitely more important things.

"Luke, honey, are you okay?" Sarah's hand brushed up his arm and held his biceps. "You look so serious." Her concern touched him.

He stared down at her. "I was just thinking about you. Us. And how we got here."

"It started with an interrogation of my motives and quickly moved to us getting to know each other for who we are."

"And what we can give each other," he added. "Not things you buy. Things that matter. Love. Support. Family."

"Exactly. All the things we need to feel connected and important." She squeezed his arm. "So why so serious?"

"Because I realized in the past I was my own worst enemy. I sabotaged so many relationships by thinking the woman I was with wanted me to buy them things or take them out to fancy dinners and on extravagant trips. After a while, I felt like that's all I brought to the table that they'd want. But you and I are building a relationship without any of those things. I've never even taken you out to a fancy dinner or whisked you away to a Caribbean island."

"I wouldn't say no to either of those things, to tell you the truth. But I don't need all of that to see you for the man you are. Kind. Generous. Caring. Understanding. Smart. Dedicated to this ranch, your family, the people and things that matter to you. Protective. And drop-dead gorgeous," she added, making him smile. "Being with you has shown me that the life I really want isn't some young, lonely girl's dream but a reality we can make together."

"I want that more than anything. I want to make you happy. For a minute I wondered how to do that. You can buy anything you want, so what did I have to give you, except to really make an effort to be kind and generous and caring and understanding and to protect you always, because I love you. And I do hope you see and feel that despite the fact I didn't give you those other things at first and I should have because you deserve them. And I feel a little rotten that I purposely didn't because I didn't want you to disappoint me. I wanted this to be real. And now I know it is."

"Wow. You were thinking all that standing over a sink of dirty dishes?"

"It started with me thinking I don't know what to get you that you can't get yourself."

"Maybe you should remember it's the thought that counts."

"People say that, but they don't really mean it."

"I do."

He brushed his fingers through the soft hair at the side of her head. "Yeah. I know that now, too."

"I love flowers. Did you know that no one has ever sent me flowers? There must be nothing like having a man send you flowers. Or a love letter." She touched her hand to her chest over her heart. "I've never been on a romantic vacation anywhere. The only trips I take are for business or camping with the boys. I've never received chocolates on Valentine's Day or held hands with a man and walked along a beach." She put her hand on his chest. "I've never made love under the stars."

He leaned in close. "I want to do and experience all those things with you."

"I could tell you a hundred more things I've never been given or done with someone I care about, but it doesn't really matter. What you have given me is more than anyone else ever did.

"You're the only man, aside from my father, who's ever loved me. You're the only man who ever gave me a gift that was so thoughtful and, well, just me. The music box is the most wonderful present I've ever received. You worry about me when I don't sleep enough, you make sure I eat well, and you are the kindest man to my boys. When you make love to me, you make me feel like the most beautiful woman ever. When you look at me, I feel wanted and loved. And every time you try to convince me that you really mean it when you say you want to spend the rest of your life with me, it tells me just how much you need me. Every smile, every kiss, every touch, every kind word, is a precious gift. Those are the things I want from you but only if you want to give them to me."

"I want to give you that and more."

"The reason I'm happy is because of you. And I want to stay happy, because falling in love with you has been so unexpected and exciting and fulfilling. But it's happened at a time when my life is crazy. The last six weeks, and especially today, have been completely overwhelming. Between dealing with Margaret, falling in love with you, finishing part of the Knox Project, and now Trish coming back into my life, I'm just stretched too thin.

"If you really want to give me something, give me time to work things out and make living here with you less complicated. I have a stack of résumés from people who would kill to work at Spencer Software. I will sort through them and hire more people and free up my time. But before I can do that, I still have the charity benefit in a few days. The press is going to be wild and the thought of facing all those people makes me want to hide out here on the ranch for the rest of my life, but I know I can't do that because people are counting on me."

He slipped his hands on her shoulders and brushed his thumbs up and down the sides of her neck. "And you'll be great. I can't wait to be your date. Do you know who this year's honoree is? It's usually someone who's donated a lot of money or raised a lot of money over the past year."

"So I've heard," she said cryptically.

"It's you, isn't it?" He didn't need her nod to know the truth. "Of course it is. Why else would you put yourself out there for public display if you didn't have to?"

"It's really not my thing. I much prefer a quiet night in. With you."

"Me, too. And your dad and his family will be there, too, right?"

"Yes. You know, I was afraid I was going to be completely embarrassed that night, but you could give me something so I won't be."

"Anything." He meant it. He never wanted her to feel uncomfortable or out of place anywhere.

"Dancing lessons."

That took him aback. "Seriously? You don't know how to dance?"

"I grew up *alone* on a ranch. I never went to school, let alone a dance or prom. The few ranch hands who came and went taught me a lot more . . . let's say, *colorful* skills."

"Like lockpicking," he said, remembering.

Her cheeks blazed pink. "There will be dancing after the dinner. And, well, I've never actually danced with a man." Her chin nearly hit her chest when she stared at the floor. "Please don't laugh at me."

He touched his finger to her face and made her look at him. "I'd never laugh at you, sweetheart. I think it's a shame you never went to prom and wore a pretty dress and had your feet stepped on by some klutzy, sex-crazed teenage boy."

She laughed and it eased the ache in his heart for all the things he took for granted as a kid that she'd never had.

"Sing me a slow song, sweetheart." He took her hand in his, wrapped his other arm around her waist and pulled her close, then started to sway right there in the middle of the kitchen.

Sarah stared down at her feet as he began to dance them around the island. "You want me to sing? I'm trying to figure out all the steps."

"It's easier if we have a song to move to. All you have to do is follow me. I'll hold on to you."

Her sweet voice rose in a lovely ballad that matched the tempo of his movements.

He held her close and lost himself in the feel of her moving with him, the sound of her pretty voice rising and falling with the poetry of the words about finding the one you love.

Luke stared into her gorgeous eyes and lost himself in her, the song, and the tender moment. He smiled when his parents, brother and sister-in-law, and Margaret, swaying with Emma in her arms, joined them. The boys stood in the doorway watching.

When the song ended everyone applauded Sarah.

"You have a beautiful voice," his mother praised. "Where did you learn to sing like that?"

"Listening to the radio in a barn not far from here."

His mother's eyes went wide. "You've never had any training? That's quite a gift."

"Thank you." Sarah's cheeks turned pink with the compliment.

His mom turned to his dad. "I think we played that very song at our wedding reception."

Sarah smiled. "I always imagined dancing to it at my wedding. I used to imagine seeing myself in a white dress and a man in a tuxedo swaying to the music and the lovely words of love and devotion."

Margaret stepped closer. "Sean said you didn't want a proper wedding and reception." Her sad gaze fell to the floor, then met Sarah's again. "But that was just another lie. He's the one who insisted the wedding take place at the county courthouse, not you." Sarah was about to say something, but Margaret cut her off. "Don't cover for him anymore, Sarah. I know he treated you poorly, but worse is that he did it without a single thought for your feelings. I'm so sorry he hurt you."

"It's in the past now." Still in Luke's arms, Sarah looked up at him. "This memory will be with me for a lifetime. Dancing with you in the kitchen with our family. How can you beat that?"

"We'll dance to this song at our wedding," he promised her. "You'll wear a beautiful gown, and I'll wear a tux. Every year on our anniversary, we'll dance to the song in the kitchen and remember the first time we danced."

He kissed her with his whole family watching and sighing over them and the love they shared.

They left the kitchen and went back into the dining room to enjoy dessert. Jack, Nick, and Emma ate chocolate cake and made a huge mess that nobody minded. The room was filled with the conversation and laughter of one big family, and it was everything Luke had in the past made even better by having Sarah and her boys with them.

Everyone left that night happy. Margaret volunteered to take the boys home and coaxed Sarah to spend the night with Luke. She was happy for them. And he saw that Margaret's acceptance lightened Sarah's heart and mind.

Finally alone, Luke led Sarah up to their room and into the big bathroom. He turned on the water and squeezed bubble bath into the luxurious tub, then took his time stripping Sarah bare and kissing every little sensitive spot he could find while the water rose to the top. He helped her into the steaming, citrus- and herb-scented water, then quickly removed the clothes Sarah hadn't already stripped off him and tossed to the floor as her hands and mouth had explored his body. He sank into the water behind her and laid back with her head on his chest and stared up at the large picture window and skylight above showing off a spectacular night sky filled with a trillion stars. And to fulfill her wish, he made love to her under that night sky until she was panting at his ear, water lapped over the tub's rim, and they both found heaven in a blaze of glory in each other's arms.

They were quiet and purposeful as they got out of the tub, dried each other, and made their way to the bed, neither of them ready to burst the intimate bubble. Luke followed Sarah as she lay back on the sheets.

He'd follow her anywhere, but especially to bed.

He steeped himself in the quiet, her scent, and the sound of her breath as he kissed and licked all her tantalizing hollows and curves. Her breasts were a temptation not to miss. Those hard nipples pressed against his tongue as he sucked each peak and made her moan his name.

Needing more of her sweet gasps and sexy sighs, he headed south, down her belly to where heaven awaited his kiss. He parted her folds with his fingertips, sweeping them over the sensitive flesh as her body wept for more. He took her pleasure on his tongue, then drove his tongue deep inside her hot core. Her legs fell wide open and he feasted with her fingers curled in his hair, holding him to her as he licked and laved and taunted that sensitive bud that made her moan for more. And he gave it to her, sliding one finger deep, then pulling it back, and plunging it inside again as his tongue circled her clit in soft sweeps that made her body go tight then quake against his lips with her release.

His pleasure hit hard and demanded he let it loose. He slid up her body, settled between her cradling thighs, and took her mouth in a searing kiss, his tongue sliding over hers as he buried his cock deep inside her. He took her hard and fast, her core tight around his throbbing dick until they both found the sharp edge of desire and fell over it.

Luke came back to himself in increments. He felt the aftershocks from Sarah's body echo through him. He held most of his weight off her, allowing her breasts to brush against his chest as her breath billowed in and out. She held him to her. He felt as close as he could get to her, and then she whispered in his ear, "I love you," and he lost a piece of himself to her. He didn't mind. She'd hold that piece of him in her heart and protect it forever.

He somehow found the strength to settle beside her and pull her into his arms. He fell asleep with her head on his chest and her soft, long hair draped over his arm, thinking nothing would ever feel as good as this.

And he'd been right, because he woke up the next morning furious and alone with nothing but a note left on her pillow.

Luke,

Had to fly to Chicago, and then I've got to go home to meet with Abby and my team.
    Call my cell.

                                                                Love, Sarah

What the hell was she thinking just getting out of bed and leaving him to go *home* without so much as a goodbye or a real explanation? He rolled over and grabbed his cell off the nightstand and tapped her picture to speed-dial her.

"Good morning, sweetheart." Her cheerful voice made him crave to have her near.

"It would be if my girlfriend was still in bed with me," he grumbled, feeling as surly as he sounded. "Where are you?"

Sarah sighed. "Chicago. I left you a note."

"I got it. The one that says you're going *home*. I thought that was here with me."

"Let me explain." She gentled her voice to soothe him. "I'm sorry I left in the middle of the night like that. I wasn't feeling well."

He sat up in bed and wiped his hand over his face, wishing his brain would boot up faster. "Why? What's wrong?"

"Just a stomach thing. I felt a bit queasy, got some water, watched you sleep, which made me think even more that you're adorable . . ."

Okay, he loved hearing that.

"Then I checked my messages."

He wished she'd gone back to bed with him instead. "And one of them said you needed to be in Chicago to put out some fire that only *you* can handle."

"Yes. Because it's for Andy's Antics. My new computer game is coming out this Christmas and the company I hired to test and debug it notified me that some nerd hoping to impress me and build his reputation broke the contract and changed *my* game. With the debut so close, and my reputation on the line, I had to take care of this in person."

Luke raked his fingers through his hair. "That sucks. I'm sure it pissed you off to find out someone hijacked your game."

"Yes, it did, because I had to leave you and the boys to take care of it."

"I wish you were here."

"Me, too, but since I had to leave for this and I'll fly back in to San Jose, I thought I'd stop by my office and put out a few other fires there. I went over a few résumés on the plane ride here and I asked Abby to set up some interviews while I'm in the office, so I can hire some help, and actually sleep six or eight hours a night. With *you*. At home. In your bed."

"*Our* bed. And I'm sorry. I woke up with plans for us and you weren't here. And I wanted you to be."

"That's very sweet. It means so much to me. I hope you know I'm trying to figure out our life."

"I know you are. You asked for time, and I'll give it to you. But I won't stop missing you when you're gone."

"I'll be back before you know it. The boys are with Margaret, but maybe if you have time, you can give her a break and take them riding. I left her a note telling her what was going on. She has my car in case she wants to take the boys somewhere, or if you want to bring them to the ranch. Their car seats are inside."

"How'd you get to the airport?"

"Car service. I took a private plane to Chicago, and I'll use the same one to get back to San Jose in, oh, about two hours. I really have to go. I'm just about to walk into my meeting."

"Okay. When will you be back here?"

"Sometime in the afternoon tomorrow. I don't have an exact time."

"A private jet, huh?"

"You want me home tomorrow, or in a couple of days when I can get a flight?"

Totally worth the money. "Tomorrow."

"I have to go. I have a lot of customers who've preordered the next installment for Knight's Revenge and I don't want to have to move the release date."

"You made Knight's Revenge III? That's my favorite game."

"Well, lucky you, I have a couple advanced copies. I'll give you one when I get home."

"You know, I could have come with you and acted as your lawyer to make them stick to the contract."

"That's sweet, but you aren't my lawyer."

"What am I, then?"

"The love of my life."

He couldn't remember ever smiling that big, but Sarah's words made him so damn happy. "That's my new favorite job. I love you. I'll see you tomorrow." It seemed like forever.

"I love you, too. Bye."

He hung up and stared at the wrecked bed and couldn't help the immediate smile that spread across his lips. He remembered their night in the tub under the stars. One of those things she'd never done. Immediately he thought of something else he could do to make her smile and let her know how much he missed her.

He rolled out of bed, pulled on a pair of faded jeans, and headed down to his office. He opened his laptop, wished he'd stopped in the kitchen for a cup of coffee first, but pulled up the website he needed, found the phone number, and dialed.

"Hi. This is Luke Thompson. I'd like to place an order for my girlfriend." It felt good to do this for her. Something nice. Something unexpected. Something that she'd love and would make her smile.

Something he hoped would make her come home sooner.

* * *

Sarah landed in San Jose, ordered an Uber, and headed straight for her office. She'd set everything right in Chicago. The nerd, whose creativity got the better of his judgment, was taken off her project, the added scenes were deleted, and the company assured her the work would still be completed on time. She'd left feeling like she'd accomplished one item on her never-ending to-do list, but added hiring her own team to debug the games to the list.

She arrived at her office to a crowd of cheering, smiling faces, all happy to see her and take a moment to celebrate the completion of the Knox Project.

Abby bumped shoulders with her. "You did it. You finished it. And you landed one of the most eligible bachelors in the state." Abby's smile went megawatt.

"It just happened." It seemed unbelievable, yet so meant to be.

"After Sean, you were destined to find a really great guy."

"How do you know he's so great?" Sarah was only teasing, but Abby held her hand out toward her office door. "Go see."

Sarah opened the door to her office, stopped short of entering, and took it all in.

Flowers. Everywhere she looked. He'd filled her entire office. And every one of the bouquets had a note that said, *I miss you.*

She clasped her hands at her chest, rested her chin on them, and just stared, tears glistening in her eyes.

Abby bumped shoulders with her again. "I think he loves you."

"I know he does." This is how it felt to have the right man send her flowers.

She finally walked into the room and buried her face in one bouquet and then another, taking in the heady scent and relishing the beauty of them and this moment.

She pulled out her cell and called him.

"I miss you, too," she said the second he picked up.

"You said you liked flowers but not which ones. I thought you might like a little of everything."

"I think you sent me the whole shop."

"Worth it to hear the joy in your voice."

"I love you."

"I love you, too. Come home."

"I'm working on that."

"Then get to it. Your family is waiting on you." In Luke's voice she heard love and anticipation, and yes, the patience he mustered to let her do her thing and return to him when she was finished.

And her heart grew too large for her chest with all the love she had for him.

Chapter Thirty-Seven

The time away from the ranch had been productive but lonely. Sarah tackled an enormous amount of work, but an empty feeling came over her when she walked into her house in Silicon Valley late the night before and realized the boys weren't in their beds, and Luke wasn't in hers. She missed them so much. And somehow, in such a short time, Luke had become an important part of her life. So much so that even a day and a half away from him felt like an eternity.

Her spirit soared as soon as the driver taking her home entered the long driveway to Luke's ranch. And as she saw the land, the stables, the house, she realized it really did feel like home.

The driver stopped in front of the house. Before she got out of the car her cell phone rang. "Hi Abby, how's the hotel?"

Abby had gone ahead to the hotel where the benefit would be held the next evening, to make sure everything was ready. "Gorgeous. And thanks for the goody basket you had delivered to my room, but it'll be gone by tomorrow. You know how much I love chocolate."

"Thanks for all your hard work over the last two days. I appreciate it and I know you'll be working your tail off tomorrow as well, what with all the meetings and press you've set up for me."

"That's why I called. I wanted you to know the organizers have combined your table with Luke's family's. I can't wait to meet him."

The driver held her door open and Sarah stepped out. "Hold on, Abby." She smiled at the driver. "Charlie, could you take the box of flowers and my bag up to the house and leave them on the porch?" He nodded and accepted the tip she held out to him. "Thank you for the ride."

"You're welcome, Miss Sarah. I'll be back for you tomorrow morning."

"Wonderful. I'll text you to let you know if I'm here or at the house we passed down the road where my kids are staying."

"No problem. Have a nice evening."

"Thank you. I plan to."

Sarah left the chauffeur to take her things up to the house and turned and walked toward the stables and continued her phone conversation. "Thanks for waiting, Abby. I can't believe my visit with Margaret is just about over and I'll be coming home."

"You sure about that?"

"Luke and I still need to come up with a plan for our future, including our living arrangements. No matter what, we'll be together."

"How are you handling the Trish thing? It's got to be hard to actually welcome her into your life, not to mention telling the boys about their sister. I seriously can't believe she had that child and never said a word to anyone."

"Luke and I plan to talk to the boys today about Trish and Jamie. As for the rest, her reasons don't really matter anymore. I don't want to keep dredging up the past and piling on the hurt and anger. I'm over it." As she said the words she knew they weren't entirely true, but it *was* getting better.

She entered the stables and smiled as several horses nickered a hello. She patted those with their heads over their stall doors and made her way to the man standing at the end of the aisle with his back to her.

"I just want to be happy." And the man in front of her made her infinitely so.

"You deserve it. Don't worry about the benefit. I've taken care of everything," Abby assured her. "See you tomorrow. You're going to knock Luke's socks off when he sees you in that killer dress." Abby had chosen something daring and different, but Sarah loved it.

She knew Luke would, too.

"Thanks, Abby. We'll talk soon." She ended the call and stuffed her phone in her purse.

Luke heard the click of her heels on the cement and turned to her, that sexy grin she loved spread across his handsome face. "You're early." Surprise and happiness filled his voice.

"Do you want me to come back later?" she teased.

"I wish you hadn't left." He hooked his arm around her waist, pulled her close, and kissed her like he hadn't seen her in a week.

She dove into the kiss, letting Luke know how much she'd missed him, too. He held her a little tighter and she felt his desperation to keep her close.

He broke the kiss, cupped her face, and stared into her eyes. "How are you?"

"A little dizzy after that kiss. And fantastic now that I'm home with you."

He pressed his forehead to hers. "This place isn't the same without you."

Her heart melted. "Thank you again for my flowers. They're beautiful."

"Sorry you only got to enjoy them for a day." Luke dropped his hands and took hers in his.

"Well, I gave a lot of them away to the ladies in the office, but I brought several bouquets home with me. I had the driver put them up on the porch."

"Really?"

"You gave them to me. I want to enjoy them as long as possible."

He held her gaze, his direct and hopeful. "And did you get everything done you needed to at the office?"

"You'll be happy to know that of the ten interviews I did, I made six offers to programmers."

His eyes went wide. "Wow. That's great."

"I also completed three more projects, shrinking my workload some."

"I love the sound of that."

"Since the Knox Project is done, except for the implementation, I also reassigned two other projects to be completed by the programmers who'd been helping with that."

"Look at you delegating instead of taking everything on yourself." Luke squeezed her hands, letting her know he approved and appreciated her effort to lessen her load so she could have more time for him and herself. "Sounds like you got a lot done. Which means you probably didn't sleep much."

"Not really. Something seemed to be missing from my bed."

"Some*one*, you mean."

She kissed him. "You."

"That's because you were in the wrong bed. You belong here. With me."

"I'm working on it," she assured him.

Luke brushed his thumbs over the backs of her hands. "I see

that. And I hope we can start making real plans to move you and the kids here."

"I was just talking to Abby about that and how this trip is coming to an end."

Luke's brow went up. "Not an end. It's a transition to our life together."

She smiled. "That actually makes me feel a lot better."

"How so?"

"I guess I feel like everything is supposed to happen at once, but if, like you said, this is a transition, that allows room for us to take the time we need to transform our lives and meld them into one life we live together."

"We'll start today with telling the boys about Jamie. Then we'll start talking about what will work best for your work schedule, the boys going to school, and where we'll live and how we'll go back and forth between here and your place, if that's what it takes."

"I love that you're open to all the possibilities of that."

He squeezed her hands. "If I get to spend my life with you, that's all that matters."

"But living here, on the ranch, we'd have a pretty great life." She knew this was where he really wanted to be. And this would be a great life for the boys. And she loved the land and the horses. They really could have it all.

All she wanted right now was him. Unfortunately . . . "Margaret should be here any minute with the boys. However, after our talk, she's taking them for pizza and a movie over at Bridget's place. She suggested I have dinner with my sexy rancher and spend the night with him."

Luke grinned. "You should take that advice."

"I was hoping to just take you to bed before they got here."

"Now, that's an idea I can get behind." Luke spun her around, wrapped his arms around her, pressed his chest to her back, and kissed her neck.

"You know we don't have time."

"I know. But I can't help myself. I've never seen you all dressed up and looking like a corporate mogul. Those heels and this suit are really sexy."

"It's a St. James. She sent me a bunch of stuff from her upcoming collection."

One of Luke's hands skimmed down her thigh and his fingers brushed back up, pulling the skirt up her leg and sending a wave of heat through her. "Let me guess, you did some work for her."

"I programmed her client database and inventory systems."

"Well, I like you in the suit, but I'll love you even better out of it." His tongue slid up her neck in a tantalizing lick.

"You'll find a matching set from her intimates line."

"Please tell me it's satin and lace."

"Would I disappoint you?" she teased.

Luke took her hand and headed for the house, pulling her along after him. When she couldn't keep up, he stopped, swung her up into his arms, and carried her.

"If you like the suit this much, I wonder how you'll react when you see my dress for the benefit."

"Maybe I should get a room at the hotel for us so I can see you in the dress and out of it."

She nuzzled her nose in his neck and softly kissed him right behind his ear. "Then I'd be wearing nothing but the jewels I borrowed for the event."

"Borrowed? Why didn't you just buy them?"

"Because, well, I don't know. There was so much to choose from I had a hard time making up my mind. I don't own any jewelry, except a few pairs of earrings. The pieces I got for to-morrow are specifically to go with the dress Abby picked out."

"I'll just have to add something sparkly to your meager collection that you can wear on your left hand and never take off."

She hugged him close as he walked up the porch steps. "I like the sound of that."

They both turned to the driveway as Margaret and the boys arrived.

Luke set her on her feet. "Rain check, sweetheart."

She pressed her hand to his chest. "We'll have all night."

Luke kissed her quick, then opened the front door, set her bag and the large box of flowers in the entryway, then turned to greet the boys.

Sarah held her arms out wide as the boys rushed up the steps and right into them. "I missed you guys." She hugged them close.

They wriggled free and threw their hands around Luke's legs.

"Can we go riding?" Jack asked.

"Not today, bud. Your mom wants to talk to you about something before you go to your aunt's house." Luke patted each of the boys on the back, then went to the steps and lent Margaret a hand coming up them.

"Thank you, Luke." Margaret looked at Sarah. "Ready for this?"

"Yes. I think so."

Margaret's gaze swept over her. "Look at you. Beautiful and strong. A business phenom and leader. You can do this," she encouraged.

Choked up by the praise and Margaret's change of heart about her, Sarah found a smile for the boys and tapped their backs to get them to go inside.

"What's this about?" Jack asked.

Nick practically attacked Luke when he sat on the sofa, rushing to climb into his lap.

Sarah sat next to Luke and patted the cushion between them for Jack to take the seat. "Well, I have some news I want to share with you."

"Is this about Dad?" Nick asked, playing with Luke's shirt.

"Yes, it is."

"And the lady?" Jack asked.

"Yes. You remember Trish."

"She made you cry." Jack folded his arms over his middle and kicked his feet.

Margaret sat in the chair beside Luke and leaned forward. "I think you know that your dad shouldn't have been seeing Trish when he and your mom were still married. That was wrong. And I'm sorry that because of what your dad did, it hurt your mom."

"He wasn't always nice," Jack said to his lap, unable to look at them.

Sarah put her hand on his back. "No, sweetheart, he wasn't. But we are all happy now. Right?"

Jack perked up. "Yes. I like it here with Luke."

"Me, too." Nick cupped Luke's face and mushed his forehead into Luke's chin.

Luke smiled and hugged Nick close, but let her go on with this difficult talk.

"We're building a family, right? Me and Luke with you boys, plus Grandma and Aunt Bridget and Sophia. We're all family now."

"And Grandpa and Grandma and Tyler," Jack added.

"That's right. They're a part of our family. And there's someone new joining our family."

"Who?" Nick asked, from atop Luke's shoulders now.

"Her name is Jamie." Sarah sucked in a breath and spilled the truth. "And she's your sister."

Jack tilted his head. "We're going to have a sister?"

Sarah took another breath and dove in. "You have a sister. Your dad and Trish had a baby together. Trish gave birth to Jamie after your dad died. I didn't know about her until just a few days ago."

"When you talked to Trish on the phone." Jack put the pieces together, helping her out.

"That's right. And because you and Nick and Jamie all have the same daddy, that means you and Nick are Jamie's big brothers."

"Where is she?" Nick asked, patting Luke on the top of the head.

The man had the patience of a saint, not seeming to mind being Nick's jungle gym.

"Jamie lives with her mommy. In a few days, we'll be back at our house for a little while, and I'm going to invite Jamie over to meet you."

"Will she live with us?" Jack's eyes clouded with confusion and questions.

"No. She'll live with Trish, her mommy. But I hope that we will get to see her lots so you and Nick can get to know your sister."

"She'll be part of the family," Nick announced with a big smile.

Sarah took out her phone and tapped the screen to get to her text messages. "Trish sent me some pictures of Jamie. Want to see?"

Nick launched himself off Luke onto her lap. Luckily she caught him before he tipped off and landed on the floor.

"Chill out, buddy," Luke scolded. "You could hurt your mom."

"Sorry, Mama." Nick kissed her.

She nuzzled her nose in his cheek. "Sit nice."

He adjusted on her lap and Jack scooted closer. She held the phone in front of them and showed them the first picture of Jamie.

"She has hair like mine," Nick said.

"I think she has your dad's green eyes, too," Sarah added, her throat tight with all the mixed emotions running through her.

Luke leaned in. "She's about a year and a half old. You guys will have to be careful playing with her because she's much smaller than you."

Sarah tapped the next picture to enlarge it on her phone.

Margaret had gotten up and stood at her shoulder. When she saw Jamie smiling big with several tiny baby teeth showing, she put her hand on Sarah's shoulder and caught her breath. "Wow. She's beautiful."

Sarah put her hand over Margaret's. "She reminds me of Nick when he was that age."

"What about me, Mama?" Jack asked.

"I think she has your nose," she said to make him happy and because their noses were very similar. "And check out the soccer ball in this picture."

"I like soccer, too." Jack beamed.

"I bet you'll find lots of things in common," Margaret said.

Sarah set her phone on the table and looked at both boys. "So, what do you think about having a new sister?"

"It's good," Jack said.

"When can we see her? I can show her my cars." Nick pulled one out of his pocket.

"Soon. Do you guys have any questions?"

Both boys shook their heads.

"Okay. Then Grandma is going to take you over to Aunt Bridget's house for pizza and a movie."

"Yay!" Jack stood and leapt over the back of the couch.

"Hey, bud, that's not how we get down." Luke snagged Nick off her lap and flew him through the air and set him on his feet on the other side of the coffee table.

"Me next." Jack jumped up and down, wanting his turn.

While Luke distracted the boys, Sarah took a minute with Margaret. "Are you okay?"

"It's just been a lot to take in, but seeing her . . . She's real. She's another part of him."

"I texted with Trish." It seemed easier for both of them to start out that way. "She's going to bring Jamie to the house to see the boys. She's also willing to bring Jamie to your house so that you and Bridget and Sophia can have some time with her, and Trish and you can talk."

Margaret nodded. "I'd like that. I know it's awkward and strange without Sean here, but I really want to get to know my granddaughter. I don't really care how she got here." Margaret caught herself. "Oh Sarah. I'm sorry. That's not what I meant at all."

Sarah put her hand on Margaret's arm. "Stop. It's okay to focus on Jamie and not put all your energy into how it happened, what happened, and all that." Sarah was tired of being mired in the past.

Margaret checked her watch. "Boys. It's time to go," she called out, then looked at Sarah again. "I'm really trying to be like you and put this behind me. It's just really hard having all this turmoil inside of me."

"Maybe you should let it out."

Margaret eyed her. "How?"

"Tell him. Say everything you'd say to him if he were here out loud. Let it out. Let him have it. Tell him you're angry and upset." She put her hand on Margaret's shoulder. "Once you've got all that out, tell him everything else. That you saw the boys. That you're going to meet his daughter. He may be gone, but that doesn't mean you have to forget him or not make him a part of your life."

"Are you able to do that?"

"Sometimes late at night I'll go into the boys' rooms and I'll look at them and say, 'Look what you're missing, Sean. I hope you can see them.'" Maybe she still harbored a lot of pain and anger, but in those moments she wanted Sean to understand what had been most important. She hoped, wherever he was now, he knew. She hoped he watched over the boys with pride and love.

He wasn't here to show them that.

They had her. And Luke. And family.

But they should have had him and he should have been the man and father they deserved.

And she would give them that kind of man, because she loved Luke, and he'd be the dad, not that the boys lost, but that they deserved.

She'd bring love into their lives. She'd started with reconciling with Margaret and Bridget. She'd add their sister, Jamie.

Margaret pushed her shoulders back. "I'll try. And I am excited to meet Jamie."

"Something to look forward to. Focus on that," Sarah advised.

Margaret went to the boys. "Let's get going."

The boys hugged her and Luke, then left with Margaret.

Luke closed the front door and turned to her. "What you said to Margaret . . . That was really honest. You gave her a way to be angry and happy."

"It's not easy to do both at the same time. I for one am done with Sean and what he left me with. I'm not going to keep carrying it around with me anymore. I'm moving on. I'm moving forward."

"With me?" Luke took a step closer.

She closed the distance and put her hands at the back of his neck, drawing him close. "Definitely with you." She kissed him softly.

Luke took the kiss deeper.

She broke the kiss and stared up at him. "We're alone."

Luke gave her a wicked grin. "I can't wait to find out what you're wearing under that suit." He took her hand, dipped his body, and pulled her toward him as he lifted her right off her feet and over his shoulder. He stood tall and carried her through the great room and up the stairs to their room.

She laughed and smacked him on the ass. "Put me down."

He did. Right next to the bed. She giggled and tried to catch her breath, but Luke kissed it right out of her again, then he stared down at her with a look of pure desire and they both gave in to the need to be close and started peeling off clothes, anxious to get their hands on the other.

Luke had his shirt off, tempting her with a full display of his broad chest and chiseled muscles. His boots went flying, but when he undid the button on his jeans, he stilled and stared at her. She let her blouse float to the floor, revealing the pink lace bra pushing her breasts up into rounded mounds that ached for his touch. The skirt slid down her legs in a whoosh of material and she stood before him in nothing but the sexy bra and matching lace panties.

"Uh . . ."

"Use your words," she teased.

"Damn."

A warm blush rose from her breasts up to her cheeks.

"Instead of words, I'd rather use my hands and mouth and tongue all over you."

She held her hands out. "Well, come and get me."

Luke closed the short distance and took her mouth in a scorching kiss as both his hands clamped onto her ass and pulled her up and snug against his warm skin. His hard length pressed to her belly and she rubbed her body against his.

Luke laid a trail of soft, open-mouthed kisses down her neck and chest. His finger slipped inside the lace cup and pulled it down and her breast popped out. His warm mouth covered her hard nipple and he sucked the peak, sending a wave of heat down low, making her clench her thighs to try to ease the ache only Luke could make better.

He released her hard nipple and licked it with his tongue, his breath making the pink tip even tighter, before he moved to her other breast and kissed the swell of it above the lace trim. His hands swept up her back and he unhooked the bra and sent the barrier flying. His hands cupped both her breasts, her nipples squeezed between his fingers as he kneaded the soft flesh and kissed her neck again.

Lost in the feel of him, and heat, her fingers slid into his hair and she held him to her.

"I love it when you let go, sweetheart."

"I want to hold on." She slid her hand down his chest and rock-hard abs and dipped it inside his jeans. She clamped her hand around his throbbing length and rubbed him up and down.

Luke hissed in a breath, leaned back, and stared down at her hand working his hard cock.

He made quick work of pushing his jeans and boxers down his hips and kicking them off his feet so she could take his silky flesh in her palm.

"That's so good." He held her hips and let her have her way with him for another few seconds before he hissed again, pushed her hand away, backed her up to the bed, and followed her onto it, covering her body with his warm one and kissing her senseless.

Somehow in the midst of hands caressing and mouths moving over each other, her panties seemed to melt away seconds before Luke joined their bodies and they were moving together in a much more intimate and primal way.

She loved the feel and weight of him on her and the taste of him on her tongue.

Luke moved, and she moved with him, meeting his thrusts and the demands of his body and hers for the release they both knew was coming but held off just a little longer so they could enjoy the closeness and tantalizing sensations coursing through their bodies until it overtook them.

They both panted with exertion and wallowed in the euphoric aftermath in each other's arms.

Sarah hugged Luke close as his body pressed her into the bed. "Now, that's what I call a homecoming."

Luke pressed a kiss to her neck, then rose up on his forearms and stared down at her. "I missed you. This. Us."

Sarah covered a yawn with the back of her hand. "Me, too. I couldn't wait to get back here to you."

Luke shifted to her side, hooked his arm and hand over her middle, and drew her back to his chest and held her close. "Close your eyes. Take a nap. I'll wake you when it's time for dinner."

Luke held her, listening to her breathe, savoring the feel of her in his arms, the way she fit just perfectly in them, his life, and his heart.

He was so damn lucky to have found someone like her. She loved him. He'd discovered he had the capacity to love just as deeply as his father loved his mom and Jason loved Michelle. It had seemed so easy for them and he'd struggled with one ruined relationship after the next. Until Sarah came into his life and stole his horse and his heart.

Now all he had to do was bring their two worlds together permanently.

Chapter Thirty-Eight

S arah, you look absolutely gorgeous in that dress. The press is going nuts over you. Can you believe all of this? . . . Sarah, I'm talking to you."

Abby's voice finally penetrated Sarah's daydream.

"I'm sorry. I was thinking about Luke. And last night. And this morning."

Abby beamed. "Tell me everything. I want details."

"I don't mean that. Well, I do, but I was thinking about how happy he was when I got home and how sweet. I took a short nap before dinner. When I woke up he'd brought up one of the bouquets of flowers and put them on the nightstand. I went downstairs to find him and saw one of the bouquets on the dining room table and another on the coffee table in front of the fireplace. It was so lovely how he'd put them throughout the house, so that no matter where I went, I could enjoy them. The last bouquet was on the kitchen table. He was at the stove making me pancakes, eggs, and bacon. We ate in front of a roaring fire."

Abby's eyes turned all dreamy. "He made you breakfast for dinner."

"He said it was the fastest thing he could make that would stick to my ribs and give me enough energy."

Abby perked up and her eyes lit with interest. "Energy for what? Come on, give."

"Let's just say I woke up in his arms in front of the fireplace this morning."

He'd given her another perfect night, with the roaring fire she'd included in her dream day.

Abby sighed. "I am so jealous. I can't wait to meet him."

"How many more meetings do we have to get through?" She and Luke agreed it didn't make sense for him to trail her from one meeting to the next before the benefit, so he was meeting her right before the actual event started.

"Two more to go. Luke, his family, and yours will meet us after that and you'll all go to the ballroom together. You have your speech, right?"

"I do. I've kept it short and sweet. I'll make a few comments about the Spencer Foundation and what we're doing, and then accept the award. Sound good?"

"Perfect. Let's get these meetings out of the way. I can't wait to meet your Luke."

"*My* Luke. I like that. Who are we meeting with next?"

"TriStar, Inc."

"Right. A security project like the Knox Project."

"Exactly. Then . . ." Abby stalled and held up her hand. "Promise you won't freak out?"

"Why?"

"Because the second meeting is actually a press conference with about a hundred reporters who all want to ask you about Spencer Software and Andy's Antics and how you, as a woman, built the companies into what they are today." Abby winced and waited for Sarah's reaction. "I've been fending off requests for months," she went on. "As soon as it was announced you were actually going to make a public appearance, the organizers set it up without asking me first. You can answer all their questions at once, then go hide out on Luke's ranch."

There was no stopping it now. And Abby had warned her they'd do a lot of press today. Meeting them all at once and getting it over with suited her. "Sounds like a plan." And after, Luke would be here, and that made her really happy.

* * *

Luke arrived with his entire family. The press snapped pictures of their arrival. Once inside the lobby, he and Jason got caught up with some old friends.

"We missed you guys at the Governor's Ball last month," Tom said.

"Jason has an excuse. He's married with a kid, but where have you been hiding, Luke?" Brandon asked.

Luke shrugged. "It's a long drive in from the ranch." He didn't go into any more detail about how his life had changed recently. He wasn't the same man who'd meet these guys at the bar after work or on the weekend and pick up women just to pass the time and fill the void that never seemed to disappear.

"You never come out with us anymore," Paul complained. "It's no fun without you."

"You mean without him picking up the tab," Jason teased.

"Whatever happened to that waitress you were seeing?" Tom asked.

Paul shook his head. "No, she was a landscape architect."

Brandon narrowed his gaze. "I thought you were seeing some Google girl."

Jason grinned at him. "Wasn't the last one the designer you hired to do your house?"

"She wanted to do *me*." He got the laugh he expected from his friends, but Jason frowned at him. "And I wasn't seeing her. I hired her to do a job."

Luke caught sight of his parents and Michelle across the lobby seconds before they got swept up in the crowd of reporters and photographers coming out of one of the conference rooms. Hundreds of flashes went off as the photographers swarmed whoever was in the middle of the melee.

"If you turn into Farmer John, you're going to lose your most-eligible-bachelor status," Paul teased.

Luke didn't respond. He stood transfixed as the sea of reporters and photogs split and his mom, dad, and Michelle greeted the woman in the middle. She had her back to him when she hugged his mom. Her red velvet dress had short cap sleeves and left her back completely exposed to her waist. She didn't wear a long gown like most of the women here at the benefit. Her gown had a full skirt that ended at her knees and showed off a pair of gorgeous legs that ended in red satin ribbons tied around her ankles, her feet encased in red heels. Her hair was piled on top of her head and secured with a ruby and diamond clip. Long tendrils escaped in waves of mahogany. A pearl necklace circled her throat and one long strand hung down her back and ended with a large ruby that sparkled from all the flashbulbs going off.

His mother stepped back from her, caught his eye, and then said something to the beautiful woman, who slowly turned to face him and stopped his heart.

The back of her dress was spectacular, but the front was even better. The dress had a deep V-neck that showed off the swell of her breasts. It was skintight to her waist, where the skirt flared out.

Sarah.

Mine, his heart called out.

"Luke can't remember who he *was* seeing," Jason said to their friends, "because *now,* all he sees is *her.*"

Truer words . . .

Luke couldn't get to her fast enough or take his eyes off her. She stared at him from across the room with a smile on her beautiful face that lit up his heart. She held her hands away from her sides and leaned a little to her left to show off the dress, which nearly stopped his heart. She did a little twirl and waved her hands down at the pretty shoes.

She knew she looked amazing. She knew he liked what he saw.

His mouth watered and his long, determined strides took him across the room and right to her.

Just before he reached her, his dad grinned and said, "Watch out, dear. That's a man on a mission."

"I love that man." Sarah's smile and eyes said it, too.

"I know you do. And he loves you."

Luke appreciated that his father saw the love between them, that Luke had finally found what he'd admired about his parents' relationship. Undying, unyielding, undeniable love.

Luke stopped short of taking her in his arms and stuffed his hands in his pockets and just took in the breathtaking woman who made his life infinitely better in more ways than he could count.

Sarah cocked her head, confused. "Aren't you going to kiss me?"

He shook his head.

"Don't you like the dress?"

"I love the dress. I just can't kiss you, because if I do, that dress is going to fly right off you, and all these people are going to get an eyeful of me devouring you."

"Oh. Oh!" She smiled at him. "I'll take my chances. Your mother and father are right behind me." She gave him a wicked grin and then leaned into him and kissed him softly. Before she could pull back, he pulled his hands free and put them around her waist and crushed her to him. Then he really kissed her.

Flashbulbs went off all around them. He didn't care how many pictures of them ended up splashed across the Internet. All he could think about was how soft the skin on her back felt and how sweet she tasted.

He ended the kiss and looked down at her. "You're beautiful."

"Thank you." A shy smile tugged at her red-tinted lips. "Another gift. No one's ever said that to me."

He leaned his forehead to hers. "I think it every day I'm with you and will remember to tell you more often."

"Son, let's get her away from all this chaos."

"Okay, Dad. I can't wait to dance with my beautiful girlfriend." He needed to change that to "wife." Soon.

He led her away from the crowd, the press calling out questions to her, and headed toward the ballroom.

Jason and Michelle, along with his mom and dad, followed.

"You look amazing, Sarah," Michelle said from just behind them.

Sarah glanced over her shoulder as he led her down the hall. "Thank you, so do you. How do you like your new job?"

"It's fantastic. My boss is really great and so understanding," she teased, because Sarah was her boss.

A woman ran up beside Sarah and smiled at the two of them.

Sarah looked back at Michelle again. "Wow! You're really lucky. Abby, here, has a horrible boss who makes her work like crazy. She gets back at me by setting up press conferences behind my back." She smiled to soften the sarcasm.

"Hey, I warned you ahead of time." Abby shrugged. "I may have kept the size and scope of it to myself."

Sarah and Luke stopped just outside the ballroom. "It's all right." His family gathered around them. "Abby, I'd like to introduce you to the Thompson family. This is James, his wife, Lila, their son Jason, and his wife, Michelle, who is our newest marketing associate for Andy's Antics."

Everyone said hello and shook hands.

Sarah wrapped her arm around Luke's and beamed at Abby. "And this is Luke."

He shook hands with Abby. "It's nice to put a face with the cell phone ringing."

Abby laughed at his silly joke. "I'm very happy to meet the man who finally put a smile on Sarah's face. I can't remember ever seeing her this happy."

"I'm hoping to keep her that way from now on."

"I'll hold you to it." Abby smiled, but she meant every word.

He appreciated that she looked out for Sarah. And when he wasn't around, he'd count on her to still do it. But now that was his job and he'd never let anything bad happen to Sarah ever again.

Abby held up a padded envelope and glanced around as everyone else attending the benefit made their way through the double doors into the ballroom. "I'm not sure where your family is. Maybe they've already gone inside. But I have the package for Tyler."

"Thank you." Sarah turned to a man who tapped her on the shoulder.

"A word, please?" the man asked.

Sarah took several steps away from all of them.

Luke watched them, tempted to go over and make the man not stand so close to her.

Abby knocked her elbow into his arm. "Don't worry. That's Jim. Our CIO. He's had a thing for her forever. He's mostly harmless. He's not stupid enough to do anything to jeopardize his job. No one who works for Sarah would do that. She's made all of the original employees millionaires. Not to mention that we all worship her."

"I certainly do."

Abby turned to look at him. "Keep treating her well, Luke. It's about time someone did."

"I have every intention of doing just that."

Abby gave him a nod.

Sarah returned to them. "Sorry. Just some business stuff to sort out."

"We'll meet you both inside," Luke's mother said, before his family headed into the ballroom.

Abby stopped Sarah before she followed. "You can't go in yet. They want to announce your arrival."

Sarah and Luke waited outside the doors.

Abby held Sarah's forearm. "Um, Sarah, you know how I surprised you with the press conference earlier. Well, I kind of gave the organizers a list of your most recent personal charitable donations."

"You did what!"

"You deserve to be recognized for everything you do for others."

"You're lucky I don't have time to replace you." There was no sting to Sarah's words.

"You love me," Abby said, all confidence.

"I do. And I need you to get the six new people I hired started on Monday."

Luke squeezed her hand. "Then maybe we can sit down and make some definite plans for our future."

"We will. I—"

Abby cut her off. "It's time to go in. They're announcing Sarah and you, Luke, right now."

Which meant everyone in the room would know they were together. He liked that.

The doors opened to a crowd standing and applauding as they made their way into the room.

Luke led her up to the podium at the front of the ballroom, where he handed her off to the head of the organization honoring her.

Luke went to take his seat at the long family table the organizers had set up for both her family and his. Her dad and stepmom both smiled at him, then stared up at Sarah. They'd do the introductions later.

Sarah took her seat next to the podium with the members of the Rockford Charity Organization.

The head of the awards committee spoke first. "We're here today to honor Sarah Anderson., CEO of Spencer Software and chairperson of the Spencer Foundation. It's a pleasure to have her join us today, because as many of you know, she rarely grants interviews, and if you've ever hired her, you're more likely to have a conference call than an in-person meeting. Not only is she the head of two growing and already highly successful software companies, she's also someone who believes in helping others. She may not like to call attention to herself, but she absolutely caught the attention of our organization for her outstanding charitable work.

"Sarah and the Spencer Foundation have helped many individuals and charities, including a school and retreat for the deaf and blind, shelters for homeless mothers and their children, food banks, other organizations that feed the hungry, and free STEM summer programs for underprivileged girls in underserved communities. Wherever Sarah travels, she is likely to discover where the greatest need for help is and fill it, most of the time anonymously. She takes advantage of business trips to identify charitable opportunities. In several communities hit hard by wildfires, she donated new fire engines to replace the ones lost. With two young sons, it is no wonder she's known to support Little League baseball teams by providing them with new uniforms and shoes. During the holidays, she donates turkeys to charity organizations to pass out to families in need. Homeless shelters also receive new blankets and coats. When she drove past an underfunded school in a low-income neighborhood that didn't have a play yard for the young children, she made sure they got one. When an employee told her about a nephew's disappointment that his high school didn't have enough instruments, she not only donated thirty new instruments, Sarah also sponsored the choir's trip to New York City to attend three Broadway musicals."

Luke had no idea Sarah had done so much for others. She sat there listening to the list of what was probably a fraction of all her accolades with her cheeks pink with embarrassment. She clearly didn't want or need the praise for all she'd done to help those less fortunate. She did it because she knew what it was to go hungry and want for what you needed most.

Her father stared up at her, pride in his eyes for all her accomplishments.

"Sarah is an outstanding example of what can be accomplished through hard work, determination, and dedication to helping others. Please help me celebrate Sarah Anderson."

Sarah stood, shook hands with the head of the Rockford Charity Organization, then faced the crowd and waited for the applause to die down and everyone to take their seats again.

"Thank you to the Rockford Charity Organization for this amazing honor. Nothing pleases me more than giving to others and encouraging others to give. I especially love helping young people have access to the things they need to achieve their dreams.

"I'd like to take this opportunity to thank a few of the many people who have helped me help others. First, I'd like to thank my amazing assistant, Abby Garner, for helping to organize the fundraiser for the Spencer Foundation, in which we raised over three million dollars at our benefit this year to help with the many charities and community needs mentioned here tonight. I'd also like to thank the Thompson family for their generous donation. The money they've provided will benefit countless people." Sarah winked at Luke.

Luke watched Jason raise a glass in salute to Sarah's thanks. Luke leaned over to his brother. "How much did we generously donate?"

"A hundred grand from the entire family, which turned out to be chump change because Abby told me Sarah donated the huge bonus she earned for completing the Griffin Worldwide Financial project. She donated the entire six hundred K to the Spencer Foundation."

"She gave up her bonus?"

"According to Abby, all of her bonuses for finishing on time are donated to the foundation. It's another way she raises money without calling attention to herself because the funds are donated by whichever company she earns the bonus from. She seems to think there are more important things in life than money. She cares about people. Especially you. Why she fell in love with your ugly mug, I don't know."

Luke jabbed Jason with his elbow.

Michelle tapped the back of her hand to Jason's shoulder. "Pay attention. Sarah is speaking."

"I'd also like to thank everyone for coming tonight. As you know, there will be an auction toward the end of the evening.

Please dig deep and give generously to the causes we are supporting tonight. They need your help. Let's all do good for others."

Everyone rose to their feet and erupted in applause. Sarah's shy
smile made her all the more beautiful as she stood in the spotlight
and gave the room a deep nod to show her appreciation. When
her gaze landed on Luke, clapping for her, his heart full of pride
and appreciation for the generous woman he loved, she touched her
hand to her chest and that smile turned megawatt just for him.

Chapter Thirty-Nine

*A*fter the congratulations from the charity organizers, Sarah walked down the stage steps and went to the table as waiters began to serve dinner to all the guests.

Luke met her a few feet from the table and wrapped one arm around her waist in a hug and handed her a glass of wine. "You were fantastic. Congratulations. How does it feel to finally stand in the limelight and celebrate everything you've achieved?"

"Truthfully, a little exhausting." She took a sip of the wine and smiled up at him. "But also really good." She'd worked hard and given back. She'd risen above her circumstances and achieved great success. It was something to be proud of, but until now, she'd never really done so. Tonight, she felt it.

And sharing it with Luke and her family made it even more special.

Luke walked with her the few steps to the table.

Tyler stood up and hugged her first. "Abby gave me the package from you. Thank you so much, Sarah." Tyler looked just like their father, with the same lean, strong build and chiseled jaw and high cheekbones. Sarah liked his hair the best. It was dark and he kept it just a little too long. His mother was forever asking him to cut it, because it constantly fell across his brow. She imagined some young girl brushing it away for him. He'd graduate high school this year and make young ladies drop at his feet in college.

"I can't wait to go upstairs to our room and check it out. How do you think it turned out?"

"Awesome. I loved all of your ideas."

"You really used them?"

"I told you I would. In fact, I have something else for you." She spotted Abby and waved her over. Abby handed her an envelope, which Sarah then gave to Tyler. "Thanks, Abby."

"Your speech was fantastic. I'll check in with you later." Abby walked off to join the Spencer Software group at their table.

Tyler opened the envelope and stared at the check. "No way! Sarah, no way. You didn't have to do this."

"You earned it. Most of that game was your idea. You deserve to be paid for your work."

Tyler leaned in close. "Dad's not going to like this."

"Tell Lyon it's my fault. You did the work, and I'm paying you."

"You're awesome! Thank you." Tyler wrapped her in a big hug.

Sarah put her arm around Tyler and he did the same with her as they both faced Luke. "Tyler, I'd like to introduce Luke Thompson of the very prestigious Thompson Law Firm. He's the lawyer slash rancher I told you about."

Luke smirked. "You forgot 'future husband.'"

She frowned at him. "You still haven't asked me."

"I will," he assured her with a grin before he looked at Tyler. "It's nice to meet you."

"Nice to meet you, too." Tyler glanced at her. "Are you guys really getting married?"

"Not before I have a chance to find out what kind of man Luke Thompson truly is," Lyon said from behind Luke.

"Lyon." Sarah released her brother and walked to her dad,

whom she'd never called by that title, and stood beside him. "Luke, may I introduce Robert Lyons. Lyon, Luke."

Lyon gave Sarah a squeeze around her shoulders and held her to him. "She's told me a lot about you." Lyon had teased her about the way she gushed about Luke during their weekly calls. "It pleases me to see her happy."

They'd lost a lot of years because her mother never told him about her. She loved that his first instinct was to claim her as his. Of course it caused a stir with his family, who also had no idea. But his wife, Norah, welcomed her to the family, even if things started off strained because Sarah disrupted the family dynamic. It took her a while to fit in, though she still felt like the outsider simply because she and her father's family didn't have a shared history. As well, she'd held back, too afraid to really get to know them at first for fear that they'd send her away or treat her badly like so many had done to her in the past. But things only got better having her dad in her life.

Luke smiled down at her. "I like making her happy." Luke shook her dad's hand. "It's nice to meet you, sir."

"Sarah's been through a lot in her life. She needs someone she can trust implicitly and count on to never waver in their support of her and her happiness."

Luke held Lyon's gaze. "She has me for all of that and more."

Lyon nodded with an I'll-be-watching-you look. "Your family made a generous donation to Sarah's foundation."

Luke shrugged. "My entire family supports Sarah. But of course I'll personally match it."

Sarah gasped in surprise. "Luke, you don't have to do that. The money Thompson Law donated is plenty."

"I want you to know that *I* support what you do and want to be a part of it."

Lyon slapped his hand on Luke's shoulder. "You're a generous man. I especially appreciate that kind of integrity."

Luke took her hand. "Sarah makes everyone around her want to be a better person. She gives loyalty and trust without asking for anything in return. I want to be worthy of that kind of rare generosity and her open heart."

"Sarah told me trust and women haven't really gone together in your life."

"I've had a few good and a lot of disappointing relationships. I couldn't seem to find what I was looking for until I met Sarah and it all became clear that having a real partner and family was absolutely possible. With her."

"And you're sure this time?"

Sarah almost rolled her eyes at her father for asking what equated to "What are your intentions toward my daughter?" Plus, they had a huge audience, including Luke's family sitting nearby.

Luke didn't balk at her father's boldness. "I think I fell in love with her the day I met her."

"Me, too," her father said, touching her deeply.

"I gave Sarah a hard time when we first met," Luke confessed. "I thought she was something she isn't and could never be. I was wrong. I told her as much. During it all, I felt this pull, something I couldn't resist or deny. A connection I'd never felt. And I knew I didn't want to live my life without her in it. She has my complete trust and loyalty. I don't ever want to lose hers. As for Jack and Nick . . . I want to be the father to them my dad was to me."

It touched her deeply that he'd be so open and honest and heartfelt with her father.

Luke brushed the back of his fingers over her cheek. "It's you and me, sweetheart. Always. Forever."

Choked up, she needed to change the subject before she cried.

Her brother became her distraction. "Tyler, show your dad your first paycheck. He'll be so proud of you for earning it."

As expected, Lyon turned to the son he doted on. "When did you get a job?"

"Sarah and I collaborated on her new project. I never expected her to pay me, but she did. All I wanted was to have an advanced copy of the game."

Lyon looked at the check. "Sarah, you can't possibly think to pay him this much."

"Sure, I can. He came up with a lot of the ideas. He did the work, so I paid him what I'd pay any other game developer."

"I think you're just being generous because he's your brother."

"If that's the case, then, I'm sure you'd agree, it's my prerogative."

Luke notched his chin toward Tyler. "Which game is that? The new Knight's Revenge?"

"Yeah, I love that game, but I thought there could be a lot more to it. So, I called Sarah and told her my ideas. And she actually used them in the new game."

"It's one of my favorites, as well. When you, your father, and mom come for Christmas this year, we'll go head-to-head."

"Luke, I'm sure Lyon would like to spend Christmas—"

"With his family," he pointedly suggested before turning to her dad. "We'd love to have you. It will be my first Christmas with Sarah and the boys. What do you say?"

Sarah's heart filled with hope. She'd never had a big family holiday and she'd love to have her family, Margaret, Bridget, and Sophia, and Luke's family all together. "Will you join us, Lyon? It would mean so much to me."

"Yeah, Dad. Let's have Christmas with Sarah, Nick, and Jack. I haven't gotten to see them in a long time. Mom will love it." Tyler looked as hopeful as Sarah.

"If it means that much to you, Sarah, of course we'll be there."

She couldn't wait. "Thank you, Lyon. It's going to be wonderful." She gave her dad a quick hug then stepped back to Luke's side.

"Well, we better sit down to dinner with everyone else," her father suggested.

She took her seat next to Luke, his family spread out around the table on his other side, hers next to her. She looked at everyone here to support her and just took it in. She'd come a long way from that lonely little girl lost in the world, with no one who loved or took care of her. Now, she'd found her own strength and used her smarts to build a thriving business and had a mismatched family she'd pulled together around her.

Luke leaned over and kissed her softly. "You look happy."

"I am because I'm here with my family."

The rest of the evening went by in a blur of people who wanted to congratulate her on her accomplishments and talk business. She loved watching Luke interact with the people he knew or who wanted to talk to him about a case he'd been involved in or about someone he'd represented. A couple people even hinted they could use his help.

At the end of the night, she finally got her dance with him, and leaned back and stared up at him. "Did I tell you how handsome you look in this tux? Sometimes when I look at you, I can't believe you're mine."

"You take my breath away in that dress."

"Don't look at me like that, Luke. There are a ton of people here and all of them seem to be watching us."

"Look at you like what?"

"Like you want me, right here, right now."

He leaned in and nuzzled his nose along her ear's outer edge. "I do." He pressed a kiss to her forehead and stared down at her, his eyes filled with desire.

Sarah swallowed hard. "You should take me home to bed."

"My favorite place to take you." He kissed her right there on the dance floor in front of everyone.

It was the best night of her life. She'd stood before a room full of reporters and taken credit for not only the innovative and unique security system she'd done for the Knox Project, but for the success of Spencer Software and Andy's Antics. She celebrated *her* accomplishments and showed everyone that she'd done it on her own through hard work and determination.

But the best thing had been standing at the podium and staring down at her dad and Luke, the two most important men in her life, and seeing their pride and love for her.

And dancing with Luke, seeing the way he looked at her and how it made her heart melt, solidified how much she wanted to spend her life with him.

Chapter Forty

*I*t turned out that escaping an event held in your honor was harder than she thought, with everyone wanting to say their goodbyes. Plus, she had to thank everyone who participated in the auction. By the time Luke sat beside her in the limo and pulled her close to his side, she was exhausted.

The drive to her home didn't take long. She was happy to be back and excited to show Luke her place.

They pulled into her driveway and Sarah spotted Luke's Mercedes. "When did you drop your car off?"

"While you were doing your CEO thing. Abby gave me the spare key to the house so I could do something for you." He glanced out the window at the house. "This house . . . it's amazing."

She loved the five-bedroom, country French cottage vibe of the place with all its tall peaks and dormers. Part of the house was done in a pale gray stone, the rest in white stucco. The massive windows were trimmed in black. And the gardens out front were simple, with miniature evergreen trees, white roses, and lavender lilacs, though they weren't in bloom now.

"I want to keep it."

"I'm thinking about redoing the ranch façade to look like this. I love it."

She loved that he didn't blink an eye or care if she sold the house or kept it. "The ranch house is already white with dark blue trim. If we added some pretty stone around the perimeter base it would look really great."

Luke brushed his hand over her shoulder and up her neck. "Yes, it would. I'm glad you see it, too."

Yes, she finally saw their future taking shape in her mind. She'd been afraid to free it to bloom into reality because it might fall apart and never be. But she didn't need to fear that anymore. Luke didn't want to take anything from her, he wanted to build on what they had.

Luke swept his fingers over her skin again, making her warm and the connection between them flare. "I've got several ideas for a tree house and playground for the ranch. Once I see what we've got here, we can make a final decision on something for there."

We. Luke was always about them.

"The kids would love to pick something."

"We'll show them the choices I bookmarked on my tablet. The kids are all going to have a blast together."

The chauffeur opened the door. Luke climbed out, then offered his hand to her and helped her out. He wrapped his arm around her. "You okay?"

"A little tired. Happy to be home."

Luke unlocked the front door and pushed it open. She stopped short in the entry and stared at the huge bouquet of red roses in a vase on the console table.

"Luke." She knew he'd done this for her.

He kissed her on the side of the head. "I just wanted you to have something nice to come home to. Something to say, 'Congratulations on all your success.'"

She promptly buried her face in the flowers, inhaling their

heady scent, and smiled. "They're beautiful. And you're . . . I love you. I love this."

"I'm glad." He stared into her office on their right, then the formal living room on the left, and finally straight ahead into the massive family room with windows overlooking the backyard. "This place is so you. Warm. Inviting. Elegance and comfort. And very similar to the ranch."

"We like the same things. Did you take a walk through the house when you were here?"

"Just the main rooms."

"Well, the kitchen is through the family room to the left. There's a bathroom off to the right. And down this hall are the kids' bedrooms. The master is through the living room on the opposite side." She pointed to the short hallway and double doors just past a cozy seating area surrounded by bookcases.

Luke took her hand and led her that way. "I already found our room." He opened the double doors, revealing her massive king-size bed made of chunky wood and covered in a white duvet with sky-blue pillows. The walls were the same shade of pale blue, the windows and closet doors trimmed in wood, and a massive crystal chandelier dominated the center of the room and its tall ceiling.

The only thing that held her attention was the huge heart made out of red rose petals at the foot of the bed. "Luke. I love it." Even better was seeing his suitcase sitting right outside the closet doors.

"It's like a five-star hotel suite in here, only better." He turned to her. "Whatever else you want to do to the ranch to make it feel like this place, do it."

"You really like it." She loved it. She'd always wanted a room just like this growing up. She thought it comfortable yet . . . elegant. Just like Luke described her.

"I can't wait to sleep with you in that bed and wake up with you in my arms." He put action into words, stepping behind her to unzip her dress. He pushed the sleeves down her arms as he planted a trail of kisses along her shoulders. "You were so smart and sexy tonight and while I loved watching you do your thing, all I could think about was getting you out of this dress and kissing every inch of you."

The dress hit the floor, leaving her in nothing but heels, panties, and the killer necklace that hung down her back.

Luke slid the necklace around so that the string of pearls and chunky ruby hung to her belly button. He took her hips and turned her around, staring down at her. "God, you take my breath away." He kissed her and did the same to her.

She slipped her hands into his tux jacket and pushed it off his shoulders and down his arms. He took a step toward her. She backed up as she undid the buttons on his shirt.

The look in his eyes held all the intent and promises of what was to come.

She welcomed it and him with a wicked grin. "I've been wanting you here with me."

"I spend every second of the day wanting you." Those words ignited a fire in both of them.

His clothes disappeared before the back of her legs hit the bed.

She scooted back. Luke undid the ribbons on her killer heels and dropped the shoes to the floor. His hands glided up the sides of her thighs. His fingers hooked in the red lace panties she wore and he dragged them down her legs.

After that, it was all hot kisses, warm hands, and making love until both of them hit that exquisite peak and Luke collapsed on top of her and she went limp.

Sarah didn't remember falling asleep in Luke's arms, but she did remember the amazing night they'd shared. And he was right, there was nothing like waking up cradled in the curve of his body behind her, his arm wrapped protectively over her middle.

"You up?" His voice rumbled at her ear.

She wiggled her rump into his hard length. "You are." She felt him smile against her head.

"I can't get enough of you." He kissed her right behind her ear, sending a delicious shiver through her. "You actually slept in."

She glanced at the clock. "Nine-thirty!"

"We got home late."

"You kept me up later," she reminded him.

The doorbell rang, surprising her. "Who could that be?"

"Another surprise." Luke turned her toward him and kissed her softly. "Take a shower. Meet me in the kitchen." He kissed her again, then rolled out of bed and walked naked to the closet and opened the doors, revealing a pile of his clothes stacked in the mostly empty portion of the walk-in. He grabbed a pair of jeans and pulled them on, then grabbed a T-shirt and walked back toward her.

She smiled at him. "I see you moved in."

"Not quite. But close."

She tilted her head and studied the small pile of clothes compared to the huge suitcase. "You'll have time today to finish unpacking."

Luke pulled the shirt over his head. "That's for something else. I gotta get the door. Shower. Kitchen."

She saluted him as he left the room chuckling.

She did what he asked, excited about another surprise. It took some doing to get the pins out of her tangled hair. She was still wearing the amazing jewelry she'd borrowed and hated to take it off and return it, but she couldn't wear it in the shower, which was heaven.

She didn't know who'd arrived, but she wasn't putting on

makeup on the weekend. The boys would be home soon and they'd probably want to spend some time outside with the friends they'd missed.

She took the time to dry her hair. She left it down because Luke liked it that way. Since Luke left in jeans, she picked something equally comfortable and pulled on a simple, slinky black tank dress, then went in search of him.

Just having him in the house made it feel different. She felt him here.

He stood at the kitchen counter sipping a cup of coffee as the same chef he'd hired to cook dinner at his place stood at her stove finishing off a pan of scrambled eggs. The whole place smelled like bacon.

"Morning, sweetheart." Luke poured her a mug of coffee from the carafe beside him.

"I would have made us breakfast."

Luke shook his head. "You're not doing anything today but being home with family." He handed her the mug.

She took a sip. "That sounds amazing."

"Let's have breakfast and talk about you and me." Luke took her free hand, came around the counter, and led her back past the dining room, through the living room, and out to the back patio where the table had been set for two.

The chef followed them out with their plates and set them in front of them as they sat. "Enjoy." He disappeared back into the house.

Luke dug into his food, starving after their night together.

She stared at him, getting his attention. "This was really nice of you to do."

"I knew you'd be tired after the festivities last night. Plus the long day you put in handling business and the press."

She appreciated so much that he understood the hard work she put in to do her job well.

She didn't know how to start this talk about the rest of their lives, so she asked Luke the simple question, "So, Luke, what do you want?"

He held her gaze. "I thought I made it clear exactly what I want." He leaned forward and put his hand over hers. "But if you need to hear it again today, tomorrow, every day for the rest of our lives, then I'm happy to remind you. I love you. I want a life with you and *our* children. And right now, I don't care if that's on the ranch, here at your place, or on the moon. I just want us to be together."

"I'm supposed to travel all over the world for the next two weeks installing my security program at all the Griffin Worldwide Financial sites," she reminded him.

"I know. I'm going with you."

Surprise and shock shot through her. "What? You can't do that."

He raised a brow. "Why not?"

She really wanted him to go with her, but didn't want to take him away from his life. "What about your ranch?"

"Thirteen people work there, sweetheart. That's how I'm able to spend three days in the office out here. That's why I can go with you on this trip and pamper you and show you just how much I love you. My dad can cover my legal cases. I think it will be good for us to spend some quality time together. Which is why I'm already packed."

The suitcase in their room.

"Abby has everything you need packed and ready to go. We'll spend a couple days here with the boys, then we'll go on our trip.

Your dad and stepmom can't wait to have their grandchildren all to themselves, especially after all these weeks apart."

While Sarah had been saying goodbye to attendees last night, he'd been speaking to her dad about this. "You and Lyon are getting along well."

"Luckily, we align on everything. I even got his blessing to marry you."

She smiled. Of course he did. Because he'd been clear for weeks about what he wanted. Her. "You haven't asked me."

"I will."

"You have a lot of plans. Travel. A proposal. A life with me." How could she not believe he loved and wanted her?

"So let's talk details about life at home."

Chapter Forty-One

The doorbell rang right at noon. Sarah and Luke had their talk about the future on the back patio and stayed out there long after they'd made the decision to make the ranch home base and use her place in Silicon Valley for the days and nights Sarah and Luke worked in their offices there, though they promised each other that one of them would always be with the boys back at the ranch, even if that meant she and Luke had to coordinate their schedules and spend more time apart than they'd like. But it was worth it to give the boys the stability they needed and deserved.

She loved that they could sit and talk about everything openly and come to a decision that worked for both of them.

She didn't need to give anything up for Luke. He didn't need to for her either. They talked about how they could have what they both wanted with a little give-and-take.

Optimistic about their future, and excited that Luke was going with her on her trip overseas, she felt like her life was finally on track and included everything she'd ever wanted.

"Sounds like the kids are home. I bet they're excited to be back." Sarah rose to get the door.

Luke followed her. "Um, I might have forgotten to mention that I have another surprise for you."

She turned in the living room and looked at him. "What surprise?"

He gave her that grin she loved so much. "Open the door and find out."

Sarah rushed to the front door and opened it to her entire pieced-together family standing on her doorstep, Jack and Nick right up front.

"Surprise!" they all shouted.

Luke stood beside her and put his arm around her back, his hand on her hip. "I invited everyone over to celebrate your big night last night and you finishing your huge project."

No wonder the chef Luke hired was still in her kitchen.

Sarah smiled at everyone, then pushed the door open wide. "Come in."

As everyone passed by, they said their hellos.

Lyon, Norah, and Tyler came in after Jack, Nick, and Margaret made their way inside. Behind them, Luke's family: his parents, brother, sister-in-law, and little Emma.

Bridget and Sophia each gave her a hug, then went to find everyone else settling into the living room.

Abby brought up the rear. "I really like your guy. You two are going to have a great trip."

Sarah hugged Abby. "I'm so glad you're here."

"Luke said it was a family event." Abby winked, because she knew Sarah considered her the sister she never had, then walked in.

A car pulled up to the curb outside.

Before Sarah closed the door because she didn't think anyone else was coming, Luke halted her. "We have one more guest."

Sarah glanced back at the car where a man stood holding a

sweet, little blond toddler. A woman stepped out of the passenger door and stared at her. Trish.

"I thought it might be easier to introduce Jamie to everyone at once."

"Trish agreed to this?"

"Like you, she wants Jamie to get to know her brothers. This way, there are a lot of us around to make it seem like a party rather than a strained introduction. At least, that's what I hoped it would feel like for everyone."

Trish and her fiancé arrived on the stoop with Jamie. Trish looked unsure of her welcome. "Hello, Sarah."

"Trish." Sarah took a breath, unable to take her eyes off the little girl who looked so much like Sean and her Nick. "Thank you for bringing her over."

"Luke made a good point. The first meeting, no matter how hard we try, will be awkward and difficult. This way, Jamie gets to attend a party and have fun and maybe that's a good way to start."

Finally Sarah met Trish's eyes and found regret and remorse, along with hope.

Trish glanced at Jamie, then her fiancé, who gave her a nod to go ahead. "I'm sorry, Sarah, for everything I did to hurt you. I look back on it and wonder how I could be so selfish and not think of you, and what you were going through. While I regret the pain I've caused . . ."

Sarah looked at Jamie. "You can't regret that it happened because you got a beautiful little girl out of it."

Trish's gaze fell to the ground. "Yes. That's true. She's my whole heart. I know one day I'll have to tell her about her father. And me. And how she came to be. My hope is that having Brett here to love her and be the father she deserves will help ease the loss for her and that she'll understand I let my feelings get away from me and didn't use my head."

Sarah glanced at Luke, the man who'd be the father her children deserved. She thought of how she'd let her heart and desires for a family override her good sense in seeing Sean for who he really was until it was too late.

"Would you like to stay?" Sarah thought Luke's idea of starting with a celebration was way better than getting caught up in the past.

Trish eyed her. "Um. Are you sure?"

"I've moved on from Sean." She looked from Trish to Brett. "You've moved on. You and I are starting something of our own today. Luke invited the family. Jamie is family. And that makes you family, too." Sarah stepped back and held her hand out for them to enter her home.

It was a big step. One she didn't know she needed to take to really put the past behind her, but it seemed right.

Trish, Brett, and Jamie stepped into the house.

Trish paused and took Jamie into her arms, then turned to Sarah. "Jamie, I'd like you to meet my new friend Sarah. Sarah, this is Jamie."

Sarah went along with the introductions. "Hello, Jamie. I'm so happy to meet you. I can't wait to introduce you to—"

"Your brothers," Trish interjected. "We told her she's coming over to see her brothers."

Sarah nodded. "They're right in here."

They all walked into the huge living room and the boys ran over.

Jack stared up at the little girl. "Are you Jamie?"

The toddler stared down at him wide-eyed.

Trish helped out. "Hi Jack. It's nice to see you again." She bent down. "This is Jamie. Your sister."

Jamie wiggled to get free of her mom's arms. Trish let her go.

Jack took her hand. "We have toys. Come see."

Nick took her other hand. "I'm bigger than her," he said to Luke.

Luke ran his hand over Nick's head. "Be careful with her."

"I will."

Luke held his hand out toward the kitchen. "Can I get you something to drink?"

"I could use one," Brett said, following Luke.

Trish hung back and stood beside Sarah as they watched the boys playing with the balls they pulled out of the toy box. Emma joined them and all four kids played like they'd been friends forever.

"It's so easy for kids to just be friends."

Sarah stood there, watching them, loving having them all together. "It's only hard for adults because we make it hard by holding grudges and not giving someone a chance. Let's not do that."

"I appreciate that, Sarah. It's more than I expected or deserve."

"And that's the last of that. You're my guest. In time, we'll be more because they need us to be."

Trish touched her arm, then took her hand back. "Thank you, Sarah. I think I'll go get that drink."

Sarah didn't move. She glanced around the huge room and took it all in.

Lyon and his wife were engaged in conversation with Margaret, James, and Lila by the back sliding doors. Tyler was on the floor, his back against the sofa where Jack had sat a moment ago, both of them with controllers in their hands as they played video games together. Sophia sat on the opposite sofa watching something on her tablet. Jason, Brett, and Luke sat on the steps that led up into the dining room, each with a beer in hand, watching over Emma and Jamie play with a ball, rolling it back and forth between them. Abby stood with Michelle, Bridget, and Trish. The ladies all had a glass of wine and conversed like they were old friends. Nick ran out of the kitchen with a cookie in his hand and slammed into Luke's back and wrapped his arms around Luke's neck. Luke reached back and ruffled Nick's hair and kept talking to Jason until Jamie stood up and put her hand on Luke's knee. He immediately picked her up and held her to his chest. Brett handed him a sippy cup, which he gave to the little girl, who didn't seem afraid of strangers. And Sarah didn't think any girl, young or old, wouldn't fall for Luke.

Sarah's eyes filled with tears.

Everyone was here. In her house. Together.

And there was Luke, taking care of and loving on the kids.

He sensed her staring and looked across the room, his eyes bright with joy.

The tears spilled from her own eyes and she brushed them from her cheek.

"Who you?" Jamie asked Luke.

Nick hung over Luke's shoulder and said, "He's my dad."

Luke's eyes went wide and met Sarah's again. She pressed her hand to her heart and gave him a nod to let him know, yes, he was Nick and Jack's dad.

Luke looked a little overwhelmed, but he smiled and wrapped his arm around Nick.

Abby came over and handed her a glass of wine. "You look like you need this."

"This . . . It's what I always wanted."

Abby bumped shoulders with her. "It took a lot of . . . I don't know what. Heart, to invite Trish to stay. I hate what she did to you."

"Me, too."

"But I get that you want to move on and make this work for the kids. And you and Luke, you're perfect together. And he's way better and hotter than Brett, so you totally win there."

Sarah laughed under her breath. "You don't even know Brett."

"I'm sure he's great. Still. Luke. Hot. Rich. Thoughtful. Romantic. Totally going to be a great husband and dad."

"Absolutely."

"He gets you, Sarah. He knows he can buy you anything you want to make you happy, but this, your family all together, that's all you've ever wanted. Still, the ring better be spectacular."

Sarah hugged Abby. "I love you." She wanted Abby to know that.

Abby squeezed her back. "I love my job because of you. You make me feel like it's us, even when it's mostly you. You always treat me like I'm your friend."

Sarah leaned back and held Abby's gaze. "My best friend," she corrected.

"Which is why I love you right back." Abby held up her wineglass.

Sarah clinked hers to Abby's, though she didn't take a sip because she had a feeling she shouldn't right now.

Bridget joined them. "Sarah, can I have a word?"

Abby gave her a smile, then walked back over to join Michelle and Trish.

"How are you, Bridget?"

"Fine. Better if you say yes."

Sarah cocked an eyebrow. "To what?"

"A job."

That surprised her. "Really? You want to work for me?"

"I was talking to Michelle. She told me about what she's doing for you, working from home, setting her own hours. You know I'm an artist. While I love what I do, it's never paid the bills. I thought maybe, if you were willing, I could draw the characters for your children's line. For like . . . on the packaging and stuff. Or I'd love to learn how to do the video games. Maybe you'd have someone train me. That would be something I could do on the computer from home, right? Then I could take care of my daughter and be there for her before and after school but still have something that's mine. I'd make my own money and not have to rely on alimony or my mom to bail me out." She looked at Sarah with such earnest eyes. "I could be more like you."

And that sold Sarah on the fact Bridget really wanted to learn and work and do this for the right reasons, not just for the money. "Okay. You're hired."

"Really? To do what?"

"Whatever most appeals to you."

Bridget looked taken aback. "Thank you, Sarah."

"I'll expect you to do your best work and be diligent about putting in the hours required to meet deadlines."

"I will. I promise. I'll work really hard. To earn your trust as well."

To ease Bridget's mind, and help Sarah really take it in that she had family, she said, "It'll be nice working with my sisters."

Sarah glanced at Abby and Michelle chatting. Abby had been by her side from the beginning. She was more than just an assistant or best friend. She was just as much a sister as Michelle and Bridget.

The handsome chef touched Abby's shoulder. She jumped and turned to the man. They exchanged a few words before the chef went back into the kitchen. Sarah caught Abby checking him out as he walked away.

Maybe there was something there. Abby worked hard and barely had a personal life. Just like Sarah's life used to be. Perhaps now that Sarah had hired some new people and evened out the load, freeing up herself, thereby freeing up Abby, Abby might take a chance and find the kind of happiness Sarah had found with Luke.

"Lunch is ready," Abby announced to the room.

Bridget walked with Sarah to the dining room. "Thank you, Sarah. For giving me a second chance."

"I think we all have a chance now to have what matters."

Bridget went ahead.

Luke met her at the stairs going up to the dining room and took her hand. "Everything okay?"

"It's a whole new beginning for all of us."

Luke kissed her hand and they walked up the three steps and joined everyone at the massive table. They were a bit squished together and extra chairs had been brought in to accommodate everyone, but no one seemed to mind.

Luke held his wineglass up and everyone followed suit. "To family."

"Family," they all chorused and everyone started passing bowls and platters.

Sarah filled her plate but didn't eat right away. Instead, she took in the people around the table, the conversations going on, and the love in the room.

Luke took her hand, leaned in, and whispered, "This is family. This is home."

Chapter Forty-Two

S arah stood in her bedroom at the ranch and stared at herself in the full-length mirror. The beautiful white gown came from St. James, designed and created just for her. She loved the draped neckline that gathered at her breasts and flowed over her shoulders and took a deep dive to her waist, leaving her back bare, much like the dress Luke loved that she'd worn to the benefit. This one hugged her hips and draped to the floor with a slit up the back so she could easily walk in it.

It was perfect.

Simple. Elegant. Just right for a ranch wedding.

Her hair was pulled into a knot on the back of her head with curls coming from it to soften the look.

She wore round rubies in her ears. Red for love.

Her bouquet had five red roses surrounded by white hydrangeas. She'd been specific with the number of roses and couldn't wait to share the reason why with Luke.

It hadn't been easy keeping her secret. Lucky for her, the morning sickness made her queasy and tired only before subsiding around lunch each day.

She'd been tempted to tell Luke on the day he proposed in Paris during their two-week trip to complete the install of the security program for Griffin Worldwide Financial. They'd spent nearly every waking hour together traveling from one country to the next, city to city, and office to office. In that time, they got to really know each other over long dinners, exploring the places they visited, and just being together without all the other distractions.

They missed the kids terribly, but they enjoyed each other.

And on their last stop, Paris, Luke took her on a tour of the city that ended at twilight in front of the Eiffel Tower, where unbeknownst to Sarah, Abby stood by recording the whole scene unfold as Luke took a knee in front of her, held up a gorgeous diamond solitaire, and asked her to be not just his wife, but his everything for the rest of their lives.

Sarah barely remembered any of it, except saying yes and kissing Luke. She loved kissing Luke.

But the video showed her in a soft flowing pink dress she'd put on to go to dinner and Luke in slacks and a dress shirt, looking too handsome for his own good, down on one knee, her smiling, tears running down her cheeks, and both of them looking so happy and in love. She remembered the applause from the tourists around them when Luke slipped the ring on her finger. She didn't remember him scooping her up and twirling her around. But the kiss. That she remembered. And the love that made her heart feel like it might explode from her chest.

Caught up in the moment, she held on to her news for today.

They wanted to be married right away.

It took three weeks to put the wedding together. And she couldn't wait to walk down the aisle to the man she loved.

Today, they'd finally be an official family.

Sarah picked up the wedding gift Luke left her. She tore open the white wrapping and found a rectangular velvet jewelry box inside. She opened the lid and tried really hard not to cry her makeup right off.

She stared in wonder at the pearl and ruby necklace she'd worn the night of the charity benefit. She took it from the box, hooked it around her neck, and let the pearls and large ruby hang down her back and checked herself out in the mirror again.

She'd liked the stunning piece when she rented it from the jeweler.

She loved it even more that Luke knew how much she'd wanted to keep it.

She was ready.

And just in time. Someone knocked on the door. She opened it and found her father standing there dressed in a black tux with a red bow tie. His gaze softened on her as he took her in. "I have the most beautiful daughter in the world."

"Thank you, Lyon."

"It seems like yesterday I bailed you out of jail." And tried to be a father to a girl who was already old enough to make her own way and be her own woman.

And she'd accomplished that all on her own.

She smiled softly. "I'm a long way from being that girl."

"You're a successful businesswoman. An amazing mother. And now, finally, you'll be a wife to a man who comes very close to deserving you."

Tears clogged her throat and filled her eyes. She blinked them away. "Dad. You'll make me cry."

He held her gaze, his filled with emotion. "That's the first time you've ever called me that."

"I'm sorry it took me this long to do it. But today of all days, I'm so happy you're here with me."

He wrapped her in a hug. "Me, too, sweetheart. I'm sorry for all the days I missed. You can bet, I won't miss any more."

She hugged him a little tighter. "I love you, Dad."

"I love you, too."

She stepped back and grabbed her bouquet. "I'm ready."

She couldn't wait to meet Luke at the altar.

* * *

Luke stood at the end of the long white-draped aisle bordered by their closest friends and family, nervous and anxious to see his bride.

His mom and dad sat in the front row just in front of him.

Margaret sat up front on the bride's side along with Sarah's stepmother, Norah.

The music began and Luke smiled at the boys coming down the aisle dressed in matching black pants, white dress shirts, and red ties, pulling Jamie in a red wagon as she dropped handfuls of red rose petals along the aisle. She looked adorable in her red dress, ruby slippers to match, and a red bow in her hair.

Trish and Brett gave her a wave as she passed their seats.

Sarah had come a long way in accepting Trish into her life. She'd fallen for Jamie. Sarah couldn't not love the little girl, who stole her heart. Every time she saw the boys with Jamie, her eyes lit up with joy.

Sarah and Trish found common ground in the kids and were building a friendship around the fact that they both wanted to be good mothers to their children.

Jason led Michelle down the aisle and took his place as best man next to Luke. Michelle stood across from them as one of Sarah's bridesmaids.

Tyler and Bridget came next and took their spots.

And then stood Abby alone at the end of the aisle in a navy-blue gown matched to go with Michelle's and Bridget's. She held a bouquet of white calla lilies wrapped in a red ribbon.

He'd gotten to know Sarah's best friend these last few weeks as they planned the wedding. Abby seemed all too willing to work with his chef friend on the menu. They seemed close, and he and Sarah were guessing there was a budding romance between them.

Abby gave him a wink when she reached the altar and took her place as maid of honor.

The music stopped for a second before the wedding march began to play.

And then Sarah appeared on her father's arm like a goddess at the end of the flower-strewn aisle.

Luke lost his breath and his heart stopped for a moment.

He'd never seen a more beautiful woman, let alone a bride. He couldn't take his eyes off her as she walked down the aisle, her gaze locked with his, a soft smile on her rosy lips.

Her father placed Sarah's hand in his, and he felt like he'd been bestowed the greatest gift in the world. "You're simply gorgeous."

She put her hand to the knot in his tie and wiggled it. "You clean up good, cowboy."

Yeah, she'd always liked the rancher a little more than the lawyer in him.

He laughed, and so did everyone else, and just like that all the tension went out of him. If possible, he fell a little more in love with her for knowing just how to make him relax and settle into this amazing moment.

They stood before their family and recited their vows. They spoke of love and friendship and vowed that no matter what, family came first.

Luke sealed those promises with a diamond eternity band, letting Sarah know his love was forever.

Sarah placed two gold bands on his finger that locked together to make one ring. One a thin gold band, the other a gold band with five diamonds across the top. Luke could take off the diamond band when he was working on the ranch and only wear the gold one.

"You may kiss your bride."

Luke didn't hesitate. He took Sarah's face in both hands and planted a steamy, but respectable, kiss on her. He leaned back for a second and said, "Mrs. Thompson."

He never expected her to take his name, but when she said she wanted it, his heart grew too heavy for his chest.

He kissed her again when the justice of the peace introduced them as Mr. and Mrs. Thompson.

They turned to their well-wishers and family and hand in hand smiled for everyone.

He walked his bride back down the aisle and straight to the raised temporary dance floor surrounded by tables covered in white linen, set with silver-trimmed white dishes, red napkins, silver place settings, and crystal glasses. Each table had a round bowl overflowing with red roses. Lights were strung on poles around the backyard garden, their shine barely breaking through at twilight, but they'd cast a soft glow once the sun fully set.

He walked Sarah up the two steps to the center of the dance floor and pulled her into his arms.

"Sing me our song, sweetheart."

She gave him a dazzling smile, looked into his eyes, and began to sing. Off to one side of the dance floor, a string quartet began to play along.

Jason and Michelle joined in, then his parents and hers, and then everyone else, just like the night they'd danced in the kitchen, but this time he and Sarah were husband and wife.

Another perfect moment.

After dinner was served and cleared, Jason stood up to give the customary best man toast before they cut the decadent white chocolate cake.

"When I met Sarah for the first time, it was obvious she'd fallen for Luke. She knew he was a lawyer, but liked him better as a rancher, because the lawyer annoyed her with too many questions. Still, she saw the real man, the one his family and closest friends know and love. That's the guy she loved. Luke had no idea Sarah was a genius. I mean, she fell for him, she had to have at least one screw loose."

Everyone laughed, including Sarah and Luke.

"Luke saw a woman who believed in the truth, helping others, and above all being the best mother she could be. She showed him a heart filled with kindness and love and a future filled with all the things Luke wanted. A partner. A family. A life like the one we'd known growing up here." Jason held his glass up to Luke. "You have it all. I wish you both a lifetime of happiness together. Congratulations. Welcome to the family, Sarah." Jason turned to the table next to theirs. "Welcome Jack and Nick. We are blessed to have you all as part of the Thompson family."

They all raised their glasses and drank to the happy couple.

Sarah stood up next to Luke and held his gaze, surprising him that she had something to say.

"Thank you for this wonderful day. Everything is perfect. You've given me so many gifts. Flowers. Dancing. The beautiful jewelry." She touched the necklace that he had given her and then picked up his hand and held it. "No gift compares to the love you show me every single day. And today, I have a very special gift to share with you." She held up her flowers. "When we ordered the flowers, we thought it special to request four roses in my wedding bouquet. One for you, me, Jack, and Nick. But—"

"Mommy, there are five red roses, not four," Jack shouted. "I counted them."

Sarah's eyes teared up and she laughed. "Yes, honey, I know." She turned back to Luke and placed his hand on her belly and looked at him with her eyes filled with love. "The fifth one is for baby Thompson. You're going to be a father." She looked at their two boys and then back to him. "Again."

"Are you serious? You're pregnant? We're having a baby?"

"Yes. We're having a baby." She ran a hand down the side of his face. He grabbed her around the waist and pulled her to him. He kissed her stomach and then stood and kissed her. He held her tight and she didn't even care that he was practically crushing her.

Everyone clapped and cheered around them.

Luke held her away from him and stared into her eyes, his filled with wonder and excitement. "I . . . I can't believe this. I'm . . . ecstatic. You're carrying our child. Are you okay?"

"Yes. You've made me so happy."

He cupped her face and kissed her softly. "I will always find a way to make you happy."

She believed him. And he did.

Acknowledgments

Thank you to my wonderfully talented and amazing editor, Lucia Macro, for finding the heart of this story in the rough draft of a story I'd written a long time ago. The rewrite you proposed seemed like a daunting task, but it was so worth it. You knew there was more here than what I'd put on the page. It was a lot of hard work during a pandemic, but you stuck with me—like you always do—and Sarah and Luke got the love story I wanted for them.

Reading Group Guide

1. Sarah manages to have a big job and raise her children. In what ways are women expected to do both competently while men are sometimes given more latitude with regard to balancing their work life and their family life?

2. Is Sarah doing herself a disservice by putting herself in the background publicly? Why do you feel she insists on this intense privacy?

3. At the start of the novel, Margaret refuses to see her son, Sean, in anything but a perfect light. Why do you think sometimes parents are willing to overlook or ignore terrible behavior in their children?

4. Do you feel sorry for Margaret? Why or why not?

5. At one point Luke comments on people who "care more about money" than anything else, even family. Why do you think people grow to have that perspective? What is it that makes some people value wealth over everything else?

6. Sarah is taken by Sean when she is younger, helping him succeed, even marrying him and saving his business. Why are women so apt to behave this way?

7. Margaret has been married three times and seems to think nothing of it, essentially living off her spouses. Yet, she

condemns Sarah for making her own way in business. Why do you think this double standard still exists?

8. At the start of the novel Luke bemoans the fact that most of the women he's met are opportunistic and after his money. Yet it stands to reason he chose these women to begin with. What in his character might make him find women like this initially appealing?

9. Luke has a fair amount of loyalty to Sean and his memory, even though they had ceased truly being close years before. Are there people in your life who you are loyal to more because of history than present-day friendship?

10. Sarah withholds the truth about Sean, their marriage, his involvement at the company, and even covers up the details surrounding the accident that killed him. Is it sometimes better to lie or withhold the truth for the sake of the feelings of others, as Sarah does with Margaret about Sean? Or, are lies always bad things?

11. The original title of the novel was *Lies and Family Ties*. Are family ties sometimes based on lies? And what do you think of this title?